S LBI R

N STR R

An Imprint of Macmillan

SPELLBINDER. Copyright © 2009 by Helen Stringer. All rights reserved.
Printed in March 2011 in the United States of America by
R. R. Donnelly & Sons Company, Harrisonburg, Virginia. For information,
address Square Fish, 175 Fifth Avenue, New York, NY 10010.

Square Fish and the Square Fish logo are trademarks of Macmillan and are used by
Feiwel and Friends under license from Macmillan.

Library of Congress Cataloging-in-Publication Data
Stringer, Helen.
Spellbinder / by Helen Stringer.
p. cm.
Summary: Twelve-year-old Belladonna Johnson, who lives with the ghosts
of her parents in the north of England, teams up with an always-in-trouble classmate
to investigate why all of the ghosts in the world have suddenly disappeared.
ISBN 978-0-312-64349-2
[1. Ghosts—Fiction. 2. Dead—Fiction. 3. England—Fiction.] I. Title.
PZ7.S9182Ho 2009 [Fic]—dc22 2008028552

For Ethan, whose adventures are just beginning

SPELLBINDER

I

The Vanishing Baby

IT WAS WEDNESDAY. The day of the week when it feels like Friday will never arrive. And it was cold. Not cold enough for snow, but that autumn cold— bright and bitter, the wind sharp with the promise of winter. It was no day to be outside. It was a day to be inside, curled up on the couch with a steaming mug of hot chocolate.

But it was Wednesday, so Belladonna Johnson was not curled up on the couch, she was walking to school, her old pink backpack slung over one shoulder, the sad remnants of the fake-fur edging on the hood of her coat clumping into spikes in the morning mist, and her eyes fixed on the pavement beneath her feet.

She stopped when she reached the end of the road and looked up. Her hair hung like two lank black curtains on either side of her face, and her dark blue eyes peered out from behind the strands, like a jungle animal peering from the undergrowth.

They were already there. Lining up on the pavement outside the school, waiting for the bus. And they were all pretty happy about it, from the look of things.

Belladonna hesitated for a moment, then trudged on, her eyes back on the ground. She hated school trips. She hated the run-down buses they had to take, the screaming and laughing of her classmates, the stapled worksheets they were supposed to complete at the end, and the fact that you never knew who—or what—you might meet.

It hadn't always been that way, of course. There was a time when she had felt the same as everyone else—that any excuse to get out of school was good. Even last term when the whole class thought they were going to Robinson's biscuit factory only to discover they were off to Dennison's assembly plant: a gray stone building full of hermetically sealed, spotless rooms where rows of men and women put PCs together. (They all liked using computers, but there's nothing particularly interesting about watching a bunch of miserable-looking people building them.) And this time the trip was definitely going to be to Arkbath Hall. It had been organized by Mr. Watson, the History teacher, and he wasn't a bait-and-switch kind of guy.

And that made it worse.

Belladonna sat down on the crumbling low stone wall confining the collection of scrubby bushes and weeds that half concealed the entrance to the school.

She pushed her hood back and lowered her backpack onto the wet pavement. It would be alright, she thought, if she could tell the difference. But she couldn't, and she lived in fear of someone (Sophie Warren, in particular) catching her talking to nothing. She bit her lip and racked her brain for an excuse that would convince Mr. Watson that she'd be better off going to see the school nurse.

It seemed to take forever. Belladonna could feel the chill from the cold stone wall working its way into her bones, and even the boisterous conversations of the other kids began to subside as they shivered in the October air, the wind whipping around the girls' pink knees, and the boys remembering that school uniform trousers are anything but substantial. It was nearly a quarter past nine before the ancient green city bus rolled up to the curb and Mr. Watson left the cozy confines of the staff room and strode down the path to herd his charges aboard.

Mr. Watson was only about thirty and imagined that the kids thought he was rather cool. They didn't, of course. To them, he seemed terribly old, with his steadily increasing bald spot, dismal ties, and graph-paper-patterned shirts. He tried to make History entertaining, but most of his students weren't really interested. For twelve-year-olds, the events leading up to the Civil War were dull as dishwater, and Charles I gave every impression of deserving what he got. (Though it seemed to be taking a long time to get to that part—beheadings are far more fascinating than acts of Parliament.)

Belladonna watched as everyone else clambered onto the bus, chatting and yelling. Once they were all packed in, Mr. Watson looked around and saw her sitting on the wall.

"Come on, Johnson," he said cheerily, "all aboard!"

Belladonna got up and walked over to him. "I don't think I can go, Sir," she whispered. "I don't feel very well."

Watson looked at her for a moment. She gazed back, her chin slightly lowered and her eyes tilted up toward the teacher. This, she knew, had the general effect of making her eyes seem huge and sad, like one of those big-eyed children with a single plastic tear on the cheaper sort of greeting cards. She could tell that he wasn't buying it this time, though. Six months ago he would have let her go, but it had been nearly a year since the accident and Belladonna had noticed that all the adults around her had apparently decided that it would probably be best if they tried the "life goes on" approach.

"Nonsense, Johnson," he said finally. "It's not like we're headed across the Sahara. This should be fun. Right up your alley, I would've thought."

And with that, he hustled her onto the bus.

Belladonna took a seat near the front and settled down to gaze miserably out of the streaky window. The bus lurched forward and the cacophony of voices rose to a crescendo as Steve Evans stole Tim Bradon's glasses *again*. Mr. Watson tried in vain to quiet everyone down, making appeals for dignity, safety, and the driver's hearing. Nothing worked.

The bus trundled through the early morning streets, past rows of tiny shops and the vast parking lots of mega-markets. Other schools full of other children whizzed by in a blur of concrete and brick. Finally, the buildings were gone, and mowed, golden fields stretched out on either side as they pulled into a winding, tree-lined drive.

Belladonna looked glumly out of the window as the lopsided black-and-white form of the half-timbered Arkbath Hall crept out from behind a knot of trees. The mullioned windows gazed blankly across the long-dry moat as the bus clanked to a standstill in the tiny car park. The kids piled out and waited while Mr. Watson counted them, before they all trudged across the lawn, crispy with frost, toward the ancient manse.

They stopped in front of a massive black gate, and Mr. Watson pressed the doorbell. He turned and looked out over his charges, suddenly nervous.

"Now, I want—for God's sake, Evans, give the boy his glasses back!—I want you all to behave yourselves. Arkbath Hall was built in the late fifteenth century—"

"Sixteenth," muttered Belladonna.

"Sorry? Yes, very good, Johnson, the late sixteenth century. Quite right. Anyway, it's very old, so I don't want any of you touching anything. Is that clear?"

Silence.

"I said: Is that clear?"

Twenty-eight dreary voices said, "Yes, Sir," in unison, though not one of them sounded even remotely like it had heard what Mr. Watson had said.

He looked at their faces as their attention wandered to the building, the grass, and the snail on the path. Belladonna suspected that in his quiet hours Mr. Watson despaired for the future of the country.

A small door set into the much larger one opened and a round, red face protruded.

"Are you the group from Dullworth's?" it asked.

"Yes!" Mr. Watson seemed relieved to have another adult to speak to. "Yes, we are. I'm George Watson."

He held out his hand. The owner of the round face stepped outside, revealing the rest of himself to be pretty much spherical as well. The buttons on his Historic Homes uniform stretched across his ample belly, giving the impression that he had been a tad more svelte when he had originally been measured for it.

"How many are there?" he asked, as if talking about bags of potatoes.

"Twenty-eight," said Mr. Watson.

The round man didn't seem pleased, but held the door open while the children marched inside, counting them off with a small shiny counter in his left hand. Belladonna was the last one through. She looked at the round man and idly wondered why he needed a mechanical device to count to twenty-eight. He seemed to curl his lip a little as she stepped through, but she thought that was probably just her imagination.

Once through the door, there was a short, darkened archway that led through to a wide, bright courtyard. In the center of the yard were two massive trees, each with a vast tangle of branches reaching up and out toward the thin autumn sun. Mr. Watson explained that they were yew trees and that yews were either male or female, so you needed to have both. The round man cleared his throat in an annoyed manner and Mr. Watson immediately stepped aside, rather embarrassed, to let the round man do his bit.

"Yew trees," he announced in an automatic whine, "were used to make longbows. Which is, of course, why they were grown *inside* the walls of the house and/or castle."

Everyone looked at the trees for a moment. Then Sarah Tisdale raised her hand.

"Yes?" said the round man.

"Is it true that you have a ghost?"

"Sarah . . ." Mr. Watson stared, and Sarah slowly took her hand down.

The round man had heard the same question a thousand times before.

"Yes," he said in a voice that conveyed his utter contempt for the questioner while also communicating his profound regret over his career choice. "There is a haunted chamber."

Excited chatter.

"Which we will see eventually," he added. "But first—the kitchens."

He led the way through a door at the far end of the courtyard, while talking about the sequence of construction and the family that built it only to lose their possessions as a result of some less-than-wise investments in merchant ships to the New World, and how that family was replaced by another family that had the wisdom to refrain from dabbling in international commerce, but had the misfortune of being Catholic during the reign of Elizabeth I, when such allegiances were regarded as somewhat less than acceptable.

It was all quite interesting, but no one heard a word that he said as he marched on toward the kitchens, nattering away, with his back resolutely turned to his audience. By the time they arrived in the kitchens, everyone's attention was starting to wander and carefully licked fingers were stretching toward the enormous sugar loaf that served as the chief decoration of the long central table.

"Don't touch that!"

The fingers shot back, while those who had managed to scratch off a bit of brown sugar grinned at each other conspiratorially. The round man glared for a moment, then directed their attention to the cavernous fireplace and the great black meat spit.

Belladonna looked around nervously, hanging back near the door. She knew that most of the other kids thought she was very strange, but because she was also the survivor of a Tragic Event, they didn't give her a hard time. They just left her alone and stared at her when she wasn't looking, which was actually worse than being the constant target of teasing. At least then she would have felt that she belonged, that she was there, but instead she spent most of her time alone, reading her books and wondering who was real and who was not.

The tour moved on. The round man led the way down a narrow hallway and into a dark, paneled room with equally dark furniture pushed against the walls, then they were off down the hall again and into a bright room with a beautiful plaster ceiling and huge bay windows that were raised like small stages. The sun streamed across the faded carpet and even Belladonna was tempted into the middle of the room and over to the big mullioned windows.

The round man told them all about the ceiling and the small stained-glass coats of arms and then led the way out into the hall and up a narrow, twisting staircase. The clatter of twenty-eight pairs of feet followed him up the stairs and into another long, narrow hallway. They went into a small bedroom, followed by a large bedroom with a vast four-poster bed, and finally into a room with a concealed priest's hole (fascinating), another four-poster bed, and a cradle.

By this time Belladonna had forgotten about wishing she was back at school and was as eager as anyone else to peer through the small piece of glass into the priest's hole, imagining what it must have been like to crouch there listening to the tramp of military feet searching the house for heretics. And she, like everyone else, just had to see exactly how hard the mattress was on the four-poster bed.

"And, of course, this is the haunted room," intoned the round man.

Everyone stopped poking about and turned to listen.

"In 1632 the Lady Mary was in this room with her baby, waiting for her deadbeat gambling husband to come home, praying that he hadn't gambled away their home. . . ."

The children were hanging on his every word. The round man loved this part.

"Finally, after two days on the town, she saw him come riding home, around that clump of trees right there. . . ."

Everyone peered out of the window. Mr. Watson stood leaning against the door and rolling his eyes.

"She knew what he'd done, and unable to take the shame of being *thrust* into poverty . . ."

He paused for effect. Twenty-eight sets of eyes grew wider by the second.

"She opened the window, *flung* the baby into the moat, and leapt in after it. And they say . . ."

He paused for effect again, lowering his voice almost to a whisper.

"They *say* she haunts the room to this *very* day,

sitting at the window and rocking the cradle . . . waiting for her husband to return."

Silence. Everyone looked at the cradle.

The round man straightened up and grinned. "Right, then. Let's go and see the Great Hall. Follow me!" He marched cheerily through the swarm of children and out of the door.

Mr. Watson straightened up. "Okay," he said matter-of-factly, "it's just a story. It has nothing to do with history. Come on. Away from the window."

Embarrassed giggles, shoves, and whoops as everyone pretended that they thought it was all stupid and had never been fooled even for a moment. Mr. Watson herded them out and set off after the round man.

They had all left the room before Belladonna realized they had gone. She was still at the window, looking down into the long-dry moat. She turned around and, with a leap in the pit of her stomach, realized she was alone. She hurried to the door, but it was too late.

"It wasn't like that, you know."

The voice wasn't angry or outraged, it just stated a fact. "The baby had gone months before. Croup, it was."

Belladonna turned around slowly.

There, near the window, was a young woman wearing a dark velvet dress decorated with pearls, a red sash, and a huge lace collar. Above the collar rose a swanlike neck ending in a beautiful oval face surrounded by shining blond ringlets.

"And honestly, do you really think a grown person could squeeze themselves out of that window?"

Belladonna Johnson shook her head slowly. "It is rather small."

"Of course it is," smiled Lady Mary. "What a sensible girl you are."

"Thank you," said Belladonna, staring at her shoes.

There was an awkward pause.

"Ah," said Lady Mary, suddenly understanding, "this is all a bit new to you, isn't it?"

Belladonna nodded and glanced up. Lady Mary was staring out of the window again, and when she looked back, she seemed troubled.

"The thing is," she said, "William is gone."

Belladonna stared at her. Lady Mary looked a bit exasperated and gestured toward the cradle.

"William," she repeated, "the baby. He vanished two days ago."

Belladonna nodded in what she hoped was a sage and knowing manner, because she had no idea where Lady Mary was going with this. Mary tossed her seventeenth-century curls in annoyance.

"Look, just let the Spellbinder know. She'll know what to do."

Whatever Belladonna had been expecting Lady Mary to say, it wasn't that. But she didn't have much time to think, as the round man suddenly appeared in the doorway.

"Hey, you!" he said. "Everyone's waiting for you downstairs."

Belladonna turned back to Lady Mary, who waved her away with a long, pale hand.

"Horrible little man," she muttered. "In my day, I wouldn't have let the likes of him cross the threshold. Off you go."

Belladonna turned and walked to the door. She glanced back to see if Mary was still there. She was.

"Don't forget to tell the Spellbinder about the baby!"

Belladonna nodded and followed the round man down the stairs, through the Great Hall, and out to the car park.

"Come on, Johnson!" shouted Mr. Watson. "Pick up your feet! Stop dragging along. I've never known a girl for hanging back like you."

He hustled her onto the bus, quickly counted heads, and nodded to the driver that they were ready to go. The engine coughed into action and the old bus heaved itself out of the car park. Belladonna looked back at the house through the streaky window. There was nothing to see, just the same dark, mullioned windows, the dip in the lawn where the moat had once been, and the gleaming white and deep black of the half-timbered walls.

And then it was gone, and they were surrounded by the concrete and brick of the modern city. Belladonna sighed. Sometimes it really did seem as though she spent more time talking to dead people than living ones. But it was so confusing. And who (or what) on earth was the "Spellbinder"?

The bus screeched to a halt in front of the school. Which was an improvement over the driver on the last trip. That driver had zoomed past Dullworth's and was headed for the city center before Mr. Morris (who had taken them to the depressing computer assembly plant) had looked up from his science magazine and realized that they were severely off course.

Of course, Dullworth's was the sort of place it was easy to pass by without ever realizing it was a school. It had been started over a hundred years before by two elderly, energetic sisters who couldn't understand why boys got to learn interesting things like History and Latin, and girls only got training in sewing, singing, and simpering. But the Dullworth sisters were not the sort who sat around bemoaning the status quo—they were the sort who leapt to their feet and marched about demanding change and scaring the horses. So they bought a house in what was then a quiet part of town and started a school for girls. Eventually the school expanded to occupy three Victorian houses connected by rickety covered walkways, and as the years passed, it finally admitted boys as well. But it still looked like a row of houses, and it felt rather like that too.

Each house had been adapted with classrooms where living rooms, parlors, and bedrooms had once been, but there was always the feeling that you were wandering around some vast gothic mansion and sooner or later the owner would turn up and demand to know what on earth you were doing there. The hallways were wide and boasted high ceilings and elegant plasterwork, while the classrooms ranged from splendid rooms with views across the grounds to tiny garrets whose windows let out onto the gray rooftops. Staircases popped up everywhere, from the broad flights that led to the science labs and the Head's office, to narrow, twisting back stairs that had once been the haunt of servants. Even the school hall had once been a ballroom and had a vast domed ceiling, painted midnight blue and stuck all over with large gold-painted plaster stars that periodically crashed to the floor in a hail of dust and tinsel, leaving pale gaps in the artificial firmament.

The rest of the day was fairly ordinary: English Lit., French, and double P.E. (which Belladonna *did* manage to spend in the sick bay—Miss Gunnerson was much more credulous than Mr. Watson). And then it was over and a horde of screaming kids raced out of school and into the late autumn dusk.

Belladonna dawdled home, glancing in shop windows and pausing at the sweet shop on the corner to buy a packet of Parma Violets, pore over the magazines, and pick up a newspaper for her father.

Then she walked past the old launderette. It had stopped being a launderette over a year ago, though all the machines were still inside. But it wasn't the rather grubby battalions of old washers and dryers that interested Belladonna; it was Mr. Baxter.

Mr. Baxter had apparently owned the shop a long time ago, and he had never left it. When he appeared in the window, the washers, dryers, soap dispensers, and slowly curling notices about the proprietor's lack of responsibility in the event that one of his machines ate anyone's clothes seemed to slowly fade away, and the bare blue walls turned a kind of yellow ochre and gradually filled with shelves from floor to ceiling. Every shelf was laden with bottles, jars, and pots of all shapes and sizes. Belladonna could see a long polished oak counter at the very back of the shop with what looked like a bright brass tea urn taking pride of place. The front window seemed to become misty, and she could just make out ". . . pothec . . ." in very fancy gold lettering across the wavy glass, from which she deduced that Mr. Baxter must have been an apothecary.

She liked Mr. Baxter. He was rather elderly with an impressive head of snowy white hair on top of which perched a red pillbox hat with a large black tassel. He wore a dark red coat, a fine yellow waistcoat, and a splendid black cravat at the neck of his freshly starched shirt.

The first time she saw him he had been at the back of the shop behind the counter and hadn't seemed very pleased to be seen. She had looked away quickly and hurried home. But since then he had become much more friendly. He always seemed to be tidying up his window display and always waved cheerily at Belladonna as she passed, as if she were a regular customer. At first, the smile had seemed odd, as if the muscles in his face were unused to stretching upward, and Belladonna thought she caught a glint of something cold in his eyes. She walked past as quickly as she could, but then she noticed that he seemed ever so slightly disappointed.

And why wouldn't he? she thought. *The poor man might not even realize he's dead.* And if she went for nearly two hundred years without seeing another face, maybe her cheek muscles would seize up too.

She began to feel guilty, as if he were a sick relative who she hadn't visited in the hospital, so one day (after looking around carefully to make sure no one was watching) she smiled back. It seemed to cheer him up no end, and for some reason it cheered her up too. So now she made sure she walked past every day, with her newspaper and her Parma Violets, and no matter how glum she'd been feeling or how dull school had been, Mr. Baxter always made her feel better.

He was there today, true to form, and she waved and he waved back and she carried on with a slightly lighter step, down the High Street, past the church and the graveyard, and up to number 65 Lychgate Lane.

"She's home!"

Her father poked his head out of the sitting room. And that was the problem right there, really.

Where most fathers would have poked their heads out of the sitting room door, Mr. Johnson poked his right through the middle of the wall.

"Did you bring the paper?"

Belladonna looked at him reprovingly. He immediately vanished back into the sitting room and reappeared in the doorway.

"Sorry," he said. "I forgot. Did you bring the paper?"

"Honestly, Dad, anyone passing by could've seen you through the window!"

He took the paper and turned back into the sitting room with a shrug.

"No one can see me. Only you."

Belladonna followed him in, exasperated.

"Gran can see you. Lots of people can see ghosts; you see them talking about it on the telly all the time."

"Charlatans," muttered her father, settling down an inch above his favorite chair.

Belladonna grunted, dumped her bag near the fire, and meandered back to the kitchen. It was a hive of activity. Pans on the stove were busily stirring themselves while bread was being sliced and buttered on the counter and plates were flying out of the cabinet and setting themselves on the table. Her mother was in a corner, examining a recipe book with some consternation.

Elspeth Johnson was everything her daughter was not; she was tall and willowy and always impeccably put together. Her hair never slid out of place over one eye or started the day sticking up on one side, and her clothes were never rumpled. And that was when she was alive. Now that she was dead, she was an absolute fashion plate. Belladonna hoped that she was going through an awkward stage and would grow up just like her mother but in her heart of hearts, she knew she never would.

"Hello, darling," beamed her mother. "Did you have a nice day at school?"

"We went on a trip," said Belladonna, helping herself to some bread and butter.

"That's nice."

"To Arkbath Hall."

"Oh, how lovely!" Elspeth looked up from her book. "Did you see Lady Mary?"

Belladonna nodded.

"I remember seeing her when I was your age. She had all sorts of useful advice about making beer and jam. Darling, could you taste that big pan and tell me if it's right? I used to make this all the time when I was alive, but not being able to eat anything is such a handicap when you're cooking."

Belladonna slouched over to the stove, grabbed the spoon in mid-stir, and had a taste. Her face wrinkled up.

"There's no salt in it!"

Elspeth slammed the book closed. "Of course! I don't know where my memory's gone."

The salt pot slid across the counter, opened itself, and slipped a teaspoon of salt into the pan. The spoon stirred enthusiastically. Belladonna watched it for a moment. When her parents had first manifested after the accident, she had thought that perhaps they'd become magical and all sorts of wonderful things were going to happen. But they weren't magic, they were just ghosts with all the usual ghostly skills (walking through walls, floating, moving inanimate objects, appearing and disappearing), but no really magical ones. And while the ghostly skills had seemed pretty impressive at first, Belladonna had to admit that they'd become a bit annoying.

"Mum . . ." she said finally.

"Hmmm?"

"Lady Mary said that her baby had vanished."

"Really?" Elspeth paused for a moment. "He wasn't in the cradle?"

"No, she said he vanished two days ago. She said I should tell the Spellbinder."

"Oh, I don't think that's necessary, dear," said her mother, but she looked thoughtful.

"Who's the Spellbinder?"

Elspeth looked at her for a moment, then smiled and nodded toward the clock on the wall. "Dinner in five minutes," she said cheerily. "Get your coat off and tell your father it's ready."

Belladonna glowered at her mother. Her parents were always doing this: not even bothering to make something up, but just changing the subject whenever she started talking about something that they didn't want to think about. Or didn't want her to think about. Which had the opposite effect, of course.

She trudged out to get her father.

Dinner consisted of everyone sitting down at the table, but only Belladonna actually eating. It was a pretty dreary experience from their daughter's point of view, but Mr. and Mrs. Johnson were great believers in the family dinner and just because they were no longer corporeal, they saw no reason to let things slide.

They were halfway through the beef stroganoff when there was a cold blast of air from the front door.

"It's just me!"

The door slammed shut and Belladonna's grandmother strode purposefully into the kitchen. She did everything purposefully, like one of those country ladies who are always walking the dogs or returning from the hunt. She looked like one of them too.

Jessamine Johnson was all tweeds and sensible shoes. She had her hair done once a week by a man in town who created a helmet of gray curls that didn't budge an inch between one appointment and the next, and she wore a pair of bright gold glasses with a fine chain that kept them from falling to the floor. But Grandma Johnson was anything but sensible.

"Hello, everyone!" she said, kissing the top of Belladonna's head on the way to the sink. "That front gate is absolutely filthy. Look at me, I'm covered in it!"

She washed her hands and turned around.

"Well, don't you look glum, Miss Johnson. How was school today?"

"Fine," said Belladonna with no enthusiasm at all.

"They went to Arkbath Hall," volunteered her mother.

"Did you now?" Grandma Johnson retrieved a bottle of wine from the fridge and pulled a chair up to the table. "Did you see Lady Mary?"

Belladonna nodded. She wished she was upstairs pretending to do her homework instead of down here talking about dead people.

"What did she say? Did she tell you about beer and jam?"

Belladonna stared at her plate.

"Oh, I see, one of those evenings, is it?"

"She told her she didn't throw the baby out of the window," said her mother.

Grandma Johnson humphed and took rather more than a sip of her wine. She gave Belladonna the beady eye and then started to recount her own day in second-by-second detail.

Belladonna got up and started clearing the table. She opened the dishwasher and rinsed off the dishes under the tap. As she put each one down on the counter, her mother whisked them into the dishwasher without touching them or even breaking the stride of her conversation with Grandma Johnson.

". . . and that Jane Lee came in this afternoon," said Grandma. "You remember her, don't you, Elspeth? Small, dumpy woman with absolutely appalling bad breath. Well, she—"

They were destined never to know what Jane Lee had done because at that moment there was an almighty crash as a plate, a cup, and one of the best glasses missed their slots in the dishwasher and hit the tile floor.

Silence.

Elspeth Johnson stared at the mess, while everyone else stared at her.

"How odd," she finally said. "That's never happened before."

"Are you alright?" whispered Belladonna.

"Yes, it's just . . ." She looked at her husband. "It felt as if someone walked over my grave."

Belladonna started to clear up the mess. Mr. Johnson patted his wife's hand.

"Well, you know, dear," he said soothingly, "maybe they did."

The rest of the evening went by as usual, but Belladonna noticed that her parents kept glancing at each other in that way that always meant something was going on. Later, as she lay in bed, she couldn't help thinking about the night everything changed. Or at least, the bits of it she could remember.

She had been in the car. In the back seat. They'd spent the day at a friend of her parents' in Wales, and it was late. They'd played "I Spy" and then sung for a while, and talked about the horrible dinner and how Phyllida's peas were always like titanium bullets. But then she'd fallen asleep.

And that was all she could remember until the hospital. The doctors said that it was normal for people not to remember after they'd been in an accident, but Belladonna was sure that she would have remembered. How could you not remember something that changed your life so completely?

And she remembered everything else. The somber faces, the sympathetic stares, the funeral, and the graveyard. She remembered the faces of everyone at school the first day she went back: sad and sorry but not knowing what to say, so saying nothing.

And she remembered coming over with her Gran to pick up a few clothes and discovering that Mum and Dad hadn't gone at all, but that the rules of haunting meant that they couldn't leave the house. They were almost the same, just ever so slightly monochromatic, as if she were always looking at them through a hazy window. There were no hugs any more, of course, but other than that, everything was as it had been.

Belladonna rolled over and looked out of the window at the clear night sky. She didn't want to lose them again.

Then it happened.

It only took a second, but as she looked up from her bed, thinking her morose thoughts, the stars went out.

They came back on again right away, but there was no doubt that for just a moment, the sky was completely, totally black.

She jumped out of bed and ran to the window. She expected to see the street outside full of neighbors, to hear the clatter of concerned voices, but there was nothing except a small movement near the bushes on the other side of the street, which she was pretty sure was just somebody's dog. It was as if she were the only one who saw it.

But she wasn't. The sound of raised voices floated up from downstairs. She crept to the door and opened it a crack, but her parents had apparently realized that they were talking too loudly and the discussion subsided into urgent whispers. She strained to hear for a while and then slipped back to the window to look at the sky. All was as it was supposed to be: The stars were in their places, the planets in theirs, and the only thing punctuating the tediously static propriety of it all was the occasional shooting star.

2

Elsie

THE THING ABOUT going to school is that it doesn't give you enough time to think about the important stuff. One moment you're mulling issues like why on earth all the stars would flicker on and off like a giant celestial night-light, and the next you're being paired off with Steve Evans for Chemistry and arguing about why the Bunsen burner won't light.

Of course, that wasn't the main problem. The main problem was that he refused to take any interest in the experiment they were *supposed* to be doing and instead made something that he said would make a "small bang."

Which is how they both came to be sitting outside the Headmistress's office. Miss Parker was not going to be amused. Belladonna glowered at Steve, who was used to being sent to the Office and was gazing about without a care in the world. Steve was tall for his age, with dishwater-blond hair that looked like it was cut by his mother (which it was). He always seemed to have a scratch or scab from some scuffle or other somewhere, and the school uniform never looked as scruffy as when he was wearing it. Steve was always in some kind of trouble, whether it was not doing his homework, tormenting the members of the chess club, or wandering off school property at lunchtime, but he was far from stupid, which frustrated his teachers and irritated his parents. Steve took it all in stride with a sort of "this-too-shall-pass" attitude that made it all but impossible for anyone to motivate him to do anything at all.

Belladonna, on the other hand, spent most of her time at school just trying to stay under the radar. She'd never been sent to see the Head, she'd never been in trouble, and she'd certainly never made anyone's shoes explode. She looked at the door to the inner sanctum of the daunting Miss Parker. There was a little device next to it with three lights. The green one said "Enter," the orange one said "Wait," and the red one said "Busy." According to Steve, if the red one came on when you knocked at the door, then you could go back to class, and sometimes she'd forget all about you. He had knocked on the door with confidence. After a brief pause, the orange "Wait" light came on.

Steve shrugged and sat down. Belladonna leaned against the wall by the door for a while, then wandered to the window. The tennis courts were below and she could hear the faint *pock . . . pock . . . pock* of the balls as the class that she should have been in practiced their backhands. She hated P.E., but she'd have given anything to be out there right now.

"What did you do?"

She spun around. The voice was right at her ear. Standing next to her was a girl a little older than she was. She wore a neat blouse, a carefully knotted tie, and a long skirt. Her hair was caught back in a ponytail by an enormous bow.

Belladonna glanced over at Steve; he was reading a comic that he'd been carrying scrunched up in his back pocket. He obviously couldn't see the girl. Belladonna turned back to the window, and the girl moved closer and peered outside.

"You're a ghost," she whispered.

"Of course I am," said the girl. "Why are you whispering?"

Belladonna glared at her. This was exactly the sort of situation that she'd been trying to avoid. It had been two years since she'd started seeing ghosts, and while her mother thought it was all perfectly normal ("Everyone on the Nightshade side of the family sees them, dear, we always have."), Belladonna knew better. Being caught talking to herself by one of her classmates would just put the icing on the cake of her miserable school year.

"Oh, look," said the girl, "tennis. I used to love tennis. That was how I died, actually."

"How can you die from playing tennis?"

"I'd just won," explained the girl cheerfully. "I nearly always won, you know. And I jumped over the net. My foot caught and I went right down onto the court—*smack!*"

Belladonna's eyes widened.

"My head cracked open. It was the most appalling mess, but quite instant. I just had time to think, 'Oh, bother!' and I was dead."

She smiled pleasantly, as if she'd just recalled a family picnic.

"That's awful!" whispered Belladonna.

"I suppose," admitted the girl, "but more awful for everyone else, really. I mean, I was pretty much past caring. My opponent, Sally Jenkins it was, went on to the next round of the tournament, which really wasn't right, because I *had* won, you know."

"I would've thought they'd cancel the whole thing," said Belladonna.

"Yes, I must say I was a bit surprised. My parents were royally ticked off, I can tell you. But there you go, no use crying over spilt milk . . . or brains."

She grinned mischievously and began to slowly fade away. Then her face changed, as if she saw something or felt something that she hadn't expected.

"Oh, really!" she complained. "This is too much!"

An almost invisible hand reached out and grabbed Belladonna's wrist.

"You've got to do something. This is all wrong!"

And she was gone. Belladonna stared for a moment

at the empty space where the tennis girl had been, and then wandered over and sat down outside the Office.

Steve looked up from his comic. "You were talking to yourself," he stated flatly.

"No, I wasn't."

The green "Enter" light buzzed on, and there was a click as the door unlocked. Belladonna leapt to her feet. Steve folded up the comic, stuffed it into his back pocket, and slouched through the door after her.

Miss Parker was austere and angular—one of those people who seem to have been born old. She was incredibly skinny and always wore navy-blue suits that seemed to have been made for a much heavier person. Belladonna imagined that her wardrobe at home was crammed with identical navy-blue suits and two pairs of black shoes. Miss Parker was the sort of person who thought black was "close enough" to navy blue, and she was certainly not the sort of person who would spend more than fifteen minutes looking for new shoes of any color. She seemed to spend quite a bit of time on her hair, however. It was always perfectly coiffed and curled around her ears in an arc of pepper and salt, ending in two sharp points just on her jawline. She wore gold half-moon glasses, which added to the general air of disapproval as she peered over the tops of them to look at her charges.

Belladonna walked from the door toward Miss Parker's dark mahogany desk across what felt like miles of dingy rose-pink carpet with such a deep pile that she felt she was about to sink right through it and into some netherworld where pupils endured perpetual detention in dark classrooms supervised by grim teachers with no sense of humor and an abiding dislike of children.

She joined Steve in front of the desk and examined the office with interest. It was much brighter than she'd expected, with gleaming white walls, certificates cataloging Miss Parker's achievements, photographs of past school events, and a large print of a Picasso painting. But pride of place went to an old wooden lacrosse stick that was mounted on a polished board along with a brass plaque that Belladonna couldn't quite read, though she imagined it was a memento of some long-gone tournament played in the days when Miss Parker herself had been a student. Two huge sash windows dominated the far wall of the office, between which there was a tall, narrow bookcase with an arched top like a church window. Belladonna tried to look out of the windows, but all she could see from where she was standing were the decaying facades of the buildings on the other side of the street. She turned her attention back to the Picasso print. It was of a crying woman and was all angles and planes, with a handkerchief that seemed more like a weapon than a comfort. She looked from that to the angular Miss Parker, and thought she could see why it might appeal to her.

She glanced at Steve, but he was examining the

carpet intently. After a few moments, he shifted his weight, shoved his hands into his pockets, and then quickly pulled them out again.

Miss Parker sniffed and put her bony elbows on the vast shiny desk, resting her chin on her clasped hands. "Mr. Evans," she drawled, "here we are again. I thought you told me you were going to stay out of my office for the rest of this term."

Steve didn't respond. Miss Parker turned her probing gaze toward Belladonna.

Belladonna thought of gorgons, creatures that could turn people to stone simply by looking at them.

"And Miss Johnson, what on earth are you doing here?"

Belladonna wasn't sure if she was supposed to answer or not, but she was generally of the opinion that getting the whole proceeding over with as quickly as possible would be the best thing.

"We . . . accidentally made some stuff. And it exploded," she explained. "But it was an accident."

Miss Parker looked at her for a moment with the same kind of expression she would probably have adopted if her cat had suddenly started reciting Shakespeare.

"An accident," she turned to Steve. "Was it an accident, Stephen?"

Steve glanced at Belladonna like a drowning man spotting a distant life raft.

"Absolutely," he said, a little too loudly. "We were

supposed to be making this stuff, but then we accidentally made this other stuff. And then Mr. Morris walked in it while it was drying next to the radiator."

Miss Parker nodded. "While it was drying?"

"Yes, Miss," said Steve, optimistic of a quick escape.

"That doesn't really sound like an accident, does it? Mr. Morris told me that as it dried, he began to experience an unsettling sensation around his feet."

"Yes, Miss," Steve burbled on. "But it was only because he had hobnailed boots on. They kept making little sparks, y'see, and setting it off."

"Setting it off?"

"Bangs." Steve was losing momentum as he seemed to realize this was probably not going to help his case. "Small . . . um . . . bangs."

Miss Parker's pale green eyes stared at Steve over her glasses and he seemed to shrivel up in front of the desk. Belladonna couldn't bear to watch.

"But it isn't our fault he got it on his shoes," she blurted, thinking fast. "We couldn't clean it off the dish, you see. And we thought that if it dried, then it would be easier to clean. We'd just been messing with different things; we didn't know that when it dried it would become explosive. And we put it right up next to the radiator, but Mr. Morris tripped over Jane Fletcher's bag and sort of stumbled into it. It wasn't like we did it on purpose or anything."

Miss Parker looked at Belladonna. The explanation had the ring of plausibility to it.

"Hmph," she grunted. "I must admit, Mr. Morris does have a reputation for a certain amount of clumsiness."

Steve glanced at Belladonna—the sun was breaking through the clouds.

"And as you have never been sent here before, Miss Johnson, I am inclined to believe you . . . this time."

She stood up slowly.

"However, in future, any chemistry experimentation should be limited to the work assigned. Is that clear?"

"Yes, Miss," they both hissed eagerly.

"Well." Miss Parker waved a bony hand. "Off you go, then."

Steve shot out of the Office as if he'd been fired from a gun. Belladonna followed him, but stopped at the door.

"Miss Parker . . ."

The headmistress seemed surprised. "Yes?"

"Has anyone ever died on our tennis courts?"

Miss Parker removed her glasses and stared at Belladonna. "Died?" she said. "On the tennis courts? What an extraordinary question. Of course not."

Belladonna looked at her for a moment. She was lying. Miss Parker was lying. Unless, of course, the girl was the one making things up. But then why would she do that when she was already dead? Belladonna smiled weakly at Miss Parker, backed out of the room, and closed the door.

Steve was waiting just outside, positively gleeful.

"That was brilliant!" he gushed. "You're a natural! I can't believe you haven't been in trouble before."

"Considering how often you're in trouble, I would've expected you to put up a better show," said Belladonna, walking away.

"There's not usually any point," explained Steve. "I reckon it's better to just fess up, take whatever they're dishing out, and get on with things. Explanations usually just extend the agony."

"Oh, well," said Belladonna sarcastically, "at least you've thought about it."

They walked down the stairs and along the empty corridors. Belladonna suddenly stopped. The tennis girl was at the end of the hall waiting for her. She looked worried and, as Belladonna watched, seemed to see something unpleasant to her left. Then she vanished again.

"Steve . . ."

"What?"

"Have you ever heard of anyone dying on the tennis courts?"

"Here?"

"Yes, here."

"When?"

Belladonna thought about the tennis girl's dress.

"I'm not sure. Early 1900s, maybe."

"Early 1900s?" he repeated, crestfallen. "How would I know? I thought you'd dug up some dirt on old Parker."

Belladonna rolled her eyes. The bell sounded for lunch and hordes of students poured out into the corridor.

Steve shoved his hands into his pockets and started to slouch toward the door to the lunch room. Belladonna knew where he was going—the chess club always met at noon in a corner of the lunch room, hunched over their games in silence except for the occasional *whap*! as they hit the small stop-clocks that timed their moves. Yesterday Steve had caused chaos by producing a matchbox and releasing a large hairy spider across their boards. It was amazing how many of them turned out to be terrified of spiders; though it was always possible that, as they never seemed to go outside, they'd never seen one. In which case, thought Belladonna, it served them right.

She was sure Steve had something equally effective planned for today, but to her surprise, he turned back.

"I know where we might be able to find out."

He spun around and marched away from the lunch room and back into the oldest of the school buildings. Belladonna followed as they made their way back past the hot drinks machine and the notice board full of paper signs telling the students to do this, and not to do that, and cataloging the dismal season-to-date record of the football team. Steve marched up the broad stairs that Belladonna knew led to the science labs (scene of former glories only that day), but he didn't stop there. Without pausing for breath, he was up again, to the top floor. This was where the sixth-form common rooms were, and the smallest, dingiest classroom in the whole school, where Watson struggled in vain to instill an interest in history to cramped ranks of bored faces.

Steve marched past the common rooms and to a tall, narrow door next to the classroom. He turned the handle. It was locked.

"Oh, great," said Belladonna, gasping a bit after all the stairs.

Steve grabbed the handle again and heaved the old door up as he turned. There was a click and it swung open, revealing a steep, narrow staircase. He turned to Belladonna with a grin. "It's a knack," he said.

"You're going to end up in jail," said Belladonna grimly, hoping he couldn't tell that she was quite impressed.

She stepped through the door and started up the stairs. Steve followed, shutting the door behind them and plunging the narrow stairwell into darkness. Belladonna hesitated for a moment, then noticed a dim gray light at the top, straining against the blackness. She started up the creaky stairs, hoping that this whole thing wasn't going to turn out to be one of Steve's famous practical jokes.

As they climbed the stairs, the sounds of the school receded and a heavy silence seemed to descend, broken only by footsteps and creaks. Belladonna reached the top and stepped into the dim gray light of a long, narrow attic.

"This is amazing!"

The eaves of the building met in a cobwebby gloom above their heads, old ribbons and pieces of newspaper dangled from the rafters, and a few faded photos stared earnestly from the walls. At each end was a dusty circular window letting in a flimsy, filtered light. The old floorboards were dirty and marked with the remains of over a hundred years of spiders and their winged victims. Belladonna crept through the dangling, dusty webs to where a series of boards were stacked against the wall. She flipped them over. They were old posters promoting coffee mornings, tea parties, choir festivals, and Christmas concerts. All held at a time before her grandmother was even thought of.

"That's not it," whispered Steve, as if anyone could hear them this far up.

He beckoned her over to the far side, where two large trunks lay side by side. She flung open one of the lids while Steve tried to clean the window with the sleeve of his jumper in an effort to get a bit more light into the room. The trunk was full of clothes, the things that people wore back in the days when they changed for lunch and tea and dinner. The colors were muted, but the contrasts strong—pale coffee shades matched with dark chocolate, sky blue, and purple. The colors that people chose when they didn't care what others thought, when they set fashions and didn't follow them.

Belladonna held them up, wanting to mock them as tasteless, but secretly longing for the confidence to stalk the halls in yellow and black.

"Not that one," Steve turned around. "The other one. It's full of papers."

Belladonna closed the lid of the clothes trunk and heaved the lid of the second one open. A hinge gave out with a crack and the lid fell against the wall with a resounding bang.

They froze. Listening.

Nothing. They were too far away for anyone to hear.

The box was full of the sort of bits of paper that people put aside but never really look at again. Programs, dance cards, reports, essays, articles from the local newspaper about dances, charity balls, and teas. There were a few letters and invitations, all dated from the early 1900s through the late 1920s. Belladonna read them and wished that she'd lived then. Perhaps if she had, she'd know what to do and say; she'd know how to dance and what to wear. She gazed at a newspaper photograph of the girls (it had been a girls' school then) who had held a charity ball for the soldiers in South Africa. Their faces seemed so grown-up and confident. Not like her at all.

"I knew it!"

Steve held up a fragile, yellowing newspaper,

breaking Belladonna's self-pitying reverie. She scuttled around to the other side of the chest and looked over his shoulder. It was a copy of the local paper from 1912. The headline read: "Local Girl in Terrible Tragedy!" And there was a picture of the victim, looking just the same as the girl outside Miss Parker's office, only a little more stiff. Her name was Elsie Blaine.

"It doesn't really do me justice, does it? I had a really nice one taken just the month before in a new lawn dress. Made me look quite ethereal, according to Mamma."

Steve dropped the paper. "What was that? Did you hear something?"

Belladonna looked at him suspiciously. "Like what?"

"Like . . . like . . ." He looked around nervously. "Like talking. Whispering."

"Saying what?"

Could he really have heard it? Could there be someone else?

"I don't know, I couldn't hear it properly. Something about a lawn and ether."

Belladonna smiled and nodded slowly. "It was her."

"Who?"

Belladonna hesitated . . . Steve looked like spiders were running up and down his back.

"Elsie," she nodded toward the paper. "It was Elsie. She said she didn't like the picture and that she'd had a better one taken right before she died. In a white lawn dress."

"I didn't say it was white, I said it was lawn."

"Did you hear that too?" Belladonna hardly dared hope. "Can you see her?"

"No. Wait. *See* her?" Steve backed away, stumbled over a pile of cardboard boxes, and fell down.

Belladonna reached out a hand to help him up. He took it, but as he scrambled to his feet, his face froze.

"Oh, my god! There's someone there! Right behind you!"

3

The Hound

"WELL, OF COURSE!" said Mr. Johnson. "Why do you suppose they hold hands at séances?"

Mrs. Johnson looked up from her béarnaise sauce long enough to remark, "Yes, but those things are nearly all a crock, dear."

"I know, but the point is that the tradition—the holding of hands—started somewhere. There had to be a reason for it in the first place, didn't there?"

Belladonna had to agree that it all sounded plausible. She tried to think back to remember if she'd ever touched anyone else when she'd seen a ghost.

"I always thought the reason was safety," said Mrs. Johnson as the silky sauce poured itself into a small bowl. "If everyone's holding hands, then you know no one's leaving the table in the dark to play the part of the wandering spirit."

"Or steal the silver," remarked Mr. Johnson, grinning.

After dinner, the family sat down in front of the television, but Belladonna's attention really wasn't on the convoluted lives of the families in the small fishing town of Staunchly Springs, where everyone was either in love with someone who didn't like them, engaged in nefarious business practices, or burying their nearest and dearest under the new patio at the bottom of the garden. She looked at her hands.

"Why should someone be able to see what I see just by touching my hands?"

"It's not just your hands," said her father, "it's anything. He probably heard just a little of . . . what did you say her name was? Oh, Elsie, that's right. He probably heard Elsie because your shoulders or arms were touching while you leaned over the chest. But with layers of shirts and jumpers between you, the signal didn't come in very clear."

"So I'm like a radio?"

"More like a hot pan," he gestured toward the television. "He's not laying that concrete very well. They'll be finding the body before it's dry."

"A hot pan?"

Mrs. Johnson was beginning to get irritated—
Staunchly Springs was her favorite show and she didn't like people nattering through it.

"You're a conductor, dear. Now be quiet while I watch my program."

Belladonna watched for a while, then got up and went into the kitchen to do her homework. She hauled the books out of her bag, spread them out, and stared at them. She did the same thing every evening, and every evening she asked herself the same question: Should she start with the Math and get it over with or go with the easier option (which tonight was History)? She opened the Math book and looked at what she had to do.

She slammed it shut. Definitely History.

Belladonna had always liked History, even before she could see ghosts. Of course, now that she could, it was much more interesting. If she ever met the shades of Charles I or Anne Boleyn, she'd be ready with some conversation. She wondered if Anne knew that her daughter had become England's greatest queen, and if Charles had ever had the least inkling that the Parliamentarians were prepared to cut his head off. She had to believe that if he had, he wouldn't have been so spectacularly dim-witted in his scheming. Although, from her observations watching the evening news, it had struck her that very few people ever lost money betting on the stupidity of politicians.

She thought about Elsie with her long skirts and that big bow in her hair. There was nothing of the Victorian fading violet about her, but when she had lived, women hadn't even been allowed to vote. Belladonna reckoned she should ask Elsie about that the next time she saw her.

She turned the pages of the book over to see how

much she had to read. Fifteen pages. Right. Better get started, then.

She leaned her elbows on the table, covered her ears to block out the sound of *Staunchly Springs* from the living room, and began to read. She'd only managed about two sentences, however, when her thoughts drifted back to the look on Steve's face when he'd seen Elsie. She wondered what he was thinking about now. Was he excited to have seen a ghost, or would he be spending the next few nights with the light on, jumping at every sound and peering into the shadows?

Belladonna pushed her black hair out of her eyes and looked up at the kitchen clock. It had been two years since she'd started seeing them. Her parents had been alive then and her mother had told her that it was just a family trait, like red hair or big ears. At the time, Belladonna had thought that, on the whole, she'd have preferred the red hair. She didn't want to be different, and she was terrified of being caught talking to something that no one else could see. School was bad enough already, what with being so skinny and having hair that hung down the sides of her face like the "before" picture in an advert for hair stuff. All she needed to cement her role as the class outcast was for someone to find out that she saw ghosts. Or thought she did. Because, of course, no one would believe that she really was conversing with the dead. The result was that she turned in on herself more than ever, which had the same effect as if her classmates *had* known about the ghost thing.

Then her parents had died, and she was suddenly grateful for the family trait. But it was still a secret. So far as the school authorities were concerned, Belladonna lived with her grandmother. Now, though, someone else had seen. It wasn't just her.

She smiled and turned back to the History book.

After half an hour, the battles of the Civil War were oozing together into a great morass of Cavaliers, Roundheads, and brave ladies defending castles. Somewhere in there, Belladonna was almost sure, were some facts that might actually show up in an exam. She counted the pages again. Six to go. She sighed, got up, and poured herself a glass of water. She sat down again, read a page, then realized she couldn't remember what she'd read. Was this important? Was there going to be a test? Because if there wasn't, maybe she could get away with just skimming over it.

She never got that far. The muffled sound of the closing theme song to *Staunchly Springs* (tinklingly cheerful, but with just enough minor chords to remind you about the body under the patio) was suddenly drowned out by an almighty crash.

And then silence.

Belladonna raced into the sitting room. Her father was standing in front of the fireplace with his mouth hanging open, but there was no sign of her mother.

"What happened?"

He didn't say anything. The chair that her mother had been sitting in (well, pretending to sit in) was on its side, the television was still wittering away, and her father was staring at a spot somewhere in the middle of the room. Belladonna detected a faint smell, as if someone had struck a match and then immediately blown it out.

"Dad," she was trying to keep the panic out of her voice. "What is it?"

He looked at her, as if he didn't know who she was. Then he was himself again.

"Something's wrong," he said.

"That's what Elsie said, but—"

"No, listen, I don't know how long I've got," he was speaking rapidly, urgently, not the way he usually spoke to his daughter.

Belladonna's eyes widened. There was a knot in her stomach.

"You're going to have to call your Aunt Deirdre. She'll know what to do. Tell her what's happened. Tell her the doors are closing."

"But what *has* happened? What doors?"

"The doors to the Other Side. Tell her there's only one left. She'll know which one. And don't go out. Whatever you do, don't go out until she gets here."

"But—"

She never got any further. The words froze in her throat as she saw her father seem to compress inward and squeeze upward until he became a thin line from floor to ceiling before both ends of the line shot together and he vanished, leaving a small bright spot, which faded to nothing.

Belladonna stared at the space where he had been, half expecting him to flash back into existence again and reveal that it had all been a huge joke. But he didn't. The room was empty and silent except for the endless cheery blather of the television. She glanced at the woman reading the news, her too-white smile cutting into the room. Belladonna turned on her heels and ran into the hallway. She pulled her mother's address book out of a drawer in the hall stand and frantically leafed through it. Her hands were shaking and tears were burning in her eyes when she picked up the phone, and it took her two tries to get the number right.

"Hello?"

The voice on the other end was brisk and no-nonsense. Belladonna felt better already. She took a deep breath.

"Aunt Deirdre," she said, trying not to sound as scared as she felt, "it's Belladonna."

There was a moment's silence on the other end of the phone.

"What's happened?"

Belladonna related the evening's events. Aunt Deirdre asked a few questions, but mostly just listened. When Belladonna finished, there was silence on the other end of the phone.

"Hello?"

"I'm here," said Aunt Deirdre in a voice that was still matter-of-fact and calm. "Right. I'm on my way. Lock the doors. Are the curtains drawn?"

"I'm not sure. Some, I suppose. . . ."

"Draw them. Don't go outside."

"But what about—"

"Don't speak. Listen. What did I just say?"

"Don't go outside. Lock the doors. Draw the curtains."

"Good. I'll be there as soon as I can."

There was a click as Aunt Deirdre hung up. Belladonna put the phone down slowly. She was glad that Aunt Deirdre was coming, but knew it would take her a while. She lived in London, where she had something to do with banks or finances. Even if she started out now, Belladonna knew it was a three-hour drive. Maybe she should call her grandmother.

She had her hand on the phone before she thought better of it. If it wasn't safe for her to be out, then it probably wasn't safe for Grandma Johnson either, and Belladonna knew that the old lady wouldn't listen to reason and stay at home; she'd be marching through the darkened streets in her sensible shoes to try and save the day.

No, the best thing to do was just wait for Aunt Deirdre.

Belladonna checked the locks on the front and back

doors and drew all the curtains. She sat in front of the television for a few minutes, but couldn't concentrate on it. She got up and decided that she'd better make sure that all the windows were closed and locked. By the time she reached the front bedroom, it was pitch-dark outside. She checked the latches, rattled the windows, and was about to turn away and check the other bedrooms when she saw a movement out of the corner of her eye. There was something in the garden.

She looked down. There was a large black shape in the middle of the lawn, right next to the water feature. It seemed to be some kind of dog, though it was nothing like any dog that Belladonna had ever seen. Its head was huge, and its body was massive and muscular. As she looked at it, it seemed to notice her and the great black head tilted up. Two cold yellow eyes met her gaze. They weren't the eyes of a dog; there was intelligence in them . . . and recognition.

They stared at each other for a moment, then the dog turned and loped out of the garden and away down the street, always keeping to the shadows until it became a part of them and was gone.

Belladonna stood at the window, frozen. Was that the dog that she had seen in the shadows the night before? It seemed bigger now, but perhaps that was just because of her state of mind. She remembered once, when she was little, she had kicked up an enormous fuss over a "gigantic" spider in her room, but when her Dad had come up and caught it in a glass, it had turned out to be quite small. Perhaps it was just an ordinary stray dog after all.

On the other hand, maybe it wasn't. She strained to see it further along the street, but there was no sign of it. She bit her lip for a moment, then turned and raced through the house, turning on every available light. Finally, she took the phone into the sitting room, turned the television up loud, and sat in front of it, her back against the fireplace, waiting.

Three hours isn't really very long. Unless, of course, your parents have just vanished and you're sitting alone in an empty house with a large, slavering, black doglike creature outside somewhere.

If that's the case, then three hours can seem more like three weeks.

Belladonna sat and waited. She turned the television down, in case the sound masked something more sinister, like scratching at the doors. She didn't turn it off because the bright movement made things seem more normal. She looked at the toppled chair and felt the tears welling up in her eyes again. She wiped them away with the back of her hand. This was no time to cry, she knew that, but the knot in her stomach had turned into a deep, dark pit. What if her parents never came back? What if this time they were gone for good?

It would be worse than the first time. At least then,

there had been the hospital and the crash and things sort of made sense. But to get them back and then just have them vanish—to be left alone again . . .

Belladonna stood up and straightened her mother's chair.

Time crept slowly by.

Gradually, she became less scared and more irritated. She wanted to do something. Sitting, cowering, and waiting for someone to come and save her seemed so spineless. If she were a character in a TV show, she thought, she'd turn it off in disgust.

She stood up and turned off the living room lights, then she went to the window and opened the curtains. Outside, everything seemed normal. The stars were out, there was no black dog, and she could see Mr. Loftus from across the road, arriving home. He always worked late. She watched him get out of his car. No evil creatures waylaid him before he got to his front door, and nothing crept from bush to bush. He just walked to the front door as he always did, turned his key in the latch, and went inside.

Belladonna pulled a chair up to the window. This was much better than sitting by the television; she didn't feel at all worried when she could see that everything was normal.

She was still watching when Aunt Deirdre arrived. She careened around the corner in a small green sports car that hugged the road and made a noise like the rumbling of the earth. She parked it outside the house and unfolded herself from the driver's seat.

Aunt Deirdre was stick-thin and very tall. She had blond hair and an imperious manner that dared anyone to get in her way. She wore impeccable suits that showed quite a bit of leg when she sat down but might as well have been trimmed with barbed wire for all the encouragement they offered the opposite sex. Belladonna had always been fascinated by her aunt and more than a little afraid. She went to the front door and opened it.

Deirdre Nightshade strode in. "Lock that."

Belladonna did as she was told and followed Aunt Deirdre into the sitting room. Her aunt marched straight to the window and drew the curtains, then she turned the lights on and the television off. She poured herself a whiskey and soda from the cabinet, sat down, and looked at Belladonna.

"Tell me what happened."

Belladonna related the events of the evening again. She also mentioned the incident with the dishwasher the night before, Elsie's concern that something was wrong, and, as an afterthought, Lady Mary's vanishing baby. Aunt Deirdre nodded.

"Well," she said, "we can't do anything tonight. Help me make up the bed in the spare room." She led the way upstairs.

"Will I be going to school tomorrow?"

"Of course. Why ever not?"

"Well, you made it sound —"

Deirdre opened the linen cupboard and whisked some sheets, blankets, and a pillow out. She marched into the chilly spare room. "Just make sure you're home before dark."

The next morning, Belladonna drifted downstairs. She hadn't slept much, tossing from one side of her bed to the other and replaying the disappearance of her father in her head. On the brief occasions when she did manage to get to sleep, her dreams were almost instantly interrupted by the yellow eyes of the black dog, looking up at her and *knowing*. She ended up spending most of the night staring at the strip of sky between her bedroom curtains and waiting for the stars to flicker off again. It seemed that they ought to, that the disappearance of her parents and the arrival of the monstrous black dog should have some reflection in the natural world. But the stars stayed where they were and everything seemed the same, even though it wasn't.

Aunt Deirdre was already downstairs by the time Belladonna got there. She had put out a bowl and a spoon with a paper napkin to one side, but most of the kitchen table was taken up with her laptop and stacks of paper, which she riffled through with one hand while holding her mobile to her ear with the other and giving some poor underling hell for presuming not to be at work at seven o'clock in the morning. Belladonna sighed and fetched the cereal out of the cupboard. She pushed it around the bowl for a while, but Aunt Deirdre showed very little sign of getting off the phone. One call followed another and they all seemed to involve the person at the other end getting shouted at for not doing something that she told them to do yesterday. Belladonna reflected that working in big business in London sounded worse than school; at least they got breaks and Miss Parker didn't call them at home at the crack of dawn to see if they'd done their homework.

She emptied the cereal into the bin, stuck the bowl in the dishwasher, and grabbed her bag. As she pulled on her coat, Deirdre covered the phone with her hand.

"I'll see you this evening," she said. "Remember, get home before dark. What?! Well, what's it doing there? I told you to handle it three days ago!"

Belladonna slipped out of the front door and marched off to school, quite cheerful, under the circumstances. Things might look grim—she had lost her parents for a second time, she hadn't done her homework, and a huge black hound seemed to be watching the house—but at least she didn't have to go to work in an office.

The morning was cold, one of those crisp, clear days when you can see your breath and the frost sparkles on the grass. A few optimistic leaves still clung to the branches of the trees that shaded Lychgate Lane, confident of a few more days of sunshine before the long winter nights and gloomy winter days condemned them to months of suspended animation. Belladonna was surprised, and a little ashamed, to realize that she was swinging her bag and listening to the birds, instead of trudging gloomily and giving in to the foreboding she was fairly sure she ought to be feeling right about now.

She pushed her hair away from her face and tipped her head up to drink in the sunshine. She'd hardly ever missed school (except for a few colds and that time she'd had the flu and been off for a week), but on days like this she could understand why some kids skived off and spent the day in the park.

Unfortunately, the walk to school wasn't a long one and, as if to bring her back down to earth, Math was the first class of the day, forcing Belladonna to make up some less-than-convincing reason why she hadn't done her homework. Mr. Fredericks hardly seemed to listen, moving right on to the next exercise. So far as he was concerned, if students couldn't be bothered to do their homework, then he couldn't be bothered to teach them. Belladonna sighed. She had only managed to keep up with Math by slogging away and making sure she did every single piece of homework. Now she'd missed one exercise and suddenly everything was a mystery. She had the sinking feeling that she would never again know what was going on in this class.

She looked over to the window. The morning light had turned thin and gray, and she could see large black birds fighting in the bare branches of the trees at the end of the football pitch. As she watched, she became aware that she was being stared at too. She turned her head. Steve quickly looked down at his book and pretended to be working. She knew he was pretending because he always sat right at the back and spent most of his time whispering with his friends. He wasn't whispering today, though.

After an interminable forty minutes, the bell sounded and everyone packed their bags and headed for French. Belladonna trudged along the corridor, wishing she'd called in sick and wondering what Aunt Deirdre was doing. Would her parents be back when she got home? Would everything be back to normal? Or was this going to be "normal" now? As she moped, lost in dismal thought, Steve caught up with her.

"Hey."

She glanced at him and managed a nod.

"Does that . . . what happened yesterday," he seemed to be trying to avoid saying the word. "Does that happen to you all the time?"

"Ghosts, you mean?"

Steve nodded quickly, glancing around to make sure none of his friends was nearby.

"Yes," said Belladonna, "all the time."

They walked on. He glanced around again.

"Are there any here now?"

Belladonna stopped. She didn't have the patience for this. She opened her mouth to speak and then realized that there weren't any. Not a single one. She looked back the way they'd come, half expecting to see Elsie loitering near the girls' toilets, or those two little boys who sometimes raced down the corridors, or that daunting old teacher with the black academic gown and the haggard expression who lurked near the stairs to the science labs. Nothing.

She looked at Steve and shook her head. "No."

"Oh," he seemed almost disappointed.

"It's really strange," she muttered as they trudged on toward their French class.

Steve grinned. "Only you would think it was strange *not* to see a ghost."

Belladonna didn't reply. She suddenly realized that something was seriously wrong. It wasn't just that her parents had vanished or that she couldn't see any ghosts in school. It was more than that. It was as if there were no ghosts anywhere. None. The whole world seemed suddenly empty.

She endured French, but her mind was elsewhere. Outside, the big black birds were still screaming at one another in the trees at the end of the football pitch. Belladonna found herself doodling page after page of doors.

"The doors are closing."

That's what her father had said. She looked at her drawings, then stopped. She turned the pages of her exercise book back. The doors were all the same, but there was something odd about them. For some reason she knew they were supposed to be red, and she knew that the squiggle in the middle was a number. But what number? It was important, she knew it was important, but even though she'd drawn the doors herself, she had no idea what the number was supposed to be.

She had just decided to draw another door and this time try to think about the number, when she realized that the room was unnaturally quiet. She looked up. Madame Huggins was looking at her, and so was everyone else. Obviously Madame had asked a question and equally obviously, Belladonna did not have a clue what it was.

She looked at the blank faces around her and the questioning yet rather smug face of Madame. Teachers only got that face when they thought they'd got you dead to rights. Belladonna thought about this for a moment, and thought about all the times she'd seen various teachers looking at Steve in exactly this way, and she decided she knew what the question had been.

"*Je dessine des portes, Madame,*" she said.

Madame looked crestfallen.

Steve's mouth dropped open in amazement.

After class he scurried to catch up with her in the corridor.

"How did you know?" he asked.

"How did I know what?" asked Belladonna innocently.

"What she'd asked. You were a million miles away. There's no way you heard a word she said."

"Because that's what they always ask."

Steve looked at her blankly.

"They notice someone isn't paying attention. Usually you," explained Belladonna with a smile. "Then they get this smug expression like they've just aced their category on *Mastermind* and they say, 'Well, Mr. Evans, if what you're doing is so much more interesting than this class, why don't you share it with us?' Or something like that. I just guessed that, being Madame, she'd probably gone one step further and said it in French."

Steve shoved his hands into his pockets and grinned.

"Brilliant," he said. "Her face was a picture! Did you see—"

He never got any further. Belladonna had grabbed him by the blazer lapels and yanked him back into an alcove near the stairs to the science labs.

"Ow! What on earth d'you—"

"*Shhhhhh!*" hissed Belladonna.

Steve was about to push her away and dart back out into the corridor, when he noticed the expression on Belladonna's face. "What is it?" he whispered.

Belladonna peered out into the corridor. Steve followed her gaze. A tall, thin, and imposingly beautiful woman was walking toward them with Mrs. Jay, the school secretary.

"Who's that?"

"It's my Aunt Deirdre."

The two women passed close enough for them to get an unwelcome whiff of Aunt Deirdre's very expensive perfume. Belladonna glanced at Steve nervously, suddenly aware that what she had done was the kind of thing that would probably only add to her "weird girl" image. He clearly had no idea why they were hiding, but his expression made it all too obvious that there was something about Belladonna's aunt that made hiding in a corner seem like a really good idea. Mrs. Jay started up the stairs toward Miss Parker's office.

"This way, Miss Nightshade," she simpered.

Belladonna waited until they had reached the first landing and started up the second flight before she stepped out into the corridor.

"Why were we hiding?" asked Steve.

"I don't know," Belladonna frowned. "It's just that . . . I mean, why would she come here?"

She gazed up the stairs, then sighed and walked away down the hall. Steve glanced around and then scurried after her.

"Well, she is your aunt. Maybe it's just something to do with school. My parents are always being hauled in for one thing or another."

"Why aren't I surprised?" smiled Belladonna.

They walked on toward the lunch room in silence.

Belladonna's mind was far away, thinking about her parents' disappearance, the black dog, and Aunt Deirdre's take-charge manner. It was becoming obvious that her aunt was going to be even less communicative about what was going on than her parents. And they were *her* parents, after all. If anyone had a right to know what had happened to them, it seemed like it should be her. Belladonna decided she had to find out more herself. Starting now.

As they passed the girls' toilets, she suddenly darted for the door.

"I'll see you later!" she said cheerily, and left Steve standing alone in the hall.

"Great," he muttered, "girls!" and shambled off for his lunch.

Belladonna waited in the toilets until she thought he'd gone. Two other girls were in there, primping in front of the mirrors, exchanging lip gloss, whispering, and giggling. Belladonna glanced at her own reflection; her long, pale face, lank dark hair, and dark blue eyes stared back. She never came into the bathroom to primp; she usually stayed as far away from mirrors as she could. And even though her mother had always assured her that she was "striking" and that being striking was much better than being merely pretty, there was a little corner of her soul that longed to have cascading curls and clear blue eyes.

After about five minutes, she poked her head out

of the toilets and looked up and down the corridor. A few stragglers dawdled along, but almost everyone was having lunch. She eased out and walked quickly along toward the stairs to the science labs and Miss Parker's office.

Once there, she ran up the stairs as quietly as she could until she reached the top floor and the door to the attic. It took a couple of tries, but she managed to heave it open, and crept up the dark stairs to the room at the top. The old posters and trunks of papers were still there, but she wasn't interested in them today. If this was the attic, she reasoned, there must be more of it. And if there was more, maybe she could find the part that was above Miss Parker's office.

She made her way to the darkest end of the room and, sure enough, next to a long-discarded wooden filing cabinet there was a narrow doorway. She stepped through and almost immediately heard the muffled buzz of voices.

She started to tiptoe across the room, when one of the boards suddenly let loose with an agonizing creak. Belladonna became a statue. Did the voices stop? Did they hear? She had no idea. No, the low hum of conversation was still there.

She started across the room again, but this time she tested each board before she put her full weight on it; if it creaked, she tried another one. Her progress was slow, but she finally reached a part of the dark, cobwebby attic where she could almost hear what they were saying. There was only one thing for it.

She looked around carefully to make sure there were no spiders in the immediate vicinity, and then carefully lay down on her stomach. A pinprick of light snuck through a tiny knothole in one of the aged gray floorboards. Belladonna put her eye up against it and was amazed to find herself looking down into Miss Parker's office! Beneath her she could see the thick carpet, the weirdly foreshortened Picasso print, the gleaming desk, and the tops of two heads bobbing in conversation. The sleek blond one was unmistakably Aunt Deirdre; the other was dark, with streaks of gray.

"It's all very well," said Miss Parker, with a twang of irritation in her voice, "but we don't know where it is. And even if we did—"

"Let me worry about that part," interrupted Aunt Deirdre. "It's here somewhere. We've always known it was here. And that's not all."

Miss Parker didn't seem to move but Belladonna knew she was probably fixing her aunt with that "get-on-with-it" stare that terrified the socks off most of her pupils.

"The Hound was out last night," said Aunt Deirdre, "not two hours after the event."

There was a long pause. Belladonna held her breath.

"I would guess that it was probably here much earlier," whispered Miss Parker, so quietly that Belladonna could hardly hear.

"What?" now it was Aunt Deirdre's turn to sound irritated.

"Didn't you see the sky two nights ago?" asked Miss Parker.

"No. Why?"

There was a pause, then Aunt Deirdre leaned forward, a new note of tension in her voice.

"Are you saying there was an intrusion? Are you sure?"

"Quite sure," said Miss Parker, as if she were describing the morning's milk delivery. "Someone is using Old Magic."

"Surely you don't think . . ."

"I don't know." Now Miss Parker was sounding impatient. "It shouldn't be possible, but it's difficult for me to find out from here. You should go to see the old woman tonight, maybe she'll have an idea."

"An idea? For heaven's sake, woman, she hosts *séances*," Aunt Deirdre's voice dripped contempt.

Miss Parker stood up. "She's not as foolish as she may seem," she said. "Besides, you shouldn't let your personal feelings affect your judgment."

"Yes, but—"

"I'll check the library. We'll speak tomorrow."

Belladonna couldn't believe that Miss Parker was ordering her indomitable aunt about as if she were an uncooperative shop assistant. As she looked at the tops of their heads, she saw Miss Parker's tilt slightly to the side.

Aunt Deirdre sniffed and picked up her ludicrously expensive patent leather designer bag. "Until tomorrow, then."

She turned on her heel and marched out. Belladonna heard the door click shut and watched as Miss Parker slumped in her chair.

The door buzzer sounded.

"Oh, go away," she muttered.

Belladonna waited until she felt Aunt Deirdre must have left the building and then made her way carefully back downstairs. She walked quickly to the lunch room and stood in line with her tray. The dinner ladies doled out a dollop of shepherd's pie and some gray-looking peas. Belladonna helped herself to a carton of fruit juice and meandered over to a table.

The room was sparsely populated by this time. Most people had eaten lunch and dashed outside to take advantage of the late autumn sunshine. The chess club was there, of course, in a far corner with their boards and their endless games. They never went outside, but spent all their spare time huddled indoors, pale and bog-eyed like cave-dwelling fish.

She stared at her plate, but all she could think about was Aunt Deirdre and Miss Parker. They knew each other, that much was obvious. And from what they said, it sounded like they had been expecting something like this. But why were they so worried? After all, she didn't want the ghosts to vanish, because it would mean never seeing her parents again, and perhaps Deirdre was bothered that she might not see her sister. But why would Miss Parker or anyone else care at all?

Belladonna looked at her lunch. The shepherd's pie had bits of diced carrot in it. She sighed and pushed the plate away. If there was one thing she couldn't stand, it was stealth vegetables.

At least she'd been right about one thing: The Hound *had* appeared when the stars blinked off, so it must all be connected. She wanted to ask someone, but she knew that Aunt Deirdre would say that she didn't have time and that her Gran would pretend that she didn't know anything about it.

Assuming that her Gran was the "old lady" that they'd been talking about, which she was pretty sure she was. And that was weird too, because Belladonna had never seen a single ghost in Grandma Johnson's house and had just assumed that the séance thing was all made up.

She opened the carton of juice and began to drink, then put it down and rummaged about in her bag, eventually coming up with three chocolate biscuits wrapped in plastic and two lonely Parma Violets. She was just unwrapping the biscuits when she noticed something—a kind of shimmering on the other side of the table. She watched with interest as Elsie slowly materialized.

This wasn't the Elsie of the day before, however. For one thing, she just wasn't as corporeal; Belladonna could see the door on the other side of the room quite clearly through her. And the confident swagger that had made Belladonna so envious upstairs in the attic had been replaced with a nervous watchfulness.

Belladonna opened her mouth to speak, but Elsie held up her hand.

"Don't say anything," she hissed. "Pretend you can't see me."

"Why?"

"They're watching. Pretend you can't see me."

Belladonna pulled her dinner plate back and began pushing the shepherd's pie around with her fork.

"Actually, I *can't* see you very well. You're transparent, you know."

"Sorry," whispered Elsie, "it's the best I can do right now."

Belladonna sneaked a look up at her while pretending to glance at the clock above the door. "What's wrong?" she asked. "I feel like . . . it seems like everyone has gone."

"I know. They have," her hand went to her chest, just below the knot of her school tie, as if she was checking that something was still there. "I'm safe . . . I think. But . . . I just managed to get through for a moment." Elsie glanced over at the window and stifled a gasp, "They're here!"

"Who? You're not making any sense."

"Look over at the window," said Elsie, whispering impatiently. "What do you see?"

Belladonna turned around and looked. The window

was long and narrow and extended the length of the lunch room. It was set high in the wall on the side nearest the grounds, so usually all you could see was sky. Today, though, the view of the sky was partially obscured by a row of five large black birds perched on the windowsill.

"Birds," said Belladonna, "really big ones. Crows, I think."

"They're ravens."

"I saw them earlier, fighting and flying around the trees at the far end of the football pitch."

Elsie shuddered. "They're Night Ravens," she said, as if that explained everything.

"They're what?"

"Oh, no! They've seen me!"

Belladonna turned to the window again. All five birds had turned around and were staring into the lunchroom. She turned back to Elsie with every intention of asking all about the birds, but the look on the ghost's face froze the words on her tongue.

"I have to go," said Elsie, slowly dematerializing. "I just wanted to tell you: Everyone is gone. Not just from here. There's no one. You have to find the door. It's here. It's red."

"What? Wait! I know that! But where . . . ?"

"You have to help us. Look for the red door."

And with that, she was gone. Belladonna stared at the space where she had been, and as she did, Elsie slowly reappeared.

"I almost forgot," she said, "the number is seventy-three."

She vanished again. For a moment the air shimmered, but Belladonna knew she wouldn't be back. She turned and looked at the birds. They were still there, only now they seemed to be staring at her.

She stood up, picked up her tray, threw away her lunch, and left the tray and her plate with the stacks of other dirty dishes. She glanced at the window again. They were still there. Staring. She stared back at them defiantly. She had no intention of being afraid of a bunch of scraggy black birds, no matter how big they were.

After a few moments of this, one of the birds spread its glistening blue-black wings and took off. The others followed, and for a moment Belladonna could see them sweeping through the autumn air. She went back to her table and picked up her bag.

Why on earth would Elsie be afraid of a bunch of birds? She trailed out of the lunch room and dawdled along to the library. And if Elsie was safe, why was she still afraid?

She sat down at a long table and pulled some homework out of her bag, but it was no use. All she could think of was red doors, ravens, and what on earth Aunt Deirdre and Miss Parker had been talking about. She took out her French exercise book and opened it with every intention of getting a head start on the next day's work, but something made her turn back the pages and look at her doodles. The endless sketches of doors marched across the pages. She had known that they were red, even though she'd only drawn them in pencil, but now she knew what the squiggle in the middle of each tall paneled door was.

It was the number seventy-three.

4

A Ham Sandwich

THE AFTERNOON SEEMED to drag on forever. Belladonna kept glancing at the clock above the classroom door and sneaking peeks at her watch, but each time it seemed that only five minutes had passed. How was that possible? How could things go quite so slowly? She sighed and fidgeted and didn't hear a word that anyone said all afternoon.

As soon as the final bell sounded, she grabbed her bag, raced to the cloakroom, snatched her coat, and headed out into the cold afternoon.

The black birds were still in the trees at the end of the football pitch, but she paid no attention to them. She just wanted to get home and talk to Aunt Deirdre. She had spent enough time wondering what was going on and knew that until she could get her aunt to talk to her about what was happening, she'd continue to have this lost-at-sea feeling.

She strode through the streets purposefully,

determined not to stop, but when she reached the newsagent's, she hesitated for a moment, then dashed inside for her Parma Violets. She almost picked up the newspaper, then remembered that she didn't need one. The thought made her stop. There was a strange feeling in her stomach and tears suddenly sprang to her eyes. They really weren't there any more. She thought of her parents' faces, smiling as she came home from school, or stern when she failed to do her homework or clean her room. Were they really gone forever this time?

A single tear rolled down her left cheek. She blinked her eyes and wiped it away with her hand. This would have to stop. If she was really going to find out what was going on, she couldn't start crying every time she thought about her Mum and Dad. She sniffed and wiped her eyes again, and as they came back into focus she noticed that the front-page story in the *Chronicle* was about a terrible train crash that had happened that afternoon. The pictures looked dreadful, all knotted steel and crushed carriages. Belladonna paused and picked up the paper. For some reason she thought she ought to buy it after all. She ran back to the counter and plunked down a few coins, then hared off again down the street.

She slowed down when she passed the launderette; perhaps Mr. Baxter would still be there. He always seemed such an "almost ghost," nowhere near as corporeal as her parents or Elsie. Perhaps he would still be waiting to wave to her through the window.

He wasn't. All she could see was broken-down washers and dryers and curling notices about washing powder and fabric softener and how the management wasn't responsible if someone came in and stole your clothes, but if you even thought about dyeing the living room curtains in one of their machines, the consequences would be too terrible to contemplate.

She picked up her pace again and in five minutes was bursting through the front door of her own house.

"I'm home!" she yelled, dropping her bag at the door and shrugging out of her coat. "Aunt Deirdre! I'm home!"

Silence.

She walked into the kitchen and saw a note on the table, propped up against the pepper grinder.

"Dear Belladonna," it said. "Gone to see your grandmother. Tea in fridge. Make sure you do your homework. Back soon. D."

Belladonna stared at it blankly for a moment, then smiled. She was right: Her grandmother *was* "the old lady" that Deirdre and Miss Parker had been discussing. It really was weird, though. As long as she'd known her, Aunt Deirdre had made fun of Grandma Johnson. And even her mother and father had been known to make the odd disparaging remark about her séances and palm reading. Why on earth would Aunt Deirdre even *think* about going to her for help, even if Miss Parker had said she should?

These thoughts passed through her mind in a flash,

of course, and within moments she had her coat back on and was dashing up the street toward her grandmother's. The going was slow, however, and the daylight was quickly fading. She slackened her pace. What about the Hound? Maybe she should go back and wait.

She turned the corner onto Dulcimer Lane and saw a familiar figure: Steve Evans popping wheelies in the road on his hand-me-down bicycle.

"Hey!" he shouted, and zoomed over, expertly spinning the bike on its back wheel as he did so. "What's up?"

Belladonna stopped, gasping for breath.

"My Aunt Deirdre," she panted, "she knows something. . . . She's gone to my Grandma's. . . . I have to find out . . ."

"Knows something?" said Steve. "About what?"

"All the ghosts have vanished. Something's wrong."

"That doesn't sound too wrong to me."

"But it is. I don't know why. . . . I just . . ."

Her voice petered off. She couldn't explain it. Couldn't explain the off-balance feeling she'd had, not so much since her parents had vanished but since she'd realized that everyone else had too. From the most imposing headless horseman to the tiniest protopoltergeist—they'd all gone.

"I have to go," she said, and took off again.

Steve easily caught up with her. "Hop on," he said.

"What?"

"The handlebars. Hop on. It'll be way faster."

Belladonna was dubious about this, but she scrambled onto the freezing handlebars and held on for dear life as Steve took off full tilt, his feet pumping the old pedals while the loose spokes created a rattling whir that bounced off the sides of the parked cars and sounded like either a roaring motorbike (Steve's opinion) or as if the whole rackety vehicle was about to shatter into its composite parts, leaving cyclist and passenger sitting in the middle of the road (the opinion of everyone else they passed).

"Where does she live?" he yelled.

"Yarrow Street. Number 3."

Steve turned a sharp right, narrowly missing a lady pushing her baby in a pushchair. The lady yelled some very unladylike things after them, but her voice soon faded in the rush of wind. They finally skidded to a stop around the back of Grandma Johnson's house.

"This is the back," said Belladonna, confused.

"Course it is," said Steve. "If you want to find out anything, you're going to have to eavesdrop, aren't you? Otherwise, all you'll get is that stuff grown-ups always hand out: Don't you worry about a thing, just do your homework, or eat your dinner, or clear the table. You know the sort of thing."

He was right, of course. Her Mum and Dad had never discussed anything serious with her, and as for Aunt Deirdre—well, Belladonna was fairly sure that she didn't even rate as a sentient life-form so far as her aunt was concerned.

The back alley was one of those old-fashioned ones with high brick walls and tall wooden gates. Belladonna slid off the bike and went to her grandmother's gate. It was locked.

Before she could even point out this fact, Steve had scrambled over the wall and dropped down silently on the other side. He opened the gate and grinned.

"You are *so* going to end up in jail," said Belladonna.

The two of them crept up the narrow garden, keeping close to the rhododendrons that lined one side. It was dark enough now for them to have a clear view into the brightly lit sitting room where Aunt Deirdre and Grandma Johnson were sitting near the fire, clutching cups of tea.

They made their way right up to the window, ignoring the thorns on the stumpy-looking roses and the sticky mud that seemed to be everywhere. The window was broad and tall, made up of five or six long panes, each of which had small stained-glass pieces at the top that opened to let fresh air in without causing a draft. Fortunately, one of these was wide open and the voices of the two women drifted out into the twilight garden.

"Well, it's all very distressing," said Grandma Johnson. "I didn't even get to say good-bye. Most thoughtless!"

"They didn't do it on purpose," snapped Deirdre impatiently. "Something's happened."

"Yes . . . something," agreed Grandma Johnson vaguely.

"And somebody is going to have to go and find out what."

"Go where, dear?"

"There. You know. Over. To the Other Side."

There was a long pause. Belladonna was tempted to raise her head and peek inside, but thought better of it.

"I think it's time for a glass of wine," said Grandma Johnson finally. "Will you join me? The sun's well over the yardarm."

Aunt Deirdre must have nodded, because there was another pause, the sound of glasses tinkling against each other, and a muffled pop as Grandma Johnson removed the cork.

"Now," said Grandma Johnson in a more cheery voice, clearly having had a sip, "where were we?"

"Someone," said Deirdre slowly (she was clearly having a very hard time keeping her patience), "has got to go over and find out what is going on."

"What is she blathering on about?" whispered Steve.

Belladonna held her finger to her lips. She had a feeling that something really important was about to happen.

"And what we need to know," continued Deirdre, "is where is the door?"

"Good heavens, child," said Grandma Johnson, "what on earth makes you think I'd know something like that?"

There was a pause. Steve looked at Belladonna

questioningly. She decided to risk a peek and slowly raised her head above the windowsill. She could see her grandmother sitting in her favorite chair, the glass of wine on a small table next to her. Aunt Deirdre was perched on a tall wingbacked chair with her back to the window; all Belladonna could see of her was one thin, perfectly manicured hand toying with a glass, but that hand positively exuded fury.

"Look," said Aunt Deirdre, "the Hound is out, there are Night Ravens in the trees around the school, and all the ghosts have vanished, so I'd really appreciate it if you'd stop the silly old biddy routine and tell me where the door is."

Grandma Johnson stared at Aunt Deirdre for a moment. Belladonna felt sorry for her—she'd once been on the receiving end of her aunt's wrath and remembered that it had made her feel like a very small animal that had been caught doing something dreadful to the best carpet.

Grandma Johnson was made of sterner stuff, however; her voice lost its comfortable tone and took on the timbre of someone who is used to being in charge.

"I'll thank you to stop using that tone with me," she said. "It might work on people in London, but this is not London, thank heaven, and I am not some office underling."

Steve pulled Belladonna back down. "Good for her!" he whispered.

"Still," continued Grandma Johnson, "the Hound. Well. A drop more, I think."

There was the sound of the cork again, followed by a brief gurgle as the wine flowed into the glass.

"The thing is, I don't know."

"Oh, don't be ridiculous—" began Aunt Deirdre, but Grandma Johnson cut her off.

"I'm serious. We lost track of it years ago. All I know is it's red and has the number seventy-three on it. It *is* here in town, that much I *do* know. But even if you found it, you wouldn't be able to go through."

"What is it?" whispered Steve, concerned; Belladonna had just got the most peculiar look on her face.

She shook her head to indicate she was fine and hazarded another peek into the room.

"But it's here?" asked Aunt Deirdre.

"Yes," nodded Grandma Johnson. "But—my goodness, is that window open? No wonder I'm freezing!"

Belladonna ducked down as her grandmother leapt to her feet, shut the window, and whisked the curtains shut. The two women continued talking, but now all Belladonna and Steve could hear was the muffled murmur of their voices.

"Well, that wasn't very useful," whispered Steve.

"How can you say that?" said Belladonna in amazement as they crept back down the garden. "The door is here. We know that."

"Where?" said Steve, who was starting to share Deirdre's frustration. "And what door?"

"The door to the Other Side!" said Belladonna. "When my Dad vanished . . . right before he went, he said that the doors were all closing. The doors to the Other Side. But apparently there's one left, and it's here in town somewhere."

"Wait . . ." Steve was staring at her. "Your Dad? Your dead Dad?"

"Yes," Belladonna decided that trying to make it all sound as matter-of-fact as possible was probably the best thing. "He and Mum are at home. At least they were. Or they were when I was there anyway, and—"

"So you don't live with your grandmother?"

Now it was Belladonna's turn to stare at Steve. Was that all he had to say? She'd just told him that she lived with her dead parents!

"No . . . Doesn't it bother you that my Mum and Dad are ghosts?"

Steve thought about this for a moment and shook his head. "Not really," he said finally. "I mean, if you can see the attic girl—"

"Elsie."

"Yes. Well, if you can see her and she's been dead for nearly a hundred years, it makes sense that you'd be able to see other people too. I mean, your parents have only been dead for . . ." His voice trailed off and he glanced at Belladonna nervously.

"It's alright," she said, managing a small smile. "I see them every day. Or I did."

Steve nodded and glanced at the window. "We'd better go."

They crept down the garden and out into the alley. Steve picked up his bike and Belladonna clambered back up on the freezing handlebars. He pushed off hard with his right foot and they rolled silently down the alley and back onto the rapidly darkening street.

They made their way back, slowly this time, passing brightly lit shops punctuated by the gap-toothed emptiness of closed businesses. The town wasn't as thriving as it had once been, and everywhere there were the signs of struggle and failure. Even the streetlights were intermittent, with repairs taking second place to other essential services, though looking at all the rubbish that was scattered about, it was hard to imagine which services were the essential ones. The little bike rolled on, passing speedily through well-lit sections, and slowing for the more dimly lit blocks where potholes lurked in the twilight.

Steve had been concentrating as they passed over the worst asphalt, but as they neared familiar territory, he was full of questions again.

"The Other Side," he said, "you mean like . . . the Land of the Dead, the place people go when they . . . ?"

"I suppose," said Belladonna reluctantly.

After their reappearance, she had somehow never thought of her parents, or any of the other ghosts for that matter, as dead. They weren't spirits either. There was something sort of ethereal and airy about the word *spirits,* and there was nothing ethereal about most of the ones she knew.

"And to get there, you just find a door with the number seventy-three on it?"

"Well, not *any* door. I mean, there are probably lots of doors with the number seventy-three on them. This is a special door."

"Special?"

"Um . . . it's red."

"So any red door with the number seventy-three on it is actually a portal to the Land of the Dead?"

She could hear the sarcasm in his voice and was just about to shoot some right back at him when she saw something in the street in front of them.

"Stop!"

"What?" he said, not stopping.

"It's the Hound!"

Steve glanced at Belladonna, then slowed down slightly and peered down the road ahead. In the distance he saw a tabby cat creep under a parked car, but there was definitely no dog.

"You're losing your marbles, Johnson," he said. "I mean, Elsie is one thing, but—"

He never got any further; Belladonna had slid one hand back along the handlebars and grabbed his left hand. The moment she made contact, he saw it.

A large black dog, teeth bared, stood in the road about six car-lengths in front of them. Now that she saw it again, Belladonna realized that it was the biggest dog she had ever seen. Not tall like a wolfhound or a Great Dane, but massive and powerful; its head was muscular and flat, with small ears pressed against its skull. The strangest thing of all, though, was the fur, which didn't seem like fur at all, but like a piece of the blackest starless night. A snarling hole into a place of nightmares.

Steve hit the brake and clamped his feet to the ground. The bike skidded to a halt, but as it did so, Belladonna lost her grip on the handlebars and shot off, hitting the ground with a thud and rolling forward along the road. For a moment, after she let go of his hand, Steve couldn't see the dog any more, but as he watched her skidding along the tarmac, the giant animal again shimmered into view.

Belladonna slid to a halt about a meter from the dog. Even in the dark, she could see the fog of its breath and the homicidal glint in its eye. To her horror, she discovered she couldn't move: She just lay there in the street, watching, as it crept closer and closer.

Just as she had decided that this really was it, something white flew past her face and landed at the dog's feet. The animal glanced down, then eagerly gobbled up the projectile before turning its attention back to the bigger prize. As it did so, it got what Belladonna could only describe as a funny expression on its face. Then, in the deepness of its fur, a sort of wrinkle appeared. No, more like a ripple, as if a stone had been thrown into a very deep, dark well.

And like a ripple, the waves seemed to spread outward, across and through the slavering beast, leaving . . . nothing. The dog simply vanished from the middle out. When the last vestige of beady yellow eye had disappeared, Belladonna turned and looked at Steve.

"What did you do?"

"Nothing," he stammered, still in shock, "I just threw it my leftover lunch. A ham sandwich . . . with mustard."

5

The Door

THE NEXT DAY was Saturday. On normal week-
ends, Belladonna would lie in bed late and look at
the sky through the narrow slit where her bedroom
curtains didn't quite meet. Her mother had made the
curtains and miscalculated by the merest scad, so a strip
of daylight always streaked into the room at dawn.

On this particular Saturday, as she blinked into the
late autumn sunlight, for a moment Belladonna imagined everything was as it used to be. She was curled
up in bed, her father had nipped out to get the paper,
and her mother was pottering away in the kitchen
inventing new and wonderful (and occasionally not so
wonderful) things to have for breakfast.

She lay very still, as if not moving would make it
true. But no amount of wishing could conjure up the
aroma of frying bacon, or the comfortable sounds of
to-ing and fro-ing with doors banging, pans dropping,
and her mother yelling after her father not to forget the

extra pint of milk. There weren't even any of the new sounds—the sounds that even the best-intentioned ghosts make: the creaking of floorboards, the sudden cold drafts, the dull thumps in the walls. Today, all was silent.

Outside, the Night Ravens cawed and squabbled in the trees. Belladonna got up and drew the curtains all the way back. The day was sunny, but there was a thinness to the air that told of cold and fast-approaching winter. She shivered, pulled on her dressing gown, and went down to the kitchen. Aunt Deirdre was already up, dressed, and finishing her breakfast. She looked up at Belladonna.

"The tea's just made," she began, then her eyes widened. "What on *earth* has happened to you?"

Belladonna was puzzled for a moment, then remembered the tumble from the bike. She had a scratch on one side of her face and a rather impressive scratch-bruise combo on her right arm.

"Oh, I fell off a bike," she said, in what she hoped was a nonchalant manner.

"You don't have a bike."

"I was riding on the handlebars of someone else's."

"Oh, very clever," said Aunt Deirdre. "I suppose you know how dangerous that is."

Belladonna shrugged and helped herself to cereal. Aunt Deirdre seemed to be having a maternal moment, however, and wouldn't let the subject drop.

"You could die doing that," she insisted, "roll under

the wheels of a car or something. Do you have any idea how inconvenient it would be if you ended up in the hospital?"

This didn't seem to require a response, so Belladonna just carried on getting her breakfast.

"No, I didn't think so," continued Aunt Deirdre. "Well, see if you can stay out of trouble for one day. I have a few errands to do."

She glanced at Belladonna and her face softened for a moment.

"I know it's hard," she said, "and we will talk, I promise. But there are things I have to do. Perhaps we'll go to the park tomorrow."

And with that, she was on her feet. She pulled on an exquisitely tailored yellow-brown jacket and grabbed her bag, her keys, and a map of the town and surrounding countryside. She ruffled Belladonna's hair with one of her long white hands and headed for the front door.

"Be good!" she called over her shoulder. "I'll be back by teatime!"

Before Belladonna could say anything, the door slammed, the car roared to life, and Deirdre Nightshade sped away up the road.

Belladonna knew where she was going, of course. She was going to look for red doors with the number seventy-three on them. But Aunt Deirdre was from London and Belladonna had lived her whole life here; she knew the roads, the parks, the back alleys (well, not as many as Steve), and the best shortcuts. If there was a red door with a number seventy-three on it some-where in town, she ought to be able to find it.

She ran upstairs and emerged wearing jeans, a T-shirt, and an old fleece-lined jacket. It had been blue at one time, but had long since faded to a kind of non-descript gray. Still, it was warm and inconspicuous— two definite assets considering the day and what she was planning to do.

She tucked her house keys and a few pounds into one of the inside pockets and zipped it closed, then she brushed her hair in the hall mirror and headed out to hunt for mysterious doors.

Of course, that was easier said than done. Common sense dictated that street numbers progressed in order, with odd numbers on one side and even on the other. But it didn't really work that way. Some houses had A's or B's after their numbers, some numbers were skipped, and some houses had no numbers at all, just names like "Rose Gables." (Sophie Warren lived there. She had a pony and entered gymkhanas. In her spare time she and her friends would smirk at Belladonna with her pale face and old clothes. Then they'd exchange makeup tips, hide in the toilets, and sneak out of school in the afternoon to go to the pictures.) Belladonna would have liked nothing better than to discover that Sophie actually lived at the gate to the Other Side, but she knew that things rarely worked out with that kind of poetic precision.

She trudged on up and down every street that

seemed hopeful—she even tried knocking on a couple of number seventy-threes that were green or blue. After all, the door might have started out red, but that didn't mean that it mightn't have been painted somewhere along the line. Each time she knocked, she half expected the door to swing open to reveal a gaping chasm, or a river with a blind boatman, or maybe a three-headed dog. But nothing like that happened. The first two times no one answered at all, and the third time the door was opened by a rather nice-looking lady in curlers. Belladonna asked if the lady knew the way to the High Street, as she was lost. It was the kind of desperate tactic she'd seen Steve use dozens of times when cornered in one class or another and she'd never found it convincing, but the lady in curlers smiled and pointed out the way, her eyes flickering with puzzled amusement.

Belladonna wandered on in ever-widening circles, up and down tree-lined streets, past the well-manicured lawns of houses where even the garages seemed to have received the television-interior-designer treatment, past rows of semidetacheds where proud gardens competed for attention, and past terraces with no gardens but really impressive shiny front steps and stained-glass panels hanging in the windows.

And then she found herself at the gate of St. Abelard's. It seemed so green and peaceful, and she really wanted a sit-down after meandering all over town.

She hesitated for a moment before pushing the gate open and going inside. She walked past the old church and on into the graveyard. The gravestones lurched, shoulder to shoulder, across the grass; there were simple stones, enormous carved angels, and stark stone sarcophagi. Some of them dated back to the seventeenth century, others seemed older, but the inscriptions had worn away after centuries of rain, wind, and sun. Belladonna could remember coming here, full of curiosity, to read the names, dates, and causes of death. Old gravestones were so detailed . . . they seemed to explain everything: when people were born, who they married, when they died, and what of.

Her own curiosity had melted away after the accident. Her parents were buried on the far side, near the trees. It was very pretty, but she couldn't go there.

Of course, she had always known that these were the final resting places of the once living, but it had never really registered until her own parents had joined their ranks.

She sniffed, tucked her hair behind her ears, and strode out toward the trees. She hadn't walked across this grass since the funeral. Today, it was wet and the long blades brushed against her trainers. She stopped near a moss-covered angel and listened, straining to hear the telltale rustle of grass. Back when she used to come here every day, she had been convinced that something else was here too. Not ghosts, not the spirits of the dead, but something alive and small. It was as if she was always just missing something out of the corner of her eye.

The last time, at the funeral, she had almost seen them, but not quite. She had felt them, though, the way you know when you're being stared at, as if they were peeking through bushes and down from the trees. But today there was nothing but silence.

She sat down on one of the great table tombs and looked at her parents' stones. They had seemed so stark and new and wrong at the funeral, but now they seemed to belong. There was a mist of green moss over them, and grass and dandelions clustered around their bases. Belladonna knew that her parents were there, but also that they weren't. The important part of them, the part that really mattered, was in the Land of the Dead. And at home, of course, when they wanted to be. But now they couldn't visit her at home any more, and if Elsie was right, they had vanished from the Other Side as well.

She could feel herself starting to drift into sadness, which wouldn't do any good at all, so she sat up a bit, pushed her hair off her face, and reached into her pocket for the remains of yesterday's packet of Parma Violets.

"They're gone. They left me behind."

Belladonna jumped. A small creature was suddenly sitting next to her. It looked like a tiny human: two feet tall, slightly built, with a tangled mass of golden curls, and an iridescent purple sheen to its pale skin that made her think of wrapping paper. It was wearing a loose gray tunic and one arm was in a homemade sling. It certainly wasn't the least bit threatening.

"Who's gone," she said finally, "the ghosts?"

"No, my family," the creature looked up at her. "There were never any ghosts here."

That was true. Graveyards were the one place where Belladonna never saw ghosts. They were always just quiet stone gardens, inhabited by rabbits, birds, and the quick-moving creatures she'd never quite been able to see until now.

"I'm Belladonna," she said, hoping that the creature would introduce itself, "Belladonna Johnson. My Mum and Dad are over there."

"Really?" The creature sounded genuinely interested. "I remember them! They didn't need any help at all—just took off right away."

"Took off?"

The creature nodded and rubbed its nose. Belladonna noticed faint dirty streaks on its face, as if it had been crying. It saw her concern and immediately drew back.

"Anyway," it said, somewhat sulkily, "my name's Aya."

"That's a pretty name," said Belladonna encouragingly. "Are you . . . an elf?"

Aya snorted at the suggestion, "An elf! Don't be ridiculous. Elves are imaginary creatures, like fairies and goblins. Do I look imaginary to you? Aren't you a bit old to be believing in that sort of nonsense?"

Belladonna stared at her. Aya was still shaking her head, a sarcastic sideways smile on her face. "An *elf*!"

"Well, if you're not an elf, what are you?" Belladonna was getting irritated.

Aya jumped off the tomb and into the long grass. "I'm a charnel sprite, of course. Don't you know anything?"

"Well, no . . . um . . . I'm sorry." She tried to look friendly. "What do . . . what do charnel sprites do?"

"Duh!" Aya rolled her eyes. "We wake them up and show them where to go, of course!"

"The dead people?"

"No, cows and squirrels. Of course dead people! Honestly! No wonder no one talks to you living people—you're so slow on the uptake!"

And with that, she was off, running through the grass and gone. Belladonna sighed and was just about to get off the tomb herself, when Aya was suddenly in front of her again.

"Watch out for the Hound," she said. "It came when we were leaving. It got my arm, and the rest of my family ran away."

"Thank you," said Belladonna, "but I think it's dead. Steve killed it."

"Can't have," said Aya matter-of-factly. "What did he do?"

"He threw half a ham sandwich at it."

"Did it eat it?"

Belladonna nodded, "And then it vanished in a sort of inside-out way."

Aya smiled, "What a good idea. Who is this Steve? Where did he learn about the food?"

"He's just a . . . just a friend," said Belladonna. "What about the food?"

"The dead can't eat food from the Land of the Living," explained Aya, as if it was the most obvious thing in the world. "It'll be back, though. I'm pretty sure it'd take more than half a ham sandwich to destroy the Hound."

She seemed very cheerful about the whole thing, particularly considering it had apparently tried to drag off her arm. She wiped the back of her hand across her face again and looked at Belladonna.

"You're looking for something," she said.

"What makes you think that?"

"You are, though, aren't you?"

"I'm looking for the door," said Belladonna. "It's red, with the number seventy-three on it."

"Why?" asked Aya.

"I have to get to the Other Side. The ghosts are missing."

"I know."

"Well, I have to . . . I don't know, I just feel like I have to do something."

Aya looked at her narrowly. "It's over there," she announced finally.

Belladonna stared at her. "I thought it was lost," was all she could say.

"Lost to some," said Aya, "and just as well, if you ask me. Anyway, it's in a building on that busy street. The one with the Chinese take-away."

"You like Chinese food?"

"All charnel sprites like Chinese food," said Aya. "We have very sophisticated tastes. Do you want to know about this door or not?"

"It's inside a building?" said Belladonna, quickly returning to the subject. "But I thought it'd be outside. I mean, with the number and everything. It sounds like a house door. Oh, I suppose it could be a hotel door."

"It could be," said Aya, "but it isn't. You shouldn't be so literal. Also, it's not really a door."

"Not really a door?"

"It *is* a door," explained Aya slowly, as if she were speaking to a very small child, "but at the same time it isn't. Though it can be. And in some ways it actually is."

Belladonna stared at her. It was the most unhelpful explanation she'd ever heard.

"You can't go through unless you have the Words, though. I mean you can, but it wouldn't be a door then. It only becomes a door when you say the Words."

At that moment there was a loud whistle over near a cluster of rhododendron bushes. Aya's face lit up. "They've come back for me!"

"Who have?"

"The others . . . my family."

"Your family? Do you live here?"

"We help the Dead, and this is where they are," said Aya.

"And you show them how to get to the Other Side?"

"Yeees," said Aya, clearly impatient, "I told you."

"Could you show me? I mean, I wouldn't need to waste time finding the door."

"It's not allowed," Aya glanced back nervously. "I shouldn't even be talking to you. I only started because I thought they'd gone. Anyway, it only works one way. I have to go."

Belladonna peered across to the long grass and thought she could make out the glinting of purplish skin. Aya waved her good hand and ran happily toward her family.

"Wait!" said Belladonna. "Do you know the Words?"

"I don't need to. Bye! Good luck!"

And with that, she turned, began to run, and was gone. The rhododendron bushes shook for a moment and then all was silent. Belladonna smiled. It was nice to think that there was someone waiting to show the Dead how to get to the Other Side. It was probably a confusing time. Her parents had never talked about it. Well, she'd never asked, and it had never occurred to her that there would be some sort of otherworldly tour guides to show the way. She'd have to ask her Mum and Dad about it when . . . well, if . . .

No. She shook her head to get the thoughts out of it. No wallowing. Wallowing never helps.

She jumped down off the tomb and walked toward the lych-gate, the grass slowly soaking her jeans. So it was somewhere on the High Street, but inside a building. That made things more difficult; the High Street was shops from one end to the other so it would have to be in a back room or something. How on earth was she going to get into the back of a shop without anyone knowing? Something like that would involve sneaking, which strictly speaking would be breaking and entering.

"You want to do what?"

Steve had to work at his parents' electronics shop on Saturdays, but spent most of his time lounging at the back near the CD players, reading comics.

"Have a look inside some of the shops. In the back. Without anyone knowing."

"But that's against the law."

"What about climbing over the gate into my Grandma's garden? That was against the law as well. At least I think it was."

"Yeah, but . . ." Steve put the comic down and shoved his hands into his pockets, the way he did when a teacher had got him into a corner and he actually had to come up with a reason for the First Reform Act or something.

"And your Mum and Dad probably know most of these people," Belladonna could sense that he was weakening.

"What are we looking for again?"

"I told you," sighed Belladonna. "A red door with the number seventy-three on it."

"A door with a number *inside* a house? That's stupid. Who told you that?"

"Aya. Um . . . she's a charnel sprite."

Steve looked at her for a moment, then picked up the comic book again. Belladonna knew she was losing him. Then inspiration struck—flattery.

"She also said she thought you were very clever. Thinking to give the Hound your sandwich."

"Clever?" said Steve. "Stupid, you mean. That thing could've eaten us both whole and had room for five more."

He went back to pretending to read the comic, but Belladonna knew he'd have to ask.

"Why was it clever?"

"Because," she said, "creatures from the Land of the Dead can't eat food from the Land of the Living."

"Really?"

Belladonna nodded. Steve put down the comic.

"That *was* pretty clever, wasn't it?"

In a few moments he had given his parents the slip and they were outside walking down the street, looking for likely shops.

"Does it work the other way around?" asked Steve after a while.

"What?"

"If you're in the Land of the Dead and you eat their food, will something terrible happen?"

Belladonna stopped. This was a really good point. "I don't know. . . ."

"Oh, well," shrugged Steve. "If we ever find our way in, I reckon we'd better take sandwiches and juice. Just to be on the safe side."

And with that, he strolled on, appraising each of the shops with a practiced eye.

The buildings on the High Street had been there for years; most of them had been built in the town's heyday back in the nineteenth century and featured stone pilasters and marble cherubs, tall windows and elaborately carved stone eaves. Nearly all of the architecture was now concealed behind billboards and neon signs, though, and the overall impression was of a busy but scruffy street that had seen much better days. None of the shops seemed to afford much prospect of abandoned back rooms, however. In most of them it was obvious that every square inch had been given over to selling space in an effort to eke the maximum income out of the property. Belladonna and Steve crossed the road when they reached the top and headed back down the other side.

"So," said Steve, "what's a charnel sprite when it's at home, then?"

"I don't really know. They live in graveyards, but I'd never actually seen one till today."

"Well, what do they look like?"

"Small," said Belladonna. "Smaller than us, and sort of untidy and slightly purple."

"Purple? Cool. What do they do?"

"She said that they wake people up after they've, you know, died."

"Like zombies?" said Steve, perking up.

"No, not like zombies. At least I don't think so. She said they wake them up and show them how to get to the Other Side."

"Ooohh. Right."

"What? What d'you mean, 'Right'?"

It didn't really make much sense to her; surely it couldn't make sense to Steve?

"It was in a film I saw at my Gran's," he explained. "There were these ghosts, but they didn't know they were ghosts, they thought they were alive and that the people who really were alive were ghosts. Someone had to tell them. It was a pretty boring film, mostly, but it picked up at the end."

Belladonna nodded. No wonder he never got any homework done; he seemed to spend all his time reading comics and watching films.

They kept walking, but she had stopped looking for possible locations for the doorway to the Land of the Dead and had begun eyeing bakeries and take-aways with a hungry eye. She hadn't had anything to eat since breakfast—and that had only been a bowl of cereal. The smell of Cornish pasties drifted across the pavement, melding with the aroma of chop suey rolls and chicken korma. She was paying so little attention that she didn't notice that Steve had stopped and was looking at something across the street. She narrowly avoided bumping into him, regained her footing, and then followed his gaze.

He was staring at his parents' electronics shop.

Evans Electrics occupied what had once been the town's best theatre. There was an enormous new sign above the door, but you could still make out the marquee behind it. Belladonna remembered her mother attending protests when it was announced that the building was to be let out for retail. The theatre had been closed for years, but the idea of it being gutted to make a shop had galvanized the whole town and protesters had camped on the pavement outside for weeks. Mrs. Johnson had spent hours in the garage painting increasingly outraged placards, but it was all no use. No financial angel had appeared to rescue the old music hall and it had finally been approved for retail space and let out to Steve's Mum and Dad for their electronics shop. Now what had been the lobby was full of shelf upon shelf of DVD players, CD combo units, and home theatre setups. Ranks of flat-screen TVs flickered at passersby, and toaster ovens and microwaves lurked at the back where uniformed ushers had once sold ice cream. It wasn't what you could call a classy-looking place, and Belladonna's Dad had frequently aired his opinion that most of the stock looked like it had fallen off the backs of trucks.

"What is it?"

Steve looked at her and smiled. "I know where there are loads of doors."

They dodged traffic across the road and darted down an alley at the side of the shop. Steve dashed around the rear of the old theatre and tried the back door. It was locked.

"Not to worry," he said, running over to where a small, dirty window looked down on the alley from about six feet above the pavement. "Give us a bunk up."

"What? Steve, this is *your* shop. Why can't we just go in the front?"

"Because my parents would have a cow. Come on!"

Belladonna made a basket with her hands; Steve put one foot in it and heaved himself up, grabbing the windowsill and dangling on one arm while he jiggled the sash with his free hand. The old latch slowly worked its way loose and the window slid open. Steve grinned at Belladonna and scrambled inside.

"Wait there!" he yelled, before vanishing into the darkness.

Belladonna wiped her hands on her jeans and hung about, visions of police stations dancing in her head. After a few moments there was the sound of bolts being slowly drawn back and the old door swung open.

"Get inside, quick!" Steve glanced nervously up and down the alley as Belladonna dashed inside.

As soon as the door was shut, Steve turned to Belladonna, suddenly serious.

"We have to be really quiet. If my parents find out we're back here, I'll be hung from the nearest lamppost."

"Why?"

"I promised. Now, hush and follow me."

He led the way down a narrow passageway that eventually turned a tight left-hand corner and widened out. Once they were away from the door, what little light there was vanished altogether. Steve put a hand up to the wall and felt his way along until he found a light switch. He flicked it on and a single bulb sparked to life halfway along, illuminating the dusty corridor and ranks of doorways on each side.

"Dressing rooms," whispered Steve, before leading the way forward through the corridor and out to a wider space, where an old standard lamp stood near a row of about eight hefty ropes that descended from the darkness above and were tied off on large wooden rods. He turned on the lamp, which cast a pool of sickly light, illuminating an area of about four square feet and revealing a huge board of switches on the wall. He hesitated for only a moment before pushing a switch near the left-hand side. There was a flicker and the space in front of them was suddenly bathed in light.

Belladonna gasped. "It's still here!"

"Well, sort of," said Steve, leading the way out onto the stage. "The seats had to go."

Below them, where the audience had once sat, was row upon row of boxed electronics. Belladonna stared out into the dimly lit theatre. Above the ranks of boxes, she could just make out the faded glory of the dress circle. Paint hung in long strips from its decorated facade and most of the gold decorations had long since dropped off, but there was still enough of a breath of former glories to make her understand why her mother had spent so many long, cold days standing in front of the place and hanging about the corridors of the town council offices. She turned back to Steve.

"It's beautiful!"

He grinned. Then suddenly reached forward, grabbed her arm, hauled her back into the wings, and turned the light off. As he did so, there was the sound of a door opening and a light in the main theatre came on.

"Quiet!" he hissed. "Don't move!"

"What is it again?" Steve's mother stood in the narrow doorway and called back to the shop in the front lobby.

"The CF-976X!" yelled his Dad from the shop. "Left side! There should be three!"

His mother strode down what was once the center aisle, muttering to herself. Belladonna peeked through the folds of what remained of the red velvet curtain and watched as the small, bullet-shaped woman examined the stacks. She had too-black hair, dragged back into a ponytail that seemed to be chiefly made of artificial hair. Ebony curls notwithstanding, there was something steely about her, and Belladonna could understand Steve's desire to stay under her radar. She finally found the box, or Belladonna assumed she had, because she had just begun to make her way back up the aisle when Steve grabbed Belladonna's arm again and yanked her back into the wings. The light in the theatre went out and the door clicked shut.

Belladonna wrenched herself free, "You didn't have to grab me! She couldn't see!"

"*Shhh!*" Steve was still whispering and genuinely worried. "She doesn't have to. If I'm doing something wrong, she just knows it. Why couldn't you just do what I said?"

They stared at each other angrily. Belladonna knew he was regretting ever showing her the theatre. She took a deep breath.

"So," she said, trying to sound calm, "where is it?"

Steve just stared at her.

"I know you want me to go, so the sooner you show me the door, the sooner I will."

He nodded, flicked the light back on, made his way to the back of the stage, and yanked a large tarpaulin to the floor. Underneath was what looked like a stack of boards of various sizes.

"What's that?"

"Scenery," said Steve, still irritated, "it's scenery. There are bound to be some doors."

He was right. Belladonna couldn't help smiling—it seemed so obvious now. She ran over and the two of them began pulling the stack apart as quietly as they could, leaning each flat back until they could see what it was and then resting it on the floor. It was dirty work, and the further they got into the stack, the more cobwebs, spiders, and unidentifiable multilegged creatures there were. Belladonna was gritting her teeth: She wasn't going to squeal (even though every cell in her body wanted nothing more) and she wasn't going to be the first one to drop anything.

There were doors in the stack, of course. Blue ones, Victorian ones, green ones, inside doors, outside doors, hotel doors, even some stable doors, but it was beginning to look increasingly unlikely that there was a red door at all, let alone one with the number seventy-three on it.

By the time they reached the last three flats in the pile, Belladonna's face was streaked with dust and dirt, and her long black hair looked worse than ever. Her lips were pressed close together as she strained to lift the heavy flats, her concentration entirely focused on the job at hand. How could it not be here? It had seemed like the perfect place. She glanced up and caught Steve staring at her sympathetically. That was worse than anything—if there was one thing that raised her hackles and made her temper flare it was the thought that other people were feeling sorry for her.

She glared at him and leaned on the stack, even ignoring the enormous spider that promptly ran across her fingers.

"You know," he said finally, "they repainted these things all the time. The door could be here, it could just be a different color."

"But I'd know," she said, her voice giving away her disappointment. "I'd know. I just thought it would be here. I was sure."

She stopped trying to pretend to be tough and looked around the ruined theatre.

"It just seemed like the place."

"It is!"

"It just felt right, I don't know. Looking around, it looks so—"

"No," Steve was pulling on her arm again. "I mean it really is!"

She turned around. There, lying faceup, was the door: a red door with the number seventy-three painted in gold on it. It was set into a piece of "wall" painted to look like it was pasted with flowered wallpaper. The whole thing was covered in years of spiderwebs, mold, and dust. Belladonna stared at it.

"That's it," she whispered. "Stand it up! Can we stand it? Will it stand?"

"*Shhhh!*" hissed Steve. "It should stand. Help me get it out."

They dragged the door to the middle of the stage and heaved it upright, then Belladonna held it while Steve went around the back and pulled out two hinged legs that allowed it to stay up on its own.

"How do you know this stuff?" she asked.

"Dunno," he shrugged. "My Dad watches a lot of documentaries."

He walked around to the front. "Not much to look at," he said, and pushed the door open.

Belladonna wasn't sure what she was expecting when the door opened, but it certainly wasn't what she saw—nothing. The door just swung stiffly ajar and revealed the back wall. She walked around it. It was just an old piece of scenery: cheap wood and struts at the back and paint and plaster at the front. The door swung shut behind her as she walked through it to the front.

She stood looking at it and tried not to feel disappointed, but the feeling welled up anyway, along with the realization that she had been foolish to believe that she could find something that her Aunt Deirdre, Miss Parker, and her grandmother had all failed to locate. So what if the ghosts were gone; for most people they didn't exist anyway. She'd been lucky to have her parents around for so long after they were dead.

Somewhere inside she'd known that one day they would go. She should leave this sort of thing to the grown-ups.

"Well," she said, trying to sound cheery, "we tried. I'd better get home and get cleaned up before Aunt Deirdre gets back."

"Belladonna . . ." Steve was standing behind her, and his voice sounded strange. "I saw the dog."

"Of course you saw the dog," she said flatly. "I was touching you."

"No," he seemed hesitant to admit it. "I saw the dog. After you fell. It vanished, and then it came back."

She turned slowly and looked at him.

"And this morning, there were black birds. Big ones. In the trees at the end of the football pitch. They're like the dog, aren't they?"

She nodded slowly.

"I think you should open the door," he said.

"But you—"

"I think it has to be you."

She turned back to the door, stepped toward it, and reached forward to push the handle. The next second it was suddenly open, though she could not recall touching it; her hand was still extended forward and her mouth was wide open, the last syllable of an unknown word dying in the air. Steve was staring at her.

"What . . . what did you say?" he stammered.

"I didn't say anything," she said, knowing it wasn't true. "What happened?"

"As soon as you touched the door, your head flew back and you said . . . you whispered something. It wasn't English . . . or any other language I've ever heard of."

Belladonna looked at him, then turned to the door and stepped through. It was no good. The other side was just the same—the back wall of the theatre and the rest of the scenery flats. She stepped back.

"Well, whatever I said, it didn't work. It's just the same."

Now Steve looked like he had that day when he'd seen Elsie, his first ghost.

"What?" she asked.

He walked past her and stepped through the door. Belladonna watched, unbelieving. She ran around the back of the flat. Then back to the front.

He stepped back through the door.

"You . . . you . . ." She couldn't get it out.

"I vanished."

"But it looks just the same on . . . on . . ."

"It isn't, though, is it?"

"No," Belladonna's voice fell away as she realized that she must have spoken the Words of Power without ever knowing what they were.

"It's the Other Side."

6

The Other Side

THEY LOOKED AT each other for a moment, then took a deep breath and stepped through the door together. Belladonna glanced back. Everything really did seem the same. It was all rather disappointing. For some reason she had expected . . . well, *something* when you crossed over. A flash of light, perhaps, or maybe some fog. Were they really in the Land of the Dead?

"Belladonna!" Steve was still whispering, but there was an urgency to his voice. "Come here! Look at this!"

He was standing at the front of the stage. Belladonna joined him and peered into the darkness. At first she didn't see anything different, just the dark empty theatre, but then she realized that it was different. Very different.

Where boxes of electronics had been stacked, there was now row upon row of red velvet seats. The balcony looked freshly painted and the cherubs and garlands were gleaming with fresh gilding. She looked up and saw that the ragged remains of the stage curtains had vanished and been replaced with billowing swathes of heavy gold-fringed velvet. It seemed that at any moment the audience would arrive and the play begin.

They stood in silence for a while, then Steve stepped back and glanced toward the dressing rooms.

"Come on," he said, "let's see what it's like outside."

Belladonna followed as he led the way through the theatre to the back door. He hesitated for a second, then pushed it slowly open.

Sunshine streamed into the dark corridor as they stepped outside. Belladonna didn't know exactly what she had expected the Land of the Dead to look like, but it certainly wasn't this. It was just . . . ordinary. The back alley behind the theatre seemed to be the same back alley as the one in the real world, and as they strolled around the side of the building to the High Street, it certainly seemed as if the only difference was the sunshine. When they reached the High Street, however, another change became apparent.

"There's no one here," whispered Belladonna.

"No," said Steve, "and what's with that tree?"

Belladonna followed his gaze. Sure enough, up at the far end of the High Street, where there should have been a statue of Nelson with a rather run-down flower stall, a newspaper stand, and several moth-eaten pigeons clustered around its base, there was instead an enormous tree.

Without really knowing why, they began walking

toward it. There was something noble about it, something that Belladonna felt she should know but couldn't quite recall. She glanced at Steve, but all his attention was on the tree as it slowly loomed higher and higher above their heads. It had seemed large from a distance, but as they got closer, the sheer bulk of the thing became apparent. The massive, knotted trunk was easily the width of a small car and the colossal gnarled roots seemed to plunge into the earth like giant fingers into clay. Above their heads, sinuous branches stretched and curled upward and out, spreading over the street in every direction, while bright green leaves rustled in the gentle breeze, filtering the sunlight and cooling the air beneath.

"I thought you'd never get here!"

Belladonna looked around. She recognized the voice, but there was no one to be seen.

"Up here!"

Belladonna and Steve looked up, and there, perched on one of the lower branches, was Elsie. She looked just as she had before, the long skirt, neat button boots, and big bow holding her long curls back, but this time she was a lot more solid. She smiled at Belladonna, but her bravado couldn't conceal the worry in her eyes.

"Hello!"

"Elsie!" said Belladonna. "What on earth are you doing up there?"

"Sitting," said Elsie, not very helpfully.

"Is that . . ." Steve lowered his voice suddenly. "Is

that the girl from the photograph? The one who died on the tennis court?"

"Yes," said Elsie proudly, "though that article didn't mention that I'd just won."

Steve looked at her for a moment. It was a bit like having the television answer back.

"Well, of course you won," he said eventually. "Why else would you have tried to jump over the net?"

"What's your name?"

"Steve."

"You seem to have sense."

"I have more sense than to try to jump over a tennis net," said Steve.

Elsie's smile faded.

"Darwin at work," he grinned.

Belladonna smiled, then tried to pretend she wasn't. Elsie stood up on her branch and yanked off a bunch of leaves in irritation. A squirrel raced down from the topmost branches and chattered at her in an unmistakably angry fashion.

"Oh, shut up," said Elsie.

"What's that?" asked Belladonna.

"It's a squirrel, obviously," said Elsie sulkily. "There are usually three women here. And a snake. The squirrel is all that's left. Everyone else is gone."

She jumped down onto the ground with that kind of graceful ease that naturally sporty people always seem to have. The squirrel waited for a moment, as if it wanted to be sure that all arboreal violence was at an end, then darted back up to the top of the tree. Belladonna and Steve glanced at each other.

"Where have they gone?" asked Belladonna in what she hoped was a conciliatory manner.

"I don't know," said Elsie. "They were the last ones, though. Everyone else went at almost the same time, two days ago."

"Six o'clock," said Belladonna, remembering her parents' sudden disappearance.

"Yes, I suppose it was. Not that time means anything much here. The little ones went sooner, of course."

"Like Lady Mary's baby."

"Who? Probably. Anyway, there was a herd of elephant-type things in the park. Massive. Very hairy."

"Mammoths?" asked Steve, suddenly impressed.

"I should say so," said Elsie, missing the point, "absolutely gigantic. They went right before the things in the tree. So now everyone's gone."

"Everyone?"

Elsie nodded, "Except the squirrel. So I thought maybe the tree was safe."

"Safe from what?" asked Steve.

"From whatever's . . . from . . ."

Belladonna sighed. "There isn't anyone here? Not a single person?"

Elsie shook her head and twirled the twig. "There's him," she said, nodding in the direction of the shops.

"Who? You said everyone had gone."

"They have."

Steve looked at her skeptically. "But you're still here," he observed. "Maybe you're in on it."

"In on what?" asked Belladonna.

"It. I don't know." He shrugged, then glared at Elsie again. "But if there's only one person left, I'd guess it was probably them that did it . . . whatever it is."

Elsie stared at him for a moment. Belladonna could see she was used to being in charge of things and didn't cotton to this boy one bit. Elsie fingered her tie and kicked at a loose cobble.

"Well, everyone except him," she said finally, "but I don't like him. He's in the apothecary shop."

"Mr. Baxter!" said Belladonna.

"Who?" said Steve and Elsie in unison.

"Oh, I know his name isn't really Mr. Baxter," said Belladonna, "but I used to see him on my way home from school. In the old launderette. He always seemed so friendly."

Steve and Elsie looked at her. Belladonna felt the wind go out of her sails.

"His name isn't Baxter," said Elsie, "it's Ashe, Dr. Ashe."

"He's a doctor?"

"I don't think so. I think he just calls himself that because it makes him feel superior." Elsie reached up and began swinging on a low branch. "Some people need titles to feel comfortable in their own skin. That's what my mother used to say anyway."

Steve rolled his eyes and nudged Belladonna.

"Yes, well, perhaps we should go over there anyhow," she said. "He might know something."

Elsie considered this for a moment, then nodded.

"Righty-ho," she said finally. "I don't suppose there's much point sitting in a tree with a squirrel. Not really my companion of choice for eternity."

Belladonna smiled.

"Besides," continued Elsie, marching purposefully down the High Street, "maybe we can get some barley sugars. They're in a jar on the counter. I really like barley sugars."

Belladonna glanced at Steve.

"She's a loony," remarked Steve.

Belladonna ignored him as they followed Elsie down the slight incline from the tree into the main part of the High Street. It was strange to see everything so clean and bright and yet so empty. It reminded her of pictures of film sets that she'd seen in magazines, as if someone was just about to shout "Action!" and fill the road with shoppers and browsers. But of course, they didn't.

"Why is everything so new?" she asked as they caught up with Elsie.

"What do you mean?"

"Everything looks . . . well, back in the real world—"

"This is a real world," interrupted Elsie, sounding a little irritated.

"Yes, I know but . . . take the theatre. In our world

it's old and the seats are gone and it's falling to bits, but here it's brand-new."

"Why wouldn't it be?" asked Elsie. "In your world I'm a jumble of bones in a grave everyone's forgotten about. Things don't decay and die here, they just sort of go on."

Belladonna thought about this. It made sense, really. After all, strictly speaking, Elsie was well over a hundred years old, but she looked the same as when she'd died.

"So the people and buildings are sort of frozen in time?"

"No," said Elsie, rolling her eyes as if Belladonna was the worst kind of dunce. "The people can be any age. Well, we can't be older than when we died, obviously, but we can be younger. I could be five if I wanted. See?"

And suddenly Elsie was gone and a small curly-headed child, decked out in white lace and a giant pale blue ribbon, was toddling beside them.

"I just don't want to," she lisped, before returning to the older Elsie they knew.

"Does that mean the buildings are ghosts too?" asked Steve. "Because if that was the case, wouldn't the only buildings be ones that had been demolished in the rea—in *our* world?"

"The buildings aren't ghosts!" laughed Elsie. "They're just the way we remembered them. Well, most of us. They're . . . I suppose they're the way we like them. I never thought about it, really."

"Okay," said Steve, "I can understand that, but if you look over there, it seems sort of . . . dark."

He was right. In the center of town and for a few streets back in every direction, everything looked bright and new, but beyond that, it was as if night had come early. The strangely dilapidated buildings seemed to loom over the streets, and the dull eyes of the empty windows stared down the sunshine. A shiver went through Belladonna's body as her gaze followed the streets out past the edge of town and into the country-side beyond. She could just make out a winding road, but beyond that the darkness closed in and storm clouds lowered over the rolling hills.

"I know," said Elsie, glancing up an alleyway nervously. "That's new."

"Well," said Belladonna, trying to sound matter-of-fact and cheerful, "fortunately, we don't have to go there. The launderette's just behind the post office."

She and Elsie sped up their walk, but Steve hung back, staring at the narrow backstreets, before running and catching up.

"Something's going on here," he said.

"Of course it is," said Belladonna brightly. "That's why we've come."

She turned left just after the post office, which had acquired an old-fashioned red pillarbox marked "VR" that had been removed from the pavement in front of the real post office years before. A brief walk down the unnaturally clean side street brought them into Umbra Avenue and the familiar landscape of Belladonna's walk home from school.

Except that it wasn't really familiar any more.

The shops were all still there, interrupted every now and then by doorways leading up to studios and flats. But the comforting predictability of the gently curving road had given way to an increasing feeling of dread as they made their way down toward the old launderette.

In their own world, the launderette took up quite a bit of the street but was somehow inconsequential. It was easy to walk right past it, with its run-down wood-work, faded sign, and curling "special offers." Here, however, it dominated everything around it. The windows sparkled and a gleaming green-and-gold sign announced: "Apothecary. Dr. H. Ashe, prop." The window itself was decorated with things that Belladonna had seen only translucently on her way home: brass containers, ranks of small bottles arranged in pyramids, and a huge white ceramic head with the bald pate divided into sections marked with words like "secretiveness," "tune," and "deceptiveness." They peered inside. It was just as Belladonna remembered; there was a huge polished wood counter stretching from one side to the other with a gleaming brass urn sitting in state at one end while jars and tall bottles clustered around an oversized brass-and-steel cash register at the other. Behind the counter were labeled drawers and hundreds of shelves of bottles and jars, extending from the floor to the ceiling.

"I'll wait out here," said Elsie, suddenly stepping back and fingering her tie.

"But—" began Belladonna.

"It gives me the willies. I don't like it."

Belladonna nodded, then glanced at Steve and pushed the door open. A distant bell tinkled as they stepped inside and into a dense miasma of aromas. The smells ranged from the delicate floral scents of roses and freesias through the earthy perfume of dried plants and tree bark, to the piercing chemical stink of sulfur and ammonia.

They paused in the doorway while their eyes became accustomed to the shadowy interior and their senses became at least somewhat used to the pong. Steve scowled into the dim recesses.

"This smell is giving me a headache," he muttered.

Belladonna ignored him and marched confidently up to the counter.

"Hello?" she called, in what she hoped was a cheery and self-assured tone.

There was a noise from the back as a chair scraped away from a table, and a small, skinny man appeared in the doorway. He was dressed in clothes that seemed a size too small, revealing bony wrists and ankles, and his face seemed somehow pointed, like an inquisitive rodent.

"Yes?" he snapped.

"Is . . . umm . . . Dr. Ashe here?"

"No, he isn't. What do you want him for?"

The man shuffled forward and pushed his face into Belladonna's. She stepped back, alarmed. He was about to speak again, but the words seemed to freeze on his lips. He peered at Belladonna, then turned and examined Steve.

"Wait a minute," he said, "you're not dead!"

Steve rolled his eyes. "Brilliant," he said.

The man stepped back and stared at them admiringly, as if he were looking at two particularly rare specimens in a zoo.

"Huh," he mused, "the old man was right. Which one of you is . . ."

His eyes narrowed as he looked from Steve to Belladonna to Steve again. He scuttled over to Steve and examined him closely.

"Get away!" said Steve, backing into the counter.

"Are you the Paladin?" asked the man.

"The what?"

The skinny man seemed surprised, then a slow smile spread across his face like a crack in an eggshell. "You don't know," he smirked. "You got all this way and you don't know. If that isn't the most delicious—"

Just as Belladonna was sure that Steve was going to hit the creepy little man, the shop door tinkled and a deep voice boomed into the murk.

"Slackett," it said, "what is going on here?"

A look of cringing dread appeared on the little man's face and he seemed to shrivel away toward the cash register. Belladonna and Steve spun around. The newcomer was standing, silhouetted in the doorway, impossible to make out.

"Nothing, Sir," simpered Slackett.

The man stepped inside and closed the door and now Belladonna recognized the familiar form of the man she'd been calling Mr. Baxter. There was something different about him here, though. He was still wearing the bright yellow waistcoat and the long red robe, but the red hat had gone and there was something not quite right about his face, as if he was wearing a mask.

"Explain yourselves," he said as he dropped his silver-topped cane into a nearby stand.

"Mr. . . . I mean, Dr. Ashe," stammered Belladonna, "we've come from—"

Ashe looked down at her and the light of recognition flickered across his face. He smiled indulgently and leaned over to examine her more closely. "You're that little girl from the Other Side," he said, his voice suddenly silky.

"Belladonna Johnson," said Belladonna.

"Indeed. Indeed. Well, well, well," he said in that annoying way that adults who seldom talk to children adopt, "and what are you doing here?"

"We came . . . um . . . through the door and—"

Dr. Ashe glanced at Slackett and scowled. "Get back to work!" he snapped.

Slackett glanced quickly out of the front window and for a moment his face seemed different, less servile, and Belladonna thought she could see Elsie peeking around the edge of the window. Was she waving? But even as the question formed in her mind, Elsie was gone and the look of the fawning toady quickly returned to Slackett's face as he scrambled back behind the counter and into the back of the shop. Dr. Ashe turned back to Belladonna, the thin smile immediately in place.

". . . and . . ." Belladonna tried to retrieve her train of thought. "And we wanted to know—"

"Did you now?" interrupted Dr. Ashe. "Through the door?" He took a small pair of pince-nez glasses from his pocket, positioned them on the end of his bony nose, and peered more closely at Belladonna. "How exceptionally clever of you."

"Thank you. Well, um, all the ghosts have vanished . . . including my parents, and so I . . . that is, we were wondering if you knew why."

Dr. Ashe looked at her for a moment, then at Steve, who was making little effort to conceal the instant dislike he had taken to the too-pale man. Ashe turned his attention back to Belladonna and leaned down in a way that he seemed to think was affable.

"I can understand your concern," he said. "I've been

watching my friends vanish one by one. It's awful, just awful. And I've been having no luck with my experiments at all."

"Experiments?"

"Yes," he straightened up. "Would you like to see? Come on back. You can bring your surly little friend with you."

He turned and vanished into the shadows at the back of the shop. Belladonna beckoned to Steve, who shook his head. She tried it again, with a little more annoyed urgency in the gesture. He shambled over.

"I'm not going back there," he hissed, "and neither should you! The guy's positively reptilian."

"Yes, but —"

"And don't you think it's odd that he's the only person left?"

"We've got to try and find out what's going on," said Belladonna. "And anyway, he's not the only one. What about Elsie? And . . . whatsisname . . ."

"Slackett," said Steve, as if just saying the name produced a nasty taste in his mouth. "Yeah, he seems the trustworthy type. Just the sort of person I'd go running to in a crisis."

"Yes, but —"

"Elsie's a kid," he continued, "and she isn't creeping about a dark shop reeking of rotten eggs. And how do you know it's safe to go back there? They could be baking children into pies, for all you know!"

Belladonna rolled her eyes and made her way into

the back of the shop. Steve hesitated for a moment, shoved his hands into his pockets, and followed her.

The narrow doorway led to a small workroom with a stained table and a single wooden chair. The table was covered with a variety of scientific apparatus, some in use and some just lying where they had been left. Books and notebooks were stacked and strewn about, and small piles of colored powder and pools of spilled concoctions littered every surface. As if this weren't enough to make the room seem the stuff of fevered dreams and midnight stories, on the far side a small furnace blazed, filling the room with an oppressive, damp heat. Slackett was crouching by the furnace, shoveling coal into its open maw and watching the newcomers carefully.

"Are you a chemist?" asked Belladonna.

"In a way," said Dr. Ashe. "I am a scientist."

"A scientist?"

"An alchemist," he announced with great dignity.

"Alchemists aren't scientists," muttered Steve.

"What? I can't hear you, boy, did you say something?" boomed Dr. Ashe.

Steve shrugged and looked at the floor.

"Dr. Ashe," said Belladonna pleasantly, "what are you working on?"

Ashe continued to glare at Steve for a moment, then smiled and turned back to Belladonna.

"I've been trying to establish what has been causing the disappearances," he said, "but it's so difficult. I don't have all my reference books, the *Rosarium Philisophorum,* the *Coelum,* the *Atalanta Fugiens* . . . classics, classics all. I had lent them to a colleague before I . . . before I passed on, you understand, so they are not available to me here. And my tools are . . . well, as you see, wholly inadequate to the task. And then, of course, I'm missing certain elements."

He sighed as if he was overwhelmed by the size of his task.

"Everyone just kept disappearing, and now . . . I don't know . . . I suppose I'll be next and that will be an end of it."

Belladonna tried to look sympathetic.

"Ah, well," said Ashe, pulling a leather-bound book toward him across the table and opening it at a well-thumbed page, "you can see here what the idea is."

Belladonna peered at the yellowing pages of the massive tome. There was a great deal of incomprehensible text and an incredibly complex diagram, labeled down to the smallest crucible and pipette. But she felt no wiser.

"I'm afraid . . . um . . . we don't start Latin until next year," she said.

"Really?" Ashe's eyes widened as though she was personally responsible for the dismal standards of the modern education system. "How are you expected to do anything worthwhile if you don't have Latin and Greek by five?"

"I don't think anyone has Latin or Greek that early," said Belladonna, somewhat defensively.

"Except Greeks, of course," volunteered Steve, grinning.

Dr. Ashe and Belladonna looked at him disdainfully, and Steve shoved his hands back into his pockets and drifted toward the furnace. He tried to ignore Slackett, but Belladonna couldn't help but notice that as soon as he was close enough, the lanky assistant started whispering urgently.

"Well, what I'm attempting here," said Dr. Ashe enthusiastically, "is basically a re-creation of something Paracelsus managed. Essentially, I suspect the disappearance of the inhabitants of the Land of the Dead can be laid squarely at the feet of a flux in the sanguineous elements. We corresponded at the time, Paracelsus and I, we were colleagues in life, you understand, and he was of the opinion that a balance of the elements was crucial to the existence of the nine worlds."

"The nine worlds?" asked Belladonna.

This whole thing was getting more complicated by the second. She had known about the Other Side for a long time, of course, her parents had spoken of it often, but . . . seven other worlds as well?

"Yes, if you take something from one world and place it in another, then the balance of both is disturbed. Tell me, have you seen any creatures from this world in your own? Aside from actual ghosts, of course."

"Yes!" said Belladonna. "Yes, we have! Haven't we, Steve?"

Steve looked up, and Slackett quickly returned to shoveling coals into the already blazing furnace. As he did so, Steve seemed to notice something inside and turned to peer into the white-hot embers.

"Well, anyway," said Belladonna, "we have. A big black dog and some huge birds."

"Ah," said Dr. Ashe, opening another book, "exactly as I thought."

"Um . . ." Steve was backing slowly away from the furnace, "is this supposed to smell like this?"

Slackett sat back on his heels and cackled softly. "Come on, pretty-pretty," he murmured.

"Um . . ." Steve bumped into the chair.

"Do you know what it is?" asked Belladonna, ignoring Steve. "My father said that all the doors were closing."

"Did he now?" said Ashe.

"Yes, right before he disappeared."

Dr. Ashe nodded as he rapidly turned the pages of the book. He cast it aside impatiently and reached up to a shelf to his left, where there was a neat row of five identically bound notebooks next to seven or eight leather- and vellum-bound books of varying sizes. He pulled an ancient-looking vellum text from the shelf and riffled through it for a few minutes before spinning the book around so that Belladonna could see. She pulled it slowly toward her; there was more Latin text but this time instead of a complex laboratory diagram, there was a detailed woodcut of a dragon.

"A dragon?" she said. "Dr. Ashe, I think we would've noticed if a dragon—"

"Not the dragon," said Ashe, snatching the book back irritably, "the jewel."

Belladonna peered at the woodcut again. There was a dark triangle in the middle of the dragon's forehead.

"It's draconite," explained Dr. Ashe.

"Dr. Ashe . . ." Steve's voice sounded odd, but Ashe ignored him.

"Draconite is only found in the brows of dragons, so, as you can imagine, it's very scarce."

"Dragons?" Belladonna was beginning to have doubts about the alchemist.

"So far as I know, there is only one jewel remaining," said Ashe, apparently oblivious to Belladonna's tone. "It was mine. I had it made into an amulet."

"Did you . . ." Belladonna hardly dared ask, "did you get it off the dragon yourself?"

"Of course not! I bought it. I'm a scientist, not a dragon-slayer. Anyway, the point is . . ."

Steve wasn't hearing any of this; his attention was focused on the furnace and the two long legs that had extruded from its depths and were currently trying to get a secure footing on the floor.

"Dr. Ashe, something's coming out of the—"

"Will you be quiet, you stupid boy! We're trying to talk!"

Steve glanced up at Slackett, who was sniggering. He scowled and returned his attention to the legs as they felt about for the floor.

"Dr. Ashe, I don't think you should talk to people like that," said Belladonna reproachfully.

"Of course, of course. My dear, I do apologize. And to you too . . . uh . . . whoever you are—"

"Steve," said Belladonna helpfully.

"Yes, Steve, I apologize," Dr. Ashe nodded in the general direction of Steve, who didn't hear him because he was too engrossed in the third and fourth legs.

"The thing is," continued Dr. Ashe, who smiled briefly and was clearly remaining calm with some effort, "the thing is, I had it made into an amulet and someone stole it and hid it in the Land of the . . . in your town."

"What does it do?"

"It goes here," said Ashe, clearing away some of the debris on the table to reveal a magnifying glass clamped to a stand. "It's held here by these fastenings and then the sunlight is focused through the magnifying glass . . . so."

"Like a laser," suggested Belladonna.

"A what?"

"Lasers focus light through rubies."

"Do they, indeed? And what do they do then?"

"Cut things," said Belladonna. "Heal people."

"Hmph," said Dr. Ashe, unimpressed. "Well, the Draconite Amulet will guide us to the element that is causing the imbalance and restore nature to its true equilibrium, allowing us to open the doors and return the nine worlds to their intended state."

"So there are doorways to all nine worlds?"

"Of course there are," he snapped, then remembered himself. "I'm sorry. I'm tired. Yes, everything is connected to everything else. Didn't you know that?"

Belladonna squirmed a little—it was a bit too much like being grilled by a teacher.

"Yes," she said slowly, "Miss Hannity used to say things like that. She taught Art, but they let her go. I overheard Madame Huggins telling Mr. Watson that it was because she was wired to the moon."

Dr. Ashe looked down his long nose at her and sniffed. "Well, I can see that things haven't changed much in my absence. There will always be doubters, but now you have seen for yourself that the doors do exist."

"*A* door," said Belladonna.

"And you think your door is the only one, do you? That in all the nine worlds, in all the vastnesses in between, there is just one door. From the Land of the Dead to your dreary little town. Is that what you think?"

"Um . . . probably not." Belladonna felt like she was failing some kind of exam.

"I should think not. Do you have any idea what would happen were all the doors to close?"

Belladonna shook her head.

"No," said Dr. Ashe, softening a little, "of course not. The future of us all — of everything — depends on the free flow between the worlds."

"And that's why the ghosts have vanished?" she asked. "Because the doors between the Land of the Living and the Other Side have closed? But why? And what about the other worlds — are the doors there closed too?"

"Not all of them . . . yet," said Ashe grimly.

Belladonna tucked her hair behind one ear and stared at him. She opened her mouth to speak, but he held up one bony hand to stop her.

"Look," he said, "I can't pretend to know all the whys and wherefores, I am but a simple alchemist."

"But . . ." Belladonna took a deep breath; she had a feeling this question was going to make him even more irritated. "If you're just a simple alchemist, why are you and your assistant the only ones left? Why didn't whatever-it-is take you too?"

"I don't know," said Ashe. "When I saw my friends being picked off like ripe fruit from a tree, I cast a circle around this laboratory; perhaps that has kept us safe. I don't really know. I just need the amulet. It's the only thing I can think of that might help solve this puzzle."

Belladonna looked at him. It all sounded plausible, in a way, but there was something about him that made her dubious. She was about to question him further when there was a yelp from the far side of the room. She turned around just in time to see a cockroach the size of a vacuum cleaner climb out of the furnace. At least it looked sort of like a cockroach, only this creature had a long articulated neck at the end of which was an appendage that looked like the head of a hammerhead shark and concluded in two swiveling compound eyes.

Steve had flattened himself against the wall and was staring at the insect with an intensity that conveyed nothing so much as the wish that he was still sitting at the back of his parents' electronics shop reading comics and waiting for his tea. The creature was craning its neck around, taking in the room and everyone in it.

"What is that?" whispered Belladonna.

Dr. Ashe glanced up without any particular interest.

"Oh, that's just an ember beetle. I was trying to get a salamander, but only got those things. I threw them into the fire and they've been breeding in there ever since. They're harmless."

"H . . . harmless?!" stammered Steve. "Have you seen the size of this thing?"

"It's just looking for a warm place. It'll be gone in a minute. Heat rises. Slackett, encourage it."

Slackett, who had been helpless with laughter up to this point, grabbed a broom and poked at the glistening beetle. Sure enough, the insect paused for a second, then took off up the wall with a clackiting of exoskeletal legs. Steve and Belladonna looked at each other for a moment, then slowly raised their eyes . . . and wished they hadn't.

The entire ceiling of the small room was covered with ember beetles, their long necks and eyepieces hanging down like so many chandeliers, the compound eyes following the movement of the strange creatures below, and their bronze carapaces glistening in the gloom.

Belladonna shuddered.

"So," said Dr. Ashe cheerily, "do you think you can get it?"

"Get what?" asked Belladonna, without taking her eyes off the beetles.

"The Draconite Amulet, of course. Oh, do stop looking at those things, they're of no importance whatsoever."

"Why can't you get it yourself?" said Belladonna, reluctantly lowering her gaze.

"Because I am dead," said Dr. Ashe, barely able to conceal his fury at her. "I chose to haunt my laboratory, so naturally I can go nowhere else in your world. Why are you wasting time with these endless questions?"

"But we don't know where it is."

"No," said Dr. Ashe, "neither do I. Happily, the Sibyl will know. You should ask her."

He returned to his books as if the matter were

closed. Belladonna glanced at Steve, who was edging his way back along the wall and didn't seem to be listening.

"Sibyl?" she asked. "Sibyl who?"

"Not Sibyl anyone," he said, looking up with exasperation and barely concealed contempt. "You see? You see? This is what happens when people abandon classical education for their children. 'Sibyl who,' indeed!"

Belladonna looked at Steve, who shrugged. She looked back at Dr. Ashe, who rubbed his temples as if he was getting a really bad headache.

"Sibyls are oracles," he explained. "They predict the future, give advice, that sort of thing. The most famous one was at Delphi in Greece."

"Greece?" said Steve. "We can't go to Greece!"

"I'm not suggesting that you go to Greece," snapped Dr. Ashe. His temper was clearly on a very thin thread. "That was just an example. There were other Sibyls. The Cumean Sibyl, for example, who just happens to reside in your school."

"Dullworth's?" said Belladonna skeptically.

"In the library," said Dr. Ashe.

Steve snorted and laughed, a noise that always irritated the socks off any adult within earshot.

"Have you seen our library?" he said. "It's practically the smallest room in the school! If some Greek fortune-teller was hiding in there, we'd know about it!"

"Obtuse child," muttered Dr. Ashe, "it's probably *under* the library."

"You mean there's a secret passage or something?" asked Belladonna.

Dr. Ashe nodded and managed a smile, "Quite so."

Belladonna thought about the small octagonal library with its rows of useless books. Most of them were so out-of-date that nearly everyone went to the big library in the center of town if they really needed to look anything up.

"How do we find the entrance?" she asked.

"Use your intelligence," said Dr. Ashe impatiently. "Now get away with you, I have work to do."

He waved a bony hand in the direction of the door and buried himself in his books. Belladonna and Steve waited for a moment, but it was clear he wasn't going to say anything else. They edged out of the room, trying to avoid knocking bottles to the floor, and watched by dozens of eyes on stalks. When they got out onto the street again, Steve gulped in lungfuls of fresh air and laughed nervously.

"What a couple of nutboxes!"

"What happened?" asked Elsie, stepping out from a narrow alley next to the building.

Belladonna looked at them both, then turned and started to walk back up the street. Steve and Elsie ran and caught up.

"You do think they're nutboxes too, right?" he asked.

"I don't know," she said. "I mean, yes, Slackett does

seem . . . odd. And Dr. Ashe is a bit scary, but . . . what if he's right? What if things *are* out of balance?"

"Yes, but are they?" asked Steve. "I mean, something's wrong here, obviously, but everything seemed pretty normal back home. Well, except for the dog and the birds."

"They're Night Ravens," said Elsie, "and if they're getting through to your world from here, then something is definitely wrong."

Belladonna looked at the ground, her hair making a curtain around her face while she thought about this. Finally, she looked up again.

"Dr. Ashe said there are nine worlds. Maybe it's not our world that's off balance. Maybe it's another one."

"Nine worlds!" scoffed Steve. "Why on earth should we believe that?"

"Well," said Elsie, "you already know about two."

"Yes, but one's for the Living and the other's for the Dead. They're like copies of each other. That's not the same as nine completely different worlds, is it?"

"They're only the same because we like it that way. Besides, you seem to think your world is better just because the people in it are alive."

"Well . . ."

"Maybe that's just practice," suggested Elsie, a humorous glint in her eye. "After all, you're dead for a lot longer than you're alive."

"But . . . so what? None of this is our problem! It's your lot who are vanishing, not ours!"

"That's a rather selfish attitude, if you don't mind me saying so," huffed Elsie.

Belladonna looked at them and walked on, heading for the theatre and home. Steve trudged behind, hands shoved in pockets.

"Did you see the beetles?" asked Elsie, catching up.

Belladonna nodded.

"He can't get rid of them, apparently. He's been spoken to, of course, but he said he can't do anything about them. He threw some eggs or something into that little furnace of his and they've been breeding in there ever since."

Belladonna stopped in front of the theatre and turned around. "There's an amulet," she said, "made out of a jewel from a dragon. He said that if we got it for him, he would be able to open the doors and fix whatever's going on."

Elsie's smile faded and she looked from Belladonna to Steve. "Wait . . . you're not going to try to find it, are you?"

Belladonna shrugged. "Dunno."

"Probably," said Steve.

Belladonna smiled and tucked her hair behind her ears.

Elsie shook her head. "It seems to me," she said, "that there are enough strange things going on here without digging up magical amulets."

"Who said it was magical?" said Steve.

"It has to be. If it wasn't, it would just be called

a necklace or a stone. When people start throwing around words like *amulet* you know you're dealing with magic."

"Dr. Ashe said it was science," suggested Belladonna.

Elsie rolled her eyes. "I know Dullworth's admits boys now," she said, "but don't tell me that standards have sunk so low that you can't tell the difference between science and magic?"

Steve glared at her.

"The thing is," said Belladonna, "that he said the problem is probably caused by something from another world being brought here —"

"Or vice versa," volunteered Steve.

"And this . . . amulet could help him locate whatever it is."

"But you don't know that," said Elsie. "What on earth makes you think he can solve anything that has to do with whole worlds? And even if he can . . . well, that could be worse."

"I just thought it might be worth a try," said Belladonna quietly.

She suspected that Elsie might be right, but she wasn't quite ready to give up just yet.

"Tell you what," said Steve, "why don't we go and see this Cumean Sybil and hear what she has to say. Then we'll decide."

This sounded like a really good idea to Belladonna. At least it was something and she really wanted to do *something*. The idea of just sitting around and waiting for things to sort themselves out reminded her too much of the time she'd spent sitting in the hospital after the accident or waiting for relatives to arrive on the day of the funeral. She nodded.

"Good idea. Let's go home."

Elsie sighed with exasperation, but Belladonna just smiled.

"See you later," she said.

"Or not," muttered Steve.

Elsie followed them around to the back of the theatre. She waited for a moment after they'd gone inside, then made her way back to her perch in the great tree and continued her watch over the town, her right hand rising unconsciously to the spot just beneath the knot on her school uniform tie.

7

The Sibyl

THIS TIME, when they stepped out of the back door of the theatre, it was what you'd expect from a late October day. The sky was overcast, a weak sun struggled to penetrate the clouds, and an icy wind was getting in practice for winter by whipping around exposed ankles and knees. The streets were crowded with shoppers and the buzz of conversations mixed with the roar of traffic, the yells of the market vendors, and the mellow tones of the town's brass band as it gave a free concert near the war memorial.

Belladonna and Steve were quiet when they emerged. Suddenly it was *this* world that seemed unreal. Steve hesitated at the corner. His parents' shop was contributing to the general cacophony with several television sets running at full volume, and they could hear his mother shouting at a customer.

"Well," said Belladonna, "I suppose I should go home and see if my aunt's come back."

Steve nodded. "Right," he said. "See you at school on Monday, then. I suppose we can check out the library at lunchtime."

"Bye," said Belladonna as she turned to make her way through the crowds.

She walked down the street a short way and stopped at a crossing, her mind racing with the day's events. The light changed and she stepped out into the road, barely thinking about what she was doing.

"Stop!"

A hand grabbed her from behind and pulled her backward just as a car skidded, screeching through the pedestrian crossing, knocked a man off his bike, and destroyed a concrete rubbish bin on the side of the road.

Belladonna froze for a second, then turned around. It was Steve.

"How did you—" she began.

"I don't know," he seemed just as surprised as she was. "I just . . . are you alright?"

She nodded and looked over toward the bicycle man. He seemed alright too—just a bit shaken. Passersby were trying to help the driver out of the car. It was a portly man in a suit and his hands were still gripping the steering wheel in shock. The sound of a siren began to whine in the distance.

Her heart was still racing when she turned to Steve and nodded her thanks. She didn't know what to say. It seemed like an ordinary accident. They happened all the time, after all. But something told her it wasn't. She turned and started to walk home again, but Steve quickly caught up.

"You know," he said, "it'd probably be much easier to root around in the library if we go now."

"No teachers."

"Exactly."

Belladonna smiled gratefully—home wasn't where she wanted to be right now.

They walked on, took a left just after the post office, and headed down Umbra Avenue toward the school. They glanced at the launderette as they passed, but there was nothing remarkable about it—no brass urns, mysterious bottles, or huge beetles. Just a dusty shop front with a "For Sale" sign in the window. It could have been any Saturday afternoon stroll, but as the school came into view, Belladonna stopped.

"This is silly," she said. "The school's closed. How are we going to get in?"

"Guess," said Steve, smiling.

"You're joking."

"Me and Jimmy McLeish snuck in nearly every weekend last year."

"Why?"

"Dunno," he shrugged. "Coz we could, I suppose."

As they got closer, the streets became more quiet, the bustle of the town center on a Saturday giving way to the weekend silence of bicycles, gardening, and car washing. Belladonna's courage began to wane, however, as the three old houses that made up the school buildings loomed before them.

"Come on," said Steve cheerfully, "the best way in's around the back."

They circled the school and squeezed into the grounds through a hole in the fence near the netball courts. Steve glanced around cautiously.

"Sometimes there's a watchman," he explained, before darting across the tarmac toward the back of the Art room.

Belladonna was not reassured by this information, and began to mentally rehearse her explanation for when they were caught. She wasn't too worried about coming up with something for the watchman, but facing her aunt or Miss Parker would take some work, and if Steve's performance after the chemistry incident was anything to go by, she suspected she wouldn't be able to depend on him for anything remotely plausible.

By the time she ran across the netball court to join him behind the building, she had decided that there really wasn't a reasonable excuse for their being there and that if they got nabbed, they were pretty much for the high jump.

Steve was crouched next to the back door of the Art room. There was a small sash window next to the door and he was enthusiastically jiggling the bottom pane up and down.

"What are you doing?" asked Belladonna, alarmed at the incredible racket it was making.

"The latch is loose," he said, still jiggling. "If you rock it like this, it comes undone."

Belladonna peered through the window. She could see the old latch moving a little further back with each movement. Finally, after what felt like forever, the window slid jerkily open.

"Ha!" said Steve. "Told you!"

He clambered inside. Belladonna glanced around and followed him into the dim interior. She couldn't believe that no one had heard.

"It's not exactly cat burglary, is it?" she hissed.

"It worked, though," grinned Steve.

They made their way past rows of old easels and the artistic works-in-progress of the sculpture class, most of which wouldn't have been out of place in one of Dr. Ashe's experiments. Belladonna opened the door into the corridor and they slipped out and along the hall toward the library.

The Dullworth's school library was not one of its best features. The parents of prospective students always reacted with surprised disappointment when they got to the part of the school tour where Miss Parker led them into the small octagonal room. Surely, they thought, this can't be it? A school with the academic reputation of Dullworth's must have a library with more resources than this? There were usually one or two parents who assumed that this was perhaps the junior library and there would be another, more impressive one somewhere else. Miss Parker would always smile kindly and explain that no, this was it. The parents would then wander around the room, with its three rectangular wooden tables and nine chairs, and examine the contents of the shelves. It didn't improve their opinion. Most of the books were old or out-of-date (frequently both) and large chunks of shelf space were taken up with tomes on subjects no longer even taught. Miss Parker would then smile cheerfully and herd everyone out and upstairs to the science labs, which were much more impressive, and then to her office, where tea and buns would be served.

Steve marched into the library and turned on the light. Belladonna turned it off again and glared at him.

"What?" said Steve.

"Someone will see the light!"

"No, they won't," he said, turning it back on again. "And if anyone does see it, they'll just assume it's a teacher or the watchman. If they see us moving around in here in the dark, they're much more likely to think something's up and call the police. It's always better to act as if you've got every right to be where you are."

"You've thought about this a bit too much," observed Belladonna.

They went to opposite ends of the library and began peering at the books.

"I suppose," said Steve, "that if we're looking for a

secret passage, the door will open with a switch of some kind. In films it's usually a decoration on the fireplace or an ornament or something."

He mimed pulling a lever, while making a creaky noise. Belladonna stared at him and shook her head sympathetically.

"Well, okay, so there's no fireplace," said Steve, "or ornaments."

"No," said Belladonna, looking around at the ranks of books. "Hang on a sec, though. Ashe mentioned the classics. . . ."

She hunted through the sections until she came to a couple of shelves full of Greek and Latin language tutors and stories of the Roman Empire. She'd been sort of hoping there would be a statue of a head or something that you could turn or whose nose would slide to the right and open a hidden panel, but there was nothing. She shrugged, but Steve was more optimistic and began pushing the spines of each book in turn.

"I've seen some films where they push on a book and when they find the right one, it goes all the way in and a door opens!"

Belladonna thought that sounded entirely reasonable, so she started on the other shelf, giving each book a sharp shove, but nothing happened. Steve stepped back from the shelves and shoved his hands in his pockets.

"It's useless," he said. "I told you that Dr. Ashe was a nutbox."

"Hmm." Belladonna put her hands on her hips and glared at the books as if it was their fault, then she clicked her tongue in annoyance. "No wonder this library is so useless. Look, these two books are in the wrong order!"

"What?" Steve looked at her like he was adding her to his personal list of nutboxes.

"See," she said, pulling one out, "Suetonius comes after Sophocles, not before."

She shoved the Suetonius back into the shelf in the right place.

"Who cares? Honestly, Belladonna, you have the attention span of—"

He never finished his sentence because, as the book hit the back of the shelf, there was a distant thud and the entire wall of bookcases slid back and then sideways with a grinding, crunching sound, revealing a small stone alcove and the top steps of a narrow, spiral staircase leading downward into the dark.

"Whoa! Cool!"

Belladonna frowned. For some reason the idea of a secret panel that only opened if the books were in alphabetical order made the whole enterprise seem less like an adventure and more like a really elaborate English test. Steve was untroubled by such worries, however, and was already standing on the top step, peering down into the darkness.

"It's really dark," said Belladonna, peering over his shoulder.

"Yeah," said Steve happily, "and cold."

He rummaged about in his pocket for a moment and retrieved a set of house keys on a ring. Belladonna had never seen so many keys — she only had one — but Steve's key ring jangled with at least six, as well as a small green cylinder.

"It's a flashlight," he explained, and clicked a small button on its side.

The light wasn't much — it more sort of trickled out than illuminated — but at least they could see as far as the next few steps. With Steve leading the way, they began their descent.

"Could you stop the keys from making so much noise?" whispered Belladonna.

"Sure. Why?"

"Because if there's anything nasty down there or anything with more legs than it should have, it would probably be a good idea not to let it know we're coming."

Steve glanced back at her for a moment and immediately silenced the rattling keys. Belladonna couldn't help smiling as they continued down the steps: She felt fairly sure that his mind had turned to thoughts of ember beetles, long legs, and chandelier eyes.

Still, even without the rattling of the keys, their descent was not very quiet — every footstep echoed into the darkness and the smallest sound was amplified to almost deafening proportions.

"Steve . . ." whispered Belladonna. "Does it feel like it's getting colder?"

He nodded. What had started out as a general chill had become icy like a winter morning. The stones on the sides of the staircase were slick with damp and their breath fogged the air in front of them. Belladonna didn't want to mention the fact that this was the opposite of the way it was supposed to be. She had seen documentaries on television and read books about caverns and they all said the same thing—it got warmer the deeper you went.

Something scuttled overhead. Steve stopped and began to arc the flashlight up to see what it was. Belladonna reached out and pushed the light back down.

"Let's just keep going," she said.

Steve glanced nervously into the darkness above their heads, but focused the light forward and moved on. The stairs seemed never ending and their knees were starting to wobble like jelly. Belladonna tried going backward for a while, but it didn't really help. Every so often something else would scuttle about but other than that, the only sounds were the ones they made themselves. They had both long since fastened their jackets tightly and alternated shoving hands in pockets and blowing on them, but it didn't help for long—the air just got colder and colder.

Belladonna was about to suggest that they turn around and go back, when Steve suddenly stopped.

"Look!" he said.

She peered into the dim light of the tiny torch and saw what she had been dreaming of for the last half hour: the end of the staircase.

They practically ran down the last few steps, through a stone archway and into a long stone corridor. The corridor walls were punctuated with small alcoves where there had probably once been candles, but now it was dark, dank, and silent except for the steady drip of water that was leaking through the wall on one side and into a small puddle on the stone floor. There was no mysterious scuttling, however, and nowhere for any surprises to hide. Steve recovered his confidence and strode forward, with Belladonna trailing behind.

"It smells funny," she remarked.

The corridor ended with another stone arch. They stepped through and found themselves in an octagonal stone chamber. Steve flashed the light around.

"It's just like the library."

He was right. Belladonna turned slowly, following the light. It seemed to be the exact size and shape as the room far above, only this room was almost empty. The only furnishings were a stone chair flanked by two tall stands with what looked like brass bowls on the top. The wall above the chair had some carving that she couldn't quite make out.

"Up there," said Belladonna, "shine the light up there."

Steve tilted the light up. There were several words

carved into the stone but they seemed to be written in Greek. Belladonna sighed and looked at Steve.

"Don't look at me," he grinned. "It's all Greek to me."

"Oh, great," boomed a female voice, "like I haven't heard that one before."

Belladonna and Steve spun around, looking for the speaker, but even by the sickly light of the tiny flashlight it was clear that no one else was in the room.

"Um . . . hello?" said Belladonna nervously.

Her voice echoed around the chamber, but there was no reply. Steve turned the light onto the Greek carving again, and as he did so, fire suddenly shot up from the two brass bowls on either side of the stone chair, illuminating the octagonal room with a flickering yellow light, but there was still nobody there.

"It's been a good while since anyone visited me," said the voice. "I've almost forgotten how it goes."

"How what goes?" asked Belladonna.

There was the distant sound of someone (or something) clearing its throat.

"Beware!" thundered the voice, bouncing off the walls and setting Steve's and Belladonna's ears ringing. "You who consult the oracle of Apollo, examine your souls! The unworthy, the abject, the abominable . . . depart! And live!"

As the echo of the last syllable died in the octagonal room, Steve sidled uncomfortably toward Belladonna. "Um . . . do you think the explosives on Mr. Morris's shoes count as . . . you know . . . unworthy?" he whispered.

"Or abject? Or abominable?" grinned Belladonna.

"Oh, right," he hissed. "You don't say three words together all year in school but now you decide you're going to be funny."

Belladonna smiled cheerfully and turned her attention back to the stone chair, imagining that the Sibyl must be sitting on it, but invisible.

"We're fine," she said.

"Basically," said Steve, adding, "basically fine. Just . . . you know, minor infractions."

There was silence for a moment, then the braziers flared up, the orange flame turning red.

"Such as the explosives on Mr. Morris's shoes?" boomed the voice.

"I told you!" whispered Steve to Belladonna.

"Or the spiders in Philip Jones's desk? Or the treacle in Sophie Warren's shoes? Or the mass release of the lab mice?"

Steve began to smile in happy recollection as his greatest hits were recited.

"You put treacle in Sophie Warren's shoes?" whispered Belladonna. "Score."

"Or," boomed the voice, "the theft of the KitKat from Mr. Robinson's sweet shop?"

Steve's face fell. Belladonna looked at him with disbelief—he had actually stolen.

"I took it back," he said weakly.

The Sibyl was silent. He shifted his appeal to Belladonna.

"I took it back. It was just a dare. You know, to see if I could. And if I would."

Belladonna looked away. She felt disappointed. Which was silly, she knew, because how could he know how to break into buildings unless . . . But still . . . *stealing.*

"Perhaps I should go," he said gloomily.

"Don't be ridiculous," said the Sibyl, who no longer seemed to be by the chair, but on the other side of the room, about halfway up the wall. "They were, as you said yourself, just minor infractions. Such trifling matters are nothing to me. I have known men who have set rivers running with blood, murdered those they should have loved, and betrayed entire nations. Stealing a small chocolate bar really isn't in the running."

Steve looked relieved and glanced at Belladonna.

"Of course"—the voice was suddenly at his right ear, sibilant as a snake—"that's on the understanding that it won't happen again."

Steve shook his head.

"Where *are* you?" asked Belladonna.

"Everywhere," said the Sibyl, "and nowhere. I was somewhere once, of course. Back then, gods marveled at my beauty."

"Huh," muttered Steve, who had got some of his nerve back, "sounds like my Mum."

"Apollo himself," she continued, clearly enjoying

the opportunity of telling the story, "offered me any-thing I wanted if I would only return his love."

"What did you ask for?" said Belladonna.

"For life, of course, fool as I was. I reached into the sand—I lived near the beach then, but that's another story—anyway, I reached into the sand and filled my hand. I asked to live as many years as there were grains in my hand."

"What did you forget?" asked Belladonna.

"Forget?"

"Well, in stories about wishes, people always for-get something."

"You make me sound so conventional," sniffed the Sibyl. "Well, as it happens, I did forget something. I forgot to ask to remain young. I also told Apollo that I didn't really love him."

"Oops," said Steve quietly.

"Oops, indeed," said the Sibyl. "I grew older and older, my beauty vanished, and after many hundreds of years, I became so small and old and frail that I was kept in a jar. Still I aged. A thousand years passed, then two thousand, until all that was left was my voice."

"How awful."

"It's better than the jar. Now, what do you want to know?"

She seemed to be back in the vicinity of the chair, so Belladonna turned and faced it again.

"We're looking for an amulet," she said. "Made from draconite. That's the stone from—"

"I know what draconite is," snapped the voice.

"It's supposed to be somewhere close by."

"We'll see. . . ."

The flames in the braziers flared blue, then green, and filled the room with a sweet, acrid smoke that made Belladonna and Steve feel dizzy. Through the light and smoke, Belladonna almost imagined she could see the Sibyl as she once was, sitting in the stone chair, gripping its arms, and throwing her head back to allow the gods entry to her mind.

> *"Peering proudly through the welkin way,*
> *The radiant raptor rends the ruddy day,*
> *Protecting the paragon in plain sight*
> *Under arches and angles in motley light."*

The flames sank to orange and the Sibyl seemed to sigh.

"Um . . . is that it?" asked Belladonna.

"Did it make sense?"

"No, it didn't make sense!" said Steve. "It was like something from one of those crosswords where the clue is a train and the answer is a caterpillar."

"Oh, good," said the Sibyl, "I was afraid I'd lost my touch."

Belladonna and Steve looked at each other and then at the empty chair.

"Oh, you'd better write it down," suggested the

Sibyl, her voice drifting down from the ceiling. "Sometimes they're difficult to remember."

"That's because they're rubbish," muttered Steve.

"If you wanted something easy," said the Sibyl icily, "you could try the horoscopes in the morning paper. They're a pack of meaningless drivel, of course, but you can understand them right away."

Belladonna scowled at Steve, who kicked the earth floor a couple of times, took a deep breath, and managed what he hoped was a conciliatory smile.

"Don't try that," hissed the Sibyl. "I have heard the honey words of great men and greater women. Lies are as clear to me as the mountains on a sunny day."

"I wasn't going to lie!" insisted Steve. "I just don't see the reason for all the secrecy."

"He has a point," said Belladonna.

"No, he doesn't," snapped the Sibyl. "This is the way it is done, the way it has always been done. When I lived in the caves of Cumae, I would write my prophesies on leaves and lay them out in front of me. Sometimes the wind would catch them and blow them about, but I never rearranged them."

Belladonna thought that was just about the most ridiculous thing she'd ever heard, but unlike Steve, she managed to keep her opinion to herself. She turned toward the door.

"Yes, well, we'd better go. It must be nearly teatime and my aunt will be worried."

"Your aunt has greater worries than whether you are home in time for tea," intoned the Sibyl. "She reads the runes and knows the truth."

"Oh, great, she's at it again," said Steve, exasperated.

Belladonna smiled back in what she hoped was the right direction, then they both walked toward the stairs.

"Wait!" cried the Sibyl suddenly. "There's more. . . ."

Steve rolled his eyes and they both turned back.

> *"As were the nights at the great Well of Wyrð,*
> *So were the dragons far Cathay feared,*
> *Likewise the worthies renowned of the sages,*
> *The thrones of the dark queen,*
> *And the stones of the ages."*

Belladonna and Steve waited, hoping against hope that there'd be a bit more. Something that might make sense.

"That's it," said the Sibyl finally. "Yes, that's definitely it. That one is separate, by the way, not part of the first one. So you got two."

"Whoopee," muttered Steve.

"Well, it's more than any of the ancients got. You might show a bit of gratitude."

"Oh, we are grateful," said Belladonna, smiling. "We really are. Thank you very much. Umm . . ."

She hesitated a moment. She wanted to ask about Dr. Ashe. He had known about the Sibyl; perhaps the Sibyl knew something about him.

"Yes?" hissed the Sibyl at her ear.

"The man who told us about you . . . that you were here, I mean. I was wondering if you could tell us anything about him."

"I have given you two oracles and still you ask for more?" The voice was beginning to sound distinctly irritated.

"It's just that . . . well, he's dead and so we don't . . ."

"You speak with the Dead?"

Now she was impressed. Steve stepped forward, clearly feeling a lot more confident.

"Constantly," he said. "Yakking away with them all the time. Get told off for it. Sent to the Head and everything."

"His name is Ashe," said Belladonna quickly, before things got out of hand, "Dr. Ashe. He lived here in town before he died. He was an alchemist."

"He was a charlatan," boomed the Sibyl.

"Told you so," whispered Steve.

"But he told us you were here and he told us about the amulet and he was right about those. It's just that he said he needed it to discover why the other ghosts had vanished and why the doors between our world and the Other Side were closing, and I just wondered . . ."

"I will not waste my oracles on a dead man," humphed the Sibyl, now clearly back in her stone chair. "For him I will give you but one word: *phatês*. Now go."

"Thank you," said Belladonna. "Could you translate that? Um . . . we don't study Greek here and—"

"Well, now would seem to be a good time to start."

"Right. Well, thank you again."

They turned toward the stairs again.

"Why don't you take the lift?" said the Sibyl. "It's faster."

There was a muffled *ping*, and a piece of wall near the stone chair slid slowly open. Belladonna and Steve sidled suspiciously toward it. Inside, the floor was tiled in onyx and terra-cotta and the walls were honey-colored marble. They stepped inside and the door closed with a whoosh. Next to the door was a small ob-sidian panel with four buttons marked *O, G, U,* and *S.* They stared at them for a moment.

"Which do you suppose it is?" asked Steve.

"No idea," said Belladonna. "*O* is probably for 'Oracle.' What about *G*?"

"For 'Ground'?"

Belladonna nodded and Steve pushed the button. For a while nothing seemed to be happening, then they became aware of the distant sound of rushing water. This was followed by a jerk that sent them stag-gering and a slow grinding sound as the lift began its painfully slow ascent.

"The stairs would've been faster than this," said Steve.

Belladonna had to agree, though sitting in the lift was a lot less hard on the knees. She slid down the wall and sat on the cold tile floor, allowing her black hair to fall in front of her face while she thought. The Sibyl's oracles were obtuse, but she had a feeling they should be able to figure them out. Perhaps the key was to break them down, line by line, like they did with poetry in English lit.

"We're here."

The sound of rushing water had dwindled to a steady drip and the lift had stopped moving. The doors showed no inclination to open, however. Belladonna looked up at the panel.

"There's usually a button for opening the doors."

Steve peered at the panel; there was nothing except the four buttons. He began to run his hands over the walls, searching for another hidden switch. Belladonna watched for a while, then stood up and turned toward the door.

"Hoige tas thuras," she said.

The doors slid slowly open.

Steve looked at her. "That was Greek, wasn't it?"

"I think so," said Belladonna uncertainly.

"Do you know what you said?"

"Not really. But I was thinking about telling it to open the door."

She had a strange feeling in the pit of her stomach that the expression on Steve's face did nothing to help. She tried to remember if she'd perhaps heard somebody say the same thing, on a travel show on television, perhaps. But she knew she hadn't. She had simply thought of what she wanted to say and it had come out . . . just not in the language she'd expected.

She stepped out of the lift, anxious to be doing something else. But instead of the sunny library, she found herself in a small, dark room.

"Where are we now?"

Steve followed her out, and as soon as he was clear of the doors, the lift whisked shut and the whole thing vanished into the dirt floor of wherever they were. He jumped back and fell over something lying on the floor.

"Great," he muttered.

He turned to look at what he'd tripped over. "Hang on . . ."

"What?" said Belladonna, her eyes slowly getting accustomed to the light.

Steve held up a small sack. Belladonna peered at it and could just make out the words "Grass Seed" on the side. As she did so, she became aware of slivers of light piercing the walls. They were in a wooden building.

At that moment the whole structure trembled as something hit the side of it hard, sending showers of dust from the roof. Steve turned, spotted the door, and flung it open, then he hesitated and glanced back at Belladonna.

"Wait here a moment," he said.

Belladonna watched him go, then stepped back and peered through one of the cracks in the wall. The lift had brought them to the groundskeeper's shed near the football field and she could see the pitch extending away past the goalposts to the clump of scrawny trees at the end. Three boys were playing football and Steve was walking lazily toward them. One kicked the ball over and he expertly checked it in midair with his right foot and fired it back before joining them in kicking it about. Belladonna quickly got bored and began hunting through the shed for a piece of paper and something to write with. She found a scrap near the back where there was an old chair and a small table with the remains of a cup of tea, several old lottery tickets, a notepad, and a pencil. She sat down and wrote out the Sibyl's prophecies. She stared at them for a few moments. It was pretty clear that the first one was the one that was about the Draconian Amulet, so she decided to concentrate on that for the moment. It did make sense, in a way. It was just that it didn't seem to reveal anything much about the location of the amulet. It didn't even mention it.

"*Phatês*," she whispered the word, then closed her eyes and whispered it again, "*Phatês*."

She had asked the doors to open in Greek. Perhaps if she said this word out loud, then the meaning would come to her.

"*Phatês*."

Nothing. It was just another strange word.

After a while she started doodling on the notepad and wondering when Steve was coming back and whether it was alright for her to go out now. That was when she realized that she could no longer hear the game outside. She crept up to the door and peeked out. There was no one there except the black birds in the trees.

She sighed, closed the door to the shed behind her, and trudged across the field. She was used to being forgotten about, but she had thought that, what with the Land of the Dead, the giant beetles, and the Sibyl, Steve might have remembered where she was.

Dusk was beginning to draw in by the time she got home. At first she thought Aunt Deirdre was still out — the house was dark and the central heating hadn't been turned on — but then she noticed the sliver of light beneath the kitchen door. She walked back and pushed the door open, in full expectation of a telling off for being out so late, but the Aunt Deirdre who looked up from the kitchen table wasn't the matter-of-fact woman who had sped off this morning.

Her face was pale and her eyes ringed with shadow. The table in front of her was littered with newspapers, from the local three-sheeter to every national paper and all the international news magazines.

"Aunt Deirdre . . ." Belladonna's voice faded away.

Her aunt waved a thin hand over the papers. "It has begun."

8

Draconite

"WHAT DO YOU mean?" Belladonna tried to keep the fear out of her voice, but the idea of Aunt Deirdre falling apart scared her more than she had imagined.

She needed to be able to rely on someone having their feet firmly on the ground and brooking no nonsense, and until this moment, Deirdre had seemed just the sort of person who would be unfazed by huge black hounds, alchemists, or doors to the Other Side. Right now, though, she looked as though she hadn't slept for days: Dark rings circled her eyes and some of her mascara had smudged where she'd been rubbing them.

"Aunt Deirdre . . ." She thought her aunt hadn't heard her, but Deirdre's eyes flashed with irritation as she gestured at the papers and magazines.

"This!" she snapped. "This! Can't you see?"

Belladonna looked down at the papers. At first they just seemed like a random collection of newspapers and magazines, but as she looked at them she noticed that they were all open at pages that reported accidents, from last week's train crash to minor traffic incidents.

"Accidents," she said hastily, not wanting to upset Aunt Deirdre further, "they're all accidents. But what does it mean?"

Aunt Deirdre sighed heavily, hauled herself up, and poured herself a glass of wine. "It's the ghosts," she said.

"The ghosts?" said Belladonna, not understanding at all. "What do they have to do with accidents?"

"Didn't Elspeth teach you anything?" demanded Deirdre. "It's not like it's new information. The Greeks knew all about it."

Belladonna stared at her blankly.

"The Ancient Greeks," said Deirdre irritably. "Honestly, what on earth do they teach you at that school? The Ancient Greeks took ghosts seriously; some of their greatest philosophers wrote extensively on the subject. Plato? Aristotle? I take it you have heard of them?"

"Yes, but—"

"Well, they believed that ghosts prevented accidents. And, as it happens, they were right."

Belladonna considered this. "How?" she asked skeptically.

Aunt Deirdre shrugged and sat down at the table again. "Sometimes they're actually seen," she said, "but usually it's just a feeling. You know, a feeling that you should sit up, pay attention, a feeling that something's about to happen."

"I didn't know they did anything," muttered Belladonna.

"Of course they do something," snapped Deirdre. "What would be the point of them otherwise?"

Belladonna bit her lower lip and stared at Aunt Deirdre. She'd had just about all she could take of people treating her like she was an idiot just because she didn't know some arcane fact or ancient language that, in the normal run of things, she would never need.

"Well, if that's the case," she said finally, trying to keep the irritation out of her voice and not really succeeding, "why did Mum and Dad die? I mean there are loads of accidents every day. Do they pick and choose?"

"Don't be obtuse," snapped Aunt Deirdre, finishing her glass of wine and pouring herself another. "Ghosts don't prevent *all* accidents, any more than doctors can prevent *all* diseases. They reduce them. Prevent epidemics, if you like. But now they've gone, and the number of accidents is skyrocketing. And that's not the worst thing."

"It isn't?"

Aunt Deirdre shook her head and began folding up the newspapers and stacking them neatly on one side of the table. "Next will be sleep," she said.

Belladonna had no idea what her aunt was talking

about, but she felt a great desire to say something, anything, to make her feel better. She crossed the kitchen
and put the kettle on, rinsed out the teapot, and made
a decision. She would tell her aunt about the door and
the Other Side and Dr. Ashe and everything. It was
clear that this was all too serious to keep to herself.

"Aunt Deirdre . . ." she began, but never got any
further.

There was a creak and a bang as the front door
opened and closed, and her grandmother marched into
the kitchen, pulling off her coat.

"Here, Belladonna, dear," she said, "hang this up,
there's a love."

Belladonna took the coat and went back out to the
hall to hang it on the pegs near the door. As she walked
back, she overheard hurried whispering.

"What did you tell her that for?" hissed her grandmother. "You're going to scare the life out of the poor
thing!"

"Well, I didn't tell her about the dreams," whispered
Deirdre.

"I should think not! You—oh, there you are!"

Belladonna slid into the kitchen and pretended she
hadn't heard anything. She knew it would be pointless
to ask—they were both so determined to keep her in
the dark. Anyone would think it wasn't *her* parents
who had vanished.

"I thought I'd come over and make you a proper
hot meal," said her grandmother, in her best cuddly-

grandma voice, "so why don't you get on and do your homework and I'll get to it."

"It's Saturday," said Belladonna.

"So it is," said her grandmother, and only a slight tightening of her jaw revealed that she was the least bit irritated by her granddaughter's tone. "Well, off you go and watch the telly, then. I'll call you when it's ready."

Belladonna sighed, trudged into the sitting room, and turned on the television. It was the omnibus edition of *Staunchly Springs*. She watched for a moment, but it made her miss her parents even more, though she did agree with her father that the patio didn't seem like the best place to dispose of a body. She changed the channel and settled for some poorly produced science fiction series instead, while the clock on the mantel ticked its dawdling way through the early evening. After about half an hour, she pulled out the piece of paper with the oracle on it and went back to trying to work it out, but by the time she was called in to dinner, she was no closer to finding the Draconite Amulet than she'd been when the Sibyl had first uttered the words.

Dinner was anything but fun. Her grandmother and Aunt Deirdre were barely speaking to each other, while trying to pretend that everything was perfectly alright. They chatted endlessly about the weather and the state of the economy and asked Belladonna how she was enjoying school. Belladonna became increasingly sullen at their refusal to tell her even a little bit about what was going on.

On the other hand, she thought, with more than a little satisfaction, she had found the door and they hadn't.

She finished her ice cream and announced that she was going upstairs to read.

Of course, once she was in her room she didn't want to read at all. She went and sat in the window, watching the comings and goings on the street below. Families who had been out for drives rolled home, children played in the street, and Jimmy Tucker fell off his bike. Belladonna wondered if he would have tumbled if there'd been a ghost to whisper in his ear and whether the accident at the crossing this afternoon had anything to do with it. And what had her aunt meant about sleep?

The moon came out and then the stars. She looked up at them and thought about the night they'd flickered out. Her parents had known why, she was sure of that, but now there wasn't anyone who would tell her the answers to the questions that were burning in her mind. She wanted to believe that Aunt Deirdre and her grandmother knew what they were doing, but something told her that they knew even less than she did. She picked at the ragged hem of one of the curtains and wondered what they thought they were protecting her from. What could possibly be worse than losing her parents twice? Tears sprang to her eyes at the thought of never seeing them again, but she wiped them away impatiently. There was no time for that. She had to be strong. She had to *think*.

And apart from the whole ghost thing, what about the nerve of Steve Evans dumping her in the groundskeeper's shed like that!

She had just decided that she would never have anything to do with him again, when the volume of the conversation downstairs began to rise. She crept out onto the landing and strained to hear what they were saying. As unlikely as it seemed, it sounded like Aunt Deirdre was crying. She kept talking about someone called Richard, and Grandma Johnson seemed to veer from sympathy to impatience and back again. Then there was a great sob followed by a lengthy silence.

"I just can't go through this again," said Aunt Deirdre finally.

Belladonna went back into her room and sat on the bed. She decided she had to talk to Aunt Deirdre. She'd just wait until her grandmother left and she heard her aunt come upstairs. Then they'd talk.

She didn't know what time it was when she woke up. All she knew was that it was pitch-dark and something was coming. Outside, in the distance, she could hear the baying of hounds. Not one hound this time, but dozens, and they were getting closer. As the baying and howling got louder, a furious wind whipped up and the clang and clatter of a hundred hooves shook the small house to its very foundations. Belladonna sprang out of bed and pulled the curtains back, and suddenly all was silence. The street looked its usual suburban self; there was even a small bird sitting on the telephone wire singing softly to itself.

As she stared, she heard the click of Aunt Deirdre's bedroom door as it opened. She ran out to the landing to find her aunt, fully dressed and ashen-faced.

"Did you hear that?" said Belladonna. "What was it?"

"It was the Hunt," said her aunt quietly.

"But there's no one—"

"I'm going out," said Aunt Deirdre abruptly. "Lock the door after me."

And with that, she marched down the stairs and out of the front door.

Belladonna stood, stunned, for a moment, then ran down the stairs and locked the door as the guttural roar of her aunt's sports car faded into the night.

She returned to her room, but spent most of the night straining to hear the baying hounds or her aunt's car. Anything but the silence of the empty house. She finally dropped off at about four in the morning, only to wake up two hours later as the car pulled up. She listened as Aunt Deirdre walked into the house, took off her coat, ran upstairs, and closed her bedroom door. Then all was silence again.

Belladonna sighed. She sat for a while in bed, thinking about how different things used to be, even after her parents died. The house was full of noise and the smell of cooking, her Mum and Dad shouted to each other from different ends of the house, and everything proceeded with a general air of happy chaos. Now, for the first time since the accident, she felt truly alone.

She rolled over and looked at the curtains that her mother had made before she died. What could they be doing now? She supposed she should have thought of it before, but they'd always been here—making breakfast, watching television, talking, laughing. What did they do in the Land of the Dead? The same things? Different ones? She should have asked. She couldn't believe she'd never asked!

Still, she thought, as she jumped down from the bed and made her way to the bathroom to brush her teeth, moping wasn't any use at all. So what if her aunt was falling apart, her grandmother was being mysterious, and Steve preferred to spend his time with his footballing friends, she still had her brains—she could find the amulet by herself.

Half an hour later she was in the kitchen, shoving a packet of biscuits and a can of Tizer into her backpack, and heading out toward the graveyard to think. The day was cold but sunny and she happily clambered up onto the great table tomb, opened the biscuits, and began to puzzle over the oracle again.

"Peering proudly through the welkin way,
The radiant raptor rends the ruddy day,

Protecting the paragon in plain sight
Under arches and angles in motley light."

She was pretty sure that "radiant raptor" meant a dragon and that "paragon" meant the stone, but the "arches and angles" part made no sense. There weren't any arches in town, unless you counted the arches in churches, and she thought it highly unlikely that a thing like the Draconite Amulet would be hidden in a church. Or what about the old market? No, they'd knocked that down last year after the big storm brought down most of the fake crenellation around the top. She helped herself to another biscuit and decided that her best option was probably to just wander around and see if anything presented itself.

"I've got it!"

Belladonna nearly had a heart attack as Steve leapt out from behind the gate. She stared at him coldly.

"Got what," she said icily, "the black death? That'd be nice."

"What? Oh, yeah, sorry about yesterday, but, I mean, you wouldn't want to get skitted by that lot. They'd make your life miserable. Listen—"

"I like being miserable," muttered Belladonna, putting her biscuits away and climbing off the tomb. "It keeps me warm."

She threw one more filthy look in his direction and stalked off, but he wasn't about to be put off so easily.

"No, seriously," he gushed, "stop messing. I think I know where the stone is."

This presented a problem. She really wanted to give him quite a bit more grief before giving in and letting him rejoin the search, but she also really wanted to know what he'd figured out. She stalked on a bit further.

"Ah, c'mon," he moaned, "don't be such a girl!"

Belladonna froze, then spun around.

"I *am* a girl," she said quietly. "But at least I'm not afraid of my friends. And I don't need anybody's help. I can do it on my own!"

And with that, she marched out of the graveyard and off toward the High Street.

Her intention was to go to where the old market building had been. There was still a sort of covered walkway left from the old buildings. Maybe that had arches. She hadn't gone very far before Steve was back at her side.

"Okay," he muttered, "I'm sorry. It wasn't very nice. I don't know why I did it."

They walked on in silence until they reached the old covered walkway. There were no arches or anything that looked even slightly like an arch. Belladonna sighed. There was nothing for it.

"Alright," she said, "what's your idea?"

"A video arcade," he announced proudly.

"A video arcade?"

"Yes," he said eagerly, the words tumbling out. "I was thinking, you know, about arches and I just kept saying the word over and over to myself. Arches, arches, arches—arches—arches. And it just came to me—arcade!"

Belladonna looked at him. For a boy who was considered a dunce by almost everyone and spent more time in Miss Parker's office than he did in actual lessons, he was really pretty bright.

"That's a good idea" was all she said, however.

Steve grinned from ear to ear. "Come on, then, there's one just down here."

He led the way down the street to a large, brightly lit arcade that spewed tinkling music and ringing chimes out into the street. Inside, brand-new machines were arranged in a maze of steel and video screens, disgorging muscle-bound avatars and thermonuclear explosions to anyone with a few coins and nothing else to do. Most were occupied by glaze-eyed gamers and a few scruffy adults. None of them had anything to do with dragons, though, and Steve and Belladonna were back on the street in a matter of minutes.

"Don't worry," he said, undaunted, "there's another one 'round the corner."

Belladonna started to follow him, then stopped as they passed Moorpark's Books.

"Hang on," she said.

"What?"

"A bookshop. Let's go in."

"Why?"

"*Phatês.* The word that the Sibyl said when we asked her about Dr. Ashe. Maybe they'll have a dictionary."

Steve nodded, heaved open the door, and led the way in.

Moorpark's was one of those bright new bookshops, full of carefully constructed displays and racks of calendars, notepads, and stuffed toys. They made their way past pyramids of bestsellers toward the history section, but there was nothing remotely like a dictionary.

"Excuse me," said Belladonna to a lackluster teenager who was stocking a shelf more slowly than seemed humanly possible, "where would we find an Ancient Greek dictionary?"

The boy stared at her for a few moments, then reached up and removed a set of earphones that Belladonna hadn't noticed. He stared at her quizzically, so she smiled and repeated the question.

"Reference," he said, sticking the earbuds back in his ears and turning back to the shelf.

Steve opened his mouth to say something that Belladonna was fairly sure wasn't going to be complimentary, so she grabbed his sleeve and pulled him away.

"Dictionary," she said, "remember?"

"What a twit," muttered Steve, glancing back, but

allowing himself to be propelled to the back of the shop where several shelves groaned under the weight of dictionaries and phrase books.

"What are phrase books doing here?" he asked. "Shouldn't they be in travel?"

"Just look for a Greek/English one," said Belladonna, refusing to be sidetracked. "Ancient Greek."

They pored over the shelves, which were packed with dictionaries of every shape and size, from massive tomes to tiny pocket versions. There were several versions of ordinary English dictionaries and at least three for each of the most popular holiday destinations, but Belladonna began to despair of finding any in languages that no one actually spoke any more.

"Oh, well," she said, straightening up after going through the bottom shelf for the second time, "it doesn't look like they have —"

"Wait." Steve had drifted around the corner to the next set of shelves. "Latin! Maybe . . . yes! Ancient Greek!"

He ran back, brandishing a small book that was almost as thick as it was wide. Belladonna joined him as he opened the book at the Ancient Greek to English section, but then their faces fell. It was in Greek. Proper, Cyrillic alphabet Greek. They stared at the strange letters.

"What's the point of that?" said Steve, exasperated.

"I suppose it's useful if you're trying to translate an

old document, or a carving or something," mumbled Belladonna, crestfallen.

Steve snapped the book shut and shoved it back onto the shelf. "Well, I just hope the stupid word doesn't mean something like 'vicious murderer who eats children for breakfast with bran flakes,'" he said, "because if it does, we're stuffed."

Belladonna had to agree. What was the point, she thought, of giving them a clue in a language that no one outside of universities spoke any more? How were they ever supposed to work it out? On the other hand, it was given to them by a creature that used to write its prophecies on dried leaves and let them blow around, and Belladonna had to admit that compared to that method of communication, an actual, real word was probably an improvement.

"Come on," she said, "let's go and look at that other arcade."

Steve nodded and led the way back out onto the High Street, 'round a corner onto Umbra Avenue, and along past the launderette to a small shop that Belladonna had always assumed sold records. The window was small and blacked out and the dark green door was chipped and festooned with dozens of stickers, which turned out not to be for bands at all, but for games. Steve pushed the door open with the authority of one who has wasted more than a few hours standing in front of CRT screens with a steadily diminishing pocketful of change.

Inside, it was dark and uncomfortably warm, though with the same cacophony of ear-piercing sound effects and thundering music as at the other arcade. Unlike the other place, however, there was a small desk and change window near the front, behind which sat an incredibly old man with a long, scraggly white beard that appeared to have much of his lunch entwined within its grubby depths. He was wearing a threadbare red cardigan with a huge white (and much-used) handkerchief hanging out of one pocket. Steve nodded a greeting to him, but the old man merely grunted and returned to counting the small stacks of coins he had laid out on the desk in front of him.

"He's always like that," whispered Steve.

Belladonna peeked back at him through the piece of hair that had dropped in front of her eyes again. He was still counting his money, but she had a feeling he was watching their every move.

Steve led the way past the newer games at the front of the shop and into the even darker recesses toward the back. Belladonna couldn't believe the place was so big—it had seemed tiny when they'd first walked in. The back of the arcade was a disorganized no-man's-land of the broken and outdated. Machines, whose screens had been smashed, electronics fried, or cash boxes jammed, shared space with fully functioning games that no one wanted to play any more. At the very back were three one-armed bandits, a dusty fortune-telling machine, and an old claw game. Belladonna's jaw dropped.

"That's it!" she whispered.

The claw game was housed in a large cube-shaped box, topped by the head of a snarling red dragon with one talon extended and two small batlike wings. Beneath the dragon in the Plexiglas box were dozens of small cheap toys of the teddy bear, toy car, and plastic doll variety. Above them, a large mechanical claw hovered above a chute that led down and out to a catch-bin on the red-painted exterior of the machine.

"But where is it?" asked Steve, squinting at the dusty, jumbled box of toys.

"There!" said Belladonna, pointing. "There! Underneath the ambulance!"

He peered at the toys and followed Belladonna's pointing finger to the far left of the machine. There, lying next to a particularly ugly kewpie doll and half underneath an old-fashioned ambulance, was a large triangular red stone set into a gold-colored medallion. The stone wasn't particularly shiny, but it had a depth and glimmer that told even the jewelry-challenged Steve that this was no plastic trinket.

"How much change have you got?" he asked, plunging his hands into his pockets and coming up with a collection of coins.

Belladonna reached into her own pockets, then stopped. "Oh, no," she said.

"What?" asked Steve, without looking up.

"Look!"

He looked up. There, just above the catch-basket, was the coin slot, and right next to that the words "Three tries for 1/-!" were written in appropriately gothic script.

"One what?" he said, squinting at the unfamiliar symbol.

"Shilling," explained Belladonna. "Old money. It only takes shillings!"

They both stared at the coin slot, suddenly deflated. Steve put his money back in his pocket.

"Wait," said Belladonna. "My Mum keeps a box on her dressing table that's full of old money. Maybe there are some shillings in there."

Steve nodded, then looked back toward the front of the shop.

"You know," he said, "there's not much point having this game here unless people can get their hands on shillings."

"Yes, but it doesn't look like it's been played in years."

"Let's ask."

Belladonna followed as Steve marched through the shop and up to the old man on the desk.

"Excuse me," he said, almost shouting.

"Yes? What?" said the old man loudly, cocking an ear toward Steve.

"We want to play the claw game!"

"Eh?"

"At the back!"

"You'll have to speak up! My hearing's not what it was!"

"The claw game!" yelled Steve. "At the back! It only takes shillings!"

The old man heard that, alright. He started laughing a wheezy, squeaking laugh that soon turned into a hacking cough. He coughed for a few minutes until his face turned red and tears started to stream from his rheumy eyes, then he took out his handkerchief, wiped his face, and was back to business.

"Shillings," he said, opening a drawer and taking out a handful of the old coins, "50p for five."

"But that's not fair!" said Belladonna. "They're only worth 5p each!"

The old man leaned over the desk and peered down at her as if he'd only just noticed she was there. "Well, aren't you the clever one, missy?" he said. "But the fact is, I have 'em and you want 'em, so they're 10p each."

"We'll take five," said Steve quickly, handing over the money.

The old man grinned toothlessly and counted out the shillings.

Belladonna and Steve scurried back to the game and then stopped, suddenly nervous. Steve held out a shilling.

"You go first," he said.

"No," Belladonna shook her head. "You go. You play more of these than I do."

"Not these old things," said Steve, but he dropped a coin in the slot anyway.

There was a clank as the shilling hit the coin box, then the whole machine seemed to lurch and the claw moved sideways. Steve grabbed the joystick and began trying to move the claw over the Draconite Amulet. The machinery clunked and juddered as it moved first forward and then to the left. When he thought he was above it, he dropped the claw and made a grab but got nothing. He started to try again but his first turn ran out. He pushed the button, but came up empty-handed on his second try as well; the third time, he managed to grab the ambulance and move it aside, opening up the approach to the amulet, then the first shilling ran out and the machine ground to a halt.

Steve solemnly handed Belladonna the second shilling, but she had no more luck than he did. She moved the ugly kewpie doll and once even dropped the claw right on top of the amulet, but couldn't actually pick it up.

"Maybe the machine is broken," she said as Steve dropped in the third shilling.

"I wish," he said, giving the joystick a yank to the right. "Me and my Dad went to the seaside once and there was one in an arcade there. It was just the same.

Even when you pick something up, half the time the claw is set to drop it before it reaches the chute."

"You mean it's rigged?" she said. "Isn't there some government agency that's supposed to regulate things like this?"

Steve looked at her like she was certifiable as the third shilling ran out. Belladonna took the fourth and dropped it in. She decided to try a meticulous approach this time, and moved the claw as slowly and carefully as she could. She dropped it on the amulet, closed and raised it, but inexplicably found that the claw had grabbed the kewpie doll instead.

"What? But I was nowhere near the stupid doll!"

"No," said Steve, squinting at the machine suspiciously. "There's something hinky about this game."

"Of course!" said Belladonna. "There'd have to be, wouldn't there?"

"Come again?"

"Well, if you're going to hide the amulet here, you couldn't risk just anyone being able to get hold of it."

"No, but that really doesn't help."

"What if it was a real dragon?"

"What?" Steve was clearly beginning to worry about Belladonna's sanity.

"Not a game. What if it was a real dragon with a real treasure? What would you do?"

"Run away, get a tank . . . I don't know. It's stupid."

Belladonna looked at him. She knew he couldn't

believe he was actually spending his time hanging around with the weirdest girl in school. He probably thought he should be with his friends, playing football and making the chess club's lives miserable.

"Okay," he said gloomily, dropping the last shilling into the machine. "If it was a real dragon, I'd have a sword—"

"And armor."

"Yes," he muttered, "and armor. And I'd ride up to its cave, dismount, and say something like . . . like . . ."

He looked at Belladonna for help. She knew it was because she was the one who kept spouting magic words in forgotten languages, but she just stared at him expectantly, biting her lower lip, her hair hanging in front of her eyes. *Maybe,* she thought, *just maybe I'm not the only one.* Steve was clearly glad there was hardly anyone else there. He took hold of the joystick and closed his eyes.

"Eliantor!" he said, in a commanding voice. He opened his eyes.

"Carry on! Don't stop," said Belladonna.

Steve rolled his eyes; this really was so dumb. Belladonna gave him a sharp nudge in the ribs and nodded him on. He closed his eyes again.

"Eliantor! As you value your life and the lives of your brood, and in the name of the Champions of Arianrhod, give up your jewel!"

He opened his eyes and turned to Belladonna, and for the first time he looked really scared.

"What was that? Is this what it feels like when you . . . ? This isn't right, I think we should go — "

He never got any further; the joystick suddenly lurched in his hand and the claw flew across the box. It hovered over the amulet, then plunged down. Then . . . nothing. Steve held his breath and slowly raised the claw. There in its grasp was the Draconite Amulet. He moved the claw back across the field of toys to the chute and let it go.

There was a clang and a rattle. Steve and Belladonna both looked down: There was the amulet, blood red and twinkling darkly, in the hopper of the machine. Steve reached down and picked it up.

"How did . . ." he began.

"It doesn't matter," said Belladonna. "Let's go."

Steve shoved the amulet into his pocket and followed Belladonna as she strode purposefully past the change kiosk.

"Win anything?" asked the old man, before collapsing in a mixture of explosive wheezes and coughs that sounded like he was about to die on the spot, but which Belladonna realized was actually laughing.

"Not really," she mumbled, pushing the door open and stepping outside. Back on the street, she turned around and looked at Steve. He still looked a little stunned, but out there, in the glare of the afternoon, she could see that he thought it seemed ludicrous to believe that any mumbo jumbo that had popped into his head could've done anything. And yet . . .

They marched up the High Street toward the old theatre. Steve took the amulet out of his pocket and looked at it. The chain and setting seemed to be gold and decorated with impossibly complicated, inter-twining geometric designs, but the stone itself was like nothing they'd ever seen. Belladonna stared into its depths. It was red, she was sure, but toward the middle it seemed to become black and to go on forever, like a bottomless well.

Steve held it up in front of his face and peered through it. Then he stopped walking and stood motionless, barely breathing.

"Belladonna . . ."

She turned back. "What?"

"Come here," he said quietly. "Tell me what you see."

He handed her the jewel and she held it up toward the sun just as he had . . . and gasped.

"Do you see it? You do, don't you?"

She did. What she had expected to see, of course, was the end of the street looking a bit red as though she were looking through cellophane, but what the amulet was showing her was not the end of Umbra Avenue leading into the High Street with Sunday shoppers and families out for a drive, but a place of arid plains and splintered mountains, where great winged creatures flew, silhouetted against a cloudless sky, while others battled on the ground, spitting flame from gaping jaws and slashing at each other's armored flanks with scythelike claws.

"Dragons!" she whispered.

"I think we're seeing it through his eyes," said Steve. "The dragon's—the one that the stone belonged to."

Belladonna nodded. She couldn't take her eyes off the scene before her; it was awful, yet mesmerizing.

"It didn't come from the Land of the Dead," said Steve.

"What?"

"Didn't Dr. Ashe say that the ghosts might have disappeared because something from one world had caused an imbalance in the other?"

"Well, yes, but—"

"Well, if the amulet wasn't from the Land of the Dead in the first place, how could it cause an imbalance there? It should be causing one here, if anything."

Belladonna lowered the amulet and handed it back to Steve.

"But he didn't say this was *causing* the imbalance," she explained. "He just said it might be able to help him locate what was."

Steve looked at her skeptically, and she had to admit he did sort of have a point. If the whole thing about imbalances caused by objects from another world was true, then surely the amulet would have created problems being here. Or maybe this world was too solid, and the ghost world was more susceptible.

"We really need to know what that word means," she said finally. "*Phatês.*"

Steve held the amulet up and watched the dragons for a few moments, then turned back to Belladonna. "We'll ask him," he said.

"Ask him?"

"Yes. Think about it—he's so impressed with himself. Didn't he enjoy making us out to be so stupid and undereducated and stuff?"

"Ye-es?" said Belladonna dubiously.

"Well, that sort of person always loves showing off. Just like Mr. Brunswick in Geography—if you let him run on long enough, he'll tell you the answers just to prove how much cleverer he is than you."

That was true, and Belladonna had to admit that Steve was certainly very good at getting Mr. Brunswick to give up the answers to almost anything, but he was a Geography teacher and Dr. Ashe was an alchemist, and she wasn't entirely convinced that he'd fall for the same ruse. Still, they really did need to find out what the Sibyl's word meant before they had any further dealings with him.

"Okay," she said, "we'll ask him. *Before* we give it to him."

"Yes. Before."

They reached the theatre and slipped around the back, being careful to avoid Steve's parents. Belladonna gave him a shove up to the window and he repeated the process of the day before. As they made their way down the old backstage corridors toward the stage, Steve turned to Belladonna.

"If we decide not to give it to him, what're we going to do?"

"I'm not sure," said Belladonna. "We'll talk to Elsie. Maybe she has some ideas."

"Huh," said Steve. "Good-bye, universe."

"She's been dead for over a hundred years. She must have learned *something*."

Steve looked unconvinced, but nodded his agreement. Belladonna smiled and tried to look confident, though she couldn't help suspecting that Steve was right. On the other hand, there was still a chance that Dr. Ashe could turn out to be okay . . . and his diagrams had looked very technical. . . .

They reached the stage and stood in front of the door marked seventy-three. Belladonna reached for the handle and once again spoke the Words of Power, although this time she was more aware of what she was saying.

Steve shook his head. "That is so strange," he said.

He reached for the doorknob, but before his fingers could close on it, a tremendous howl echoed from the back of the theatre.

"Oh, no," he whispered.

Belladonna turned around and saw Mrs. Evans racing down the aisle toward the stage, her clip-on black ponytail flying behind her like a distress flag.

"Stop!" she panted as she reached the stage. "What are you doing?"

She started to scramble up onto the stage. Steve

looked at Belladonna and gripped the amulet firmly in his fist.

"Come on," he said, and stepped through the door.

"Noooo!" screamed his mother, running toward them with a speed that was impressive, considering her size.

Belladonna turned to follow Steve, but it was too late—Mrs. Evans's pudgy hand closed around her arm like a steel vise.

"What have you done?" she screamed. "You stupid girl!"

Belladonna struggled to free herself, twisting every way she could while trying to edge toward the door. Mrs. Evans raised a hand to strike her, but the backward swing of her arm caught the door, and even as Belladonna flinched, expecting the blow, the scenery flat toppled over and hit the floor of the stage with an almighty crash, splitting the flimsy door into two pieces.

Mrs. Evans gasped and stared at the fallen doorway while Belladonna stopped struggling as the realization suddenly hit her: Mrs. Evans knew.

Mrs. Evans seemed to realize that she had revealed something she hadn't intended. She turned her attention back to Belladonna and her eyes narrowed as she pondered the new situation, but the hesitation was all Belladonna needed; she wrested herself free and took off down the labyrinthine backstage corridors of the theatre.

She ran back, past the dressing rooms and the

wardrobe rooms, past all the offices and cubbyholes that populate the less glamorous environs of theatres everywhere. The heavy steps of Mrs. Evans were never far behind, but Belladonna knew that she had to get out. She raced down the last corridor toward the door, grasped the handle, and turned. It was locked! She looked back; Mrs. Evans was at the other end of the corridor, a lumbering silhouette, closing in.

Belladonna looked around frantically. Where was the window Steve used to get in? There was a door to her right; she pushed it open and found herself in a tiny office. The window was high on the wall, but there was an old wooden desk nearby. She pushed the desk under the window and started to climb.

The pale autumn sun hit her face as she pushed herself up and out. She swung one leg over and was straddling the window, when the office door burst open.

"Oh, no you don't!" said Mrs. Evans.

But it was too late. Belladonna dropped to the ground and took off like a greyhound. As she rounded the corner into the High Street, she could hear Mrs. Evans trying to get the stage door open, but she didn't hang around to find out if she was successful. She just ran, and didn't stop running until she was nearly home, when she finally slowed to a walk.

At the front gate, she stopped. Steve was trapped on the Other Side and she was fairly certain she'd never be able to use the door again. She really had to tell someone now.

She thought about Aunt Deirdre and the way she'd looked when she went out after the Hunt last night. Somehow, Belladonna felt this latest piece of news might tip her aunt right over the edge. No, she needed someone who wasn't fazed by anything, someone who took everything in her stride and for whom Mrs. Evans would be no more challenge than a naughty child.

She turned away from home and headed for her grandmother's house.

9

The Eidolon Council

BY THE TIME Belladonna reached Yarrow Street, it was late afternoon and a chill had descended on the town. The sky had turned overcast and the cold breeze of the morning had become an icy wind that pierced through to the bones. Belladonna pulled her jacket tight and zipped it up, but it didn't really help. She walked the last few yards to Grandma Johnson's house trying to think about what she would say. She knew she'd get in trouble for not telling her about the door, and even more trouble for actually going through to the Other Side, but none of that mattered now. Steve was trapped. There was no way through and people all over the world were in danger.

She walked up to the front door of number 3 and rang the bell.

The front of Grandma Johnson's house was the same as all the others in her row, but unlike the others, she had a sign in her front window: a large drawing of a hand with the lifelines marked out and the words "Fortunes Told" in bold blue print above it. Belladonna blew into her icy hands and rang the bell again. There was no answer. She looked at the windows and noticed that all the curtains were drawn. That was strange—it was nowhere near dark yet. She rang the bell a third time, and then knocked for good measure. This time the curtain in the front room twitched and she thought she saw someone's eye peeking out at her, though she was pretty sure it wasn't her grandmother's. She waited, shivering, on the step, but nobody came to the door. Now she was getting angry. She rang the bell again and leaned on it extra long. The door flew open.

"Go home, Belladonna," said her grandmother sternly. "I'm busy. I'll come by later."

She started to close the door, but Belladonna reached forward and held it open.

"No," she said. "This is important."

"I'm sure it is, dear, but—"

"I've been to the Other Side!" she blurted. "I found the door!"

Grandma Johnson stopped. She opened the door slowly and looked down at her granddaughter. "You what?"

"I . . . that is, *we* found the door. Number seventy-three. Painted red. And we went through. It's really cold, can I come in?"

Grandma Johnson stepped aside and allowed her

into the narrow hall. The door to the front room was closed, but she could hear muffled voices inside.

"I'm sorry," said Belladonna, lowering her voice. "Do you have a client?"

"No," said her grandmother, "just a few friends. Now what's this about the door?"

"It was in the old theatre. In a pile of scenery."

"But . . . the Words of Power . . ."

"I said them. I didn't know them but I said them. They just came out. And the door opened, so we went through."

"We?"

"Steve Evans and me. And that's the thing, really . . ." She hesitated — this was the difficult part — "he's stuck. We were going through again — "

"What? Why?" Grandma Johnson rolled her eyes. "Oh, never mind. You'd better come in and tell everyone at once."

She opened the door to the front room and ushered Belladonna in.

The front room was where Grandma Johnson usually met her clients. The walls were covered in a dark red flocked wallpaper, huge dark green plants lurked in the corners, and in the middle was a large round table covered with an old silk carpet. Usually there were only two chairs in the room, one for the client and one for Mrs. Johnson, but this afternoon it was full of chairs that had been brought from all over the house, and Belladonna found herself being stared at by eight sets of curious eyes.

She recognized a few of the people: Mr. Philips from the corner shop where she bought her Parma Violets, Mrs. Kostopoulos from the hairdresser's, and Mr. al Rashid from the petrol station at the end of the High Street, but the rest were all strangers. They all looked very serious, though, and most had dark circles under their eyes as if they hadn't been getting much sleep.

"This is my granddaughter, Belladonna Johnson," announced Grandma Johnson. "Some of you know her, I think. She has something she'd like to tell us."

Belladonna glanced at her grandmother, taken aback. Who were these people? She had thought that the whole ghost thing was peculiar to her family, but now there was a room full of people who apparently sat around discussing it.

Grandma Johnson gave her a gentle nudge and smiled encouragingly. "Don't be shy," she said.

Belladonna looked at the people again, took a deep breath, and told them everything right from the beginning, including about the Hunt and Aunt Deirdre's disappearance the night before. There was silence when she finished, then Mrs. Kostopoulos leaned forward.

"What makes you think Mrs. Evans knew about the door?" she asked.

"The way she looked when she knocked it over,"

said Belladonna. "And she knew that I knew. She gave me a really peculiar look."

Mrs. Kostopoulos settled back in her chair and a chubby lady near the window cleared her throat slightly.

"This girl—"

"Elsie," said Belladonna helpfully.

"Yes, Elsie. You say she is the only one who hasn't disappeared?"

"No, there's Dr. Ashe too. And Slackett, his assistant," said Belladonna. "Oh, and everything away from the High Street seemed dark."

"Dark?" asked the woman.

"Not dark, exactly, sort of run-down."

"Decaying, perhaps?" asked Mr. al Rashid.

"Yes, decaying. But . . . more than that . . . sort of rotting."

The people in the room looked at one another with serious faces.

"What does it mean?" asked Belladonna.

The people in the room ignored her and a few whispered to one another and frowned.

"We need to find another door," said Mr. Philips finally. "We need to send someone to the Other Side to get a look at the situation and report back."

That's typical, thought Belladonna, flashing a glare at Mr. Philips—she'd just told them that she'd been there and what she had seen but still they wanted an adult to go. She was really tired of grown-ups treating her as if she was somehow unreliable.

"We should consult the books," said a pale man near the back.

"Good idea," said Grandma Johnson. "I'll just see Belladonna off home and we'll get right to it."

She steered Belladonna firmly out of the room and closed the door.

"Who are those people?"

"The Eidolon Council," said her grandmother, zipping up Belladonna's jacket again.

"The what?"

"We supervise relations between the Living and the Dead. There's a similar organization on the Other Side, the Conclave of Shadow."

"Why do they all look so tired?"

"Because of the dreams."

"Aunt Deirdre mentioned dreams. What is it? Are they having bad dreams?"

"No, dear, it's not that," she hesitated. "Look, just go home, we'll take it from here."

Belladonna could feel her anger rising again. "Tell me!" she said grimly. "I found the door and went to the Other Side. I lost Mum and Dad for the second time and was nearly eaten by a huge Hound. I think I can take whatever it is about dreams without bursting into tears."

Grandma Johnson stepped back, as if she was seeing her granddaughter for the first time.

"Alright," she said finally. "You're right. The Council . . . well, everyone really . . . everyone looks tired because they're not having dreams. No dreams at all."

"Why?"

"Dreams are sent by the ghosts."

"Ghosts send dreams?" Belladonna rolled her eyes. "And prevent accidents? What else do they do? Control the weather?"

"You've been spending too much time with that Evans boy," said Grandma Johnson testily. "They send dreams to the living through an alabaster doorway in the House of Mists."

"Is this according to the Ancient Greeks as well?"

"Partly. But it was confirmed by the Conclave of Shadow. Belladonna, I really don't have time to—"

"What happens if we don't have dreams?" interrupted Belladonna, looking narrowly at her grandmother. "It's bad, isn't it?"

Grandma Johnson glanced back at the door to the front room and lowered her voice conspiratorially. "We die. All of us. There. I said it. If we don't find out where the ghosts have gone, accidents will be the least of our worries. Now, off you go home."

"No! Wait!" Belladonna wriggled free of her grandmother's determined push toward the front door. "You can't say that and just send me home! Why would we die if we don't have dreams?"

"Lower your voice! Dreams are the most important

part of sleep . . . everyone knows that. We have them during our deepest sleep, our most important sleep. People . . . all creatures need to sleep or they sicken and die."

"So if you don't die after accidentally falling off the cliff, you'll die from not dreaming about it?"

"I suppose."

Belladonna stopped and stared at her grandmother. There was something new in her tone of voice and in her eyes: a nervousness and uncertainty that she had never seen before.

"You're not sure, are you?"

"It's in the books," said Grandma Johnson hastily. "The books explain it all."

"What books? The books they were talking about?"

"Dr. Ashe's books of magic. Yes, we know all about him. A thoroughly unpleasant man when he was alive, and by the sounds of it, no better since he's been dead. The notebooks were found in his apothecary shop after he died. There are four of them and we consult them from time to time. Now, come on, off you go!"

She opened the front door and began gently pushing Belladonna toward it.

"But what about the Hunt and Aunt Deirdre?"

"Aunt Deirdre's a grown-up. If she wants to act like a fool, that's her lookout, but you stay away from them. Just cover your ears and let them ride by."

Belladonna reckoned it would take more than covering your ears to ignore the Hunt, but she was about to do as she was told and leave when suddenly she froze.

"Mrs. Kostopoulos!"

"What?" Now her grandmother was really confused.

"Mrs. Kostopoulos. She's Greek. Can I ask her a question?"

Grandma Johnson clicked her tongue irritably, but stepped aside. Belladonna burst through the door into the séance room. She had left out the part about asking the Sibyl about Dr. Ashe when she'd told them what had happened, but there was just a chance . . .

"Mrs. Kostopoulos," she blurted, "do you know any Ancient Greek?"

"A little," said Mrs. Kostopoulos, taken aback.

"Do you know what the word *phatês* means?"

"*Phatês?* Um . . . I don't . . ."

Belladonna's heart sank, but the portly hairdresser suddenly smiled.

"Yes!" she said. "Yes! It means 'liar.'"

"Liar?" whispered Belladonna.

"Why do you want to know that?" asked her grandmother.

"Because that's what the Sibyl said when we asked her about Dr. Ashe: *phatês.* Liar."

Grandma Johnson looked grim. "And the Evans boy is trapped over there with the amulet?"

Belladonna nodded. She had a sick feeling in her stomach.

"Right," her grandmother's usual no-nonsense manner had returned and she wheeled Belladonna around and out into the hall again. "We need to get to work. We have to find another way to the Other Side before Dr. Ashe gets the amulet."

"But you don't know what it's for!" said Belladonna.

"That doesn't matter. If *he* wants it, well, it can't be good, can it?"

"But—"

"You've done very well, Belladonna. Now go home and ask Aunt Deirdre to make you some hot soup. She's not up to much in a kitchen, but even she should be able to open a can. We'll talk tomorrow."

And with that, she gave Belladonna one last push out onto the front step.

"It's getting dark," she said matter-of-factly. "Go straight home. Tomorrow's a school day."

The door clicked shut. Belladonna stood on the step for a moment, then turned and began to walk slowly home.

The wind was still cold, but she wasn't feeling it any more. Her mind was racing with the few snippets of information she'd managed to glean from the Council. She tried to remember if she'd dreamed last night. She certainly didn't look like them, with dark circles under her eyes, did she? She stopped in front of a shop window and examined her reflection. She did look a little tired, but was it because she hadn't been dreaming or because she hadn't had much sleep last night?

She dawdled on. Dr. Ashe's notebooks. Something bothered her about that, but she couldn't think what.

The house was dark when she let herself in. She turned on all the lights, turned the central heating up, and leaned against the kitchen radiator until she felt warm, then she made herself some tea and went and sat down in front of the television. It was six o'clock and the news was on. Once again, it was a catalog of freak accidents and motorway pileups. She glanced at the clock and settled down to wait. At seven o'clock she went and stood at the window, peering down the road for any sign of Aunt Deirdre's car. By eight she decided she had better call her grandmother, but just as she picked up the phone, Deirdre's car roared up to the curb outside.

"Where have you been?" she demanded as her aunt walked in the door.

"Not now, Belladonna," said Aunt Deirdre. "I'm shattered. What time is it?"

"After eight."

"Right." She took off her coat and hung it on the hall pegs. "Did you get your own tea? There's a good girl. I've got work to do."

Belladonna followed her into the kitchen as she powered up her laptop. "But—"

Deirdre drew in her breath sharply and fired a

warning glare at her niece. It was no use. Belladonna drifted back into the sitting room and watched a film about gangsters and nightclub singers that she was fairly sure neither her parents nor her aunt would want her to watch. At ten o'clock, she turned off the television, said good night to her aunt, and went upstairs to bed.

Sleep was out of the question, of course. She just lay there, staring at a small damp patch in the ceiling over her bed and thinking. She wondered if Steve was alright and hoped he'd managed to find Elsie again. Or perhaps Elsie had vanished now too.

The whole thing made her feel so helpless.

And then it happened again. The distant baying of hounds, the thundering of hooves, and the clanking of iron bridles as the Hunt bore down on the small house on Lychgate Lane. Belladonna sat up in bed and saw their shadows through the closed curtains, raging past in a maelstrom of horses, boots, and dogs. The noise grew almost unbearable, the howls and clatter melding together until it almost seemed like a single agonized cry, and then, just as suddenly as they had appeared, they were gone and all was silence again. Belladonna sat, listening, hardly daring to breathe. Then she heard the click of the front door closing and the roar of the car as Aunt Deirdre set off after them once more.

Belladonna ran to the window and watched as the small car disappeared around the corner. What would she do if she caught them? She tried to picture Aunt

Deirdre stopping the Hunt, holding up one of her long white hands and demanding that they cease making such an unconscionable noise and settle down and talk like civilized human beings. She smiled to herself. If anyone could do that, it was probably her aunt.

She closed the curtains again and got back into bed, but no sooner had her head hit the pillow than she sat bolt upright again.

"There's another notebook," she whispered to herself. "There were five on the shelf!"

She closed her eyes again and pictured Dr. Ashe's laboratory. There was the big book he had shown her first, then the second one—the one with the picture of the dragon—he'd taken that one from a shelf. There were other printed books on the shelf, and next to them were the notebooks. Five notebooks. They had to be the books her grandmother was talking about! She jumped out of bed, ran downstairs to the phone, and dialed her grandmother's number.

"Hello, you have reached the home of Jessamine Johnson. I can't come to the phone right now, so please leave a message and I'll return your call as soon as I can."

Belladonna listened to the beep, hesitated, then hung up. She thought about it for a moment—she knew her grandmother was there. She picked the phone up and dialed again. She got the machine. She hung up and dialed once more.

"What?!" said Grandma Johnson, clearly furious.

"It's me," said Belladonna nervously.

"Belladonna? Why on earth aren't you in bed?"

"The Hunt came again and Deirdre's gone, but that's not why I'm calling. I was thinking about Dr. Ashe's books." The words tumbled out, but Grandma Johnson wasn't listening.

"Belladonna, stop. Stop. You've done very well up to now. Except for getting your little friend trapped in the Land of the Dead, of course. But it's time to leave things to the grown-ups."

"Yes, but—"

"No. Go to bed." Her voice was kind, but there was no mistaking its firmness. "It's school tomorrow."

"Don't you want to hear—"

"No, I don't. What time is it?" There was a pause while she must have glanced at her watch. "Oh, good heavens! It's after midnight! Go to bed. I'll talk to you tomorrow. Sleep tight."

And she hung up.

Belladonna stood in the hall, holding the silent telephone to her ear for a moment before she slowly returned it to its cradle. She walked slowly up the stairs and into her bedroom and stared at her bed for a few minutes, then she turned on her heel and started to get dressed.

10

Casting a Circle

FIFTEEN MINUTES LATER, Belladonna slipped out of the house, her pink backpack slung over one shoulder and sagging slightly from the added weight of two ham sandwiches, two packets of crisps, and two cans of Tizer (just in case she got through and needed to eat). She hesitated for a moment at the gate, then walked away down the dark streets toward the town center.

It was cold and silent in the town, with the kind of stillness that can only be found in the hours after midnight, when everyone is asleep and the traffic lights blink through their changes on empty streets. Occasionally a car or two would speed down the road, and once she glimpsed a police car cruising its beat. After that, she kept to the shadows, walking swiftly toward Umbra Avenue.

She passed the arcade where they'd found the

dragon game, closed up tight with an enormous padlock on the door, and walked up to the empty launderette. She looked up and down the street, then crept up to the door and tried the handle. As she expected, it was locked. She peered inside to make absolutely sure there was no one there and then walked around to the alley at the back. As she walked, she heard the distant squeal and crunch of two cars crashing. Another accident. She hesitated for a moment, listening, but all was quiet again. She continued to the back; that door was locked too, but there was a window right next to it that looked like it might not be quite so resistant. It was an old sash window like the ones at school, so she decided to try Steve's trick of slowly jiggling the latch free.

She got a firm grip on the top of the lower pane and gave it a sharp shove up and then down. There was a horrifyingly loud creak with the first movement and she froze, expecting the police car to come screaming around the corner and into the alley with sirens blazing, but there was nothing. She tried it again—there was still a noise, but it was much quieter, and by the fifth or sixth shove it had almost ceased making any sound at all. Every so often, she would stand on her toes and check on her progress with the latch. She could just make it out through a clean smear on the dirty window, and it did seem to be moving, but soooo slowly.

The time ticked by, and still she worked the window up and down. Her arms ached and she had to keep stopping and shaking them out to get the blood moving again. Finally, after what felt like hours, she gave a final shove and the window slid open. She looked carefully up and down the alley, pulled an old plastic crate over from a nearby pile of rubbish, and climbed inside, closing the window behind her.

Inside, the launderette was much as she expected. She was in a small back office with crushed cardboard boxes stacked on one side and discarded bits of paper scattered about as if someone had simply emptied the contents of a now-vanished desk onto the floor. The only remaining furnishings were an ancient gray metal file cabinet that crouched in the shadows and a broken wooden chair that someone had leaned against the far wall. A streetlight outside filled the room with a strange blue-green light, casting long eerie shadows across the room and into the main part of the launderette beyond. Dust was everywhere and old washing powder crunched underfoot. She closed her eyes and tried to picture it the way it was in the Land of the Dead. The fireplace was where the chair was, and Dr. Ashe's workbench . . .

She opened her eyes. It was where the cardboard boxes were! She began moving them across the room, clearing the space. She closed her eyes again and visualized the bench, with its experiments and papers . . . and his stool was . . . right here! She stood in the spot and looked around.

In the Land of the Dead he had kept his notebooks

on a shelf near the desk, but she suspected that when he was alive he had been far more cautious. Still, she knew that he would have kept even his most secret books close at hand and from what he'd said, the only books he could have in the Land of the Dead were the ones that were here in his shop when he died. The Eidolon Council had four of them, so the other one just had to be here. She looked around and sighed: It had been so many years since the alchemist had been here, nothing was the same.

She stood for a moment, discouraged and wishing she had gone back to bed like her grandmother told her to. Then she thought about Steve trapped on the Other Side with Dr. Ashe and who knew what else, and her parents, who really might be gone for good this time. She closed her eyes once more, pictured the workshop, and stretched her arms out as wide as she could. Her left arm almost touched the wall. She opened her eyes and peered at the rotting plaster to her left. She might not be able to reach it, but she knew that Dr. Ashe's long arms and languorous hands would have easily accessed anything there.

She stepped over and looked at the wall more closely: The plaster was riddled with hairline cracks and every so often there was a small black gash where a piece had fallen away. She began to work at one of these, pulling the surrounding plaster down. It crumbled easily, but only revealed old wallpaper, beneath which was more old wallpaper. This wasn't working.

She looked back again to where Ashe had sat and realized that she hadn't factored in the height of the stool or his lanky stature. If he reached out from where he had actually been, his hand would brush the wall nearly a foot higher than where she'd been working.

She dragged the broken chair over and stood on it, swaying slightly as she tried to maintain her balance on its three remaining legs. None of the plaster was broken here, but she hit at it a few times with her fist, pausing between each strike to make sure no one was coming. Eventually a small piece of plaster fell to the floor.

She worked her fingers into the hole and began pulling the rotting stucco away. Once again there were layers of aging wallpaper, but her fingers began to detect something else. Something lumpy. She continued working until the last yellowed layer of wallpaper came away from the wall and she could make out what was there—a small door! She excitedly removed the rest of the crumbling plaster and paper, ignoring the sound it made as it cascaded to the floor. By the time she was through, she was covered in white dust and the tips of her fingers were red and raw from working her nails under the brittle old wallpaper, but she had exposed what seemed to be a small wooden cupboard. The handle was long gone, but the iron hinges were still there, black and shining like new.

Belladonna flinched slightly as she worked her sore fingers under the door and slowly pulled it open. The feeble glow of the streetlight outside didn't reach inside the cupboard: It was just a black, rectangular hole cut into the white plaster wall, like a missing tooth in a mouthful of gleaming ivories. Belladonna took a deep breath. She was reasonably sure that there would be spiders in there, or at the very least things with wings and articulated segments. She steadied herself with one hand against the wall and extended the other toward the hole.

The first thing she felt was a shelf bisecting the cupboard. There was nothing on the top of it except some small things that broke up at her touch. She shuddered slightly and wiped her hand on the front of her jacket before reaching into the lower shelf.

Her hand immediately touched something cold and hard—a box! She steadied herself on the broken chair and removed her left hand from the wall, then she carefully removed the box, jumped down, and placed her prize on the floor near the window where the light was best.

It was black and glistening, though the hinges were rusted and all but one of the rivets holding the ornate clasp in place were gone. The last one gave way easily and Belladonna slowly lifted the lid, revealing two dark leather pouches. She removed the largest and opened it. Inside was a silver bell, about twelve centimeters high, covered with flowing ornate decoration. It seemed to shine with its own light, but was mercifully silent. She turned it upside down and saw that it didn't have a clapper.

"What's the point of a bell that doesn't ring?" she whispered to herself.

She placed the bell on the floor and moved on to the second pouch. She reached inside and felt the soft touch of leather—it was a book! She pulled it out slowly and, holding her breath, opened it at a random page, then another and another. The whole thing was full of notes and drawings in the spidery hand she recognized from the apothecary shop on the Other Side. It was the missing fifth book of Dr. Ashe.

She was about to settle down for a read when there was the unmistakable sound of a car driving slowly down the alley. She froze until the crunch of tires faded away, then shoved the book and the bell into her backpack, opened the window, and scrambled out into the alley. She made her way quickly to the churchyard and made herself comfortable on her favorite table tomb. The security lights that shone from the church at night (much to the irritation of the people who lived nearby) provided just enough illumination as she opened the book and began to leaf through.

Much of it was in Latin, with a few notes in Greek, but there was enough written in English for her to be able to understand that this was actually a book of spells. As the book progressed, the initially neat handwriting became more and more difficult to read. He was obviously becoming more excited about what he was writing, as if he had discovered something he had spent half a lifetime searching for. Or perhaps someone else was telling him what to write—the hurried penmanship and frequent abbreviations looked like the kind of thing she did when Mr. Watson dictated notes in History. But if he was just taking dictation, who was telling him what to write?

Belladonna began to feel a chill in the pit of her stomach that had nothing to do with the freezing weather. She had thought Dr. Ashe was daunting, but there was something manageable about him, with his apothecary shop, overly complex "experiments," and bad temper. Even finding out that he was lying about the amulet was good in a way—at least she was sure he couldn't be trusted. But now it looked like someone else might actually be in charge. It was just like the old man in the gangster movie she shouldn't have been watching this evening, and there was something much more frightening about that.

She continued leafing through the pages but it was clear to her now that she really ought to take it to her grandmother and the Eidolon Council. They had the other books, after all, and Mrs. Kostopoulos spoke Ancient Greek, so they'd be able to read all the bits she couldn't make out. She quickly riffled through the remaining pages and was just closing it when she saw something she recognized. There, on a page near the end of the book, was a drawing of a bell—the same bell she had found in the box. She leaned over and examined the text more closely. It was in English, and appeared to be instructions for summoning the Dead.

Belladonna closed the book for a moment and sat back. Should she try it? Maybe she could get Steve back. Okay, so he wasn't actually *dead* (at least she hoped not), but he was in the Land of the Dead, which might amount to the same thing so far as spells were concerned, and if she could get him back, then she wouldn't need to find another door, then she could take the book to the Council and they could figure out how to get the ghosts back. She wanted to see her parents again. She wanted the world—both worlds, or all nine, if there really were nine—to return to normal. She wanted to come home from school and smell the dinner cooking and hear her Mum and Dad bickering. But right now she was wracked with guilt. It was her fault that Steve was trapped on the Other Side and she somehow felt that she ought to at least try to set that one thing right herself. And even if this spell didn't get him back, maybe she could summon Elsie. She'd at least know if he was okay. Belladonna looked at the leather cover of the book. On the other hand, it was also possible that she might get Dr. Ashe. It was his book, after all. She opened it again and reviewed the spell more closely. Apparently, you had to draw a magic circle and so long as you stayed within the circle you would be safe. She tucked her hair behind her ears. It was worth a try.

She jumped off the tomb and read the first instruction. You had to find a graveyard (check!) and then locate the exact center. She walked to one corner of the old cemetery and crossed to the other, dragging her feet so that they left a clear line in the wet grass. Then she went to the third corner and walked to the fourth—where the two lines crossed was the center of the graveyard. She opened the book again. Now she needed a stick made of yew. Belladonna remembered being told that yews were always grown in graveyards. She looked at the various trees around her; there was a willow, a couple of scraggly pines, and a large, gnarled tree with dark green foliage that she recognized from the tour of Arkbath Hall. She ran over and struggled to remove a spindly cane that was shooting up from one of the roots. The tree was reluctant to let go, but eventually she tore it free and returned, panting, to the center of the graveyard.

Following the instructions in the book, she drew a wide circle around herself and placed the bell in the center. She looked at the book again and turned the page. There was a brief note instructing the alchemist to strike the bell three times with the stick of yew and repeat the sacred text.

Belladonna scanned the page, looked at the next page, then flicked back to see if she'd missed anything on the first page.

"What sacred text?" she said to no one in particular. "Where's the stupid sacred text?"

She stood there for a few moments, feeling increasingly like a total banana and hoping that no one would wander by and see the strange girl from school standing in the middle of the graveyard at night with a bell and a stick. Then she thought about what her mother would say (once she had stopped laughing) and shrugged her shoulders.

"Oh, well," she said, "in for a penny, in for a pound."

She leaned forward and hit the bell with the stick.

Instead of the dull thunk she had expected to hear, the bell tolled with a mighty sound that seemed to reverberate from deep within the earth itself. She held her breath for a moment, then hit it twice more. Each time, the bell rang with a deep sepulchral roar that echoed around the graveyard until it seemed that the air itself was vibrating. Belladonna stepped backward and put her hands over her ears. It didn't help: The ringing was in her bones and inside her head; it made all coherent thought impossible and seemed to fill her brain with rusty nails. Slowly the ringing died down and she lowered her hands and sighed with relief. All was silence once more.

She looked around, but everything seemed the same: The graveyard was just as it had been, the circle was unchanged, and the bell was sitting in the wet grass right where she'd put it. She had just decided that maybe she'd better try hitting it again, when the bell began to emit a new sound—a sibilant rasp like rain hitting a fire. As she watched, it started to glow with a greenish light and the elaborate decorations around its rim began to shift and move.

Belladonna stepped closer as the ancient engravings slid around the rim of the bell, winding sinuously together, splitting off and then recombining. She stared, almost hypnotized by the serpentine movement, but even as she marveled at the beauty of the undulating silver, she realized that it wasn't just random—it was forming words.

She stood close to the bell, and whispered the words as they appeared. The language was strange and the script unfamiliar, but she knew what it meant. She knew she was summoning something old. Older than Ashe, older than the dragons in the amulet, and far, far older than anything her grandmother knew existed. Yet it had a familiar ring, as if she knew the language, knew the words, and knew who it was she was calling and had just forgotten. Like she sometimes forgot the name of the postman, or what that stuff is that you put in a cake along with the baking soda to make it rise. But how could she have ever known this?

"Lamashtu of the seven names, daughter of heaven, keeper of the seal and the dark hounds, send to me one from your own realm to answer my call and obey my command."

No sooner were the words out of her mouth than a wind began to whip around the tops of the trees. The weather vane on the top of the church spire began to spin, twirling faster and faster as the speed of the wind picked up. Dark clouds and fog descended with the wind, picking up leaves, branches, and paper as it whirled. Inside the circle, however, all was calm and Belladonna watched with fascination as a tornado seemed to form around her as if she were at the very eye of its fury. Now, this was a spell! It was all very well saying Words of Power in front of a plywood door, but winds and fog and glowing bells . . .

But as the wind continued to scream around the circle, she began to have second thoughts. She looked at the bell and chewed on her lower lip. Lamashtu. The name seemed familiar but she didn't really know who or what Lamashtu was. Though apparently she had dark hounds, which, based on her recent experience, probably wasn't a good thing. "Send to me one from your own realm." That wasn't good—she probably should have been more specific.

And then, as quickly as it started, the wind stopped. Belladonna gasped and took a step back—Slackett was standing about four feet away from the edge of the circle.

He had his back to her and turned around slowly. He was holding a small jug in one hand, as if he'd been caught in the middle of doing something. When his eyes met Belladonna's, he smiled slowly.

"The living girl," he said. "You are playing a dangerous game."

Belladonna tried to conceal her disappointment; Slackett was definitely at the bottom of her list of potentially helpful people. She wasn't sure if it was even worth mentioning the problem.

"Something has happened," said Slackett, his eyes narrowing in his angular face. "What have you done?"

"Nothing," said Belladonna. "That is . . . Steve is . . . I think he's stuck."

"Who is . . . ? Ah, the boy who is frightened of creepy-crawlies. The Paladin."

"You keep saying that," said Belladonna. "What do you mean?"

"You are the Spellbinder," said Slackett. "Stands to reason he's the Paladin."

Belladonna stared at him for a moment. The Spellbinder—Lady Mary had mentioned the Spellbinder; she had seemed to expect the Spellbinder to help somehow and to know what to do. It couldn't be her—Slackett was either confused or deliberately winding her up.

"No, I'm not," she said. "Really, I'm not. Look, he went through the door again and I was stopped and now the door is broken."

Slackett grinned. "You shouldn't be here," he said. "The game is too dangerous. Ashe is—"

Before he could tell her what Ashe was, his face suddenly changed. He looked down.

"No!" His voice was suddenly hoarse and its smug simper had given way to the unmistakable strain of fear. Belladonna slowly became aware that he was sinking into the earth. She instinctively ran forward.

"No!" he yelled, his voice suddenly strong. "Don't leave the circle! It's your only hope."

"But—"

Shafts of light began to spring up beneath him, as if he had broken through the ceiling of a room below. As he continued to sink, he scrabbled in his pockets. "Here," he said, "take this. Give it to the Paladin. He will know what to do with it."

He threw something small toward her. It seemed dark and heavy when it landed at her feet, but when she picked it up, it was nothing but a rather beaten-up six-inch plastic ruler.

"I don't understand!" she yelled.

"He will," shouted Slackett as the ground reached his shoulders. "He will! Keep it safe! Don't let my master see it! Don't let—"

But it was too late. He had disappeared beneath the soil and where he had stood, there was nothing but a shaft of greenish light. Belladonna watched as the light stretched up toward the tops of the trees, then began to fall again, like the water from a fountain. An inexplicable sensation of gloom gripped her stomach and she stepped back toward the center of the circle. The light continued to fall, then stopped at about six feet and formed itself into a familiar shape.

Dr. Ashe looked up slowly. Belladonna hadn't remembered him looking quite so gaunt and unfriendly;

she couldn't believe that this was really the same person she had waved to on her way home from school.

"You certainly are a clever girl," he said, smiling. "If a very foolish one."

Belladonna couldn't speak. Her mouth felt dry and her breath was coming in gasps. She held up the book by way of explanation.

"Ah, my book!" Ashe stepped forward. "Of course, the spell to call the Dead. How very enterprising. Now, did you find the amulet?"

Belladonna stared at him and shook her head slowly. A part of her had been clinging to the hope that Dr. Ashe, while irritable and somewhat pompous, would still turn out to be alright, in spite of what the Sibyl had said, and that he really was looking for a solution to the vanishing ghosts. But seeing him here now in the graveyard, with his steely glare and rictus smile, she suddenly knew that the oracle had been right and that the worst thing she could do was to let him know that Steve had the amulet and was lost in the Land of the Dead.

"I summoned you. I—I want to know . . ." she began nervously.

"You did not summon me," said Ashe, with the unmistakable dripping sarcasm of the worst kind of Math teacher. "You issued a general call to the Dead. You got Slackett. He always was easily led. I merely followed his trail."

"I want to know—" repeated Belladonna, but Ashe was having none of it.

"*You* want to know?" boomed Ashe. "I don't give a fig what you want! What are your desires to me? You have my property. Return it at once."

"No," Belladonna shook her head firmly. "It isn't yours. It belonged to the dragon."

Dr. Ashe looked taken aback for a moment, then smiled his thin, humorless smile again. "And I suppose your shoes still belong to the cow who gave his hide to make them?"

"Well, no, but . . . we saw the Sibyl. I asked her about you. She said one word: *phatês*. Liar."

"Hmph," said Dr. Ashe. "I never liked that woman."

Belladonna felt more confident and took a step closer to the edge of the circle.

"You don't want to find out what happened to the ghosts," she said. "You don't need to. I think you made them vanish in the first place."

Dr. Ashe looked at her as if he was considering a response, but after a few moments he clearly decided not to bother: The smile fell from his face and his voice became heavy with menace. "Idiot child," he hissed, "give me the amulet."

"No."

He nodded slightly, then lowered his head, stepped closer to the circle, and began muttering words which she couldn't quite hear. As his lips moved, the whispered words seemed to seep into her head and grow louder, blocking everything else out of her mind. Belladonna knew it was some kind of counterspell to break the circle, and shook her head sharply to try to clear her brain. She stumbled back to the center of the circle and began frantically turning the pages of the book, looking for something, anything, that would make him go away, but Ashe just kept coming, closer and closer to the circle, and she knew, in spite of everything the book had said, that he would be able to cross inside and that she was anything but safe. Yet even as she knew it and even as she knew that her only hope was to find something in the book, the words and figures on the pages began to dance and fade before her eyes. The murmured words were becoming more than one voice, more than ten; it felt like a thousand tongues were crying urgently in her brain, but none was speaking loud enough to hear, each was just an endless supplication without reason or hope.

She shook her head again and tears started stinging in her eyes as she realized that the battle she was fighting was hopeless and the light of life was closing into a narrow tunnel. She looked down, and with what she knew would be her last living glimpse, saw the wet green grass glistening in the moonlight, and the silver bell with its still undulating decoration.

A particle of hope glimmered in her mind, and she summoned the last speck of strength she still possessed, took a deep breath, gritted her teeth, and kicked the bell out of the circle. It was a titanic effort, and it took all she had. She saw the bell fly across the graveyard and dimly heard it clank as it hit something not far from the yew tree.

And then all was black.

The first thing that woke up was her sense of touch, then her sense of smell: the feel of the wet grass on her back, the smell of rain and the faint aroma of burning wood.

Belladonna opened her eyes. It was still night. The moon was still high in the sky and the freezing breeze reeled around the church spire and whipped down into the graveyard. She sat up. The circle was still there, but Ashe was gone and where he had been was a crawling pile of bronze-colored beetles, suppurating in the moonlight.

She jumped to her feet, shuddering and brushing herself down, just in case one of them might have skittered nearby. The book was still there. She picked it up and put it into her backpack, then tried to remember where she'd kicked the bell. It took a while, but eventually she found it, lying in a puddle next to the grave of someone called Albert Beeston, who had died in 1836, along with most of his family. Belladonna guessed that there must have been some sort of epidemic and thought that she should probably ask Mr. Watson about it. If she ever saw him again.

She put the bell into her backpack and looked

around. Her head was splitting and for the first time she really felt afraid. What was she thinking? Why did she presume to believe that she knew more than her aunt or her grandmother or the . . . thingy Council? She'd summoned the Dead and found out nothing. Steve was still trapped, accidents were still multiplying like bacteria, and her parents were still gone.

She looked at the houses that pushed up against the walls of the old churchyard. The windows were all dark. Everyone was asleep. Was it really possible that not one of them was dreaming?

And then the sound came again.

The howling. The crash and clatter of hooves.

Oh, great, she thought, *the perfect end to a simply super evening.*

She turned and looked up, over the trees at the far end of the graveyard and up into the sky. The night was pockmarked with storm clouds that suddenly seemed to move, not with the steady pace of the wind, but with deliberate speed. As she watched, they converged and appeared to take on a form, the tops becoming heavy and the lower parts extending downward like legs, hooves, and paws. Belladonna staggered back against Mr. Beeston's grave as the Wild Hunt descended from the skies.

As it came closer, the cloud cover dissipated and the images of horses, men, and hounds became more clear. The colossal hounds she was familiar with by now, but the horses were not the flimsy Thoroughbreds she was used to seeing on television; they were massive and muscular, their necks like the knotted cable that hauled concrete slabs on building sites, and their legs like the bases of dockyard cranes. The men who rode them, by contrast, seemed average in size, if not in manner. Each, in his own way, was superficially ordinary, yet had abandoned the spark within himself that made him feel, love, long. They were no longer human in essence, only in form, and had the wild look of creatures who hunt without any hope of capture, and strive without any expectation of satisfaction. Their Leader set the standard and beat his horse to a foaming frenzy while charging at the front of the stampede. His glare was fire and his skin stone; his cape flew out behind him like black wings as his whip hand tore at his horse's flank.

Belladonna watched, unable to move as the Hunt galloped closer, expecting any moment to be ground underfoot. But when they reached the graveyard, the Leader of the Hunt held up a hand and brought them all to an improbably rapid halt.

Now that he was close, she could see his pale face, the skin stretched tightly over the bone. His eyes were yellow, with black centers, and were examining her closely. He removed his hat with a flourish and dark hair fell into his eyes, giving him an almost friendly appearance. Almost.

"Greetings, milady," he said. "Well met, indeed."

Belladonna pushed her hair out of her eyes and

looked at him, and then at his men, their eyes sparkling hungrily in the night.

"Um . . . hello," she said.

"You know," he leaned forward in his saddle with a conspiratorial air. "You don't really belong here, with *these* people."

He waved his hand in the direction of the darkened houses with disdain.

"We have a spare horse. A lively creature, eager to run."

"I don't really . . . I haven't had any lessons. . . ."

"No lessons!" He leaned back and looked at his men, who joined in the expected guffaw. "You don't need lessons, Belladonna, you'll take to it like a duck to water."

He held out a gauntleted hand. "Come, join the Hunt."

Belladonna stood up. There was something tempting about the idea.

"What are you hunting?" she asked.

No sooner were the words out of her mouth than it became clear it was the worst thing she could have said. The Leader frowned his disapproval and his men began an angry muttering that made her flatten her body against Mr. Beeston's stone again.

The Leader held up his hand and, with an effort, smiled again.

"We're hunting for the lost," he said, "for those for

whom this paltry thing called life is no life at all. Come. Come."

He held out his hand again. Belladonna looked at him, and his yellow eyes called her forward even though every ounce of common sense told her to run in the opposite direction. She stepped away from the relative comfort of Mr. Beeston's grave and extended a hand. The Leader smiled and showed white teeth that were a little too sharp.

"I knew you would," he murmured.

He removed the gauntlet from his right hand and reached down with long white, waxy fingers.

Belladonna, her eyes glazed, reached up.

"No!"

A small hand grabbed hers and, with surprising strength, pulled her away.

"Get out, you half-dead creatures! Go!"

The spell was broken and Belladonna looked down in surprise. Aya's purple eyes flashed in anger at the riders of the Wild Hunt and, in spite of her size, they all shrank back, the hounds whimpering as they sought cover among the legs of the horses, and the black steeds whinnying in fear of the tiny creature.

"Hah!" said the Leader. "Another time, then. Give your aunt my regards!"

And he wheeled his horse and took off toward the east, climbing into the sky pursued by his baying pack of hounds and his cursed men.

Belladonna stared at Aya.

"It's been a long night, hasn't it?" said the charnel sprite.

"I have to get to the Other Side," whispered Belladonna. "I mean . . . sorry . . . thank you."

Aya smiled.

"Steve is trapped," said Belladonna urgently. "I have to get to the Other Side."

"What about the door?" asked Aya.

"It's gone . . . broken. Please. He doesn't know about Ashe. Well . . . he suspects, but that's not the same, is it?"

"There are other doors," said the charnel sprite, "other doors in other places. Lots of doors."

"But I don't know where they are, and anyway, my Dad said that they are all closing. I don't have time to find another one. I need to get there, I need to warn Steve now. He can't give Ashe the amulet!"

Aya looked at her for a moment, then took her hand and led Belladonna across the churchyard to the yew tree and down a staircase near its roots that Belladonna was pretty sure had never been there before.

"Come with me," she said. "There's another way."

Belladonna hesitated, but Aya smiled and squeezed her hand.

"It's alright. Come on."

The stairs were narrow and made of wood, polished to a shine by hundreds of years of running, rough-clad feet. They descended steeply beneath the tree at first, then settled into a steady, gentle incline, winding beneath the earth. After a while the wood steps gave way to stone and then to packed dirt as Belladonna and Aya walked into the depths of the charnel world. The roots of the tree twisted around and down on either side of them, writhing through the packed earth and pushing the lumpen profiles of rocks and stones into the narrow corridor. Aya didn't notice them, but Belladonna's height meant she was constantly ducking and dodging to avoid being beaned by a chunk of rock.

After a while, she realized that many of them weren't just rocks, but the jagged remains of ancient tombstones. Letters and fragments of phrases glistened on the damp stone, as epitaphs, carefully crafted by grieving families, themselves long dead, slowly crumbled to dust.

Belladonna had just settled into a contemplation on the transitoriness of life, when more solid reminders of the fate awaiting us all began to emerge from the walls and between the roots of the tree. Bones jutted from the clay: femurs, ribs, and convoluted spines. As she ducked to avoid a larger-than-usual chunk of tomb, she noticed the bones of a single finger beckoning her into the earth.

"Are these . . . um . . ." she began.

"Dead people," said Aya matter-of-factly, "and a few ex-cats and dogs. People bury all kinds in graveyards."

Belladonna nodded and pressed her lips together. Aya looked at her.

"They're not *people*," she insisted.

"I know, but . . ."

"They're just . . . I don't know. Bones."

The tunnel seemed to contract as they descended, and though Aya still stepped bouncily, Belladonna became less sure. She wondered whether following a vaguely purple charnel sprite down a tunnel deep into the earth was any wiser than accepting the invitation of the Hunt. She glanced back the way they had come, but couldn't see very far before path, root, bones, and stone disappeared into the all-enveloping blackness. Aya was humming softly.

Belladonna stopped.

"You know," she said, "I really think I should be getting back."

"We're here!" announced Aya, smiling.

She took Belladonna's hand and led her gently around a sharp right turn and under a piece of root so low that even the charnel sprite had to duck.

Once around the corner, Belladonna found herself near the top of a vast cavern lit by the phosphorescent glow of thousands of bowls of cave-dwelling fish suspended from the roof by cobweb-covered chains. A narrow staircase, cut into the rock, led to the cavern floor. The stair didn't have a rail on the outside but Aya trotted down as if it were no more dangerous than the front steps at home. Belladonna followed much more carefully, making sure to stay as close to the wall as she could.

As they got closer to the floor, she noticed hundreds of small alcoves in the stone walls. Most were dark, but a few seemed to be dimly lit from within.

"Is this where you live?" she asked.

"Here?" said Aya, surprised. "No. This is just . . . what's the word you use up there? It's where we work, where we . . . it's the office!"

She grinned triumphantly at finding the word.

Belladonna smiled thinly. It wasn't like any office she'd ever seen, though there were a few desks on the far side where enormous piles of paper were stacked. The rest of the cavern was taken up with long tables, potted plants, jugs, glasses, and plates of sandwiches.

Once she reached the floor level, Belladonna could see the alcoves more clearly. Each alcove had two or three beds or couches inside, on which were what appeared to be sleeping people. She glanced at Aya.

"Are they—?"

"They're transitionals," explained Aya, as if that made it all perfectly clear.

"Transitionals?"

"They're not dead. I mean they are dead. Just not *dead* dead. You see?"

Belladonna stared at her, mystified. "Not *dead* dead," she repeated.

"They died up there, then they were buried. Then they emerge. Then they need to rest . . . and then they go."

"To the Other Side?"

Aya nodded and led the way to a recess in the cave wall. It was surrounded with iridescent draperies and bits of beads and crushed-up foil and sweet wrappers.

"This is the way they go," she said, "only we can't send any now, obviously."

Belladonna peered into the black opening. "Because the ghosts have vanished."

"Yes. We can't be sure . . ."

"Is it safe?"

"Charnel sprites are forbidden access to the Land of the Dead," shrugged Aya. "But all the dead people go this way and I'm sure someone would have told us if no one was getting through."

She pulled aside one of the draperies and peered into the darkness, then quickly dropped it again.

"I shouldn't let you do this," she said. "It's forbidden. It's always forbidden for the Living. But now . . . we've all been told not to let anyone through until we know everything is alright."

Belladonna smiled at her and stepped forward into the tunnel. Aya watched for a moment, then rushed forward again. Belladonna felt the soft touch of her small hand and turned around. Aya thrust a small green lamp into her hand and tried a smile herself, though the upturn of the corners of her mouth was contradicted by the concern in her wide eyes.

"Good luck," she whispered.

"Thank you," said Belladonna, and she walked forward again, holding the lamp ahead of her.

When she had gone a few meters, she glanced back, but the entrance to the tunnel was already just a pinhole of light. She held her breath for a moment, before deciding that no, she would keep going. It wasn't like she hadn't been to the Other Side before.

Last time had been different, however. The transition through the door in the theatre had been instant; there was no passage, no sense of moving from one place to another at all. The tunnel, by comparison, was narrow, low, and dark. The walls felt like thick velvet and the sound of her footsteps was swallowed by the blackness. Belladonna felt apprehensive. The silent darkness seemed to weigh her down, filling her mind with shapeless fear.

As if this weren't enough, she slowly became aware that the air was growing warmer and more stale, though the tunnel itself was growing higher. At least she could straighten out of the half-crouch she'd had to assume so far. She paused and stretched her back, then raised the lamp and carried on.

Was this really the route that the Dead took? It seemed more than a little mean to force them through a narrow tunnel like this when they'd already been through whatever it was that led to their deaths. Belladonna's mind wandered back to family funerals and the deaths of others she'd heard of or seen. Images of lines of hearses, dark hospital rooms, and grim news reports played and replayed through her mind with increasing detail and sharpness as she began to breathe in great gasps. She shook her head in an effort to dispel the dizziness and realized that the air really was disappearing. And why shouldn't it, she thought, the Dead didn't need it.

Her feet kept on walking forward long after all conscious effort at locomotion had ceased. The fog in her mind spread until even the dim light of the green lamp had closed in, leaving a narrow peephole in her perception. Her face felt hot, but the fingers holding the lamp were icy. She tried to blink away the feeling, and thought that perhaps she saw some light. But it was too late. The velvet darkness closed in.

The last thing she remembered was the sound of the lamp hitting the ground.

11

The Yarrow Street Ghost

*S*HH! QUIET! I think she's waking up!"

Belladonna felt like she was lying at the bottom of a deep pit and the only way out was to open her eyes. Except she didn't seem to be able to do that.

"No. Look, I told you, I can't eat those things!"

"They're really good."

"Shut up. Come on, Belladonna—breathe!"

"Is she cold?"

"A bit."

"Maybe she's dead. We're always cold. See?"

"Ow! Keep your clammy hands to yourself!"

Belladonna took a deep breath, mustered all her strength, and strained to open her eyes. It felt like the hardest thing she'd ever done, like she was wading through treacle, digging out of a snowdrift, lifting an enormous weight from her chest. Her eyes opened slowly and the sun streamed in. She closed them again.

"Belladonna!"

She opened them. Two shadows were leaning over her. Her fingers moved over something soft. It was grass.

"It's Steve," said the worried voice. "Can you hear me?"

"Yes," her own voice was suddenly husky.

"I told you she'd be alright," said a no-nonsense girl's voice.

"You said she was dead."

Belladonna tried to push herself up, but her arms seemed to be made of jelly. Steve reached forward and helped her to sit.

"We heard you," he explained, "down there. Then you fell."

"There was no air," she rasped.

Looking around, she realized she was sitting at the base of the great tree in the town on the Other Side. Steve was looking at her, genuine concern on his face, while Elsie ate lemon bon-bons from a quarter bag.

"You shouldn't have come that way," she pointed out. "It's for the Dead. We don't need air. Or light, for that matter."

"Then why is there light here?" asked Steve, who had clearly had just about all he could take of Miss Personality 1912.

"It's nice," shrugged Elsie. "I said we don't need it, I didn't say we didn't like it. Are you sure you don't want a sweet? Belladonna?"

She held the bag out, but Steve pushed her hand away.

"I told you," he hissed, "we can't eat the food of the Dead. Besides, I'm pretty sure taking sweets from a shop is still stealing even if it is the Land of the Dead."

"It was the only way through," whispered Belladonna. "Your mother destroyed the other door."

"On purpose?" Steve looked confused.

"I don't know. Things are getting complicated. Where's my backpack?"

Steve handed her the backpack and she rummaged through it, removing a can of Tizer and Dr. Ashe's book. She popped the can and handed the book to Steve.

"It belonged to Dr. Ashe," she said. "I found it in the old launderette. I tried to conjure a ghost. I thought you might come, or Elsie. But first it was Slackett and then Ashe. He tried to . . . he's not—"

"We know," said Steve. "Turns out they really did start them on Latin and Greek early."

"I wasn't very good at it," said Elsie, "but we had to read bits of *The Iliad* and I always liked Odysseus. He was a liar too, though not like Ashe, who is an absolute rotter, if you ask me."

"I got rid of him, but then the Hunt came. Aya took me into a cavern beneath the graveyard. Where the charnel sprites work. The tunnel is theirs."

Steve exhaled slowly. "You've been busy," he said.

"That's not all." Belladonna got to her feet carefully

and tried walking around a bit. "According to my Gran, the ghosts bring dreams to the Living. With no ghosts, no one's been dreaming."

"So?" asked Steve, eyeing the can of Tizer hungrily.

"Without dreams, we die. That's what she says anyway. Aunt Deirdre says so too."

"We do? Can I have a swig?"

Belladonna handed him the can.

"That's interesting," said Elsie, licking the powdery coating off her last bon-bon. "It makes you wonder who the target is, doesn't it?"

"What d'you mean?" asked Belladonna.

"Well, we . . . that is, the ghosts, we've been disappearing and it looked like that was the problem, but if the Living need us to survive, then it's not just us, is it? It's something bigger."

"You mean, is someone after the ghosts, or are they really after the Living?" suggested Steve.

"Or possibly both," said Belladonna.

They looked at each other with grim faces. Belladonna picked up her backpack and stared up into the tree as her eyes slowly got used to the light and the details around her came into focus. The leaves were turning brown.

Not brown like autumn, but brown like they'd got some sort of disease. She looked out at the High Street—every tree and bush was suffering from the same blight, and the decay that was destroying the plant life seemed to have turned the remainder of the buildings into semi-derelict shells of their former selves, like fruit in a bowl that's been left too long.

"It's getting worse," she said. "I think we should go back. I only came to help you get home, but look at the tree . . . and the houses. Whatever it is seems to be spreading."

"I know, but how can we get back now?" said Steve. "We can't go the way you came."

"I think we'll have to."

"You could hold your breath," suggested Elsie brightly, "and run."

"We need to speak to my Gran and I need to give her Dr. Ashe's notebook. Are you coming?"

Elsie shook her head.

"I don't think I can," she said. "I haunt the school — it's the only place I can go."

Steve looked at Belladonna doubtfully. "Are you sure about this?"

"Uh-oh," said Elsie, "nasty-looking alchemist at two o'clock!"

Belladonna and Steve whirled around. There, down the hill, about a hundred meters away, was Dr. Ashe. He was marching purposefully toward them, his Hound by his side and a smirk on his face.

"Huh," said Steve grimly, "I should've known it'd take more than half a ham sandwich to kill anything that size."

"Come on!" Belladonna turned and led the way back to the entrance of the charnel sprite's tunnel.

Only it wasn't there.

She glanced at Steve and they both started digging through the piles of dead leaves that suddenly littered the roots of the great tree.

"It was here, wasn't it?" asked Belladonna, a note of panic creeping into her voice. "I thought it was here."

"It was," said Steve.

"Well, it isn't there now," said Elsie, jumping down, "and Ashe is getting closer. I suggest running."

They hesitated for a second and then took to their heels, racing up the street, away from Ashe. They ducked down a side street and stopped for a moment.

"Where are we going?" asked Steve. "We can't just run."

"The graveyard," suggested Belladonna. "The one near my house."

"Why?"

"The tunnel," she said, taking off again and doubling back, "the one that leads to the charnel sprite's cave."

"But that's where you came from," said Elsie, "and you ended up under the tree."

Steve nodded. "If that end of the tunnel is gone, why on earth would the other end still be there?"

"I don't know, but it's all I can think of!"

They were at the bottom of the hill now, near the old theatre. Steve darted down the alley and peeked out into the street. He ran back and urged them forward.

"He's coming this way," he said. "Let's go."

Belladonna led the way, but it wasn't long before her ordeal in the tunnel started catching up with her — she was gasping for breath, her ears were ringing, and the darkness seemed to be closing in again. They ran down street after street, places that in the Land of the Living were as familiar to Belladonna as her own back garden. But this wasn't the Land of the Living — it was the Land of the Dead. What if the graveyard wasn't even there? Why should it be? Everyone here was already dead, after all. Steve reached out as she stumbled and helped her keep going, but it seemed hopeless.

"I don't think I can . . ." she gasped.

"Wait a minute," said Steve. "Isn't this Yarrow Street where your grandmother lives?"

Belladonna nodded. "Number 3. On the end."

"We're there."

Belladonna looked up. Sure enough, there was the familiar row of terraced houses; even the fortune-telling sign was there, though for some reason the door was painted a different color.

"Maybe we could hide in there. Just till you feel better."

Belladonna hesitated. Her hair was sticking to her face with sweat, but she was beginning to feel better again. Then she saw Ashe, off in the distance, marching with the unhurried confidence of someone who knows that his quarry cannot escape.

"Yes," she said, "come on."

Steve and Elsie helped her up the steps and Steve turned the doorknob.

"It's locked!"

He peered through the narrow windows on either side of the door.

"Why on earth would it be locked? It's the Land of the Dead! Who's going to steal anything? This is so—"

He was still peering through the windows when the door was suddenly flung open. An elderly man stood in the doorway.

"Get inside!" he ordered. "Quickly!"

Belladonna stared at him.

"Quickly!" he repeated.

She lurched forward and ran inside, followed by Elsie and a completely flummoxed Steve. As soon as they were across the threshold, the man slammed the door shut.

"Kitchen," he said, sticking an unlit pipe into his mouth. "Tea, I think."

And with that, he marched into the kitchen, leaving Belladonna, Steve, and Elsie standing in the hall with their respective mouths hanging open.

"Who is that?" hissed Steve.

"And why is he still here?" whispered Elsie.

"I think we should go," said Steve. "He could be another one of Ashe's helpers. This could be a trap."

Belladonna bit her lower lip. "No," she said, "I think we should stay."

Steve and Elsie looked at each other and then at Belladonna.

"Why?" they asked in unison.

"I think he might be my grandfather."

"Might?" said Steve. "Don't you know what your own grandfather looks like?"

"He died when I was a baby."

"Oh. Sorry."

Belladonna smiled and walked back to the kitchen, trying to remember the face in the picture on the mantelpiece in the living room at home. It was a small, faded snapshot of an elderly man at the seaside hoisting a baby up into the air. He had a mustache, she remembered that, and a rather baggy cardigan. But . . .

He clanked around with the kettle while Belladonna, Steve, and Elsie hung back by the door. The kitchen was far too small to accommodate all of them.

"I've got a cream cake here," he said, removing a packaged cake from the fridge, "just . . . you know . . . if you're hungry."

Belladonna felt she should say something, but before she could decide exactly what that should be, the man's expression changed and he eyed her narrowly.

"Wait," he said. "You're alive."

Belladonna nodded.

"And you," he added, looking at Steve.

"Not me, though!" said Elsie cheerily. "Dead as a doornail."

"What is . . . what is your name?" asked Belladonna.

"Oh! Rude of me," he said, holding out a thin, muscular hand. "Phil. Phil Johnson."

Belladonna shook his hand and peered into his face. "I think you might be my grandfather."

The old man stared at her but didn't let go of her hand.

"Belladonna?" he said at last, his voice cracking slightly. "Are you Belladonna?"

She nodded, and in an instant he scooped her up into his arms with a hearty yell. "Belladonna! As I live and breathe! Or, well, actually, I don't . . . but . . . Ha!"

Belladonna gasped and then grinned. It had never occurred to her that they could touch, but of course why shouldn't they? This was their world, the Land of the Dead, and they lived here just as they had when they were alive. At home, her parents were little more than shadows, but here . . . her stomach did a little flip . . . here she might be able to hug them again. And they could hug her back. If she ever found them.

"Um . . . sorry to interrupt," said Steve, a little embarrassed at all the emoting going on. "But what about Ashe? He'll be here any minute."

"Oh, I imagine he's here already," said Grandpa Johnson as he put Belladonna back on the floor. "Have a look."

Steve and Elsie glanced at each other and ran to the front room. They were back a moment later.

"He's just standing there," said Steve. "On the path in front."

"And look!" Elsie ran to the kitchen window. "There's the Hound!"

Belladonna spun around. Sure enough, Ashe's Hound was standing there, right in the middle of the back garden, its mouth slightly open, showing a fine set of really big teeth and drooling slowly onto a patch of lawn.

"Why don't they come in?" she asked.

"Witch bottles," said her grandfather cryptically. "Now . . . let's get into the back room. I've got a nice fire going and we can sit down and make ourselves comfortable. No tea and cake for you or your friend, I'm afraid. But you, young lady—"

"Elsie. I'm Elsie. And, yes, please! One sugar."

Steve plonked himself into one of the chairs in front of the fire and sighed, "I'm starving."

Belladonna sat down and nodded, then suddenly jumped up again and opened her backpack.

"I nearly forgot! Sandwiches! I made sandwiches!"

She pulled one of the packets of sandwiches out.

"I made two," she explained, sharing it out, "but I think we should save one for later. Just in case."

Steve wasn't listening; he just grabbed his half of the sandwich and devoured it hungrily. Elsie carried two mugs of tea in on a tray and Grandpa Johnson handed glasses of water to Steve and Belladonna.

"It's alright," he said. "You can drink the water."

Belladonna looked at the glasses suspiciously. "How do I know you're really my grandfather?" she asked.

Grandpa Johnson smiled. "Good girl. Never take anything or anyone at face value."

He leaned over and whispered in her ear. A smile spread across Belladonna's face. She turned to Steve and Elsie.

"It's him."

Steve looked at Elsie and then at the old man, then he picked up the glass of water and drank deeply.

"If you're dead," said Elsie, still not satisfied, "why are you still here? All the others have vanished."

"That'll be the witch bottles too, I rather imagine."

"What will?" said Steve. "And what's a witch bottle?"

"It's a small bottle, usually blue or green. Ours were green. You put some things inside: hair, a few trinkets, some wine. Then you bury it under the doorstep or in a wall and it stops spirits from entering. Jessie and I made two when we bought this house, just for a laugh, you know. We put one under the front door and one under the back."

"And that's why Ashe can't come in?"

"Yes, you have to be invited, you see. Unfortunately, they work a little differently in the Land of the Living."

He smiled ruefully and stirred the sugar in his mug slowly.

"In what way?" asked Belladonna.

"They keep spirits out. All of them."

Belladonna looked at him for a moment, then the

penny dropped. "Ohhhh! That's why there are no ghosts at Grandma's house!"

Grandpa Johnson nodded. "So I've never been able to visit. I couldn't let her know that everything was alright."

"But she knows," said Belladonna. "Mum and Dad, they . . ."

"I know, I know," he said, patting her hand. "But it would've been nice to talk."

"Well . . . hang on," Steve leaned forward. "If no ghosts can appear in your grandmother's house, how can she have séances? I mean, that's her main business, isn't it?"

"Duh," said Belladonna, rolling her eyes. "She does it the same way everyone else does, of course. She makes it up as she goes along."

"You're kidding."

Belladonna and Grandpa Johnson shook their heads slowly. Steve looked from one to the other, then burst out laughing.

"That's brilliant!"

"Well, it would be if I hadn't picked that house to haunt. It never occurred to me back then that the witch bottles did anything. It was just a bit of fun. But we only get to have one place to haunt, you see, so naturally I picked this house. I thought Jessie and I could just carry on. But I can't get through."

"I picked the school," said Elsie proudly.

"You're just weird," said Steve.

"Would you like us to dig up the witch bottles?" asked Belladonna. "When we get . . . I mean, if—"

"A week ago I would have said yes," said her grandfather, "but I think they're the only things that have saved me from whatever's happened to everyone else. And in any case, I send her dreams as often as I can."

"You mean it's true?" asked Belladonna. "Ghosts really do send dreams to the Living?"

"How?" asked Steve skeptically.

"There's an alabaster doorway, a door frame, in the House of Mists and a chair. They're both very old. Anyway, you just sit in the chair and . . . I don't claim to know how it works, but you can send messages, memories, dreams to whoever you like. Once you get the hang of it, they give you an alabaster bowl to keep at home and you can use that. I've got one in the front room but, of course, it won't work from here so I always have to go to the House of Mists."

"Who's 'they'?" asked Steve, still suspicious. "And what's the House of Mists?"

"The Conclave of Shadow," said Belladonna.

"Yes!" said her grandfather, surprised. "How did—"

"Grandma mentioned them."

"It sounds very ominous," said Grandpa Johnson, "but it's just a collection of the older ghosts. Truth be told, they never really had much to do. Until recently."

His attention seemed to wander and he began stirring his tea in an absentminded way.

"What changed?" asked Steve.

"Um . . ." Grandpa Johnson squinted at Steve. "I don't think I got your name. . . ."

"Oh, sorry," said Belladonna. "This is Steve. Steve Evans."

"Really? Any relation to Roger Evans?"

"Who?"

"Young chap. Died in the First World War, I think."

Steve shrugged, "Dunno. Anyway, what changed?"

"Oh, well . . . the bowls stopped working. That was the first thing. Everyone had to go up to the House of Mists to send their dreams. You should have seen the lines! Chaos! Then sometimes instead of the dreams going through from here to . . . you know, wherever . . . things started coming through the door from other places to here. Well, it simply wasn't designed to work that way. The Conclave appointed a commission to research the door, to see if it had ever happened before."

"Why didn't they stop people using it?" asked Steve.

"They couldn't—the Living have to have their dreams."

"Gran said that we die without dreams. And Aunt Deirdre—"

"Oh, she's showed up, has she?" said Grandpa Johnson, clearly unimpressed. "Well, she's right. Without dreams, you don't sleep properly and if you don't sleep properly, eventually . . . well . . ."

"What's the House of Mists?" said Steve.

"It's a big house," said Elsie.

"No? Really?" said Steve sarcastically. "What's it for?"

"Don't know," shrugged Elsie. "It's big, though. Very impressive . . . and the gardens are the cat's meow."

"It's for government," said Grandpa Johnson, sensing Steve's irritation, "not that we need much, but disputes occasionally arise. There is a library housing all the records of the Shadow Lands, of course."

"The Shadow Lands?"

"That's where we are. You call it the Land of the Dead. There are feasting rooms on the third floor — the Vikings are very fond of those. And the Dream Door is there. In a room on the ground floor, just to the right as you go in."

"And sometimes there are garden parties," said Elsie, "with swingboats and jellies!"

"Well," said Steve, ignoring Elsie, "if all the doors back really are closed, then perhaps we should go to the House of Mists. Maybe their commission has found something. They could already know what's happening and why."

"Hmm," said Grandpa Johnson, "that's probably the best thing. We certainly can't sit here. We'll set out in the morning, but for now I think you two need some sleep."

"But how will we get past Ashe?" asked Belladonna.

"You leave that to me. I'll see what I can think of." Grandpa Johnson smiled encouragingly, but

Belladonna had a feeling that he had no idea what to do. She reached into her backpack and handed him Dr. Ashe's book.

"Maybe there's something in here."

He took the book and leafed through it. Then his eyebrows shot up and his pipe nearly fell out of his mouth.

"Good heavens! It's spells and . . . ooh, that one looks dangerous. And that one. Where on earth did you find this?"

Belladonna told him about the launderette and the hidden cupboard in the wall, and once she'd started, the whole story came tumbling out, from Lady Mary right through to the Draconite Amulet and the charnel sprites' tunnel. It felt good to tell a grown-up even though she knew he probably couldn't do much about it.

Grandpa Johnson sucked on his unlit pipe, lost in thought for a few moments.

"Where's this amulet now?" he said finally.

"Here." Steve pulled it out from inside his T-shirt and handed it over.

Grandpa Johnson turned it over in his hands, a look of awe on his face.

"Well, I never!"

"If you hold it up to the light, you can see dragons," said Belladonna.

Her grandfather glanced at her, then held it up to the lamp in the corner of the room. Belladonna couldn't help but feel a little bit pleased as his mouth dropped open.

"Good gravy and dripping! So you can! I wonder how old Ashe knew where it was."

"He didn't," said Steve. "Well, not exactly."

"He must have thought all his birthdays had come at once when he persuaded you two to go fetch it for him."

"Why?" asked Belladonna. "What is it for?"

"Well," said Grandpa Johnson, holding it up to the light again, "unless I'm very much mistaken, this is one of the Nomials."

"Nomials?" said Elsie, suddenly interested.

"Yes," Grandpa Johnson handed it back to Steve. "Nomials."

They all looked at him expectantly, certain that he was about to say something really important, but all he did was chew on the stem of his old pipe, lost in thought.

"Grandpa," said Belladonna quietly, "what are the Nomials?"

"Stones," he said finally. "Gems, I suppose . . . um . . ."

"You don't know, do you?" said Steve, who was more familiar than most with the look of someone who doesn't know the answer.

"No one knows," said Grandpa Johnson, looking a little offended. "There are just stories. After the last Dark Times, the Nomials were created, d'you see?

And they were hidden. I don't know why. The stories don't go into detail. I imagine they have some individual powers, but together . . . together they somehow form a multiversal orrery."

"A what?" asked Belladonna.

"An orrery," said Elsie, as if it was the most obvious thing in the world. "It's a sort of mechanical map of the solar system. My Papa had one in his study at home. It shows the relative positions of all the planets."

"Well remembered," said Grandpa Johnson, clearly impressed. "An ordinary orrery shows the planets that make up the solar system in the Land of the Living. The multiversal orrery, on the other hand, is said to show the relative positions of all the nine worlds."

"Is that all?" said Steve. "It's just some sort of model? Why go to all the trouble of hiding the pieces, then?"

"Because . . . well, the legend has it that whoever possesses the multiversal orrery has power over the nine worlds and all the spaces in between. That's why it was broken up and the pieces hidden throughout the worlds."

"Duh," said Steve, rolling his eyes. "Don't you have movies or comics in the Land of the Dead? Special doodads with the power to destroy the universe *always* fall into the hands of the bad guys."

"I didn't say they had the power to destroy the universe."

"I bet they do, though. Ow!"

Belladonna had kicked him under the table. She couldn't see much point in making the old man angry and there were a lot more questions she wanted to ask.

"What makes you think it's one of these Nomials?" she asked, smiling in a way that she hoped was encouraging.

"Um . . ." Grandpa Johnson glared at Steve for a moment. "It's . . . uh . . . well, I'm fairly sure that's Pyrocasta. The place that you see with the dragons. There are legends about one of the Nomials being made from a jewel given by a dragon."

"The dragon gave it?" asked Belladonna, surprised. "They didn't kill it?"

"Of course not." Grandpa Johnson seemed taken aback. "Why would you kill one when you can just ask?"

Belladonna felt suddenly ashamed, as if she'd advocated killing baby bunnies or something. "I don't know . . . I just . . ."

"Well, if that's so," began Steve, who hadn't lost any of his former skeptical tone, "then why—"

"We can talk about all this tomorrow," said Grandpa Johnson, suddenly standing up. "It's a two-day walk to the House of Mists. There'll be plenty of time, and I can see you're feeling tired."

"I'm not—"

Steve winced as Belladonna's shoe made contact with his shin again.

"I'll make up the beds," said Grandpa Johnson, striding out of the room.

"What do you keep kicking me for?" hissed Steve. "We need to find out about these Nomial thingies. It's bound to have something to do with the ghosts and the doors."

"I know that," whispered Belladonna, "but you were just winding him up. Old people don't like being talked to like that."

"That's true," said Elsie. "My grandmother once gave me a proper clip 'round the ear when I told her that times had changed and that children didn't have to be seen and not heard anymore . . . and that her new hat made her look like a mushroom with a bird sitting on it."

"She hit you?" said Belladonna, shocked.

"I'm not surprised," said Steve. "I'll bet Granny got a round of applause from the rest of your nearest and dearest for that one."

Elsie bit her lip and glared at Steve, giving Belladonna the distinct impression that he might have hit the nail on the head.

"Let's go to bed," she said quickly. "It sounds like this House of Mists thing is going to be quite a trek."

She turned and walked through the hall, but couldn't resist a peek through the sidelight of the front door.

"Is he still there?"

Steve was right behind her. Belladonna nodded but didn't turn around. She could see Ashe standing near the front gate, but he wasn't staring at the house any more. He seemed to be holding something small in his hand and he was staring down at it, his jaw set in concentration.

"I hope your Granddad comes up with a plan for getting past him."

"He will," said Belladonna as brightly as she could. "Come on, let's get some rest."

"D'you reckon there are aspirins in the Land of the Dead?" asked Steve, following her up the stairs.

"I doubt it. Why?"

"I've got a headache. It's probably lack of food."

"You had a ham sandwich!"

"*Half* a ham sandwich."

Grandpa Johnson was standing on the upstairs landing waiting for them.

"You take the front room, Belladonna," he said, gesturing to what she had always thought of as her grandmother's room. "And I've put you in the back bedroom, if that's alright, Steve."

Steve mumbled his thanks and disappeared into the spare room, closing the door softly behind him.

"Thank you," said Belladonna, suddenly feeling awkward. "It's very nice of you to help."

Grandpa Johnson smiled at her for a moment, then scooped her up into his arms again and gave her a huge hug.

"Oh, Belladonna," he whispered, "it's so wonderful to see you. Don't worry about a thing, we'll have your Mum and Dad back here and you back home where you belong before you can say Jack Robinson! Now, give me a kiss good night. Or don't children do that any more?"

"Of course we do!"

She kissed his cheek and then wiped her eyes. She hadn't even realized she was crying.

"Good night," she said finally, smiling.

"Good night. I'll give your book a read and we'll see what we can do in the morning."

She went into the room, leaving the door slightly ajar so that she could see the light from the landing. As she scrambled into bed she could hear her grandfather's footsteps retreating down the stairs and, for the first time in what seemed like ages, she felt safe.

12

The Green Box

I T WAS STILL dark when Belladonna woke up. She
waited for a few moments while her eyes grew accustomed to the light, then sat up. Something was wrong.

She glanced at the window. There were no stars in
the velvet black sky, but a sliver of strange blue moonlight sliced across the floor. The night was so much
quieter than the nights at home. There, if she woke
up in the small hours, she would hear the distant hum
of cars and the occasional bleating of a horn; there
would be sirens sometimes, and the lonely warbling of
solitary birds. But here there was nothing, just the all-
enveloping silence of death. She disentangled herself
from the blankets, tiptoed to the window, and peered
out, trying not to move the curtains.

Ashe was still there and still staring at whatever he
had in his hand, but now it seemed to be giving off a
faint glow. The light was sickly and faint, but it was
enough for Belladonna to see that the alchemist was

smiling. Suddenly the sense of safety that she had felt in bed vanished and was replaced by an anxious knot in her stomach. Then, as she watched, a strip of light poured across the meager front garden. Someone had opened the front door.

For a moment she was puzzled, but then she knew. "Steve!"

She turned and ran out of the room. When Ashe had started mumbling to whatever was in his hands, Steve had complained of a headache. It couldn't be coincidence. At the top of the stairs she felt the chill of the night air and could just see the lower half of Steve's jeans as he stood in the doorway.

"Steve! Stop!" She clattered down the stairs as Steve stepped out onto the front step.

She had just reached the open door, when she was yanked back by a strong hand.

"Stay here," commanded her grandfather. "Don't move."

His voice was stern, like army commanders in old movies. He strode to the open door, then hesitated for just a moment as the full horror of the situation dawned on Belladonna.

"No!" she yelled. "Don't!"

He turned, gave her a wink, and then shot out of the door.

By this time Steve was halfway between the front door and Dr. Ashe, but Grandpa Johnson crossed the ground in three long strides. He grabbed Steve, turned, and half threw, half shoved him across the threshold and back into the house, but just as he was about to step back inside himself, the door slammed shut.

Belladonna yelped, jumped over Steve, and started straining at the door.

"It won't open!" she cried as Elsie appeared out of the kitchen. "He's trapped outside!"

Elsie sprang to her aid and they both heaved on the door, but it was locked tight. Belladonna peered through the sidelight, then dashed into the front room and threw open the curtains.

Grandpa Johnson and Dr. Ashe were facing each other. Ashe was no longer staring into the thing in his hand, but was glowering at Grandpa Johnson with a face like thunder.

"How dare you!" he yelled, his voice cracking with fury. "They are mine!"

"They are not," replied Grandpa Johnson, completely unruffled by the alchemist's rage.

Ashe looked at him for a moment, then a smile slowly spread across his face, like mud cracking in the sun.

"Well," he said finally, "you've stepped beyond your witch bottles. You know what happens now, don't you?"

"I have an idea."

Ashe stepped forward and threw his arms wide, muttering words that Belladonna couldn't hear but that she knew were Words of Power. Grandpa Johnson turned back and smiled at her again. Then, like her father, he seemed to squeeze in and up until he was nothing but a thin line of light. And then he was gone.

Belladonna and Elsie stared out of the window, pale, horrified faces framed by faded flowery curtains. Ashe seemed to relish his final victory over Grandpa Johnson for a moment, then turned his steely gaze onto Belladonna.

"You may as well come out," he called, his voice like cold stone. "Living creatures like you need food from the Land of the Living, and I'll wager the old man didn't have so much as a pancake in his house."

Belladonna stared at him, unable to respond.

"Come out, my dear, do come out. You know that all I want is my little jewel."

Elsie clicked her tongue and closed the curtains with a flourish.

"Awful man," she said, "an absolute stinking rotter."

Belladonna looked at her. She could feel the tears burning in her eyes but was determined not to cry. She was about to say something when there was a low moan from the hallway.

"Steve!"

They ran back to the door where Steve lay crumpled against the wall at the foot of the stairs, the Draconite Amulet at his feet and his head in his hands.

"Are you alright?" asked Belladonna.

"My head . . ." he groaned.

"It was Ashe," explained Belladonna, "but it doesn't

make any sense. Grandpa said the witch bottles kept him out. He said he couldn't even send dreams to Grandma."

"It's the amulet, I suspect," said Elsie matter-of-factly. "Apparently it works like an amplifier. That's one of the things it does anyway, according to that book of Ashe's."

Belladonna stared at her. Elsie sat down on the stairs.

"According to your Granddad, each of the Nomials has a special power. According to the notebook, Ashe had only managed to locate one. He seemed to think that this one would help him find the others, but he was most interested in its ability to amplify. He went on and on about that, apparently."

Steve looked up and rested his head back against the wall.

"Feeling better?" asked Belladonna.

"What happened?"

"Well, if Elsie's right—"

"Which I am."

"If Elsie's right, the amulet probably amplified Ashe's magic so he was able to get into your head and control you in spite of the witch bottles."

Steve looked blank, so she explained the events of the last fifteen minutes, concluding with the disappearance of Grandpa Johnson.

For a moment there was silence.

"I'm sorry," said Steve quietly.

"It wasn't your fault," said Elsie. "It was Ashe."

Steve shook his head. He looked frightened. "I don't remember any of it," he said. "Just going to bed. And my head aching."

He reached for the amulet and slowly slipped it around his neck again. Elsie watched him, her mouth a thin line of determination.

"Right," she said. "We have to get out of here."

Steve looked up at her, his fear rapidly being replaced by the irritation he always seemed to feel whenever Elsie opened her mouth.

"Oh, right," he said, his voice dripping with sarcasm. "I'll get my jacket. Which way would you like to go? Out the back into the jaws of whatever kind of dog that is, or out the front door? I'm sure that alchemist won't be a bit of trouble."

"Oh, *ha*," said Elsie. "For your information, Belladonna's grandfather had a plan."

"He did?" said Belladonna and Steve in unison.

"Yes. He said we should go up to the roof and sneak out across the roofs of the other houses. He said we could get down at the end terrace and then head for the House of Mists."

"How do we get up there?" asked Steve.

"There's a trapdoor to the attic at the top of the stairs!" Belladonna felt suddenly optimistic. This could work.

"Right," said Steve, standing up. "It's a plan."

Belladonna ran into the back room to retrieve her

backpack and Ashe's book, which was lying open where Grandpa Johnson had left it on a small table near his chair. She shoved it into her bag and turned to leave, but as she did so, she noticed something on the floor near the door — his empty pipe, abandoned in the rush to save Steve. For a moment she just stood and stared at it, then she bent down and picked it up carefully. It was an ordinary pipe, not fancy or special in any way, but now it was all that remained of the grandfather she had never known and then found. She could feel the tears burning in her eyes again.

"Are you coming?" Elsie's voice echoed down the hall.

"Yes! Just a sec!"

She wiped the tears from her eyes, took a deep breath, and marched out into the hall. She was walking back to the stairs, shoving the pipe into the front pocket, when she felt something hard.

"The ruler!" she said suddenly. "I nearly forgot!"

Steve and Elsie both looked at her as if she had finally and totally gone to ga-ga-land.

"What?" said Steve.

"Slackett gave it to me. He seemed to think it was important. He said you'd know what to do with it."

She scrabbled about in the pocket of the backpack and handed Steve the plastic ruler. He stared at it and then at her.

"It's a ruler," he said flatly.

"I know," said Belladonna, "but Slackett said that

you were the Paladin and that you'd know what to do with it."

"Underline something?" said Steve sarcastically. "Or . . . oh, I know—I could measure the exact length of the Hound's teeth, right before it uses them."

"You could draw a right-angled triangle," suggested Elsie, grinning.

"No," said Steve, "I'd need a protractor for that."

Belladonna could feel her cheeks burning and she tried to control her irritation.

"Look," she said, "haven't you noticed? Slackett isn't out there with Ashe. He risked everything to get that ruler to you. He could be dead now—"

"He's already dead," pointed out Elsie, not very helpfully.

"Yes, but . . . well, he's not here and I think Ashe did something to him and he said that ruler was important!"

"Alright, alright, keep your hair on," said Steve, shoving the ruler into his pocket. "I'll keep it."

Belladonna nodded, then felt suddenly embarrassed by her own fury over a six-inch plastic ruler.

"Have you finished messing about?" said Elsie sternly. "Can we possibly escape now, d'you think?"

"Sure," said Steve, clearly feeling much better. "Off onto the roof, down a drainpipe, and away to the House of Mists, where the Conclave of Shadow will explain everything. I don't think."

"But maybe the Spellbinder will be there," said Belladonna.

"The what?" said Elsie and Steve in unison.

"The Spellbinder," Belladonna looked from one to the other. "Lady Mary told me to tell the Spellbinder. At Arkbath Hall. And I think my mother and father knew something about her, but they wouldn't tell me because . . . well, because . . ."

"Because they're adults," said Steve, "and they never tell us anything."

"And then Slackett thought I was the Spellbinder, but obviously I'm not, so—"

"Why?" said Steve.

"Because I'm not."

"But maybe you are. I mean, you're the one who knew the words to open the door."

"Yes," said Elsie, the excitement rising in her voice, "and you were able to summon the Dead. That's not a normal thing to be able to do, you know."

"No!" cried Belladonna suddenly. "It's not me! It can't be me!"

Elsie and Steve looked at each other. Elsie tried to put an arm around her shoulders but Belladonna shrugged her off angrily.

Silence. They looked at each other, and then at the floor.

"Why?" said Steve quietly. "Why can't it be you?"

"Because," Belladonna wiped her hand across her eyes. "Because Lady Mary told me to find the Spellbinder because she'd know what to do."

"So?"

"And I don't!" she blurted. "I don't know what to do! If everyone's expecting the Spellbinder to save the day and I'm the Spellbinder, then . . . my Grandpa would still be here." Her voice trailed off.

Steve and Elsie glanced at each other. Belladonna could see the disappointment in their eyes . . . and the pity. She wished she hadn't said anything.

"Well," said Steve finally, "if you're not the Spellbinder, then maybe she's at this House of Mists place."

"Maybe," mumbled Belladonna.

"Either way," said Elsie in her best brisk, no-nonsense way, "the first order of business is to get out of here. Where's this trapdoor, then?"

They crept up the stairs to the landing and stared at the square in the ceiling that marked the entrance to the attic. The edges were grubby from decades of fingers, but there was no obvious way to get to it, let alone remove it.

"How are we supposed to reach that?" said Elsie.

"There's a chair in the front room!"

Belladonna ran off and returned with an old chair. Steve took it off her, placed it squarely underneath the trapdoor, and jiggled it. One of the legs promptly fell off.

"Why don't you just climb on the banister?" asked Elsie.

"Because I might fall off and plummet to my death," said Steve drily.

"I'll do it, then! I'm already dead."

"So you keep saying," muttered Steve.

Elsie heaved herself up on the banister, teetered there for a moment, turned a funny color, and quickly got down.

"What's the matter?" asked Belladonna.

"Apparently you can still have vertigo even when you're dead," said Elsie unhappily.

"That doesn't seem fair," said Belladonna, peering over the banister and down into the hall. It didn't seem all that far—maybe she could do it. She glanced up at the trapdoor and tried to calculate how much of a stretch it would be from the banister.

She had just decided that if she could get some kind of a stick, maybe a broom handle or something, she could probably reach the trapdoor and knock it away (assuming it opened inward, of course), when Steve emerged from the second bedroom, dragging the bedside table.

"Found this," he said. "Help me get it over there."

They dragged it under the trapdoor and he clambered on top, but he still wasn't high enough. They looked at each other, then at the trapdoor, then at the disappointing bedside table.

"Hang on," said Belladonna, "what about this?"

She took out the drawer, spilled the contents onto the floor, and handed it to Steve. He set it on top of the table and stepped onto it.

It only gave him a few extra inches, but it was enough to reach the trapdoor. He pushed on it and it gave way with a soft click, swinging gently down into the hall like a loose tooth.

"Yes!"

The triumph was short-lived, however. The hole into the attic was black and impenetrable, and none of the dim light on the landing seemed to reach it at all.

"Come on," said Steve to Belladonna, after a few moments' silence, "I'll give you a bunk up."

"Me?" said Belladonna. "Why me?"

"Because I don't think you could lift me up there."

"Well, what about Elsie?"

"She's afraid of heights, in case you didn't notice. Look," he rummaged through his pockets and produced his key-chain light. "You can have this."

Belladonna turned the tiny light on. Somehow it seemed even less effective than when they'd used it to find the Cumean Sibyl. Still, there was probably nothing for it. She reached up and took Steve's hand. For a moment, they both teetered on the drawer, then he clasped his hands together and smiled encouragingly. Or Belladonna imagined it was supposed to be encouraging; what it actually looked like was some sort of grimace. She put her right foot into his hands, her hands on his shoulders, and pushed off with the left. He heaved her upward with a grunt and she flew up into the attic, grabbing the edges of the opening as she went and pushing herself on through. She landed with a thump just as she heard an almighty crash below.

"I'm okay! I'm okay!"

She peered over the edge and saw Steve lying on the floor, the drawer next to him and the bedside table on its side.

"Yes, he's fine!" laughed Elsie. "He fell on his head! No damage!"

Steve glared at her for a second, then failed miserably at maintaining his scowl and burst out laughing as well. Belladonna grinned as she leaned out of the attic, putting off the awful moment when she'd actually have to explore.

"What's it like?" asked Steve, scrambling to his feet.

"Dark," said Belladonna.

She turned on the tiny flashlight and shone it into the attic. The pinprick of light showed roof beams, swags of cobwebs, and long-abandoned bird nests.

"Can you tell if there's a way out onto the roof?"

Belladonna sighed: Now she'd have to leave the relative security of the trapdoor opening and walk around. She stood up and tested the strength of the floor with her right foot. It *seemed* strong enough. She took a few steps in. Down below, she could hear Steve reconstructing the tower and arguing with Elsie about who should go up next. She felt the cobwebs as she eased past, like hands stroking her hair, and flinched as something crunched underfoot. Why did she always have to be the first one into the dark, creepy places?

This attic was nothing like the ones at school. Those were really like rooms, large and spacious with proper walls and even polished floors in some places. But this attic was never intended for people; it was like the inside of an insect's exoskeleton: brown, dry, and dismal. Belladonna couldn't get rid of the feeling that she was in someone else's domain and that sooner or later the pinprick of light from Steve's flashlight would reveal something dreadful—probably involving compound eyes and four-part jaws.

Which is why she nearly jumped out of her skin when she heard a thump behind her, followed by frantic scrabbling. She whirled around, but it was only Elsie, hauling herself up and into the attic.

"Oooh, creepy!" she said, not very helpfully. "Look at these cobwebs! Have you found any spiders yet?"

"No," said Belladonna, trying not to think about it.

"I'll bet they're corkers!"

"Hello? Could I get a hand?"

Belladonna looked down the opening. Steve was standing on the rickety bedside table, holding up a hand.

"Hmm," she said, "how are we going to do this?"

"How about grabbing my hand and pulling?"

"You're too far down."

She looked around for inspiration, but there wasn't much in the way of potential tools in the attic. Then her eyes lit on the back of Elsie's head.

"Undo that ribbon," she commanded.

"What!?" Elsie spun around. "No! I've worn this for nearly one hundred years!"

"Well then, you're overdue for a change."

Elsie opened her mouth to object further, but thought better of it and turned her back to Belladonna, offering up her head. Belladonna reached up, untied the massive bow, and watched as Elsie's curls cascaded over her shoulders in shining corkscrews. She tried to suppress a pang of envy. Her mother had tried to curl her hair once, but as soon as she'd taken the curlers out, it had fallen into limp waves and within half an hour was hanging in its usual lank black strings.

"What?" asked Elsie, turning around and noticing the strange expression on Belladonna's face.

"Oh, nothing," mumbled Belladonna. "You have nice hair."

Elsie smiled and pushed a mass of curls back. Belladonna turned away, looped the wide ribbon around her hand, and shook her head. It was broad, but she could see that it would never take Steve's weight. She looked around again.

"Your belt," she said finally. "Let's try that!"

Elsie grumbled that she couldn't see why all these experiments had to be made with articles of *her* clothing, but she unfastened her sturdy canvas belt and handed it over. Belladonna lay on her stomach over the edge of the opening and dangled it down toward Steve.

"Can you reach this?"

Steve stretched his hand out and got a good grip. "Yes!"

"Good. Now, come on, Elsie—pull!"

Belladonna and Elsie heaved on their end of the

belt and hauled Steve up to the point where he could grab the edge of the opening with his other hand and scramble up.

"Brilliant!" he said as he stood up.

Belladonna smiled and gave Elsie her belt back. Elsie clipped it around her waist, retrieved the ribbon, and tied up her shiny curls.

"Nice hair," said Steve.

"Thanks," said Elsie, tying it back in a perfect bow again.

Belladonna glanced darkly from one to the other before turning back to the gloomy attic. As she did so, she felt a sudden sharp gust of wind on her neck and quickly aimed the flashlight at what seemed to be its source.

"Is that a door?"

Steve took the flashlight and made his way carefully across to the far angle of the roof. He brushed the cobwebs away from the beams and revealed a rusty deadbolt.

"Yes!"

He heaved back the bolt and pushed. There was a screech of wood and metal and the small door slowly swung open, revealing a perfect rectangle of starry sky. Elsie ran across the attic and leaned out.

"Oh, doesn't it look gorgeous . . . ohhhh . . ."

She suddenly looked ill and shrank back inside.

"It's the roof," said Steve. "It's high. What did you expect?"

"Does it look like we can get across?" asked Belladonna.

"Sure. I think. Come see."

Of course, he didn't turn around to try and light the floor, so Belladonna was left to feel her way over. The fact that Elsie had made it without any difficulty didn't fill her with any confidence—Elsie was one of those surefooted, sporty types. Her kind never tripped over their own feet, bumped into the furniture, or dropped the cut-glass trifle bowl that had been handed down in the family for years all over the brand-new beige carpet.

Sure enough, Belladonna walked about four steps before she tripped and landed flat on her face. Elsie laughed, but Steve was less amused.

"Belladonna!" he hissed. "Quiet! He'll hear us."

"Oh, right, he'll hear *me*," she muttered, standing up and brushing away as many of the cobwebs as she could find, "but he won't have heard you crashing about on the landing like a bull in a china shop! Anyway, I tripped over something."

"What," said Elsie, still sniggering, "a piece of spiderweb? A dead insect?"

Belladonna ignored her. For once, it hadn't been her innate clumsiness; she really had fallen over something quite big. She tried to feel around in the dark, but it was no good.

"Shine the light over here."

Steve turned around and pointed the light onto the floor with the attitude of someone who's fed up messing about with girls and really just wants to get out on the roof, thank you very much. He wafted the light back and forth impatiently and then stopped.

"What's that?" he said, suddenly interested.

There was a large, faded green box in the middle of the floor. It was covered in dust and cobwebs and looked as if it hadn't been touched for years. Belladonna peered at it—there was a single yellowing label in the center of the lid. Steve brought the light over and she crouched next to it, squinting at the overly florid script.

"What does it say?"

"It says 'Hunt' and there's a date: October 1753."

"Open it!" whispered Elsie excitedly. "I love presents!"

Belladonna hesitated. There was something about this simple green box that seemed dangerous . . . and tempting. She reached forward and removed the lid.

"What is it?"

"Tissue paper . . . hang on . . ."

She folded back the crumbling paper and revealed a small brass horn, about a foot long and almost black with tarnish.

"Hmph," said Steve, "is that all? Come on, we'd better get going."

He returned to the door and leaned out.

"We'll have to climb up here, onto the top. Then I think we can get all the way along to the end."

"There is no way that I can—" began Elsie.

"Hang on," interrupted Belladonna, still staring at the horn. "I think I know what this is. We should be able to go out the front door."

Steve and Elsie looked back as Belladonna took the horn out of the box.

"It's a hunting horn," she said.

Steve thought about this for a moment.

"So?"

"I think it will call the Hunt. The Wild Hunt."

"The who?"

"The Wild Hunt," explained Elsie. "It's a legend. They're hunters or knights or something and they're cursed to ride the night sky for all eternity."

"They didn't seem very cursed to me," said Belladonna. "They seemed quite happy about things, really. They've been showing up at home in the middle of the night for the last few days and every time they do, Aunt Deirdre takes off after them. She hasn't caught them yet. At least . . . I don't think she has."

Steve looked at her in disbelief. "Cursed?" he said finally. "Erm . . . are you sure that calling them on purpose is a good idea?"

"No," Belladonna stood up and joined them at the window. "But it would make a fantastic diversion, wouldn't it?"

"I suppose . . ."

"Wait a minute," said Elsie. "What if it just produces another problem and blocks us off from this exit as well?"

Belladonna and Steve thought about this for a moment.

"It's worth a try," announced Steve. "I mean, it's not like you can get onto the roof at all without having an attack of the heebies, and it's entirely possible that Belladonna and I will plunge to a sticky end way before we reach the last house. And even if we do reach the last house, what if the door into that attic is locked? This one was."

Belladonna leaned out of the window, put the horn to her lips, and blew.

The result wasn't quite what she'd expected. Instead of a clarion call to the night, what emerged was more the sound of a wet raspberry.

"Oh," she said, crestfallen, "there must be some kind of knack."

"Purse your lips up," said Steve, "like this."

His face looked so ridiculous that Elsie started to snigger again and this time Belladonna couldn't help joining in. The more she tried to straighten her face, the less likely it seemed that she would ever manage to purse her lips in the approved fashion.

"Stop it!" she squealed at Elsie. "You're making it worse!"

She raised the horn to her lips once more, caught a glimpse of Elsie making the "purse your lips" face, and collapsed in giggling hysterics again.

"Oh, give it here!" said Steve.

He snatched the horn from her hands, raised it to his lips, and loosed a deep, brassy peal into the sky. The long note started low, but soared upward until it seemed to reach to the horizon, clawing at the clouds and splitting the air itself. It was still echoing around the rooftops as he lowered the horn and handed it back to a stunned Belladonna.

"Trumpet lessons," he said. "My Dad's idea."

"What's that?" asked Elsie, pointing toward the horizon.

Out where the gray dawn was just beginning to prowl around the skyline, clouds were starting to gather. At first it seemed as though a wind must be moving the small night clouds toward a single point, but as they reached their destination, they started to swell and roll outward, like smoke billowing from a wet bonfire. Huge black thunderheads formed and the distant, deep sound of thunder itself rumbled across the sky.

"Um . . . whose idea was this?" said Steve.

The words were hardly out of his mouth when there was a deafening crack and the great thunderheads began to take on form as the Wild Hunt stampeded into the Land of the Dead, their hounds baying for blood and their great steeds foaming at the mouth and kicking up fire and sparks with their steely hooves. The black cloaks of the riders billowed behind them, and leading the pack was the tall man with the flashing, bottomless eyes and the mirthless smile.

"Get inside!" said Belladonna suddenly, as the Hunt bore down on the tiny house. "Get inside!"

Steve and Elsie were frozen with fascination and terror as the riders came closer. Belladonna grabbed first one and then the other and shoved them both back into the attic. Then she reached out and slammed the door shut, shooting the bolt and sinking to the floor with her hands over her ears as the Wild Hunt circled the house, shaking the whole terrace to its very foundations. The walls boomed and cracked and dust fell from every crevice as if a hurricane were bearing down from the tropics intent on reducing every decaying structure in the Land of the Dead to a pile of rotting splinters. The sound of the hounds and the rattle and crash of horse, bridle, and man filled their ears until they thought they could bear it no longer.

And then there was another sound. Far below the noise of the Hunt itself—the whimpering of a dog.

And then silence.

Belladonna, Steve, and Elsie looked at one another, straining to hear. Finally Belladonna stood up, slowly slid the bolt back, and pushed the door open. It swung out easily, revealing the rising sun and a clear sky. Steve and Elsie joined her and they each scanned the horizon for any sign of the black riders, but there was nothing.

"What about Ashe?" asked Steve.

Elsie turned on her heel, marched across the attic, and swung down to the floor below, temporarily forgetting her fear of heights. They heard her feet clattering down the stairs, then running to the back of the house.

"He's gone!" she yelled. "And the dog too!"

Belladonna and Steve joined her downstairs. Sure enough, the street outside was empty and the only sign that the Hound had ever been in the garden was a small patch of dead grass where its drool had fallen.

Belladonna picked up her jacket and shoved the horn into her backpack.

"Right," she said, "let's go."

"Now?" said Steve, not entirely convinced that Ashe was really gone. "He could be hiding behind a bush or something!"

"No," Belladonna shook her head. "He's gone. Which way is the House of Mists?"

"Um . . . west," said Elsie, who tended to agree with Steve on this one. "That way."

She pointed up the street. Belladonna flung open the front door and marched outside. The fresh air felt good after the stifling fear that had filled the house all night.

"Come on."

Steve and Elsie stepped outside and they started up the street toward the edge of town. As they put distance between themselves and the scene of the night's events, their strides became quicker and more confident. In the morning light, it seemed entirely possible that all their problems would be solved when they reached the House of Mists.

Belladonna was glad to be on the move and to be doing something definite, but behind her decisive action and breezy attitude something darker lurked. It was the memory of the last thing she saw before she bolted the door against the Wild Hunt: the face of the Leader, his smile flashing and his eyes glistening with recognition as he nodded slightly toward her. Belladonna had understood in that moment that although he had allowed himself to be used this time, there would be a price and he expected her to be the one to pay it.

13

Night Ravens

THEY HADN'T GONE far before the changes to the streets around them turned the town into something strange and unfamiliar, and for the first time Belladonna felt that she really was in a different world. The rapidly spreading decay had reduced the familiar buildings to an alien landscape. All around them, brick was rotting and flaking, plaster and stucco had fallen off in vast powdery sheets, and windows were cracked and broken. All plant life had succumbed to the spreading blight that had struck the great tree and been reduced to nothing more than dead, dusty compost and gaunt skeletons.

And then there was the silence.

Not a bird or insect sang or thrummed, no cars could be heard in the distance, and no planes flew overhead. The almost-imperceptible sounds that are all around wherever people live: the brush of bodies pushing past each other, the murmur of voices, the whisper sounds of jeaned legs walking. All this was absent. There was just the emptiness of the streets and the echo of their own footsteps on the crumbling tarmac.

After about half an hour, the road became narrower and the buildings were replaced with a long, high wall of pale brick. It reminded Belladonna of the grim Victorian warehouses she'd seen at the docks on a school trip last year. But unlike the warehouses, this wall was unpunctuated by windows and no effort had been made to add some decorative contrasting brickwork.

"I don't like this," said Steve.

"It wasn't like this before," said Elsie, her voice hushed as if someone might overhear. "The bus stop was just over there and it was all green fields and wildflowers."

Belladonna knew that they were all feeling the same oppression. She thought about going back, but when she turned to look back toward the town, she discovered that she couldn't see it at all, just miles of wall receding to a pinprick.

Elsie was squinting into the distance ahead. "You know," she said, "I think the walls stop up ahead. I can see sunlight."

She was right. The walls blocked out most of the early-morning light, but up ahead they could clearly make out a strip of sunshine lying across the path. They sped up, eager for some relief, and as they did so, the crumbling tarmac of the narrow road gave way altogether and they found themselves walking on a sandy country lane. Then the walls ended, but instead of the feeling of release they had expected, they found themselves hemmed in by towering hedgerows that were almost as high as the wall. The sunlight, it turned out, was the result of a few holes in an otherwise solid parapet of thorn and bramble. They stared at it in disbelief.

"Well," said Elsie finally, "at least there's one good thing."

"Which is?" asked Steve.

"It isn't dead," said Elsie, "so whatever is infecting the town hasn't got this far."

That was true, and did give Belladonna some hope about their destination. Perhaps the decay hadn't reached the House of Mists and the Conclave of Shadow was still there. She tried to feel optimistic, but somehow she kept returning to the thought that the reason these hedgerows weren't dead was because it was convenient to someone to keep them alive . . . and to keep travelers on the approved path.

"D'you remember that trip to the farm last year?" she asked.

"Yeah," said Steve, "it was miserable. And cold. And the smell!"

"This is kind of reminding me of that."

"How so?"

Belladonna looked back at the way they'd come, and forward down the narrow lane.

"The sheep," she said.

Steve looked at her, nonplussed, then a light suddenly dawned.

"Yes!" he said. "The way they herded them through the gate and into that narrow channel before they sheared them."

Belladonna nodded. Steve looked back and ahead, grimly aware that such methods weren't only used for things as benign as shearing.

"Shall we see if we can get through this hedgerow?" he said.

"I think that would be a really good idea."

They ran to the hedgerows on either side of the road and searched for anything that looked like a thinning of the branches, but the hedge might as well have been made of concrete. Some light filtered through from the other side, but the gaps were too small to even give them a glimpse of what lay beyond the narrow lane.

"Ow!" said Steve, after reaching in too far. "These things are sharp . . . whoa!"

"What?"

Belladonna and Elsie stopped what they were doing and turned to look at Steve, who was standing in front of the hedge with a strange expression on his face.

"Come here," he said quietly. "Watch this."

There was something in his voice that sent a chill through Belladonna. She and Elsie walked over to him, half expecting to see some particularly nasty insect.

"Watch," he said again.

He reached his hand into the hedge and deliberately scraped it against a thorn. Belladonna flinched as the blood trickled from his wrist onto the green hedge, but she was completely unprepared for what happened next.

As they watched, the branch where the blood had fallen began to absorb it. And as if that weren't creepy enough, the surrounding branches pressed toward the site of the blood, eagerly straining for a share of the bounty.

Belladonna's eyes opened wide. She'd seen plants that ate insects before; she'd even had a small Venus flytrap in her bedroom for a while. But plants that devoured human blood were something else altogether. She looked up and down the lane at the thick bramble hedge and wondered how much blood it had taken to grow so huge.

"That could work!" said Elsie suddenly.

Steve and Belladonna stared at her blankly.

"Didn't you see?" asked Elsie. "When the other tendrils were trying to get the blood, they made a thin patch. Right there. We could get through!"

"Elsie," said Belladonna, "that would take a lot of blood, and we sort of need ours."

"But it *would* work," insisted Elsie.

Belladonna rolled her eyes in frustration. Elsie's unbounded enthusiasm about everything was starting to grate and she had begun to wonder if she really did die in an accident or if perhaps her friends had helped her along the way. Strangely, Steve, who usually found everything that Elsie said irritating beyond words, was prowling in front of the hedge, as if looking for a slightly thinner spot.

"Steve," said Belladonna, suddenly concerned, "you can't be thinking . . ."

"We wouldn't need much," said Steve, "just a few good splashes."

"Well, where would . . . you're not going to cut yourself on purpose? What if it got infected? You could get tetanus!"

Steve shook his head, sat down on the dusty road, and rolled up his right jeans leg. Elsie and Belladonna walked over and looked down.

"Perfect!" announced Elsie. "That thing should bleed like a stuck pig!"

"You're kidding, right?" said Belladonna, knowing that he wasn't.

Steve grinned. The scab really was impressive. There was a good-sized central wound and several satellite scrapes that combined to create a mini planetary system on his knee.

"I fell off my bike two weeks ago," he explained. "My Mum was always on at me to stop messing with the scab, but if I had, it would've been better by now."

"How fast were you going?" asked Elsie, eager for all the gory details.

"Dunno," said Steve, starting to pick at it in an exploratory fashion, "but I hit Foster's grocery van and made a really good dent, so pretty fast, I think."

Belladonna couldn't bear to watch, but didn't want to seem girly about the whole thing.

"So," she said, marching toward the hedgerow, "what's the plan?"

"Well," said Elsie, joining her and examining the hedge critically, "if he stood here and hit the hedge there, then the branches would zoom in from either side and you and I could get through the thin spots."

"Okay," said Belladonna, nodding, "that could work. But . . ."

"But what?" asked Steve.

"Well, how are you going to get through?"

"I'll just have to be quick," grinned Steve. "Oh, hang on . . . we've got a gusher!"

The scab was off and blood was pouring down his knee. Steve stood up and half hopped to the hedge while trying to catch as much of the blood as he could. Belladonna and Elsie stood on either side and waited.

"Ready?"

"Of course we're ready!" said Elsie impatiently. "Go! Go!"

Steve flicked the blood at the hedge. For a moment it just sat there, dripping slowly down the thorns, then there was a rustling and a sort of high-pitched, barely there whine, and the branches on either side shot toward the site of the feast. Belladonna shuddered, but there wasn't much time to think about it as the hedgerow in front of her suddenly thinned and she could make out a piece of field and daylight through the knotted bramble.

Elsie went first, charging toward the hedge with her head down and ribbons flying. With a yell loud enough to raise the Dead, if there had been any except herself around, she launched through the gap. Belladonna watched, then took a deep breath and ran forward, getting up as much speed as possible before covering her head with her hands and diving in.

She landed with a thump next to Elsie, who was flushed with the thrill of it all.

"That was great!" said Elsie, adjusting her ribbon.

Belladonna smiled thinly and noticed that a nasty gash on Elsie's forearm was rapidly healing itself. In a moment she looked the perfect Edwardian girl again. Belladonna sighed. There were definitely some advantages to being dead. She had scratches right down both arms and the beginning of a bruise on her left knee and she knew they wouldn't be vanishing anytime soon.

"Are you okay?" yelled Steve from the other side.

"Yes," said Belladonna, "we're fine!"

She tried to peer back through the hedgerow, but the brambles had all returned to their usual positions and there was no sign of Steve or the path.

"Oh, come on," she heard him mutter, "bleed. *Bleed.*"

"Are you—?" began Elsie, but at that moment

there was a yell of triumph, a sort of splatting sound, and the whine and rustle of the thorn tendrils as they rushed toward the blood. Then there was an almighty crash as Steve rocketed out of the hedge and onto the ground next to them.

"Brilliant!" he said gleefully. "Did you hear that noise it made?"

"Yes," said Belladonna grimly as the branches returned to their original positions once again.

She stood up and looked around. As she had expected, the hedgerow was the only green thing around. The grass where they had landed was brown and dead and the few bushes that crouched in sad clumps across the hill were gray and decayed.

"Ew," said Steve, standing up and looking around, "what's that smell?"

"I think it's the plants," said Belladonna, "dying."

They tried holding their noses, but the putrid, composty smell just found its way in through their mouths instead.

"It's this way . . . I think," said Elsie.

"You think?" said Belladonna. "You mean you're not sure?"

"Well, not exactly. I mean, I usually take the bus."

"Why don't you just disappear and reappear where you want to be?"

"That only works in the Land of the Living. It's more ordinary here."

"Ordinary," said Steve. "Just the word I'd use for

a place with alchemists, huge hounds, flying hunts-men, and blood-eating shrubbery."

"The bus goes on the road," continued Elsie, ignoring him, "but some people like to walk and make a sort of camping trip out of it. I've heard them talk about crossing a plain. They said it was really pretty. The House is in the middle of a small wood and it has a garden. That's where they have the garden parties."

Belladonna and Steve looked at each other. They had no choice—they'd have to follow Elsie.

"Okay," said Belladonna finally, "lead the way."

Elsie smiled and marched off in what they all hoped was the right direction. Belladonna and Steve followed, but as they walked, Belladonna let the black curtain of her hair slip down to conceal her face. Something was wrong about this. She knew it, deep in her bones. If the House of Mists was so important, if it held the Dream Door and the Conclave of Shadow met there, then surely anyone with evil intentions would know that too. But on the other hand, her grandfather had seemed so sure. And after all, what else were they going to do?

"I wonder what happened to Ashe," said Steve, to no one in particular.

"Maybe they got him," said Elsie cheerfully. "Maybe those dogs ripped him to pieces!"

"They probably just scared him away," said Belladonna gloomily. "He'll turn up again."

Elsie glanced at Belladonna, taken aback by the pessimism, but she couldn't see her face for the hair.

"She's always like that," explained Steve drily. "Belladonna's known for her relentless cheerfulness all over school. Gets us all down, actually, the way she constantly looks on the bright side."

Elsie looked at Steve, who tried to maintain a straight face, but couldn't stop the smile that tilted one side of his mouth. They both grinned and started to do imitations of Belladonna's walk, stomping along behind her with their chins down.

They were still stomping and whispering when the target of their teasing tripped over and tumbled down a stinking, slimy bank of what had recently been daffodils.

"Ew!" said Elsie. "That looks disgusting!"

"You're lucky," said Steve. "You can't smell it. You okay, Belladonna?"

Belladonna looked back up and was about to say that she was fine, when the words froze on her lips. Steve's smile vanished too.

"What is it?" he whispered.

"Behind you," said Belladonna.

Steve and Elsie turned around slowly. A few meters away, near the top of a small rise, Ashe's Hound was watching them.

"Oh, no," Steve whispered.

Belladonna scrambled to her feet.

"Maybe we should run," suggested Elsie.

Steve shook his head. "That would probably just

encourage it. Besides, I don't really want to turn my back on it, do you?"

"So we just wait for it to run down the hill and rip our throats out?" said Elsie. "That doesn't sound like a particularly good plan either."

They stared at the Hound and the creature stared back but didn't move a muscle.

"Look," said Belladonna, "why don't we walk away slowly? That's what they always say on those wildlife programs on the telly. If, you know, if a grizzly is after them or something."

Elsie and Steve thought about this for a moment.

"Okay," he said finally, "yeah. Slowly."

They began to move away from the dog, through the narrow gulley and up the opposite rise. The Hound didn't move; it just watched them go and drooled.

Once they'd reached the top of the next rise, they began to feel more confident—maybe it was just watching. They walked down the other side with more of a spring in their step.

"Maybe he can see through the eyes of the dog," suggested Steve. "I saw a film like that once. There was this scientist. It was on an island, I think. Or was that another film? Anyway, the point is, he had all these animals that were in his power and—"

"My mother says films are vulgar," volunteered Elsie. "She says educated people don't go."

"Your mother sounds like a whole heap of fun," said Steve.

"Steve . . ." Belladonna yanked the sleeve of his jacket. "He's back."

He turned around and sure enough, there was the Hound on the crest of the rise they'd just come down. They looked at each other and carefully repeated what they'd done before: They walked slowly through the valley and up the next small hill. The Hound stayed where he was until they vanished from sight and then ran after them until he could see them again.

"I hate this," said Steve. "What is he waiting for?"

"Maybe he's waiting for this," said Belladonna.

They'd just reached the crest of the next rise, but instead of more undulating peaks and valleys, there was only flat ground ahead. The perfect place for a dog to run.

"Better and better," said Steve.

Belladonna nodded hopefully as they started their descent into the flat ground, but they hadn't gone far before the Hound was at the crest of the last rise. This time, however, he didn't just watch, but loped slowly down toward them.

They picked up the pace a little, but the dog was getting closer, and now they could hear the low guttural growl that they'd first heard on the night they'd eavesdropped at Grandma Johnson's.

"What are we going to do?" said Steve, casting about for cover.

"We're going to have to stand and fight," said Elsie grimly.

"Easy for you to say," said Steve. "You're already dead."

Belladonna stopped. "Use your ruler," she said.

"You *are* joking, right? That dog would snap it like a twig!"

"Maybe not. Try it."

Steve rolled his eyes and pulled the sorry-looking plastic ruler from his pocket. If anything, it looked even more flimsy now than when Belladonna had handed it to him.

They all looked at it.

"Look—" began Steve dubiously.

"Maybe we should run," said Elsie. "It can't be that far to the forest. We might make it."

"Point it at the Hound," said Belladonna.

By now the Hound had picked up speed and was running across the dead grassland toward them. Steve sighed and pointed the stick at the black beast.

"There. Happy now? Whoa!"

He dropped to one knee with a thud. The ruler was no longer a ruler but a four-foot-long sword, the blade gleaming in the fading light and the guard and handle inlaid with gold and precious stones. Steve could barely lift it. He hauled himself to his feet as the dog leapt toward them and swung it with all his strength.

The Hound flew over their heads and landed behind them. Steve spun around, carried by the momentum of the sword, before lowering it slowly to the ground. Belladonna could see that it was far too heavy. How on earth was he supposed to fight anything with this? Yet even as she watched him, the sword seemed to become less unwieldy. He lifted it up again and bounced it in his hand a few times, then he tried a few small practice swings. The more he held it, the more comfortable he seemed to be and the more the sword became like an extension of his arm, as if he'd trained for years for just such a moment.

"My hat!" said Elsie. "Good show!"

"Right," he muttered, ignoring her. "Right. Come here, you rotten Chihuahua!"

The Hound circled them, waiting for that split second when Steve would lose concentration or drop his guard. It felt like hours—only a fingernail of blood red sun remained above the horizon, and a fetid wind had started to blow from the distant forest. Finally the great Hound took his chance and with a blood-curdling howl, he leapt at Steve's throat.

Steve swung the sword and hit the Hound squarely across the neck, but instead of the expected blood, nothing but black dust spilled from the wound. Steve hesitated for a second, then struck again, hitting the dog in the stomach. Again, nothing but dust spewed forth, as if the dog were a bag of soot. The Hound wasn't prepared to give up, however, and made one last attack, not at Steve but straight at Belladonna.

She dropped to the ground and covered her head

as Steve stepped forward and slashed at the Hound again.

And then it was gone. The black dust filled the air and clogged their lungs, and there was the stench of death and rotting eggs, but no Hound. Steve pulled Belladonna away from the cloud of dust and stared in admiration at the sword, but even as he watched, it shriveled back to a frail plastic ruler.

"That was amazing!" he said. "Did you see that? Whack! Whack! Brilliant!"

Belladonna nodded.

"Thanks for not letting me throw this thing away!" he said as he slid it back into his pocket. "Too brilliant!"

"What did it feel like?" asked Elsie, her face flushed with excitement. "You know, when you sliced into it?"

"It was just—"

"We ought to move," interrupted Belladonna. "He might send something else. You know, if he was watching us through the Hound."

"Yes, yes, right. Wow. Did you see that? That thing was heavy too. I didn't think I was going to be able to lift it at first and then—whang!"

They walked on through the dark toward what they hoped was the forest and the House of Mists beyond.

"I suppose this means you *are* the Paladin, doesn't it?" said Belladonna after a while.

"Whatever that is," said Steve, still flushed with

excitement. "We must be really close to the forest. I can hear the trees."

He was right. The silence of a moment before had been replaced with the rustle of leaves in the breeze. Belladonna stopped walking to listen. She pushed her hair behind her ears and cocked her head. Something was wrong. There wasn't a breeze. And there wasn't a tree in sight. She turned and looked back, just in time to see a great black cloud bearing down on them out of the sky.

She yelped and pulled Steve and Elsie down to the ground. The black Night Ravens raced overhead, the moonlight glancing from their murderous beaks and claws. They swooped by, narrowly missing their quarry, then wheeled around far above the ground and prepared for another attack.

"Ow!" yelped Elsie. "They're not supposed to do that!"

"No? What are they supposed to do?" Belladonna ducked again as a single huge bird zoomed by her head.

"They're supposed to watch. That's all, just watch. That's what I was told anyway."

"Oh, yeah?" said Steve. "Who told you that?"

"Slackett," said Elsie.

Belladonna and Steve almost forgot about the birds. They both turned to her in utter amazement.

"Slackett?!"

"Yes," said Elsie, a little sheepishly.

"And you believed him?" Belladonna couldn't

believe that Elsie had trusted Slackett even for a moment.

Elsie shrugged and then dived to the ground as the flock came screaming down at them again.

"Oh, great," said Steve. "How are we supposed to fight them? You can't even see them!"

"Let's run," said Elsie, jumping to her feet.

Belladonna and Steve hesitated for a second and then nodded. They all sprang to their feet and tried to get as far as they could before the birds swept down again. Belladonna estimated they'd gone about a hundred meters before the sound of the wings bore down once more. They dropped to the ground and the birds missed their target, then leapt to their feet and ran again. Once more the birds tore in and once more they dropped to the ground, but this time Belladonna felt a wing brush past.

"They're getting better."

"I know," said Steve. "I think we're going to have to take a stand. We can't do this all night."

He was right. They were nowhere near the forest, so far as she could make out, and even if they were, the birds would get them long before they reached the shelter of any trees. When she turned back, Steve already had the ruler in his hand and was waiting for the telltale sound of the great black wings. There was silence.

They strained to make out anything in the starless sky, but nothing could be seen.

"Maybe they've given up," said Steve.

"I should cocoa!" scoffed Elsie. "Look out! Here they come!"

Belladonna looked up. The great black birds were circling far above. They seemed to stop moving for a moment and then, like a single guided missile, they shot toward the earth.

Steve pointed the stick but this time, instead of a sword, he found himself holding a great longbow, six feet of seasoned yew. He looked around, desperate.

"There are no arrows!" he yelled.

Belladonna froze for a moment as the Night Ravens screeched in their descent, then she reached down, tore a handful of rotting grass from the ground, held out her right hand, and yelled, straining to be heard above the birds.

"Naðu ti am!"

No sooner had she said the words than there was a slight hissing sound, like air escaping from a balloon, and her hand was full of arrows.

Steve didn't say anything; he just grabbed an arrow, strung it into the bow, and strained to pull it back. At first it seemed that the bow was not going to bend. He grunted with the effort, then relaxed, took a deep breath, and pulled on the string again. This time the bow bent back and the arrow screamed toward the birds, hitting one. The wounded bird let out a great cry of anguish and dissolved into a green vapor that fell to the earth like foul-smelling rain.

"Right," he muttered. "Right."

The birds had wheeled away in surprise after the first had died, but now they regrouped and poured out of the clouds toward them again. Belladonna handed some of the arrows to Elsie.

"Here," she said, "keep giving them to him."

Elsie nodded and fanned the arrows out in her hands to make it easier for Steve to grab them.

"This is like *Ivanhoe*!" she said. "I can be Rebecca and you can be the drippy Rowena."

Belladonna rolled her eyes and passed Steve another arrow.

Steve fired. Again. And again. And again. The arrows filled the air like hail and every one found its mark. Soon the cloud of Night Ravens was reduced to three huge birds, no longer flying as a single attacking weapon, but dipping and weaving overhead like fighter pilots in a dogfight. Belladonna could see that even with the magic of the mysterious ruler, Steve was beginning to feel the strain. Sweat poured down his face and he was finding it more and more difficult to raise the great longbow toward the sky. Still, he grunted, pulled back the bow, and fired twice more.

Only one Night Raven was left. It circled lazily in the sky, getting lower and lower. By the time Steve realized it was within attacking distance, it was almost too late. He fired, but this time the arrow failed to fly true—it only tipped a wing and the bird was still coming. He reached for another arrow, but even as

Belladonna handed it to him, she knew it was too late. The screeching black bird flew into his face, claws raised and beak agape. Steve dropped the bow, ripped the bird off his face, threw it to the ground, and stabbed it with the arrow. The bird screamed and vanished into a small pool of green sludge.

Steve sat down on the ground, gasping for breath.

"Ew," he said, wiping the green goo from his fingers. "Yuck. That was close, wasn't it?"

Belladonna nodded and pulled him away from the slimy remains of the bird as the ruler returned to its true form.

"You're bleeding," said Elsie matter-of-factly.

"I am?"

Steve raised a hand to the long scratch that the last Night Raven had left down the right side of his face.

"Huh, so I am! Oh, well. That one when I fell off the bike was worse. Come on, let's get to the House of Mists before any more nasties come after us."

Belladonna and Elsie marched off across the plain, but Steve hesitated and took one look back to where the Night Raven had met its end. The green slime had nearly all vanished into the ground, leaving a black mark that steamed slightly and seemed to sizzle softly like water on a hot griddle. He put his hand to his face. The scratch wasn't deep, but the bird had hit with some force. It felt like a bruise was coming.

He ran and caught up as the three of them walked across the flat plain, the dead ground crunching underfoot as unseen creatures of the blighted land skittered around them.

The inky blackness of the starless night made it difficult to see, but at least the flatness of the plain meant that there was little to trip over.

"Um . . . are you sure this is the way?" asked Belladonna.

"No," said Elsie, "but it has to be. I mean, we'll get there eventually, won't we?"

"I've heard stories about people who were lost in the desert and thought they were going in a straight line," said Steve, "but it turned out that they were just walking 'round and 'round in circles."

"Oh, that's helpful," said Belladonna.

After going a few more meters, it became obvious that they wouldn't get anywhere in the all-enveloping darkness.

"Here," said Steve, pulling his keys and the tiny flashlight out of his pocket. "Whoa!" He lunged for the keys, but they fell clanking to the ground.

"Oh, great," he muttered, dropping to his knees and feeling around among the sludge of rotting undergrowth.

Elsie bent down and pushed the ground cover around until she heard the jangle of metal on metal. She retrieved the keys, turned on the flashlight, and started to hand them back.

"Are you alright?" she asked.

Belladonna turned. There was something in Elsie's

tone of voice that was different. It had lost its flip edge and sounded genuinely concerned.

One look at Steve told her why. His face was pale and there were dark circles around his eyes.

"I'm fine," said Steve, "just tired. Let's keep moving."

Belladonna glanced at Elsie. She didn't look happy and it was with an unfamiliar gentleness that she helped Steve to his feet. She looked at Steve again. He stuck the flashlight under his chin and made grinning zombie noises before handing it to Belladonna.

"Here," he said, "you go first."

Belladonna nodded and took the key ring. It was probably nothing. And why wouldn't he be tired after fighting off the Hound *and* a flock of dive-bombing Night Ravens? She led the way across the grassland, peering ahead in the desperate hope of seeing the ragged outline of the forest on the horizon. The hours stretched on, and still there was no sign of trees. What if Steve was right? What if they *had* been walking around in circles?

"Can we stop for a bit?" said Steve. "I feel a little sick."

Belladonna turned around. She had been going to tell him that they were nearly there, but what she saw turned her words to dust.

Steve seemed barely able to stand, and his face was white. Not pale, but white. The scratch on his face seemed larger than it had been, and something was trickling out of it. She thought it must be blood, but from where she was standing it looked black, like oil.

"What?" he said, barely able to keep his eyes open.

"We're . . . we're nearly there," she said, managing a smile.

He nodded wearily. Belladonna looked at Elsie, her eyes wide with fear, but Elsie tried not to look at her and walked a little way ahead, as if trying to see how far they had to go.

"Why don't we stay here for the night?" she said. "We'll make much better time in the daylight."

Belladonna nodded. It was obvious that Steve wasn't going to go very far and maybe a rest was all he needed. Maybe the exhaustion was just a side effect of the magic.

"I'll see if I can find anything dry," said Elsie, "for a fire."

She wandered off as Steve sank gratefully to the ground.

"You really don't look well," said Belladonna.

"Funny that," said Steve, his eyes sparkling for a moment, "because I feel positively chipper."

Belladonna smiled and started to clear away some of the rotting grass.

"Nice work with the arrows, by the way," said Steve.

"Thanks."

"Mind you, if you really were the Spellbinder, you probably could've come up with something really spectacular."

Belladonna glanced up. Steve was grinning and almost looked like himself, but the moment was brief. Soon he was lying back, sweat running down his pallid face and the black goo seeping from his wound.

"What did he say?" he mumbled.

"Who?" Belladonna tried not to sound as afraid as she felt.

"Your grandfather. What did he say that made you believe it was him?"

"My name. When I was little, I couldn't say my name. He knew what I called myself."

"What was that?"

"Jelly Bun," said Belladonna.

Steve smiled. "Now there's some ammunition."

Belladonna smiled back, but even as she did, his eyes closed as if the sheer effort of keeping them open was too much.

"I'm really tired," he mumbled. "I'm just going to sleep for a bit."

Elsie returned with an armful of twigs and sticks. The flickering light only made Steve look worse. After about an hour of fitful sleep, he woke up, and Belladonna broke out the last of the ham sandwiches, but he shook his head.

"I'm thirsty." His voice was barely a whisper.

She nodded and fished about in her bag for the last can of Tizer. She helped him drink it and waited while he drifted off to sleep again. As she moved back to her seat near the fire, she caught Elsie's expression as she watched.

"You know!" she whispered. "Tell me! What's wrong with him?"

Elsie tried to ignore her, but Belladonna's eyes bore into her soul.

"I think he might be poisoned," she said. "I think . . . there's a possibility . . ."

"What?" Belladonna's voice was flat. She knew what was coming, but for some reason she needed to hear Elsie say it.

"He could be dying."

"No, that can't be!" Her voice caught in her throat. "It's just a scratch!"

"Look," whispered Elsie, "there's no point arguing, I'm just telling you what I know. Slackett said the Night Ravens' beaks and claws are poisonous. If they get you, you're dead. But I thought he meant for us, not for you. Not for the Living."

"But that doesn't make any sense," said Belladonna. "Everyone here is already dead. What's the point of a poison that does that?"

"Not dead like dead in your world," explained Elsie, "dead as in *dead*. Wiped out. Erased from the nine worlds. Gone."

Belladonna stared at her, but saw nothing. She heard nothing. She couldn't feel the cool of the breeze or the heat from the fire. She glanced at Steve and her mouth felt dry. Could it really happen as quickly as that? One minute everything is fine and the next . . .

"Maybe he's wrong," she said, turning back to Elsie and trying to sound confident. "Slackett didn't look like the sharpest pencil in the box to me. Besides, when did he tell you all this? I thought you didn't like Ashe?"

"I don't," said Elsie, "and neither does Slackett."

"Then why doesn't he do something?"

"I don't know. I think he's waiting."

"For what?"

"To see what Ashe is really up to. But he's only one person. . . . What can one person do?"

Belladonna stared at her. It was heartening to know that they weren't the only ones who knew that Ashe was behind the disappearance of the ghosts, but she really would have preferred a more substantial ally than Slackett. And Elsie was right, what could he do? All she'd actually seen him do was sweep the floor in Ashe's laboratory. Although he did give her Steve's stick.

She felt confused; on the one hand she wanted Slackett to be on their side and to have a plan to save the ghosts, but that would mean that he had probably told Elsie the truth when he said the Night Ravens were poisonous. In her heart she knew that he was an ally, but she couldn't help but cling to the desperate hope that perhaps he wasn't. She looked at Steve and felt the tears burning in her eyes.

"I can't leave him here," she said. "I can't go home and . . . I can't tell his Mum and Dad . . . There must be something! What about . . . what's it called? A—"

"An antidote?"

Belladonna nodded frantically.

"I don't know," said Elsie. "I just don't know."

Belladonna looked up at the starless sky. How could this be happening? How could she have let it happen? He had wanted to go home. It had been her idea to stay. And now . . .

She took off her jacket and laid it gently over him. His eyes flickered open.

"Something's wrong," he said.

"I know," she said.

He tried to sit up, but she easily pushed him back down. He raised his right hand and touched the suppurating scratch on his cheek.

"It was the Night Ravens, wasn't it?"

"Yes. Their claws and beaks are poison, apparently."

"Information that would have been helpful a while ago," he grinned, and for a moment Belladonna saw a flicker of the Steve who had given Elsie such a hard time.

"It'll be alright," she lied. "You just need to rest."

"I know," he whispered.

"Belladonna! Belladonna! Wake up!"

Belladonna opened her eyes and sat up, alarmed.

She couldn't believe she'd fallen asleep. She had meant to stay awake, just in case Steve felt better or wanted something to eat or . . .

"He's gone," said Elsie, fighting back tears. "I couldn't do anything! It was so quick! I couldn't do anything!"

"Dead?" cried Belladonna, jumping to her feet. "He can't! He—"

"No," said Elsie, "gone."

Belladonna spun around. Elsie was right. There was no sign of Steve. Where he had been lying there was nothing but her old jacket with the fake-fur collar.

"But how . . ."

"I'd been out to get more sticks," sobbed Elsie, "for the fire . . . you know. And when I got back . . . he was sinking! It was . . . like a . . . like a . . ."

Elsie's face crumpled as she gave in to her fear and guilt. Belladonna walked over to her jacket. There was something not quite right about it. She reached down to pick it up and then gasped.

"Elsie! Look!"

Elsie ran over as Belladonna held up the jacket by one sleeve.

"I know!" she said. "It swallowed him! The earth . . . it just . . ."

Fully half of the jacket was buried in the ground, the earth set hard around it as if it had been there, half buried, for years.

Belladonna hesitated for only a moment and then

started frantically digging. Elsie watched, then suddenly seemed to snap out of her distress and remember that she was a no-nonsense Edwardian girl and blubbing was for babies. She threw herself at the patch of ground and joined Belladonna in heaving handfuls of earth away. They quickly released the jacket, but that was all—there was no sign of Steve. After a few more minutes of fruitless excavation, Belladonna stood up, brushed herself off, and slipped the jacket back on.

"Come on," she said grimly, blinking back the tears. "Let's find the House of Mists."

"But . . ." started Elsie.

"He's gone. And so is the amulet. Ashe has what he wanted and we have to try to stop him. That's all we can do."

14

The House of Mists

BELLADONNA AND ELSIE trudged on across the plain in silence. Every so often Belladonna could feel Elsie sneaking a peek at her. She knew she expected her to cry, and maybe she would. But later.

"Elsie . . ."

"Yes?"

"You said the Night Ravens were supposed to watch. Does that . . . I mean, does that mean that Steve was right about the Hound as well?"

"About it being Ashe's eyes?" Elsie kicked at a slime-covered stone in her path. "I suppose. I didn't know about the Hound, though. Slackett only mentioned the Ravens. Why?"

"If he can't see us through their eyes any more, he'll know we killed them. And that we're still on our way to the House of Mists."

Belladonna saw Elsie shoot a quick glance in her direction, as if she expected her resolve to falter, but she had just wanted to be sure. If Ashe knew where they were going, he was probably on his way too. They just had to make sure that they got to the Conclave of Shadow first.

After a few hours, Belladonna began to feel her steely determination wane. It seemed that they would never get there, that surely they must have come the wrong way.

"There it is!" cried Elsie. "Look! The forest!"

"Are you sure those are trees?" said Belladonna dubiously.

They certainly didn't look much like trees. The trunks were twisted and black and their roots rose above the ground in stark arches as if they were struggling to break their connection with the earth. Above them the thin branches strained upward, wrenching the trees away from the ground. Anywhere seemed preferable to staying in their native earth, even the inevitable death and decay.

"Yes!" said Elsie. "We're nearly there!"

Within an hour, they were on the edge of the forest, though it turned out to be more of a small wood. They made their way carefully, picking their way over gnarled branches and through slimy black undergrowth. Every so often they'd hear the unmistakable sound of something skittering through the trees, but they never saw anything.

Then, suddenly, they were through, standing on a small rise above open ground. They peered through the hovering mist that shrouded the ground and saw it. A garden.

Not just any garden, though. This was a vast formal landscape of trees, shrubs, and flower beds, all connected with a complicated interlocking latticework of paths. Vaulting arbors shaded narrow footpaths, and lanes of artfully trimmed topiary shapes drew the eye forward to elegant fountains and long, narrow reflecting pools. Near the center was a small pavilion with tall windows and welcoming glass doors, on either side of which were lollipop-shaped orange trees in huge terracotta pots.

Of course, all the plants were dead, but that only added to the architectural qualities of the garden. Instead of being a knot of greenery and color, the garden was a symphony of black, brown, and gray. Each plant, bush, and tree had decayed in its own way, some leaving only skeletal remains while others still boasted full heads of crisp foliage. The effect was one of pared-down beauty, like an old lady who still has the fantastic bones that made her admired in youth.

Belladonna led the way silently through the black trees and onto the garden path. They walked along the gray gravel lane, gazing at the plants around them. White marble stones marked the edges of the well-turned flower beds where gray shrubs rustled in the light breeze and the glistening, composty remains of flowers slowly sank back into the earth. The gurgle of the fountains was the only sound, but far from being crystalline and sparkling, the water was green with algae and smelled of fever ponds. Inside the pavilion, a table was laid for tea, but the cakes and scones had crumbled to dust and mold was growing up the sides of the teacups and out of the spout of the pot.

They made their way on slowly, down narrow paths and up wider boulevards. Once, Elsie tried touching a topiary lion, but the black leaves crumbled away as if her hand were poison. And still there was more: lattice-work arbors, covered in dismal tendrils and long-dead spiderwebs; the stark beauty of the bushes and flowers; and the brittle grace of well-pruned cypress.

"That's it!" said Elsie suddenly, as they emerged from yet another rose-trellised bower. "It's the House of Mists!"

Belladonna joined her and looked out across a brown sunken lawn to a sweeping marble stair that led up to a balustraded terrace. The terrace sur-rounded what was obviously the back of the kind of house Belladonna had only seen on school trips or period dramas on TV.

It was massive and stately, built of a white stone that gleamed in the late-afternoon light. Tall windows gazed across the garden like unseeing eyes, and massive urns decorated the pediments. They walked toward it across the sunken garden and past a stand of trees, which turned out to be concealing yet more of the imposing building. Two wings stretched out from the central structure, each apparently housing a long gallery on the second floor, where the windows were even taller and more unblinkingly impressive.

"This is the back," said Elsie. "Maybe we should go in the front."

She led the way around the terrace to a brick wall planted with espaliered pear trees. They walked out of the garden through a wooden door, along a narrow path past what appeared to be a dead herb garden, and out to the front of the house.

If the back had seemed impressive, the front was truly daunting in its splendor.

Two sets of marble steps curved around to a large covered porch that was guarded by eight soaring white pillars. The pillars ended in cascading carved acanthus leaves, above which was a stately pediment with a long marble frieze showing what Belladonna assumed to be gods and goddesses reclining in a variety of poses. At the center of the frieze was a statue of a woman on a chariot, ready to gallop out of the stone and away.

"Who's that?" whispered Belladonna.

"The Queen of the Abyss," replied Elsie, awestruck. "I saw her once. Only from a distance. She has a chariot drawn by a pterodactyl and bats follow her wherever she goes. She rules the Land of the Dead."

"Well, she's not doing a great job at the moment," remarked Belladonna, staring at the beautiful yet grim marble face. It reminded her of someone. Someone she'd met.

"Let's get on with this," she said finally, reaching for the huge brass doorknob.

Elsie hung back, looking at the blank windows and listening for a sound, any sound.

"What is it?" asked Belladonna.

"It's just . . . well, at first I thought the garden was dead because, you know, everything else is."

"Yes," said Belladonna, "it's been spreading from the town."

"But what if it isn't?" said Elsie. "There was something about the garden that seemed sort of . . . established."

"You think it started here," said Belladonna.

"Yes. I don't know. But maybe."

Belladonna looked up at the imposing polished mahogany front doors, then turned on her heel and came back down. If Ashe was already there, then strolling in the front door would be a really bad idea.

"Let's go in the back," she announced grimly.

Elsie nodded and they retraced their steps to the rear of the house. The door there was almost as imposing. Belladonna turned the handle.

"Locked," she said.

"What about the windows?"

Belladonna glanced at Elsie and began to examine the windows. They all appeared to be locked, but she gave each one an exploratory jiggle, just to be sure.

"No good," she said.

She sighed and wandered away, trying to take in

the whole house to see if there was anything like a sturdy drainpipe near an open window. She knew that Steve would've found a way in already, but she lacked his crucial sneaking skills. She pushed her hair back from her face, turned, and looked out over the garden. It was so beautiful in its monochromatic way, and the silence made her feel calm even amid all the sorrow and dread.

A small breeze swooped across the lawn and stroked her face. It was slightly warm and smelled of summer. She tried to imagine the garden in all its glory, green and fragrant, with flowers bursting from buds and the steady drone of ever-industrious bees. The Conclave of Shadow had chosen a nice place for their meetings—it certainly knocked the socks off Grandma Johnson's front room where the Eidolon Council met. So much so that Belladonna was finding it hard to believe that the two really consulted on anything. Grandma Johnson had said that the two councils supervised relations between the Living and the Dead, but in the normal run of things, there couldn't really be much to supervise, and Grandpa had said that the Conclave of Shadow didn't really do much of anything. She hoped that he was wrong and that the Council was already working on a way to return the ghosts to the Land of the Dead and open the doors so they could once more move freely between their home and the Land of the Living. She smiled a little at the thought of her parents waiting for her again after school, her father anxious for the paper and her mother waiting on tenterhooks for the next episode of *Staunchly Springs*. But no sooner had the happy image floated into her consciousness than it was pushed aside by the memory of Steve, slowly dying in front of the small fire on the plain, and her Granddad sacrificing himself to save them from Dr. Ashe. Belladonna shook her head quickly, pushing the memories aside. Dwelling on the past wasn't going to help and right now she needed to think clearly. Even if it was more than likely that the Conclave of Shadow had gone the way of all the other ghosts, she and Elsie still had to try to find them—they had to be sure.

She strolled down the steps toward the brown grass. It was when she reached the bottom that she saw it: a small window set into the bank.

"Hey!" she yelled. "Over here!"

"What?" Elsie ran over.

"A window," she said. "The terrace must be over some part of the house."

Elsie grinned and examined the window. It was small but had the air of something that had been forgotten. The wooden frame was damp and rotted and the glass was thick with years of accumulated dirt.

"Someone hasn't been looking after this," she said quietly, taking hold of the frame and giving it a sharp tug up.

There was a loud crack as the latch gave way and the lower sash jerked upward, breaking the glass in the upper pane.

"Oops."

"Where does it lead?" asked Belladonna, peering into the blackness.

"Only one way to find out," said Elsie matter-of-factly.

She stood up, made sure her ribbon was secure and her skirts smooth, then clambered over the sill and let herself down into the room below. This was immediately followed by a yelp, a thump, and an impressive metallic crash.

"Elsie!" hissed Belladonna. "Are you alright?"

"Yes," she whispered back loudly, "but you should watch that second step!"

Belladonna smiled, tucked her hair behind her ears, and lowered herself into the darkness. She felt around with her right foot, peering into the blackness for something solid. Eventually she located something hard and reasonably sturdy and crept in.

"It's the top of an oven!" whispered Elsie. "See?"

As her eyes slowly got used to the dark, she could see that she was perched on what was presumably the air vent, with the actual cooktop about three feet below. Elsie was standing on the floor, surrounded by upended saucepans and lids.

"Is it on?" she asked, nodding in the direction of the six huge gas rings beneath her.

"Yes, so you'd better hotfoot it down here," said Elsie, cracking up. "No, of course it's not on!"

Belladonna scowled as she lowered herself carefully down onto the top of the stove and dropped lightly to the floor.

Once she was down, they both turned around and had a good look at where they were. The kitchen was like nothing either of them had ever seen — it seemed to take up acres of space, with dozens of ovens around the walls, as well as three huge fireplaces with massive iron spits ready to go the next time anyone showed up with a wild boar or a whole moose. The center of the room was occupied by ranks of long wooden worktables littered with bowls, chopping blocks, condiment boxes, and spoons. Gleaming copper pans hung in graduated ranks from massive racks above their heads, and huge sinks stood ready for the truckloads of washing up that would be needed for even the humblest tea prepared in this colossal kitchen.

"Wow," said Elsie.

"You could feed hundreds out of a place like this," said Belladonna.

"Thousands," added Elsie. "Come on, let's go upstairs and find the Conclave."

She marched off toward the door. Belladonna followed, but there was a knot in the pit of her stomach telling her to take care.

The kitchen door led out into a narrow hallway that seemed to stretch interminably in either direction. Elsie looked up and down, then just picked a direction and marched off. Belladonna followed, cautiously glancing out of the small grubby windows that lined one side of the corridor as she went. The windows revealed nothing more than an empty cobblestoned courtyard. Belladonna noticed that the cobbles were wet and looked up at the narrow patch of suddenly iron-gray sky. The whole setup reminded her of scenes in those depressing Victorian novels they were always making them read at school.

"It seems so empty," she murmured. "Are we too late?"

They turned a corner and started down another equally unpromising corridor, but they hadn't gone far before a movement across the courtyard drew her attention. Belladonna looked out and there, on the second floor of the opposite wing, she saw a light, moving slowly.

"Elsie, look," she whispered.

Elsie stopped and returned to Belladonna. "There must be someone there," she whispered. "Maybe the Conclave is still here after all."

"I have a bad feeling about this," said Belladonna.

Elsie tried to smile encouragingly, but Belladonna could tell that she had exactly the same feeling. They had been so much better off out in the open where they could see what was coming. Here, they could turn a corner and be done for.

"Come on," said Elsie finally. "In for a penny."

"My mother used to say that," said Belladonna, following. "It's a pretty stupid saying when you think about it."

Elsie stopped in front of a door and opened it carefully, making sure that it didn't creak. They peered inside. There was a narrow staircase leading steeply upward.

"Servants' stairs," said Elsie.

The stairs were old and wooden and curled upward in a wide spiral. Elsie started to climb, but Belladonna winced as the old stairs groaned beneath her feet.

"Quiet!" hissed Belladonna. "Will you be quiet! We don't know what's up there!"

"The hall, I should imagine. Come on!"

She disappeared around the first bend. Belladonna quickly caught up, grabbed her belt, and yanked her to a halt.

"Let's at least *try* to be quiet," said Belladonna.

Elsie nodded and the two of them started up the stairs again, feeling each step and trying to avoid creaks. Five more minutes brought them to a large wooden door. Elsie glanced back at Belladonna, who nodded. She pushed the door open slowly and they both stepped out.

They were on a wide landing above the entry hall, bounded on one side by vast portraits and on the other by a sturdy mahogany balustrade. Looking down, they could see an elaborate marble floor and a sweeping grand staircase. Above them, an enormous stained-glass dome sent shards of colored light across the walls and floors. The landing itself had four doors, carved with images of life and death, each surmounted by a different looming carving of death personified.

"It's not very cheerful, is it?" whispered Belladonna, her voice dropping into the silence like a rock into a lake.

They froze until the last lingering echoes of her voice had faded and all they could hear was the steady ticking of the great long-case clock in the entry below them.

"This way," whispered Elsie, gesturing toward a door on their right.

"Why that way?" asked Belladonna.

"There's a sign. See?"

Elsie pointed at a small wooden sign with lettering picked out in peeling gilt. It read "Long Gallery," then right below that, "Hall of Argument," followed by a small arrow pointing to the right.

"The Hall of Argument," explained Elsie. "That's where the Conclave meets. I imagine that's where they are. It's where we saw the light and it would explain why it's so quiet."

"Yeah," said Belladonna dubiously, "so would a few other things that leap to mind."

Elsie rolled her eyes and strode toward the door. Belladonna watched for a moment, expecting her to fling the doors open in yet another bravura Edwardian

gesture, but instead she hesitated, bit her lip, and fingered her tie.

"What is it?" said Belladonna.

"Nothing . . . that is . . ."

Belladonna smiled and joined her at the door. Then
she turned and slowly twisted the handle. The great
door swung inward slowly and without a creak, but all
sense of relief faded when they saw what was inside.

"What on earth is that?" whispered Elsie.

Belladonna felt along the wall, located a switch, and
turned the lights on. Above their heads, chandelier
after chandelier burst to life down the long gallery, the
crystal drops scattering light throughout the room,
glancing off mirrors and shooting out of the tall windows. The whole of the left-hand wall was made up of
windows, stretching from floor to ceiling, while on the
right, the walls held mirrors of exactly the same size
and shape. Under normal circumstances, this would
have made the gallery an almost magical place, but
someone had turned it over to another use; shelves had
been installed against the mirrors, all the way from the
door to the fireplace at the far end, and on each of the
shelves, so close that they were almost (but not quite)
touching, was row upon row of glass jars. There were
jam jars, pickle jars, wine bottles, water bottles, every
size of glass receptacle imaginable, even bell jars like
the ones they used in physics class to create a vacuum.
The jars were all clean, but there were no labels or

signs to indicate what had been or what was now inside them. And something was definitely inside them—each jar seemed to be full of smoke or mist that moved slowly around like a self-stirring soup.

"Are they . . . ?" asked Elsie. "No! Oh, no! It's us! It's us!"

She ran to the shelves and touched jar after jar. She picked one up and began straining with the lid.

Belladonna looked at her, then at the ranks of jars. The milky, misty contents moved slowly. Then she knew.

"That's . . . the ghosts?"

Elsie nodded.

"All of them?" Belladonna stared at the ranks of jars. "But . . . if it's the ghosts of everyone who ever lived . . . shouldn't there be more?"

"A spirit doesn't take up much space," whispered Elsie, "no space at all, really."

Belladonna walked over to the jars and touched one. It was cold as ice, and the gray-green mist inside seemed to move faster at her touch . . . or was that just her imagination? She pulled her hand away—perhaps it wasn't respectful—and tilted her head back to take in the rows of jars and bottles. How many ghosts were in each one? How many lives? She reached forward again, lightly touching the cold glass. Were her parents perhaps in this one? Were other ghosts with them? Were they at least together?

"All of them," she repeated to herself, "every ghost who ever was."

"Except me. I'm the only one left." All Elsie's efforts to remain calm deserted her and she suddenly sobbed, "What is he doing, Belladonna? What's going to happen to us?"

Belladonna opened her mouth to speak. She thought she ought to try and say something comforting, but then she noticed something else.

"What are the wires for?"

She examined the jars more closely. A wire had been placed in each bottle or jar and held in place by a cork. They then ran along the shelves to the far end of the room where there was some sort of workbench. Belladonna froze. She'd seen that bench before, and she instinctively tipped her head upward to look at the distant ceiling. It was so high that it faded into darkness, in spite of the chandeliers, but something was moving up there and she knew exactly what it was—ember beetles.

Belladonna took a deep breath and followed the wires down the room.

"I can't open them!" cried Elsie, tears springing to her eyes. "I can't . . . I'm so sorry. . . ."

She ran further down the hall to another shelf and began struggling with the jars there.

"Elsie," said Belladonna gently, "come and look at this."

Elsie put the jar down and joined Belladonna at the far end of the room near the workbench, where all the wires had been neatly gathered together and inserted into a roughly drilled hole in the back of a large marble chair.

"That's the Seat," said Elsie, "from the Room of Dreams. But where's the Door?"

"The Door?"

"The alabaster door. The Dream Door. We sit in the chair and send dreams to the Living through it."

Belladonna chewed her lip and examined the wires going into the chair. "One at a time?" she asked finally.

"What?"

"D'you do it one at a time?"

"Well, of course . . ."

"So what would happen if all the ghosts . . . all the ghosts of all the people who had ever lived . . ."

"I don't know," said Elsie, a note of desperation creeping into her voice. "It would be very powerful, I suppose. Maybe . . . maybe instead of sending dreams we could send something else. Something real. But why? And who would sit in the chair? Someone has to sit in the chair."

Then Belladonna heard it. A sigh. It was so faint that it could have been mistaken for a draft, or the sound that the wind might make through a tiny crack in one of the tall windows. But there was another element to it, a low shuddering groan, hopeless and longing.

Belladonna forgot about the chair, about the ghosts,

about Ashe, about everything. She just ran toward the sound. It seemed to come from the darkest corner of the room.

She ran so fast that she almost crashed into it, a huge cage, crouching in the corner, lurking like a bad dream. She raised her hands to stop herself and created yet another noise that echoed through the empty rooms of the House of Mists. And then, for a moment, her heart sank. It was empty.

She scanned the interior. There was nothing there! But there had been . . . she was sure of it.

"Belladonna?" The voice was barely a murmur, but there is something in us that always hears our name, no matter how quietly it is spoken.

She peered into the cage again. And then she saw him, huddled into the farthest corner, curled tight, as if that would protect him from anything in the Land of the Dead. His face was white without color, almost translucent, and there were dark rings around his eyes. The cracked lips had a tinge of blue about them, and a fresh rivulet of black liquid was spilling from the corner of his mouth, over the dried remains of many more.

"Steve?" she whispered.

"Please . . ." he said.

"Yes?"

"Kill me."

She looked at him, and the black despair in his eyes brought hot tears to hers.

"How did you get here? What has he done to you?"

"I don't know . . . I was there, with you, by the fire . . . and then I was sinking into the ground . . . I couldn't breathe. And then I was here. He brought me. He's keeping me alive," said Steve, his voice pained and dry. "He gives me enough of the antidote so that I can't die . . . I can't die."

The sentence seemed to exhaust him and he fell back into the shadows for a moment, then wrenched himself up slightly.

"Please . . ." he breathed. "I want to die."

"No . . . no, I can't."

"Belladonna, he needs me alive. . . . I don't know why, but he does. If you kill me, it will be over."

Belladonna felt her way around the cage to the far corner and threaded her fingers through the bars to touch his hand. He was cold and clammy, and there was something not quite alive about his skin. Her instinct was to let go, to recoil and shrink away, but she couldn't leave him here like this and she knew, in the moment that she touched him, that she must either save him or kill him.

"No," she said again, "I can't."

Now that she was close, she could see that he was barely there. Even the effort of turning his head was almost too much.

"Please . . ." he said, his voice disappearing into a whisper, "please . . ."

"No." She suddenly felt stronger; she would not permit this to happen. "Where's the antidote?"

"I can't . . ."

"Where?" she repeated, her voice betraying the desperation she felt but didn't want him to see.

His eyes flickered open, "On the desk . . . blue bottle . . ."

And then he was gone again. Elsie crept over to the desk and started going through the collection of bottles and vials that littered the desk.

"Here it is!" she yelled.

"*Shh!*" said Belladonna, joining her at the desk. "Is there anything we can put it in?"

"What?" said Elsie. "Why don't we just give him the bottle?"

"Because Ashe might come back and if he sees the bottle is gone, he'll know someone is here."

She quickly looked at the other bottles. Every one had something in it.

She swung down her backpack and rifled through it, knowing there was nothing. If only she'd kept the Tizer can!

"Hang on," said Elsie. "I've got something."

She unzipped a small purse that was built into her belt and removed a pen.

"A pen?" said Belladonna. "What use is that?"

Elsie smiled, unscrewed it, pulled a lever in the side, and expelled the ink into one of the other bottles.

"It's a fountain pen," she said.

Belladonna grinned and held the bottle while Elsie siphoned out as much of the antidote as the pen would hold, but as she turned to go to the cage, there was a loud bang outside the door. They both dived under the desk.

"It's him!" said Elsie, her voice trembling with an unfamiliar fear.

Belladonna bit her lip; she looked from the jars to the cage. *He has the Dead*, she thought, *and he has the Living*. It made sense that he'd need more of the Dead—they would have far less energy than a living person. But what was he trying to do?

At that moment there was another bang and the door at the far end of the gallery flew open.

"Be careful, you idiot! You'll damage it!"

Belladonna and Elsie crept further under the desk at the familiar sound of Dr. Ashe's voice.

The reprimand was followed by a crunching, grinding sound, as if something large was being dragged across the floor. Belladonna crept to the edge of the desk and peeked out.

It was something large. Something huge, in fact, and carefully wrapped in blankets tied into place with ropes. Ashe was pushing on one side, but there was someone else there too. Belladonna waited, then gasped—it was Slackett!

The two men carefully positioned their package

about three meters away from the chair. Then Ashe stepped back, satisfied.

"Unwrap it," he said to Slackett, "and check the connections."

He spun on his heel and stalked to the door, then stopped suddenly and turned back for a moment. Belladonna held her breath and darted back under the desk. But it was alright. A second later, they heard the door close and footsteps receding down the hall outside.

"What are we going to do?" whispered Elsie.

Belladonna shrugged and peeked out again. Slackett had undone the ropes and the collection of blankets fell to the floor, revealing a plain white doorway.

"It's the Door!" gasped Elsie.

"Why would he want the Dream Door?" said Belladonna quietly.

"It can only send dreams," shrugged Elsie. "Nothing else."

"Unless it has some other powers," said Belladonna, looking at the jars and the cage. "Powers no one else has thought of."

She heard Steve make a muffled sound. She glanced at Slackett, waited until his back was turned, and then crept over to the far side of the cage. Steve looked at her, his eyes fever-bright.

"I'm supposed to sit in the chair," he whispered. "The chair is meant for the Dead. I was thinking . . . if the Dead send dreams . . . things . . . through the

Door to the other worlds . . . then maybe the Living can . . ."

"Maybe the Living can bring things from other worlds here!" said Belladonna, her eyes opening wide. "He's combining the power of the Dead and the Living! He's reversing the Door and bringing something here!"

"Very good," said a voice behind them, "but what are you going to do about it?"

Belladonna spun around, her heart in her throat. Slackett was standing behind her, clutching a handful of wires, a familiar smirk on his face.

"Do about it?" she said.

"That's what I said."

She looked at him carefully; there was something in his eyes. . . .

"Why are you here?" she asked. "I thought he'd . . ."

"No," he said, "he thought I was weak and pulled by your spell. He doesn't know about the Rod of Gram."

"The what?"

"The ruler. Not that it did any good. Looks like your Paladin will be dead before the night is through."

"No, he won't!" said Belladonna, standing up. "Tell me what Ashe is doing. What does he want to bring here?"

"So, you've worked out that much," said Slackett, clearly impressed. "With a living person in the chair and the dream-power of the Dead, the Door no longer sends mere dreams, it can bring solid corporeal creatures from any of the nine worlds and any of the spaces in between."

"The spaces in between?"

"The Darkness," snapped Slackett. "Didn't they teach you anything?"

"No . . . no one's explained anything." Belladonna could feel tears of frustration burning in her eyes. "Tell me. I need to know."

"The Darkness is the Void," said Slackett, after taking a deep breath. "It's the spaces where the worlds are not; it's minuscule and infinite at the same time. To be banished to the Darkness is to become nothing, neither Living nor Dead for all eternity. Well, that's the way it's supposed to be, at any rate."

"What happened?"

"They thought when they banished her there that it was over, that she would be lost to the nine worlds. It took her a while, but she has become stronger than ever she was before. Consuming knowledge from the other drifting souls, she grew in strength, and in time became ruler of them all, the Empress of the Dark Spaces."

"Good name, isn't it?" said Elsie.

"And Ashe wants to use the ghosts to get her out?" asked Belladonna. "How did he work out how to do it? And . . . and . . . why would he want to? Who is she?"

Slackett laughed. "Ashe didn't work it out!"

"Then who—"

"Ashe was nothing but a bitter failure until his

scrying ball suddenly started working. He thinks it was his years of study and devotion that finally gave him some ability, but it wasn't . . . it was her. He is to prepare the way for her return, and it begins tonight."

"But . . ." Belladonna struggled to understand. "Why close all the doors to the Land of the Living if that's what he's going to do?"

"He doesn't want to take any chances," said Slackett, lowering his voice. "And he hasn't just closed the doors to the Land of the Living. All doors to all other worlds are closed; the people of the nine worlds are deaf and blind, vulnerable as baby birds as the hawk circles the nest. He has to be sure that the Dream Door brings the right person, that it opens into the Darkness. For that, he needed there to be only one possible route; he needed all the Dead, a living creature, and the Draconite Amulet to amplify his spell and carry it into the Void."

"And you've just been spying on him? Why didn't you try to stop him?"

"I was sent to watch, not to act."

"Wait," said Belladonna, "sent? Sent by who?"

"The Queen of the Abyss, of course," said Elsie.

"Who?"

"She is one of the Old Ones," said Slackett. "She rules the Land of the Dead."

"Well, she's not doing a very good job!"

"I was to warn her when he began to get close," explained Slackett, "but it all happened much faster than I'd anticipated. The doors closed and she was trapped on the Other Side."

"In the Land of the Living? The ruler of the Land of the Dead is in the Land of the Living? What on earth is she doing there?"

"I am not at liberty to say," said Slackett, suddenly getting all huffy and sounding a little like a politician on the television, "but all will be well now that you are here."

"Me? What can I do?"

"You must close the Dream Door and reopen the doors to the nine worlds."

Belladonna stared at him like he was certifiable. "Did you get knocked on the head? I'm twelve! I'm just trying to get my Mum and Dad back! I can't take on empresses! I can't even take on Sophie Warren at school and she's just an ordinary girl!"

"You are the Spellbinder," said Slackett confidently.

"No . . ." began Belladonna, but before she could protest any further there was a rattling gasp from the cage.

She spun around. Steve's eyes were no longer bright, but dull and dry. They closed slowly. Belladonna fell to her knees next to the cage where his head lay against the bars.

"What is it?" she cried.

"He's dying," said Slackett. "I told you. If Ashe doesn't hurry up, he'll have to find a new live one. Hmmm . . . wonder who that could be?"

"No." Belladonna ignored him. All her attention was on Steve. "No, no, no. You won't give up. I won't let you."

She examined the cage. There was a small door near Steve's head, fastened with a metal pin through a rusty hasp. Belladonna reached forward, eased the pin out, and opened the door slowly. Steve didn't even look up. She gulped back her tears and gently opened Steve's mouth, raised Elsie's pen, pulled the small lever, and released the antidote into his mouth.

"Hope it's not too late," said Slackett, in the tone of one who really didn't care one way or the other.

Belladonna glowered at him. "Alright," she said, "what do I have to do?"

"Use the other Nomial," said Slackett.

"But I don't have it."

"Oh, for cryin' out loud. Elsie!"

Elsie stood up and backed away nervously, her hand to her tie.

"No."

"Come on, Elsie, you knew this time would come."

Elsie hesitated, then nodded. She loosened her tie, unfastened the first two buttons on her blouse, and pulled a gold chain from around her neck. On the end of it was a glistening jewel, the color of honey.

"The Silex Aequoreus," said Slackett, "the Stone of the Sea."

Elsie handed it to Belladonna, who stared at her in disbelief.

"But . . . this has been protecting you?"

"Yes," said Elsie, "but only until the Spellbinder came."

Belladonna didn't know what to think, but her first instinct was to be a little annoyed with Elsie. "Why didn't you say something?"

"I wasn't sure," she said. "I mean, he said it was you, but you didn't really seem like much to write home about—"

"Oh, thanks."

"Well, you didn't. Until we were on the plain and Steve killed the Hound and you made arrows out of grass. That was all really impressive."

"I'm the Spellbinder. . . ." whispered Belladonna. "But what does that mean? What is a Spellbinder?"

"Not *a* Spellbinder," said Slackett, "*the* Spellbinder. The Spellbinder comes when the nine worlds are in danger. Though last time was a bit . . . well, anyway . . ."

"The last time? What happened last time?"

"It's complicated," said Slackett, who obviously thought he'd already said too much. "There's no time. We have to stop wasting time! There's a door, it leads back to the landing. Wait until Ashe is in here and has begun the spell. There'll be a sound. Then run around and come in the other door. You *must* be on the opposite side of the Dream Door. It's not just for the Land of the Living or the Land of the Dead, you understand, it's for every living thing in all the nine worlds."

Belladonna looked at the jewel in her hand. "But what do I do then?"

"You have to say the Words. There are Words of Power that must be spoken."

"Why does everyone expect me to know words all the time?" said Belladonna. "I don't know any words!"

"You always know the Words."

Belladonna whirled around. It was Steve! He still looked deathly ill, but at least he didn't seem to be dying any more. She hesitated for a second, then reached into her backpack and retrieved the trumpet. It just fit through the bars of the cage.

"Okay," she said, "I'm going. But take this. If it looks bad, call the Hunt."

"I can't." He was still gasping for every breath. "Belladonna, I can't."

Belladonna ignored him and turned to Slackett. "Where's this door, then?"

Slackett nodded and pressed a small piece of molding in the fireplace. There was a moment's hesitation, a brief grinding of gears, and the fireback slid away. But even as it did, footsteps could be heard approaching the main door.

"It's too late!" Slackett spun around, fear on his face.

"No, it isn't," said Elsie. "Go on, Belladonna, I'll distract him."

"No!"

"Yes. My father always said it was better to die for something than nothing."

"But you're already dead!"

"Go!"

Belladonna hesitated for a second, then smiled quickly at Elsie and crawled through the door. Slackett pressed the molding again and as the fireback slid into place, she saw the great door at the other end of the room open and Elsie step out from behind the desk.

"What-ho, Ashe!" she said cheerfully. "Bit of a rum setup you've got here."

And with a click, the door closed and Belladonna was alone in the dark.

15

The Name of the Darkness

ELLADONNA WAITED until her eyes grew used to the dark. The space was small, but there seemed to be a passage on the far side. She crawled toward it. It was another door. She pushed on it, hoping against hope that this one didn't require a hidden button.

It didn't. It swung open easily and Belladonna found herself back on the great landing under the gleaming stained-glass roof. But even as she stepped into the corridor, she stopped cold. Someone had screamed. A loud, sustained, painful scream that ended with a groan and then . . . nothing. Belladonna's hand flew to her mouth. It was Elsie. She was gone.

She took a deep breath and began to run toward the gallery. There was still a chance for Steve. She reached the door, but as she held her hand out to open it, the whole house suddenly seemed to gasp and a booming throb sent a shudder through to its deepest foundations. Belladonna, too, gasped, clutching at her chest. It was as if something was trying to pull her heart out of her body using sound alone, a thrumming, sonorous sound that was felt rather than heard. She stumbled and fell, but quickly scrambled to her feet and flung open the door.

If the sound was difficult to endure outside the room, once the doors were open, it became very nearly impossible. Belladonna staggered back, then gritted her teeth and stepped into the gallery, but what she saw made her despair of ever seeing the Land of the Living again.

In front of her was the alabaster Dream Door, shimmering like water on a hot day. Down the sides of the room, the jars jangled on the shelves, their misty contents pulsating rapidly in time with the lowering thrum. But it was the chair that made her blood run cold.

Steve was sitting in it, his white-knuckled hands gripping the arms and his head flung back. Around his neck was the Draconite Amulet, sparkling brightly — not reflecting the chandeliers or the moonlight, but giving off its own light as if the stone itself were alive.

Dr. Ashe stood, triumphant, behind the chair, his gaunt face stretched with a rictus grin, and as she watched, he raised his hands upward and spoke.

"Lamashtu of the seven names! Empress of the Dark Spaces! I, your servant, call on you to leave your abode and take up your rightful place in this and all worlds. The seal is broken! The sleeper awakes! Let the darkness run free and dispel the frail light, that the creatures of the Dark Spaces may come to me so that I may serve you through them. All this I ask, Lamashtu, with the power of your first name: Meslamta!"

The thrumming seemed to decrease for a moment, and Belladonna hoped that perhaps his incantation hadn't worked. She held her breath, waiting.

It was a few moments before she realized what was happening. It was the stone.

The Draconite Amulet was rising, floating up from Steve's chest until it hovered in front of him. Then, with a sound like the sigh of a thousand souls, a red stream of light hurtled from it and smashed against the brilliant white of the alabaster Door. As she watched with growing dread, the Door turned slowly black, as if some unseen hand was pouring ink from above.

She took another step into the room, hoping that if she got closer, perhaps she would know what to do. Dr. Ashe saw her, but he just smiled. It was far too late.

An inky mist began to pour from the Door, with a stench like rotten meat and stagnant ponds, and slowly, slowly a great black wing could be seen, unfurling into the room.

Belladonna watched, frozen, as a woman, incredibly tall and slender, with skin as white as paper and long straight hair the color of blood, stepped into the room. Her black dress hung straight to the ground and pooled on the floor like oil, and her jet beads and bracelets rattled softly as she moved. But it was her ebony-feathered wings that amazed Belladonna. They were enormous, bigger than any she'd ever seen in paintings or films, but far from seeming unwieldy, they moved easily behind her, like a black silk cloak.

"Who calls the Empress of the Dark Spaces?" she said in a voice that was soft like velvet, but tough as steel.

"I, Heironymous Ashe, her loyal servant. Are you she?"

The woman looked at him disdainfully. "No," she said, "I am but one of her court. How do you come to know the name that binds and frees?"

"I obeyed her summons! I alone was chosen! I recovered the Nomial, lost in the first of the nine worlds."

The winged woman glanced at the spinning amulet, but Belladonna had stopped listening. The Nomial! She looked at the honey-colored gem in her hand. Slackett had said that was a Nomial too. She turned it over in her fingers, examining it closely, looking for anything that looked like writing. As she looked, it caught the light and flashed with a brightness that made her blink. She looked again, then the strange feeling crept over her. The feeling that always seemed to come when she was about to do something she shouldn't know how to do. She lifted the Silex Aequoreus high above her head in both hands.

"Lamashtu!" Belladonna's voice echoed through the gallery.

The winged woman spun around. "What is that?" she spat.

"Nothing!" said Ashe, a note of fear creeping into his voice. "A child. Kill her!"

"Do not issue commands at me, worm!" said the woman. "I am one of the Keres, bringers of death. We obey no voice but our own and none shall command us but the Empress of the Dark Spaces!"

"Lamashtu!" repeated Belladonna. "Lamashtu of the seven names, I bind you by the Order of the Elders of Annu, and with the name that is second . . . the name . . ."

She hesitated, and a slow smile spread across the face of the Kere.

"Yes?" she said with the delighted menace of a teacher who knows her student hasn't done her homework. "Oh . . . the child doesn't know it."

She stepped closer to Belladonna and brushed her face with the tip of a black wing. "Poor thing," she simpered, "you must be so tired."

Belladonna was about to protest that she wasn't tired at all, but as soon as the wing brushed her face, she realized that she *was* tired, deeply and profoundly tired, more tired than she'd ever been. Every muscle suddenly longed to rest, and her brain yearned for the oblivion of sleep. Her arms grew heavy and the small golden amulet was almost too heavy to hold.

"Belladonna!" Slackett jumped up from his hiding place behind the desk. "Get away from her!"

Belladonna looked at him languorously, hardly taking in who he was or what he was saying. The Kere's wing swept toward her again, but with a supreme effort she took a step away to the right, avoiding its satin tip, and breathed deeply.

The cold air filled her lungs and her eyes narrowed as she looked at the hungry face of the woman in black. She raised the amulet again.

"Lamashtu of the seven names!" she yelled. "I bind you by the Order of the Elders of Annu, and with the name that is second. Chalmecatl, the unseen, begone!"

"Ha!" crowed the Kere. "The second name is not enough to bind me or close the door! They chose poorly. You are too young and too weak. Observe the power of one who is not worthy to prostrate herself before the Empress of the Dark Spaces and think upon her strength before you die!"

The Kere's wings shot up, forming an arch above her head as she waved one hand in a circular motion in an almost careless manner.

As she did so, the room seemed to start spinning, and Belladonna watched as Slackett lost his footing and Ashe clung to the marble chair. The Kere smiled calmly, revealing two rows of pointed teeth, as a dark cloud began to form near the ceiling and ember beetles crashed to the floor, squirmed, and died. The black cloud gathered strength and began to crackle, then launched a single bolt of lightning at Belladonna. She jumped backward just in time, and as she looked at the smoking piece of floor, she began to feel something else. Not fear, not the helplessness of one who seemed to be controlled by unseen forces, but the strength of one who controls the forces herself, by sheer will. And by anger. How dare this woman, this thing, come here and claim dominion over them? How dare she steal her parents for the second time? How dare she and her servants try to maim, kill, and destroy?

She raised the amulet over her head again and this time, she knew what she had to say.

"Lamashtu!" she yelled, her voice rising above the crack of the lightning. "Lamashtu of the seven names! I bind you by the Order of the Elders of Annu, and with the name that is hidden, the oldest name. I bind you by Gretak! Begone!"

"You idiot!" The Kere turned on Dr. Ashe. "You did not prepare the way! She *is* the Spellbinder!"

A green light shot from the amulet Belladonna was holding and struck at the core of the spinning red draconite. There was a buzz, then a deep, hollow chord, as if a thousand machines were suddenly switched off. The room lurched to a standstill and the dark cloud vanished like smoke. A white mist rose from the base of the Dream Door and began to spin slowly, enveloping it and returning it to its original alabaster white.

The Kere stepped back into the Door. "You have failed, alchemist, but we will find another. And another. And another. Until the Empress of the Dark Spaces and all who reside with her return to their rightful place."

And then she was gone and the gallery was quiet once more. Belladonna sank to her knees, exhausted, the Nomial still clutched in one hand.

"You have destroyed my work," said Ashe quietly, his voice shaking with fury. "You have destroyed everything."

He began moving toward her, removing a small vial from his pocket as he did so.

"Hundreds of years of preparation . . . gone. All my work, alive and dead, leading to this one moment, this one purpose. All gone. But don't think you will live. Not here and not there. Your day is done, Spellbinder."

He raised the vial and removed the stopper, then grabbed Belladonna by the hair and pulled her head back, but before he could pour its contents down her throat, a steady clear peal sliced the air of the room. A trumpet blast, long and lingering, insinuated itself through the gallery, out through the windows, across the dead garden, and toward the twilight horizon.

Belladonna smiled as she noticed that the chair was empty and that Steve was at the back of the room, holding on to the cage and staggering to the shelves, the horn grasped in one hand.

Ashe looked at him with disdain. "Stupid boy," he said, and prepared to pour the contents of the vial down Belladonna's throat, "it's far too late for that."

But the rumbling had already begun, and through the tall windows of the gallery Belladonna could see the clouds gathering on the horizon, roiling and dark, moving toward the House of Mists, the sound of hooves, bridles, and hounds swooping across the sky.

By the time Ashe realized that the Wild Hunt was already there, it was too late. The windows shattered and the dark horsemen thundered into the room. The Leader stopped, his hat shading his sparkling black eyes, and took in Steve with the horn, Ashe with his vial, and Belladonna as she wrenched herself free and stood. He rode over to her.

"You called us again," he said, his voice friendly but stern. "This time I must add to my band. Are you ready to join us?"

Belladonna shook her head.

Dr. Ashe laughed and returned the stopper to the vial.

"Yes!" he cackled. "Yes! Take her! Take the Spellbinder to the outer reaches of Hell, or wherever it is you demons ride!"

The Leader turned his head and glanced at Ashe. "Who is this?" he asked.

"It's . . . um . . . Dr. Ashe," said Belladonna, her voice low. "He's an alchemist."

"Is he now?" said the Leader.

He looked around the room at the jars, the cage, and the Dream Door. "And what has he been trying to do?"

"He was . . ." began Belladonna.

"He was trying to free the Bound Ones," said Slackett, stepping out from behind the desk.

"Really?" said the Leader, turning toward Ashe with a smile.

"Yes, really," snarled Ashe. "And don't tell me you don't wish for their release as much as I. Or do you want to ride the night sky for all eternity?"

"Hey, boys, the alchemist thinks we're cursed!"

The men of the Wild Hunt threw back their heads and laughed, and the room trembled with their guffaws and the stamping of their horses' hooves, and for the first time Ashe looked afraid.

"Are you scared, little man?" asked the Leader, leaning toward him, his yellow eyes flashing. "As well you should be."

He held out a gauntleted hand. "Come."

Dr. Ashe shook his head and backed away. "No," he whimpered. "What do you want with me?"

"A price must be paid," said the Leader, "and I've taken a shine to the young Spellbinder and her Paladin, so I'm afraid you're the one. You're a pretty poor excuse for a man or a ghost, after all, so I doubt anyone will miss you much."

"No! T-t-take him!" shrieked Ashe, gesturing toward Slackett.

"Slackett?" smiled the Leader. "Why would I take Slackett? No, it's you, my boy. Stick him in a bag, Rodolfo."

And with that, he grabbed Ashe by the hand and swung him easily to a burly rider behind him. The rider thrust the screaming man into a sack and secured it with a rope to the pommel of his horse.

"Come, lads, this indoor air is too stale for my blood!"

He wheeled his horse around to face the shattered windows, then turned and touched his hat in salute. "And farewell, young Belladonna Johnson, we shall meet again."

As the bag on the burly man's horse struggled in vain, the Leader spurred his horse up and out of the window. His men followed with a great yell and howling of hounds and galloped to the horizon and away with the thunder.

16

Home

BELLADONNA WATCHED until the last of the Hunt had vanished and the sky was still and quiet. She wondered where they went, what they did, why they rode, and why Aunt Deirdre pursued them through the night.

She was still deep in thought when the silence of the long gallery was suddenly shattered with the crash of breaking glass. She spun around.

Steve was standing next to the shelves with a large bat. He still looked a little pale and tired, but the glint in his eyes that meant trouble for teachers was back. He grinned at Belladonna.

"What's that?" she asked, trying not to show how pleased she was.

"Dunno," said Steve, hefting the bat lightly. "I think it's a baseball bat. It's what the ruler turned into. Elsie's in here somewhere."

He swung at the glass jars again, shattering another four or five and releasing their misty contents. The freed ghosts were without form, just breaths of icy air that shot out and up to the ceiling, circling the chandeliers. The cold spirits were not to the ember beetles' liking and the few huge insects that hadn't fallen during the Kere's storm began dropping from the ceiling like moths.

"Amazing!" said Slackett.

"Ember beetles," said Steve, "can't stand 'em."

"Not that, the Rod."

"The what?" said Steve, obliterating another bunch of bottles and jars.

"The Rod of Gram! I've never seen it actually working."

"The Rod of Who?"

Another bunch of jars released their prisoners.

"The ruler. You just pulled it from your pocket and . . . wham!"

"Oh, yeah, pretty cool, huh?"

Steve swung at another row of jars, but the effort was beginning to tell.

"D'you think you two could lend a hand?" he said. "It's just jars, you know, not dragons or anything, and I have been a bit under the weather."

Belladonna grinned and looked around for something heavy. She picked up a piece of broken window frame and joined Steve in demolishing the glass prisons. They were about halfway down the final shelf when a small jam jar crashed to the floor. Most of the released mist rose to the ceiling, but one piece lingered, then congealed, darkened, and brushed itself off.

"Elsie!" yelled Belladonna and Steve in unison.

"Right you are," said Elsie, as if nothing much had happened. "Bit of a rum do. Thanks for the help."

Steve and Belladonna looked at each other, taken aback, then burst out laughing.

"Stiff upper lip and all that," said Steve, putting on a posh accent.

"What-ho, chaps!" giggled Belladonna.

"What?" said Elsie. "Well, honestly, you are odd!"

Steve tried (not very successfully) to stifle his laughter and got back to finishing off the rest of the jars.

"Why are they all going up there?" asked Belladonna. "Are they going to . . . you know, become people again?"

"Of course we are."

Belladonna spun around. "Mum! Dad!"

Her parents were there, really there. Standing right in front of Ashe's desk, looking slightly tired but pleased as punch. Belladonna couldn't stop smiling as she looked from one to the other. They were fine. They were back.

And then she did something that she knew she would only be able to do here. Something she hadn't been able to do for nearly two years and something she thought she'd never be able to do again—she hugged them.

"And how about something for the old man too?"

Belladonna grinned, wiped the tears from her eyes, and embraced Grandpa Johnson.

"You were so brave," she said.

"Not as brave as you, Belladonna," he said, his face suddenly serious. "It's easy to be daring in the spur of the moment when there's no time to think, but you came here to save us all when you could easily have turned the other way."

Belladonna smiled, but felt a little embarrassed by all the praise. She just wasn't used to it and she was suddenly very, very tired.

"Go home," said her Dad, stroking her hair.

"We'll be there when you get back. I'll put the kettle on," said her mother.

And with that, they vanished into the mist again.

Slackett patted her shoulder. "They'll be fine," he said.

Belladonna nodded happily. Slackett smiled, and even though Belladonna now knew he was not working for Ashe, she still found the expression on his face strange. As if it hadn't been designed for comfort but was streamlined for sneaking.

He strode to the chair and picked up the Draconite Amulet from the floor.

"Do you still have the other one?"

Belladonna nodded.

"Good. Take this one too."

"But why—?"

"Now I'd better get you home. Come with me."

He marched off toward the door. Belladonna looked at Steve, who stuffed the plastic ruler back into his pocket and shrugged. They ran to catch up with Slackett.

"Are the doors open again?" asked Belladonna.

"Not yet," said Slackett, "but this one should be. It's the oldest and the strongest."

He led the way down the stairs and into the vast entrance hall of the House of Mists. On one side, next to the largest grandfather clock Belladonna had ever seen, was what looked like a lift. Slackett pressed the button. There was a moment's hesitation and then the doors slid open with a familiar hiss. Belladonna and Steve stepped inside.

"Hang on," said Steve, "we've been here before!"

Belladonna looked at the honey-colored marble walls, the onyx floor, and the cryptic buttons and recognized it at once.

"It's the Sibyl's!"

"Oh, good," said Slackett, "then I don't have to explain the buttons."

"Wait—!" said Steve.

But it was too late. Slackett had hit the outside button and the door had closed before the word was even out of his mouth.

"Oh, great."

"What's the matter?" said Belladonna. "It's not like we don't know the button to press to go home."

"Yes, but I wanted to know what the U and the S were for."

"U is probably Underworld."

"And S?"

Belladonna smiled, shrugged, and hit G. The lift hesitated, then suddenly took off sideways, lurching to the left for what felt like a few meters and then slamming to a stop. The doors whispered open and Belladonna and Steve stepped out into the grounds-man's hut at the end of the football field.

As soon as they were clear, the doors snapped shut and the whole lift vanished into the floor, leaving nothing but a small cloud of dust. For a few moments, they both stared at the spot where it had vanished.

"Well," said Steve finally, "I suppose that's that."

Belladonna nodded and was about to open the shed door when there was the unmistakable sound of about thirty boys running onto the field. She looked at Steve.

"What day is it?" he asked.

"I don't know. It was Sunday when I came through from the graveyard. Um . . . Wednesday, maybe."

Just then the door flew open, nearly knocking Belladonna to the ground. Frank, the groundskeeper, shambled in, one hand in his pocket and the other clutching a newspaper of the sort her father would never let in the house.

"Here!" he growled. "What are you kids doing in here? Get out of it before I report you both. Skiving lot! Out!"

Belladonna and Steve stepped outside and Frank slammed the door. They pressed their bodies against the shed, trying to stay out of sight.

"We'll have to go through the school," whispered Steve. "There's no chance of getting out across the field with this lot lobbing them about. Oh, did you see that? Bill Russell's just rubbish! I don't know why he's even on the team!"

Belladonna nudged him sharply to get his attention back to the matter at hand. He grunted disgustedly and led the way back toward the school, avoiding the netball courts and the large windows of the art room. They crept inside through a back door—fortunately classes were in session, so the corridors were almost empty.

"Look like you've been sent to fetch something," whispered Steve, holding his head up and marching confidently.

"That always worked for me," said a familiar voice.

Belladonna and Steve spun around. Elsie had manifested right behind them, looking just as she always did, curls perfect, high-button boots polished, and eager for some fun.

"Elsie!" Belladonna beamed.

"Your Mum said to get some milk on the way home," said Elsie, "and your Dad said not to forget his newspaper."

"Are you alright?" asked Steve, a genuine note of concern creeping into his voice.

"Of course I am," said Elsie confidently. "My grandfather was at Roarke's Drift, you know. It'll take more than one rotten alchemist to see off a Blaine!"

Steve rolled his eyes, but Belladonna could see that he was really pleased and more than a little impressed.

"Well, I'm off. Your Granddad's making raspberry jelly. Be seeing you!"

And with that, she was gone.

By this time they were almost at the front door and Belladonna was already imagining herself sitting at home with a cup of tea and a slice of cake, when the door to the school secretary's office flew open.

"Mr. Evans, Miss Johnson . . . in here at once!"

Their hearts sank. Mrs. Jay was the eyes and ears of Miss Parker and was popularly supposed to sit in her office near the front door just waiting to pounce on hapless students. She looked like a gatekeeper too. Even Belladonna's mother had once remarked that there was something of the bulldog about Mrs. Jay, with her wrinkled jowls and her heavy black glasses.

Belladonna and Steve trailed into her office. Mrs. Jay shut the door, marched to her desk, and sat down.

Her office was huge, a great gray box of a room, with no decoration except for a long calendar of the school year marked with different colored felt tips showing all the major events, trips, and exams. The desk itself was small and wooden with stacks of papers, but no computer. Mrs. Jay left tasks like that to her own assistant, a mouselike woman who worked in a cubbyhole beyond a small glass door on the far side of the office.

"Sit down."

Belladonna and Steve sat in the two uncomfortable wooden chairs that were the room's only other furniture.

"Right," said Mrs. Jay, in her usual no-nonsense way, "hand them over."

She held out her right hand as if asking for gum or water pistols or some other form of contraband.

Steve stared at her. "Hand over what?"

Belladonna squirmed on her seat, unable to imagine what the old lady was on about. Mrs. Jay just gave them her best gimlet stare and waited. Steve glanced at Belladonna, who shrugged, mystified. She looked at Mrs. Jay, and then at her desk: her pen holder, her cup of pencils and felt tips for doing the chart, and her name plate. It was all very ordinary, yet not quite right. Like an office in a play.

Belladonna reached into her backpack and pulled out the two amulets.

"Belladonna, no!" said Steve, his eyes wide.

"It's alright," said Belladonna, "isn't it?"

She handed the amulets over. Mrs. Jay nodded and then looked disappointed.

"Where are the others?" she demanded.

"The others?"

"I thought the Sibyl told you," tutted Mrs. Jay. "She was supposed to. Didn't she give you two prophesies?"

"What is this?" asked Steve, irritation creeping into his voice. "A test?"

Belladonna reached into her jeans pocket and pulled out the piece of paper with the two rhymes on it. She looked at the second.

> *"As were the nights at the great Well of Wyrd,*
> *So were the dragons far Cathay feared,*
> *Likewise the worthies renowned of the sages,*
> *The thrones of the dark queen,*
> *And the stones of the ages."*

A light dawned and she looked up at Mrs. Jay.

"There are nine," she said.

"What?" said Steve. "How do you make that out?"

"The Well of Wyrd is where the Norse god Odin had to hang for nine days and nights to gain wisdom. There are nine worthies. . . ."

"And nine Chinese dragons," said Steve, starting to get the gist. "But what about the dark queen?"

"The Queen of the Abyss," said Mrs. Jay. "She is in all worlds, wherever there is death. I didn't think you'd get that one. I said so, but nobody ever listens to me, of course. So, where are the others?"

"There were two," insisted Steve, getting irritated. "There weren't any others. The Draconite Amulet and that, that yellowy one."

"Hmmph," said Mrs. Jay, sliding the two amulets into a drawer of her desk and locking it. "We thought . . . we assumed that the alchemist had them all."

"Well, he didn't," said Steve sullenly.

Mrs. Jay looked at him with obvious distaste, then turned to Belladonna. "Are you sure he is the Paladin?"

"Oh, yes," said Belladonna brightly.

"And what is with this Paladin-Spellbinder stuff?" said Steve. "More like reckless child endangerment, if you ask me."

Belladonna sniggered.

"Oh, this is perfectly dreadful," shuddered Mrs. Jay. "It wasn't like this last time at all. Well, you can go home. There are seven more Nomials out there. I have to consult with . . . I have to find out what we're going to do next. Go on. Off you go."

"Can we have the rest of the week off?" asked Steve hopefully.

"No, you can't. You've missed quite enough classes as it is."

She scraped her chair against the floor as she rose, then crossed the room and flung open the door to her office.

"Wait," Belladonna looked at Mrs. Jay. "I have a question."

"Yes?" said Mrs. Jay, closing the door slightly.

"At the beginning, the night I first saw the Hound, I saw the stars go out. Just for a moment."

"The stars didn't go out," began Mrs. Jay.

"But they did, I saw them."

"There was our night sky and for a few seconds there was a different sky. The sky in the Land of the Dead."

"There are no stars there."

"Quite right. It happens sometimes if something is being sent from one world to another without using the proper doors. The alchemist used an ancient rite to rend a hole between the worlds to send something from that place to this."

"The Hound and the Night Ravens," said Belladonna.

"Just so."

She opened the door wide again and looked at them with the kind of bored expectation that adults often use when they're already thinking of the next thing they have to do.

Belladonna and Steve walked out slowly. As soon as they were safely in the entrance hall, the door slammed shut behind them.

"I reckon it was her personality got her that job," said Steve, grinning.

"But she knew," mused Belladonna, "she knew about the Nomials . . . about everything."

"Well, not quite everything."

"No . . . but who is she going to consult with? And what do you think it means?"

Steve opened the huge front door. "I think it means we're going to need lots of sandwiches," he said. "Come on, let's go home."

Belladonna smiled. They walked out of the school into the late autumn sunshine. She looked up at the trees and the clouds and listened to the sounds of the busy street: the cars and bikes and impatient pedestrians, the blaring music, the drills of the men working on the road and the clattering conversations of the people passing by. In a window at the top of an old house encased in scaffolding, a gray face looked down, a mob cap on its head and a soot smudge on its nose, while below a woman in a 1920s cloche hat glanced at her watch and hurried away, the Louis heels of her shoes glinting in the sunlight as she ran.

Belladonna felt a warm glow. A few days ago the world had seemed so empty, populated only by the living. It wasn't until they had gone that she realized how much a part of her life the ghosts were. It wasn't just her parents, it was the glimpses of all the lives that had been lived and that, in a way, continued to be lived. Perhaps she had resented her ability to see them at first, fearing exposure and ridicule, when she was yearning to fit in, but those few days without them had made her understand that her ability wasn't some weird family curse, it really was a gift, just as Grandma Johnson always said. Steve was right, they would probably need to go back. But for now she was going home through a town full of familiar faces, and when she got to 65 Lychgate Lane her parents would be waiting, just as they always were.

She turned right and headed up the street. Steve caught up to her, his hands shoved deep into his pockets.

"Hey," he said, "d'you think that ruler thingy will work in this world?"

"I doubt it," said Belladonna, smiling.

"Didn't think so," he said. "Too much to hope for."

They walked away up the street, said a perfunctory good-bye at the top, and turned their separate ways. Neither of them looked back at the school.

Which is why they failed to notice the large black feather that circled slowly down from the great horse chestnut tree on the other side of the road and landed on the pavement, black as jet and soft as silk.

GO FISH

HELEN STRINGER

Diana Brown

What did you want to be when you grew up?
I wanted to be a film director from a very early age, though I didn't get my first camera until I was about thirteen. I was constantly writing scripts for films or plays and I used to sit around writing down everything that everyone said (which, by the way, is a really good way of irritating people!).

When did you realize you wanted to be a writer?
I've always told stories, starting with ones for my sister. The only purpose of Barbie dolls was to act out complex dramas on the bedroom floor. Crashes and explosions featured prominently.

What's your first childhood memory?
Going on holiday to the Isle of Anglsey in North Wales when I was about six. My mum and dad rented a cottage near the sea and we visited lots of castles. It was really fun, right up to the point when I got the mumps. Of course, that didn't halt the visits to castles, cliffs, and prehistoric settlements! I just had to soldier on, trailing behind everyone else.

What's your most embarrassing childhood memory?
I couldn't possibly tell you!

What's your favorite childhood memory?
I have lots of favorites, really. Going to the movies on birthdays, seaside vacations, the last day of every single school semester . . . that sort of thing.

As a young person, who did you look up to most?
Queen Elizabeth I and Emma Peel. They were both very strong women but were still sort of stylish and interesting. Elizabeth Tudor became queen of England at a time when it was thought women couldn't govern countries, and she survived many attempts on her life, including being thrown in the Tower of London by her older sister. Emma Peel was a character on the old TV series *The Avengers*. She was a nuclear physicist and spy. She always dressed perfectly, drove a white sports car, was never scared, and always had a witty remark ready.

What was your worst subject in school?
Math. My brain would just check out as soon as numbers were put in front of me. Let alone those "a train leaves Liverpool heading for London at the same time as a donkey sets off from Cumbria for Manchester" types of questions.

What was your best subject in school?
My best subjects were English, History, and Art.

What was your first job?
I had a great first job. It was at a huge house called Croxteth Hall, which had been the home of the Earls of Sefton. The

family had died out and the massive house was empty. I was hired to help research the family's history and prepare the house to be opened to the public. I was like a kid in a candy store! Some days I'd just pick up the massive set of keys and wander around in the house seeing what they opened. The House of Mists is based on Croxteth Hall and the kitchens are exactly the same (in my head, anyway).

How did you celebrate publishing your first book?
I took myself and a couple of friends out to Gordon Ramsay's restaurant for dinner! We didn't hear any shouting, but the food was really fantastic!

Where do you write your books?
On the kitchen table

Where do you find inspiration for your writing?
I find inspiration in all sorts of things. Books I've read (particularly history books), real-life stories I've heard, and most of all in places that I've been. The theatre at the back of Evans's Electronics is based on a real theatre behind an electronics store in downtown Los Angeles. I couldn't believe it when I saw it—it's just amazing.

Which of your characters is most like you?
Probably Steve—I was always in trouble at school, too!

When you finish a book, who reads it first?
My mum and dad. Usually I send it to them in chunks as I write it and sometimes I read it aloud to them. Reading aloud really helps in finding mistakes and also to see the reactions (or lack of reactions) from the listeners—it gives me a good idea of the flow and pacing.

Are you a morning person or a night owl?
Definitely a morning person. I usually start writing quite early but seldom produce anything worth reading after 2 PM. Not that I write from the crack of dawn until 2 PM—some days I might, but on others I might only manage a paragraph or a sentence. I always leave the file open on my laptop, though. That way, I'm walking past it all day and thinking. . . .

What's your idea of the best meal ever?
I really love cooking, so my idea of a great meal is in a restaurant where they serve food that I couldn't make myself and that arrives looking completely different from what I'd imagined when I ordered it.

Which do you like better: cats or dogs?
My sister and I couldn't have cats or dogs when we were growing up as my dad was horribly allergic (the bigger the animal the worse it was). I've sort of made up for that now— I have seven cats. I'd like to have dogs, too, but I suspect my dad would never speak to me again!

What do you value most in your friends?
Just friendship, really. Oh, and understanding when I don't call for weeks at a time.

Where do you go for peace and quiet?
Home

What makes you laugh out loud?
Lots of things! I laugh a lot.

What's your favorite song?
"Shine" by Take That. It really kept me going when I thought my book would never get published!

Who is your favorite fictional character?
Elizabeth Bennett from *Pride and Prejudice*. I know, I know . . . a terrible cliché. But true.

What are you most afraid of?
It used to be spiders, but they don't bother me much anymore. I really can't stand crane flies (I think they are called mosquito eaters in the US—even though they don't have digestive tracts . . . hmm) because they fly so erratically and have sort of uncontrollable legs.

What time of year do you like best?
Autumn and winter. It's cozy and you can have the fire on. Plus, I'm a pale redhead so the sun doesn't like me very much.

What's your favorite TV show?
Doctor Who

If you were stranded on a desert island, who would you want for company?
My friends and family. Anyone else would be an unknown quantity. I mean, you could say you'd like to be stranded with someone you admire but they might turn out to be a total pain and you'd be stuck listening to them talking about themselves for years and years until a boat came to rescue you.

If you could travel in time, where would you go?
The late 1700s—it was such an interesting time and so much happened then: the Enlightenment, the American Revolution, the French Revolution, the Industrial Revolution, the beginning of newspapers and magazines, the birth of the novel . . . I don't think I'd be bored!

What's the best advice you have ever received about writing?
It wasn't about writing, but applies just as well. An old film teacher once told me that you should be careful who you show your work to. Some people mean well and really try to be encouraging but somehow they suck all the energy out of a project and you just don't want to work on it anymore. He called them Black Holes. He was right and I'm very careful now—I have a couple of friends who I really like in every other way, but I'd never let them read any early drafts.

What do you want readers to remember about your books?
I'd like them to remember them as fun and exciting and interesting. That's how I remember my favorite books.

What would you do if you ever stopped writing?
I can't imagine not telling stories in some way. Maybe I'd wander from town to town telling tales to anyone who'd listen, like a medieval minstrel.

What do you like best about yourself?
I like people and really, really enjoy meeting new people.

What is your worst habit?
Talking. Yak-yak-yakkity-yak. (Oh, and procrastination.)

What do you consider to be your greatest accomplishment?
Actually finishing this book!

Where in the world do you feel most at home?
In England

What do you wish you could do better?
I wish I could play the piano. I refused to take lessons, though my sister did. I can play the saxophone, trumpet, and flute, but I would really love to be able to sit down and play the piano. . . .

What would your readers be most surprised to learn about you?
I have no idea! A lot of people I meet ask me about "rules" for writing. I don't have any. I think the idea that you have to write so many hours a day or so many pages is . . . well . . . rubbish. I think you should write when you feel like it and don't get in a tizwoz. That surprises some people. Oh, and I love TV. A lot of people seem to think that because I'm British I'll only watch PBS—ha! I'll watch anything so long as it has a good storyline and starts after 5 PM. (I do have a rule about not watching before 5—I'd never get anything done!)

Will Belladonna ever learn how to be a good Spellbinder?
The Queen of the Abyss could explain it to her,
but Belladonna can't just go and ask her questions, can she?

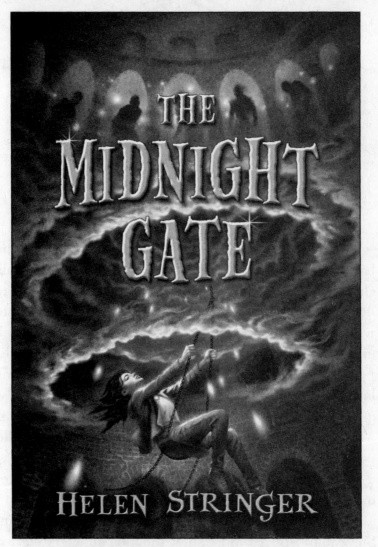

Belladonna and Steve's adventures continue in

THE MIDNIGHT GATE

I

The Visitor

"MR. EVANS!"

No answer.

"Mr. Evans!"

Belladonna sneaked a look over her shoulder to the back of the classroom where Steve and his friends usually clustered. He was far away, gazing out of the window and down at the football field below. The cloud-cloaked sun was low in the sky, throwing the trees at the end of the field into stark relief and making the frost on the grass sparkle.

"Am I talking to myself?" Madame Huggins suddenly had that dangerous sarcasm in her voice, the tone that generally went before a detention, or worse—a trip to Miss Parker's office. Not that Steve was a stranger to either penalty.

Silence settled on the classroom like a heavy blanket, but still Steve was oblivious.

Jimmy Wright shoved a bony elbow into his ribs and Steve jumped back to life, first shooting an angry stare at Jimmy, then gradually becoming aware of the silence in the classroom. He slowly turned his head to look at Madame Huggins. She had drawn herself to her full height, a difficult feat for someone so resoundingly round.

"Good morning," she said, her voice dripping with sarcasm.

Titters from the rest of the class.

"Did you have a good rest?"

Steve just stared at her, sullen indifference writ large on his face.

"Now, give me an example of a genitive charge."

Steve stared and then cocked his head to one side and shifted in his seat.

"In Latin?" he said finally.

"No, in Greek. Of course in Latin! This is a Latin class, you stupid boy!"

Madame Huggins's face had turned entirely red, except for the very tip of her nose, which was as white as snow. Belladonna began to suspect that she might explode, but instead she took a deep breath.

"Look," she said, her voice strangely calm, "you don't know how lucky you are. Most schools dropped Latin from the curriculum years ago. But it's a great foundation, it really is."

Belladonna bit her lip: Dr. Ashe had said the same thing the first time they'd seen him on the Other Side and that hadn't ended well at all, what with the Hound, poisonous Night Ravens, and the imprisonment of all the ghosts. She glanced back at Steve again to see if he registered the same memory, but he was busy staring at Madame Huggins, his face a mask of obstinance.

"Alright," said Madame Huggins finally, "let's see if you have even managed to grasp the basics. A genitive charge—in English."

"He nearly died of boredom."

Madame Huggins opened her mouth to pour scorn and then stopped. A barely suppressed giggle ran around the classroom.

"Um . . . yes," she said, clearly amazed. "Yes, that's right. But if you know that, then why didn't—"

But she was destined never to know what made Steve Evans so impossible in class when he was clearly one of the brightest students in it. The bell rang for the end of the lesson and the end of the day. Steve scooped up his backpack and was out of the door in a flash and on his way down to football practice with the rest of his cronies.

Belladonna packed up her Latin grammar, her exercise book, and her pencils. She glanced at Madame Huggins as she stuffed them into her pink backpack. The old lady had slumped into her chair behind the desk, exhausted by the sheer effort involved in trying to get a bunch of twelve-year-olds to take any interest in Latin. Belladonna smiled as she passed by, but Madame Huggins didn't notice; she just stared toward the back wall of the class.

Belladonna walked through the empty corridors of Dullworth's, her steps echoing on the old wooden floors and the crisp tile of the entrance hall. It was amazing how quickly several hundred students could vacate a building when they were really motivated. Of course, not everyone had gone—there were always the after-hours classes. Tonight it was orchestra practice, and the sound of chairs being dragged across the parquet floor of the assembly room was soon followed by the whining, huffing cacophony of twenty erstwhile musicians attempting to tune up. Belladonna winced as she hurriedly retrieved her coat from the cloakroom, stepped out into the late afternoon gloom, and headed home.

She hadn't gone very far before it was completely dark. She kicked at a stone lying in her path and pondered the misery that was February. It may be the shortest month of the year, but it always felt like the longest. By February she always felt as if winter would never end, days would always be short, and the sun would never shine again. It didn't get light until close to nine in the morning and by three it started to fade, all without the actual sun putting in a single appearance, just the endless lowering, lead-gray sky.

At which point in her reverie, the skies opened and a freezing rain began to descend.

"Oh, great," muttered Belladonna, pulling her hood up, "that's just great."

By the time she got home, her fingers and nose were almost blue with the cold, her feet were soaked, and her black hair was hanging in dripping strings down the sides of her face.

"I'm home," she said, hanging her coat up on its hook in the hall.

"Oh, my heavens!" said her mother, materializing near the sitting-room door. "You're soaked to the skin! Get those wet shoes off and get in front of the fire. Dinner will be in five minutes."

Belladonna pulled her shoes off and left them at the

bottom of the stairs before wandering into the sitting room, where her father was sitting, or more accurately hovering, an inch or so above his easy chair, watching the television. He took one look at her and let go with a single guffaw.

"Ha!" he said. "You look like a drowned rat!"

Belladonna glared at him and sat on the floor in front of the gas fire. The news was on, of course, but it wasn't very interesting. She looked up at her father, who was watching attentively, and wondered why he was so fascinated. It wasn't as if any of it affected him—he'd been dead for nearly two years.

After dinner, she went up to her room to do her homework, but her heart wasn't in it. She just couldn't bring herself to care about the establishment of the monasteries. Her thoughts kept going back, instead, to Dr. Ashe and his efforts to open a doorway to the Dark Spaces. Sometimes, at night, when everything was at its most silent, she would still wake up, her heart racing with the awful sensation of the thrumming, pounding power that had changed the Dream Door to a door of nightmares. She remembered the smooth, cold surface of the second Nomial, the honey-colored Silex Aequoreus, as she had raised it above her head. And most of all, she remembered the way the Words had made her feel as she defeated the dark emissary of the Empress of the Dark Spaces and reclaimed the Dream Door for the ghosts and for the living. It had seemed like such a great victory, but the uneasy feeling she'd had since then just wouldn't seem to go away.

She shook her head and tried to make herself

concentrate. She carefully traced the outlines of a typical medieval monastery and started labeling the various buildings. Then she stopped and glanced out of the window. The rain was beating against the glass like impatient fingers and she could just make out the trees on the road, bending and lashing about in the wind.

She watched it for a while and the reason for her mood slowly dawned on her.

It was because everything was back the way it was. She walked to and from school alone and was still the "weird girl," the one no one really wanted to talk to. Sophie Warren and her friends still lay in wait and poured scorn on her every chance they got. She was still only an average student and she wasn't showing any signs of "blossoming," as her mother had promised. And to cap it all off, Steve, the only person who knew her as anything other than the girl whose parents had died, had apparently stopped speaking to her.

Which, of course, was the way things had been before they'd found the door to the Other Side.

She chewed on the end of her pen and looked at the diagram of the abbey. Things must have been so simple then. You just became a monk or a nun and spent the rest of your life reading books and copying them out. And praying. There was a lot of praying, and an unreasonable amount of it seemed to take place in the early hours of the morning. That wouldn't be so great. But still . . . they didn't have to worry about exams, and some of them got to work on the farm. Although perhaps that wouldn't be so great either, seeing as there wasn't any farm machinery.

Belladonna sighed. She still didn't know what the Spellbinder really was, even though she was it. There had been others before her, she knew that much. Had they been left in the dark as well? Or had they known exactly what to do and when? It seemed that all she had done was react to something that had happened, and that really didn't strike her as the best way to go about things. It was like her dad with their old car—every time something went wrong, he would get it fixed, but he never did any maintenance (unlike Peter Davis's Dad, who spent so much time under *their* family car that Belladonna suspected Peter didn't even know what his own father looked like). The result was that the Johnson family car slowly fell apart. More slowly than if he'd done nothing at all, of course, but it fell apart all the same.

It all gave her the feeling that something was missing, that there really ought to be someone who could explain what she should do. Or perhaps it really would just come to her—maybe she'd sort of ripen, like an apple in a brown paper bag. Though, if that was the plan, it was a very haphazard one. She sighed again. Everything seemed so complicated and yet dull at the same time. She filled in the names of the kitchen, the dormitory, and the chapter house. But perhaps it was always like that, no matter what time you were born in. The past always seemed simple, the present was always slightly disappointing, and the future was always just a little bit scary.

The next day it was still raining, so she pulled on her boots, at her mother's insistence, shoved her shoes into her grubby pink backpack, and trudged off to school for another dismal day. She hung up her coat and was just taking off her boots when Lucy Fisher suddenly appeared at her elbow. Lucy was probably the only girl in school who was even more shy than Belladonna. She was tiny for her age, and pale as a charnel sprite, with a tangled mop of blond hair surrounding an ethereal face.

"Hey," she said, "did you hear?"

"What?"

"Mr. Watson's taking us on a field trip to some old monastery next Tuesday. It's an all-day thing, so you know what that means!"

Belladonna looked at her blankly. Lucy glanced around to make sure no one was listening, then leaned in.

"No Latin," she whispered, grinning lopsidedly. "Isn't that great?"

Before Belladonna could answer, Lucy was gone, off to spread the good news in her endless, futile efforts to be accepted. Belladonna sighed and hoped against hope that she didn't give the same impression.

Sure enough, when History rolled around, Mr. Watson handed out permission letters to be signed by parents and informed everyone that they had to be at the school by seven in the morning the following Tuesday and to bring sandwiches for lunch because they would be gone all day.

Belladonna shoved the note into her bag.

As soon as school was over, she walked to her grandmother's house on Yarrow Street. Approvals, permissions, and sick notes all had to be signed, and seeing as her parents were currently residing (so far as anyone else was concerned) in a shared grave in the churchyard, their signatures didn't carry much weight. Everything of that sort had to be handled by Grandma Johnson, who took her responsibilities very seriously.

Belladonna rang the front doorbell and saw the familiar twitch of the curtains in the séance room, shortly followed by the sound of the latch and the sight of Grandma Johnson flinging the door wide.

"Well, Belladonna!" she said, beaming. "What a surprise! Come in, dear, come in. Get your wet things off and go into the back room. I've got a client. Won't be a mo."

Belladonna nodded, relieved that it was just an ordinary séance. Ever since she'd discovered that her grandmother was a senior member of the Eidolon Council, she was never quite sure how many people she'd find in the house. The Council were supposed to work with their opposite number in the Land of the Dead, the Conclave of Shadows, on things that affected both worlds, but Belladonna was still not entirely convinced that they really achieved anything much at all.

She took off her coat, hung it on the end of the banister, and squeezed past all the assorted junk in the hallway to the back sitting room. Grandma Johnson smoothed Belladonna's dark hair with her hand as she passed, then winked and returned to her séance room, resuming a session that involved rather more than the usual amounts of hooting, table thumping, and moans, while Belladonna tried to find something to watch on the television.

Grandma Johnson was the only person Belladonna knew who still had an indoor aerial. Her parents had been dead for two years, but at least they had satellite. She pushed the wires of the rabbit-ear antennae from side to side, up and across, until she managed a configuration that brought in a grainy picture that she thought might be a cooking show. Or something about cars. No . . . interior design.

She sat in a hard wingback chair and squinted at the screen as the rain stopped outside and silence settled over the house. Except for the moaning next door, of course. Belladonna smiled—whoever the client was, they were getting the full four-star treatment, though she knew that the witch bottles hidden under the front and back steps meant that there wasn't a ghost anywhere in the building.

After about fifteen minutes, she heard the front door click shut, and her grandmother bustled into the sitting room.

"Right!" she said, rubbing her hands together. "What about some cake?"

"Yes, please," said Belladonna. "I'm starved!"

She followed her grandmother into the ridiculously small kitchen at the back of the house, and watched as she took a box out of the fridge and unpacked a small sponge sandwich cake. Grandma Johnson never cooked. If you couldn't get it pre-made at the local supermarket, then she wouldn't have it. Belladonna had a feeling that her Dad had never had a home-cooked meal until he married her Mum.

Grandma Johnson cut two huge slices, made them each a cup of tea, and herded Belladonna back into the warm sitting room.

"Now," she said, once they had each had a few bites of cake, "what brings you here? Does something need signing?"

"Yes," said Belladonna a little sheepishly, aware that she hadn't been seeing her grandmother as often as she should. "There's a trip to Fenchurch Abbey next Tuesday."

"Ah," said her grandmother. "Establishment of the monasteries, eh? Or is it dissolution? I can't remember where you're up to."

"Establishment," said Belladonna, pulling the permission slip out of her bag.

Her grandmother took it and then spent about ten minutes looking around for her glasses, which turned out to be inside a particularly ugly pottery vase in the shape of a yellow-eyed cat.

"Let's see . . . hmm . . . sandwiches, eh?"

"It's an all-day trip," explained Belladonna.

"I can see that," said her grandmother, peering at her over the top of her glasses. "Well, it all sounds alright. Though I can't imagine why they have to have these trips in the middle of winter. You're going to absolutely freeze up there. Make sure you wear two extra pairs of socks."

Belladonna shuddered at the thought of anyone seeing her bundled up like a four-year-old. She'd be suggesting mittens on a string next.

"And mittens," said her grandmother, right on cue. "They're so much warmer than gloves."

Belladonna smiled and took another bite of cake.

"Now," said her grandmother, leaning forward, "how are things going at school?"

"It's boring," said Belladonna.

"Boring? How can it be boring?"

"It just is," said Belladonna.

"Nonsense," said her grandmother, handing her the signed permission slip. "These are the best years of your life. You'll see. It'll get better."

Belladonna finished her cake and wondered if her grandmother had ever been to school and if it had been different then. Maybe things really were interesting in the olden days. Maybe everyone had been nice and played hockey and had midnight feasts and ripping adventures, but Belladonna doubted it. Something told her that once people left school, a sort of selective memory kicked in and all the bad stuff, all the teasing and humiliation, all the tedious classes and endless mounds of homework, were forgotten in favor of half-recalled sunny summer afternoons filled with laughter, tennis, and surprise picnics.

"I'd better get going," she said.

"Goodness, is that the time?" said her grandmother, leaping to her feet and nearly knocking over a nearby occasional table crowded with china figurines. "I've got a new client coming at five! Off you go. Say hello to your Mum and Dad."

She hustled Belladonna out of the sitting room, helped her into her coat, and practically shoved her out the front door. Belladonna sighed and zipped up her coat. The rain might have stopped, but the wind was still icy cold and cut to the bone. She hoisted her backpack onto her shoulder and walked down the front steps just as the new client arrived.

It was a woman. Belladonna could tell that from the shoes, but almost nothing else was visible behind the capacious black coat with its high collar and the wide plaid scarf that encircled her neck and the lower part of her face. The woman swept past Belladonna, and for a moment, as the fabric of the coat brushed against her hand, she shuddered, her feeling of February gloom somehow magnified. She glanced back and saw the woman reach up and ring the doorbell with a long leather-gloved hand. Grandma Johnson opened the door and ushered her in, all smiles and happy conversation, but Belladonna noticed that as she did so, something fell from beneath the woman's coat and landed on the top step.

She waited until the door had clicked shut and the orange "séance light" had come on in the front room, then she quickly scrambled up the steps to see what the mysterious new client had lost.

It was still there, gleaming slightly in the sickly glow from the old streetlamps. Belladonna hesitated for a moment, then reached down and picked it up, a knot forming in her stomach.

It was a large black feather.